Also by Stephen Swartz

Contemporary Literary Fiction

After Ilium

Aiko

A Beautiful Chill

A Girl Called Wolf

Exchange

Fantasy & Science Fiction

The Stefan Székely Vampire Trilogy

I. A Dry Patch of Skin

II. Sunrise

III. Sunset

*Epic Fantasy *With Dragons*

The Dream Land Trilogy

I. Long Distance Voyager

II. Dreams of Future's Past

III. Diaspora

The Masters' Riddle

The Flu Season Trilogy

I. The Book of Mom

II. The Way of the Son

III. Dawn of the Daughters

THE BOOK OF DAD

Sequel to the FLU SEASON Trilogy

[Book 4]

A Novel

Stephen Swartz

MYRDDIN PUBLISHING GROUP

UNITED STATES ◆ UNITED KINGDOM ◆ AUSTRALIA

ISBN-13: 978-1-68063-016-9

www.myrddinpublishing.com

Cover design by Iris Schaeffer

NOTE

This is a work of imagination created for entertainment purposes and is not intended to convey any medical advice or provide health care information for readers.

What characters may state on the pages is solely a product of their fictional personalities and should not to be construed as the Author's own views on any particular facts and opinions whether accepted or contested.

FLU SEASON

a pandemic trilogy

I.

The Book of Mom

Part 1

Journey

Part 2

Destination

II.

The Way of the Son

Part 1

Exile

Part 2

Vengeance

III.

Dawn of the Daughters

Part 1

Births

Part 2

Deaths

(Sequel to the Trilogy)

The Book of Dad

Table of Contents

1 Home

2 The Game

3 Ideal City

4 Obituary

5 The Remains

6 Family

7 Motivations

8 Darker Secrets

9 Li'l Miss Demeanor

10 A Grandiose Larceny

11 Arrested Development

12 A Chicken Coup

13 Lucky Thirteen

14 Feast & Famine

15 The Department of Social Order

16 Contestants

17 The Gray Lady

18 Little Lies

19 Rank & File

20 Island Holiday

21 Transformation

22 Transportation

23 Sibling Rivalry

24 Tuba Tuesday

Genealogy

Acknowledgements

About the Author

Pandemic (n.) – when a disease spreads to various populations over a wide area.

Plandemic (n.) – the belief that a pandemic has been deliberately engineered to intentionally harm people or to provide a means of control over a population.

THE BOOK OF DAD

1

HOME

I HAVE TO GET OUT. I'm beginning to realize how much I hate this place: this cold, gray city straining at the cusp of winter, ready to bite back anyone who dares smile or lets show the happy thought born of some unexpected joy (an unapproved word no longer allowed); nor the anticipation of a holiday break and welcome time spent with family. Forbidden.

It isn't that I hate living in a city, or even the concept of a city. It's that I hate this particular city, the dark capital of a fifteen-state nation that once was more, that seeks to be more.

Most citizens accept this way of organizing a city, its paramount purpose to produce. We must get back to where we once were, they say: peak efficiency, like clockwork machinery, no matter the human cost. We needed to rebuild, to resurrect the triumphs of humanity, they say, despite a ten-year pandemic that crushed our social graces and the decades of lawlessness and war that followed. Yet it's worse than we want to believe, the way we've arranged the world in these brave new ways of existing, almost as though they've intended from the start, from the dark depths of their twisted minds, to create a cold, gray world so perfectly suited to drown our spirits, to suppress all enjoyment – the outlawed sensation which deters participation in the government's well-defined rigor.

This somber, morose, oppressive city.

This prison. My home.

I break from my trance, deciding this is not my home and I want to escape.

"But how?" I mutter, low enough that none passing me can hear. I gaze up at the gray sky: a hint of the drizzle.

Despite being late, I stand frozen on another cold, gray sidewalk, thinking of my mother. Nearly two years since her passing. I keep remembering random moments with her. She would hate this city. She wouldn't stand for the things they've done here. She would rant and rage and *do something*.

What could I ever do to change this?

It's not unusual, my counselor says, to dwell on familial trauma. Yet he cautions me to keep my thoughts to myself. My wife didn't think anything was wrong with that, either, but a few people at the station noticed my work had fallen off. I no longer did my tasks with enthusiasm. I seemed more pathetic than usual, so I was required to meet with a counselor. They whispered that I was having depressive thoughts, forgetting that my mother had just died.

Most citizens will find themselves assigned to a counselor. Many of us continue suffering the effects of the prolonged pandemic and the period of anarchy and war that followed – can't ever forget it. A lot of torn minds, anxiety-riddled and violence-prone. They need to be calmed and their energy redirected. It's what you get with a 'plandemic', some say – and those people are quickly collected and sent away for rehabilitation. Like I was.

I'd put it off as long as I could but my manager finally decided I needed 'adjustment' and filed for an appointment. He shared it with authorities so my record would show I complied. They said it was a favor, something helpful, not a black mark against my credentials. I only half-believed that. Everything we said or did was noted.

Yet I can't go. Not today. Feelings overwhelm me and all I can think of is Mother's funeral, the eulogy, the weeping of all her kin – as I stood apart, not weeping.

"Mother died?" asks a voice too close to me.

Hearing the strange words, I shake my head, clearing my mind of thoughts I'm not supposed to have.

I notice the monitor standing nearby, addressing me.

"You look glum, citizen," the monitor admonishes. "Like your mother has just died. Everything right with you?"

"I'm going to...." I stare up at the tall office building before me, as though I can see into the windows high above. "Up there. To see my counselor."

"Counselor, eh? Good for you. Take care of yourself."

"I was collecting my thoughts."

He pulls out his tablet. "I observed you standing here for nearly twenty minutes. Did you exit your assignment early? Did you inform your supervisor?"

"I arrived early so I decided to wait out here. In the drizzle. Fits my mood. That's not a crime, is it?"

"Not a crime." The monitor opens his tablet, taps his finger on the screen. "You have unused minutes you are not allowed. You will need to repay those. We can't have minutes wasted by just 'standing around'...can we?"

I give a sigh, which isn't smart. "I'm here for my counseling session. I arrived sooner than expected. Everything is all right."

"It isn't 'all right', *citizen*. You should have calculated the route better, gone the most efficient way, monitored your walking pace in order to arrive precisely on time."

More taps on the tablet, a ding. "Account number?"

"What?" I cry out, then catch myself.

"Standard deduction."

"For what?"

"You've wasted twenty minutes here on the sidewalk. Time you could have been engaged in gainful employ or conducting business or preparation for your counseling session. Instead, you stood and stared at the sky. Twenty minutes."

"That *is* my preparation for my counseling session."

"Granted, a certain 'grounding' may be helpful. I'll give you five minutes for that. Which still leaves fifteen unassigned minutes to repay. Account number?"

I know when not to argue. I say my account number and the deduction is done with a tap on the tablet. Fifteen credits deducted.

"Fritz Baumann, correct? Age forty-one."

"Yes." I hate being who I was, who I have to be by law. "But I go by Frank."

The monitor gives a nod, staying focused on his tablet.

"I see you were incarcerated previously. Nine months. Hmm. For a video? You were a broadcast producer." He reads on down a screen full of details, nodding at each one.

"I interviewed an old woman, that's all. I let her talk about her life during the pandemic. And after. Oral history."

"I think I saw that." The monitor grins illegally.

"It was well-received," I speak proudly. "That is, until someone decided we shouldn't know what happened during that time. A big secret about how cruel people can be to each other. It needed to be exposed—"

"Careful. I'm detecting emotive ebullition. Might add a charge."

"Sorry." I clam up.

More taps on the screen, then a soft beep to end it.

"You will receive a receipt in your e-box," says the monitor as he closes the tablet. "I suggest you enter the building now so there are no additional fines for loitering. Must remain productive if we are to continue creating an ideal society."

I can only nod, unwilling to risk further smear to my reputation.

The monitor waits for me to put my hand on the door, push it open, watches me as I step inside, then stalks away.

The large lobby of this office building smells of freshly scrubbed upholstery, a sharp plastic scent that makes me want to sneeze. Yet doing so might get me hauled to a sterile examination room where I'd be given all manner of tests, then taken away to one of the harsh quarantine camps for who knows how long. So I endure it.

I glance around, see others waiting glumly, dressed in proper public attire: a woman in a plain gray dress, gray raincoat folded over her knee. A man in a gray suit and tie, still wearing his gray raincoat, hands in its pockets. Both stare into space, awaiting their appointments. The others, mostly in gray, do not look at me.

As I turn to the elevator doors, I note the marks on the floor that indicate where I should stand while waiting so the cameras can get a good look at me, scanning my record until the elevator arrives. I stand at the appropriate distance.

When the doors open I step in, alone within the box and feeling anxious. Just as *they* want us to be: always on edge.

They: the authorities, the powers that be, the higher-ups, the élite, the great leaders of the world, the State.

Us: the simple-minded masses, workers of the world, the cogs in the machinery, the cattle, sheep, worm food, the stumbling dead.

Me: an observer, cast aside and yet, so far, not condemned.

How did we get to this horrendous situation? I almost utter the words, risking a sound device picking them up.

If Mother could see me now, I muse, almost smiling then biting my lip. The camera in the elevator might catch my smile and inform an attendant. This very thing, a box to lift people to higher floors, would amaze her, basic woman that she was. It wasn't her fault. She was born in the seventh year of the pandemic, faced a lot of danger growing up in the forest of a national park, hiding away with her young parents. Then the terrible part of her life happened. She never tired of telling stories of her life, all the things she did, how she got by, the bad with the good. She never went to school, learning only from her parents. She didn't experience the reconstruction era following the war, isolating herself on an island in the marshes down south. At least she had a happy life there at the end. I made a video of her telling her stories. Now it's for me to 'carry on' – her final words – and she gave me that old gray tuba she loved to play and a stack of notebooks as a parting gift.

I smile to myself, looking away from the camera as the elevator comes to the twelfth floor, doors opening with a soft *humpf* to invite me into reality. Another day in a life not of my choosing.

+   +   +

"Session number seven," the artificial voice intones as I sit down in the appointed place, within the camera's view. The voice speaks my full name, age, last address, account number, and gives a summary of the previous session – mostly accurate.

To begin the session, I apply the sanitized electrode to my finger, another one to my temple. The chair is plastic, hard, uncomfortable

– as it should be. Never want to get comfortable.

Standard greetings. Simple questions. Easy answers. Small talk and chit-chat – and I remember Mother telling me about the chit of woodland critters at night, how the noise helped her go to sleep, knowing they would watch over her. And I go on and say it, give the tale, then stop, my mind rushing back through time, visiting spots of memory I'd forgotten.

"Any more?" asks my counselor after a moment of silence.

Dr. Richards is assigned to look after me. He listens and gives advice. An older man, he is customarily clean-shaven, unnecessarily balding, with small glasses perched on his large nose. He often looks over the top of his glasses. He's left-handed when typing notes on the tablet balanced on his knee, legs crossed. He sits opposite to me – not squarely opposite but a bit to the side so as not to block the camera's view although he's not so large, being rather slim but tall, hunched slightly more than may be appropriate. His disposition is pleasant; we could have a good conversation over tea if not for us being put together for the purpose of him keeping an eye on me on behalf of the State. We all work for the State – or for someone who works for the State.

The camera looks like a neatly designed mirror; I can see myself: my tired, unpleasant face, trying to appear satisfied with my lot in life yet without a smile which would tip off the camera to my lie.

I take a long breath, as required. All part of the therapy.

"Breathe in...and breathe out," Dr. Richards instructs.

"I don't know what else to say," I offer.

The doctor clears his throat, checks his tablet, tapping.

"In our previous session you mentioned your mother. Most of our sessions eventually come around to your mother. Feelings of guilt. Regrets. The moments you recall. How you continue to think of her. Unwelcome distractions from your assignments, no doubt. Is that still an issue?"

Sure, but who doesn't think about their mother? Especially when she died and I missed that moment. It was at a family gathering. I didn't see her until the funeral, but that was unsatisfying. And I felt guilty for not crying. And my older siblings looked at me like I was a monster. They questioned why I made that video of her, why I dared show it to the world, making our mother into a clown.

"Yes, I suppose so."

"Is there more you wish to say on the topic?"

More? As though anyone's life is ever done. There's always more to tease out. Another anecdote.

Mother had a hard life. I would've had a hard life, too, if she hadn't taken us south. That was where my life really began, being a little boy. She never talked much about her early life, focused more on her young adult experiences. All I remember is her sitting on her cushion in the shade of her shack in the marsh. Her and my sisters who enjoyed teasing me like I was a forlorn puppy. But I didn't mind too much; I knew they loved me, though we had different fathers.

And that tuba she had! You wouldn't know it to look at the old gray thing now, but it had been through a lot of troubles, too. Passed down for generations, used and abused, until it fell into my hands and I promised Mother to make a go of it, try to make use of it if only for my own pleasure. She insisted I learn to play it, saying the words her father told her, words that her grandmother told him.

It was like that tuba was the most important thing in the family, our most prized possession, the only thing to help survive the Great Pandemic, the Great Reset, the Great War, the Great Rebuilding, or whatever — the way everyone divided the past century into eras like they were months on a calendar. A full century lost in the chaos of widespread illness and targeted oppression.

"Fritz?" my counselor calls softly.

It's Frank. I've gone into another trance. A rabbit hole. Mother did that. She said her father did it, too. Something about her having a set of imperfections we shouldn't mention these days. They put people like us away.

"Just thinking," I respond, awakening to reality.

"Care to share?"

"I...." Have to shake my head, clear the webs. "I was just a little boy when I first heard about all that happened in the world and how my family survived. I know my mother's father wrote in notebooks about their experiences, passed them on to her and her to me. My own father didn't write. Maybe he didn't know how to write. But he did enough, according to Mother. He did a lot – got caught up in the war, for example. She was still in her thirties while he was by her account an old man, broken by the war. She pitied him and that was the main reason she gave him a child."

"And that is you, correct?"

"Yes – apparently." My throat tightens uncomfortably. "He lost his other children. And his wife. Had nothing left until my mother arrived, returning to her childhood home on that mountain. In that national park. It's a memorial site now."

"Like in the video."

"Yes, like the video." My lips firm, holding back the urge to say more. I don't want to return to the rehabilitation facility.

As a broadcaster, I made videos for the station. I interviewed people who had interesting lives or did something special. Mother fit both of those. So I interviewed her, let her talk about her life. She had a way of speaking which was compelling. She also played the tuba. The video streamed and got good reviews.

Until it was taken down by order of a few anonymous people who didn't like being reminded of the bad things that happened. We were awful, yes. No need to remind us. Like we could ever forget. You can't mention the pandemic; people will shush you, or a monitor will charge you. Repeat offense will land you in jail. I spent nine months in a facility, reciting commandments over and over, because I made the video. But I don't regret making that video.

"What feelings do you have when you think of that place?"

More breaths. A beep from the monitoring device.

"Level ten," the artificial voice intones.

"Stress, obviously," Dr. Richards responds.

I take several breaths.

"Level eight," the voice informs us.

"I remember living in that forest, on that mountain," I say in a rush to stop the annoying beeps, "having kids to run around with, playing games. You know how kids can be, loose in a forest. We were care-free. Then one day Mother decided we should head south. She got us ready and pulled us down the mountain but my father didn't make it. His heart gave out and we...we left him there. Mother said he wanted us to go on, to forget about him, but I can still see in my mind him laying on the ground, hand over his heart, his other hand pointing on, and Mother crying, saying the angels would take care of him, just like they did for her father."

A moment of silence.

"That was before I was born, how her father died. She explained later – many times – how she had to leave her father unburied after he died, murdered. She was pulled away – the capturing of her and the other women. They were taken to a town and sold."

I have to take a long breath, experiencing again all the feelings my mother stuffed into me.

"The servitude contracts," my counselor confirms.

I nod. "She always regretted not seeing to his grave, not being allowed to bury him proper. Not until she returned ten years later and his bones still lay there." I can't go on, have to take a moment, then I barely get out the words: "Then she buried him. Buried him together with her mother's ashes. She brought them in a pickle jar."

Moments of silence.

"Again, that was before I was born."

"It hurts you?" asks Dr. Richards.

I give another nod. "Wouldn't it?" I stare straight at the camera. "Shouldn't it?"

"Yes," Dr. Richards says. "A standard reaction. Well within the parameters for normal responses."

"I guess there's a lot that hurts."

The counselor nods twice. "Tell me."

I gaze across the room at the camera behind the mirror. Just a record for administrative purposes, they say.

Pursing my lips, I regret what I said. How will my words affect my disposition? Will I be assigned additional time in counseling? I might not be cleared for new employment. I'm out of the broadcast business anyway. Banned.

"Yes, go on."

"She kept telling her stories, saying how bad things were, like she lived through a fable about monsters. Oh, I believed her. I was a little boy and she was Mother. But she told her stories as though she wanted to make me feel bad for being born, like being the last of her children was a sacrifice she was willing to make and I should be grateful. I never asked to be born. None of us do. That was part of why I had to get away, leave the marshes and make my own way."

"And you did. Is that the source of your regret?"

A rush of memories fight to escape, banging on my mind's vault, crying to be let out. I have to shake my head to put them away.

"She was a crazy woman by the time she died at seventy-nine, with most of her kin gathered around for a birthday celebration. She sure liked preaching to her grandchildren. Couldn't remember their names. I wasn't there on that day, I told you, but I visited several times. I made that video of her, returned to show it to her. She knew I loved her. I suppose she also loved me. It's always difficult between mothers and sons."

"Yes, perhaps." He thinks it is common these days: mothers and sons, fathers and daughters, the generations in conflict as always, particularly over how the past is defined. The younger generation blaming the older generation for everything that's happened. The same down through history. Everyone adapts to this post-pandemic life and the way everything has changed.

Changed? From what? We don't remember how it used to be. We aren't allowed to know. Nobody wrote anything. Mother had a lot to say, mostly quoting from her ancestor's diary a century past and her father's notebooks. She talked a lot about her grandmother, the tuba player, even though the woman was killed when Mother was a baby. We went through a lot. We accepted how messed up we were. Seeing a counselor is an upward career track. For me, it is a requirement, a condition of my freedom in our ideal society.

"Tell me what you feel," he demands.

"I feel apprehensive. At being here. Forced to be here."

"As you know, it's a condition of your release," he says as if he is reading off the tablet.

I want to sigh to demonstrate my displeasure.

"Then you might tell one of your mother's stories," my counselor suggests. "A new one."

So I tell him about something from my grandfather's notebook. I repeat the adventure about trying to save his aunt, getting caught up in the rebellion in my grandmother's town but escaping. I read those pages many times, practically memorized them, the only text I had for learning to read. Mother taught me, going over those pages line by line. Everything was a lesson, she liked to tell me.

"I feel the weight of my family pushing down on me," I say.

"We see that quite often," says the doc. "Many people today feel guilt for what's happened – without feeling any responsibility for it. Generational guilt, perhaps."

"That's it," I say. "And you?"

"Me? What, guilt?" He smiles like he is thinking up a good story. "It isn't appropriate for me to share my experiences. But my family had some bad times, too."

He seems satisfied I've fulfilled my obligation, giving him a new story to analyze. Back next week for more. We'll continue discussing my complicated relationship with my mother, and perhaps start to unpack my relationship with my wife. Talking about our children will have to wait.

"Enough for today," says Dr. Richards, tapping on the tablet. "I'll approve the session. You'll see your weekly funds released to your account within a few hours. Enjoy your dinner."

"Dinner, huh?" I shake my head, try to laugh. "The situation we've come to where I have to sing for my supper."

"Yes," my counselor says. "But it's the twenty-one-aughts now, so what are you going to do?"

2

THE GAME

COLD, GRAY CITY, a reflection of its distant past. Built to look similar to a previous age's architecture. Colorless concrete rising high, small fixed windows, wide steel awnings. The flaws are hidden in the dark corners and under roofs, behind mirrors or in plain sight as traffic lights and street signs. Always watching, always listening. Now we know. It took years for people to realize what had been constructed after the pandemic and the lingering anarchy. Society's collapse was an opportunity to build a completely new society based on models proposed by tyrants. Government for the government, the only way for the loathsome league of leaders who live lavishly on the labor of losers.

I smile to myself, enjoying the sounds in my head.

Then came the class of clowns with their communal cadence: 'If you don't do anything wrong you have nothing to worry about' – well before they began inventing crimes out of thin air using what they see and hear to build cases against people who display a less than enthusiastic acceptance of their lot. Or who dare question anything about the way things were, are, or should be. We've learned that any crime can be invented from scratch, witnesses hired, and evidence manufactured. It's a kind of game now.

Or they pull it directly from your legitimate work product. Like me editing a plain video from the raw footage, making a story from pieces which, on their own, mean very little. Yet the whole thing, presented as a singular historical document matching the history most people experienced, standing as a monument to our cruelty? What then? It's not the story we want to share. And off you go, sent to a rehabilitation facility – or worse.

It wasn't too bad being there. Boring, for the most part. I learned what to say, how to answer questions. Learned how loud I needed to shout my affirmations to get them off my back for a while. And lots of hours reading the propaganda literature or sitting still before the screens. Only approved material, naturally. I kept a lot to myself. I seldom spoke with other 'guests'. Always watching my back, keeping the cameras fixed in the corners of my eyes, knowing where they were, searching for that one spot where no camera viewed – a game of mine. I wrote sensible confessions, got high marks.

The food was adequate but I still lost weight. We exercised in formation. We showered and slept together, all part of the training. They said it was to prepare us for dormitory-style living as single workers. But I expected to return to my wife and children. After all of it, the dumb guys, the rebellious fellows, stayed while I, quickly learning how to please the authorities, said the right things and got out at my first check-up. Stay bland and productive another year, they told me, and this nine month visit would be wiped from my record.

My video had long since been wiped from every storage venue at the station and anywhere else. They took the back-up copy hidden in my home. Wiped it off my tablet. But I have another copy, in deep hiding, waiting for the day I can show it again, hoping technology in the future can play it. Then I'll show it again for the whole world and shout: "See? This is how it really was, the world we survived!"

+   +   +

"Session number nine," the voice intones, drowned out by the oily rain dripping down outside.

"You didn't say much in our previous session," Dr. Richards says.

I sit squarely before the mirror with the camera, still composing myself, waiting for my counselor's signal. Enough details shared and I will earn a fresh set of credits.

I stare at Dr. Richards, letting my mind fall open to the past.

"Mother sometimes spoke of another doctor she knew when she was a baby. I questioned how she could know so much at that age but she insisted she had great wisdom as a baby. She just couldn't tell anyone what she saw. That doctor went with Mother's aunt and her kids and another woman, heading south to the marshes where Mother eventually took us decades later. Later that other woman's daughter, seeing the video we should never mention, came there and found her in the marshes and gave her their story."

My counselor taps on the tablet, looks up.

"That's why we went there," I continue. "Looking for them. They weren't there, or no longer there. But we stayed and made a home in the marshes. Had a shack on an isle, took what we needed from the water and trees, got by just fine. Mother had few complaints."

I debate whether to tell stories of conflicts between Mother and me. Could be used to make a case of domestic violence against me, another way to put me away. But, no, I never hurt her. I never threatened her physically although I felt angry at her many times. I would shout, shake my hands, storm out of the shack, expecting her to chase me, bring me back, but she never did. She said she was too tired of 'minding kids' to worry about me, her last one, so I was left to fend for myself.

Then I had to make friends with her lover, a tanned boy from the marshes who wasn't much older than me. Julio was like an older brother who slept with my mother. I imagined her with my father in that hut in the national park. You know it was renamed Sorrow Mountain National Park? Because of having so many graves there. Guides take you around, tell you stories of each person buried there. Mother said it was her father's idea to hide in the forest until it was over. Then come out. Start living again. But you know how plans tend to go....

"Fritz?" calls the doc. "You seem to have ventured off for a bit. Memories? Would you like to share?"

"Yes, memories...."

"Anything could be relevant to your therapy."

"Yes, relevant." I have to catch my breath.

"Take your time."

All right, taking my time. Time to recall my mother's stories of the bad years. She would begin with her father's notebooks.

Dr. Richards glares at me. Too long lost in my thoughts.

"My mother's father, Grampa Sandy, and his mother, the tubist. In the sixth year of the Great Pandemic. Their city was in constant lockdown, food and supplies scarce, irregular electricity, rampant crime, and they had to keep up with school and work using what they called a 'computer' with 'virtual service'. It's hard to imagine how bad things got back then. We don't have anything like that now but I've seen pictures. We have these tablets, which I guess are like computers. They do the same things but on a smaller scale. And connections via interstream are shaky at best, only reliable between government agencies." I blink, realizing where I am. "I can't even call over to my wife in her posh sector to ask about the kids."

"Yes, I see," says Dr. Richards blandly. "Go on, Fritz."

I try to explain more about Mother and her peculiar ways, what I know of her life before I was born. Her quirks might excuse mine, give me a pass. Or condemn me as a defective person and shuttle me off to a labor camp where people like me can be coddled yet provide some productive effort. And my father's life, what I can remember of it. His war stories. That isn't much. Mother told me a lot more about *her* father. That was the common thread: Sandy – Isla – Me.

"And again," Dr. Richards groans impatiently.

I shake myself from my thoughts. "Yeah...."

He taps on his tablet.

"Please don't note that," I say. "I could lose my job."

"It's a private matter," he says, "not to be shared outside of this room." He glances at the camera. "Go on."

Nodding, I feel a little more relaxed. I can only study the mirror, wondering how I appear on camera. Such devices are common in all buildings and outside, always watching people come and go, looking for signs of illness, rebelliousness, individualism. A response squad will arrive to deal with the situation, keeping us safe and secure. It is for our own good: for our safety and health.

"Why the need for that?" I ask, glancing up.

The doctor does not look. "For safety."

"Safety? Like if a client gets worked up, does something...*umm*, violent?"

"One reason, yes." He types notes on the tablet.

"I hope our discussions are private."

"They are." He makes another note. "However, we need to record them. In case an issue arises later. Then we can review it."

"Who? Who reviews it?"

"That would be the Communications Protocol Department. Or, if necessary, someone assigned from the Mental Health Council."

"Oh." I run down the list of officials who have an interest in me. "Making sure I use the correct words? Never say anything different than official policy. Like that?"

"You should never be concerned with your grammar and syntax. Misspeaks will never be a cause for arrest."

I chuckle. "Let's hope not. My mother was a great user of *ain't* and *y'all* – which I've lost through my northern education."

More notes. "You've done well for..." checks his notes "...what you call yourself: a 'country boy'. Your success should bring happiness. That is the end goal, is it not? Happiness?"

"Yes, I suppose I'm happy," I have to admit. "Can I say that?"

"Certainly. There's nothing wrong with being happy."

"But there are issues I struggle to make sense of. My mother is top of the list."

"You wish to understand how your mother's set of traits have influenced you? Do I have it? To the end goal of dismissing them?"

I nod again. For a couple minutes.

"Yes," I say at last. "I used to handle the production of video for the station. We used cameras to record scenes like fires, crashes, as well as interviews with people. It isn't anything more than creating a visual reference. There's no opinion given. The station uses videos in their reports, often as background imagery. It's not political."

"Nor should it be," says my counselor with a smirk.

Mother had a smirk sometimes. She got it from her mother. *She* got it from my mother's grandmother. I never thought a facial tic could be passed from mother-in-law to daughter-in-law but it did. Of course, her parents being cousins, who knows? Half cousins, she was quick to point out: same grandfather, different grandmothers. In a pandemic, when you think the world is ending, you get with people you feel safe with, who will protect you, and that's how those cousins got together and had my mother: Isla Augustine – named because she was born on an island in August, she liked to remind everyone.

Mother wasn't one to write a lot. She learned to read and write from her mother but found it tiresome. She had read a bible and the notebooks my grandfather wrote, and a journal from our ancestor, the man who brought the tuba. But Mother talked an awful lot and sometimes I got it into my head that I should write that down, too, so I did. Just to try to fix our family, which turned out to be large and quite convoluted.

"I hope you don't think it's too weird," I say. "Things were kind of desperate in those days. Nobody knew if they would survive, or if they needed to repopulate the world. You know? Crazy times."

"Much has been written about that era," says my counselor. "I've heard of programming on your station which depicts the events of those decades. Dismissed now, of course."

"But not any of us. Not real people," I counter. "Generic people, unnamed, for illustration purposes only."

It never seemed strange to me – not until I entered society as it was being re-established. Only upon reaching the city did I realize how others had fared. We all had stories of the 'time of troubles' or what some called the 'pandemic pause'. Mother was forthcoming about her parents' affairs.

"They've got me overthinking everything."

"They?"

"Society." I fidget a bit. "I mean, my wife knows the names of my parents and other associated people."

"Let's talk about this extended family of yours...."

After Isla, my mother, was born, Grandma Hannah got together with their neighbor Frank while Grampa Sandy got together with Lorraine, the twin sister of Frank's wife Louann, and both pairs had daughters. Hannah and Frank had Cherie. Sandy and Lorraine had Polly, named after Sandy's mother who died on the island where

Isla was born. One big happy extended family. And that's not even the weird part. Grandma Hannah and her daughter, my mother, having a child with the same man, that Frank fellow, decades apart. I'm just lucky to be born at all, the way life went for Mother. That was life on the mountain, hiding away in a national park.

Dr. Richards agrees. "You might dismiss it, but your situation is not unique today. A pandemic, with the lockdowns and restrictions, shortages of food and fuel, desperate times, put people in different circumstances. They found different ways to cope. A lot of 'pandemic babies' were born, not all of whom were standard issue. Incest, for example. Those born from rape. Age-gap relationships. Interracial pairings. You see, love and comfort from anyone was a good thing during those hard times."

I had to nod. We are whatever our parents make us. No choice in the matter. And the other aspects we share with parents, whoever they may be, handed down through biology. I have the quirky traits of my mother, who got them from her father. I don't seem to have any traits of *my* father, none that Mother ever pointed out, except my appearance. I have his face and frame but her hair and eyes.

"It's funny how people from the past can stay with you," I say in a low voice. "Like they're walking beside you today."

Like Frank, my father. I still recall looking up at him, standing tall when I was a toddler, dirty from playing in the mud, and this giant reaching down and picking me up like I weighed nothing, and carrying me over to a stream, dunking me in it to wash me. I roared with terror as he pushed me into the cold water, laughing at me. He peeled off my soaked diaper, made from random cloth, and handed me over to my older sisters to wrap me again. Then he stalked off, complaining about *these dang kids* like he never wanted me.

Frank was a broken man, Mother told me as I was growing up. He was fine when he was young and going with Grandma Hannah. But marauders came. Eventually Mother returned to the national park with her daughters and sister. Frank was there, back from the war but full of anguish and now alone. Being a soldier in the Southern Command, he'd gotten wounded, was still in shock from what he'd seen and done. Mother pitied him. One night he asked if they could be a couple and she finally agreed.

I remember her going down the mountain almost every day and climbing up again before dusk. She found employment in a store by the highway. My sisters took care of me, played with me while she worked. The girls teased me, called me Fritter instead of Fritz. It took Mother three years to earn enough of the new money to buy us tickets on a bus. My father, Frank, didn't make it. Died there at the bottom of the mountain after making his way down the long trail.

"Then we traveled south to where she spent the rest of her life," I say, checking my counselor for his reaction. None.

I finished growing up in the marshes, caring for Mother, putting up with her amusements. But I had to leave. I knew I wouldn't be doing any good there. Heading north, I worked at odd jobs as I went, buying another ticket, continuing north. I worked where I could, and eventually I was able to pay for school. I learned video production – the renewed technology. We needed electricity to run the technology, of course, but the power grid was gradually coming on. I was able to get a job with a broadcast station.

That was where I met my wife, Sandra Dubinsky, second of four daughters who'd survived the pandemic without any parents. Their mother died early in the pandemic, the father died later of the virus. She was like me: a survivor of an odd family. So we immediately connected, finding something in each other that was familiar and comforting. As soon as I was hired full-time by the station, we had our wedding. We actually found a priest. He was surprised anyone came to him now for wedding vows. We didn't tell him our first son was on the way. We named the boy Frank after my father, the least I could do given how little Mother told me about him. The next year we named our second son James after my wife's father.

Every day I arose happy, went to the station with the sun in my heart. It was exciting seeing the world coming back to life, the cities running properly, people smiling, well-fed and free of the pandemic chaos. But nagging thoughts, a few from the station, interfered with my happiness. Sandra agreed I should talk to someone. Therapists popping up to care for the disillusioned people. It wasn't that I felt awkward in this growing society. It wasn't even my discomfort with the restrictive society forming around us. The authorities made sure nothing like what happened before would ever happen again. No, it was my secret sensations about my *heritage*, let's say, and the way my mother instilled such guilt in me.

"She used to take me over to her father's grave, on the mountain, there close to our hut, and made me kneel with her as she cried and prayed over Grampa Sandy."

"That's not so unusual. To mourn?"

"It was a daily ritual for her until we left the mountain. But it was more about her guilt. She seemed to want to pass it on to me. Her guilt about leaving him to die there."

"Why did she do that?"

"Well...." I turn down a dark alley, try pulling myself back. "She didn't actually *leave* him. She and other girls of the mountain were taken away by slavers. Can you imagine that? Taken off their land and marched away, raped on the way, then sold to others and forced to bear children for them? And now they say it never happened."

"There is some evidence," my counselor says.

"My mother carried her baby with her – my big sister Amy – and took care of her mother, Grandma Hannah, who was raped by them. And Grandma managed to save her baby, my aunt Allie. And my mother's sisters: Cherie, Polly, Iris, and Jenny. All taken. But they left my sister Ellie and my brother Raymond to die along with other young kids inside a dug-out home filled with smoke."

Dr. Richards shakes his head, rubs his brow.

"Are you sure you want to say that, Fritz? It could be considered controversial." He pinches his lips a moment. "Besides, what exactly is the truth seldom matters years after the fact. Time marches on. We gain new perspectives."

"It did happen," I say. "My mother said so, and I believe her."

Dr. Richards rolls his eyes as if indicating the camera. "I see you need to work out the best wording for this hypothetical situation."

I want to shout, but I don't.

After I calm myself, I try to speak but my voice is hoarse: "They left his body there, unburied. Because my mother was taken away with the others. Didn't want to take time to dig a grave. Years later, however, when she finally returned, a skeleton remained, overgrown with forest plants, and she buried him then." I take a long breath, let it out. "Then, about five years later, I was born."

The doctor stirs uncomfortably in his chair. "Yes.... I see."

"And we visited the grave daily. She always wept. She got me crying, too. It was real. This is what they sent me away for saying. Someone didn't like it being told in a video."

3

IDEAL CITY

COLD, GRAY HOME. What's been assigned after my release from my rehabilitation. The room slightly larger than my cell but stuffed with everything a modern worker needs. There is an aisle running from the entrance door to a small window. To one side is the bed, more like a bunk on a ship, barely enough for one. Cabinets opposite it and above. I fill them with books and a few precious items they allowed me to keep, clothing in approved style for workers. The walls are gray; cabinet doors also gray; floor and ceiling, and curtains for the window, are of different shades of gray. "A neutral color to match the neutered neutrality of our neutral existence," the manager explained while showing me identical units, "for are we not our best when we are a neutral influence on the world, never upsetting the balance, staying neutral?" Each unit he showed was gray but different shades. The female dormitories, I've heard, are all pink and white.

Toward the window, my lone view of a cold, gray city, fits a small kitchen station: single hot plate, a basin, a faucet, and the chill box large enough for eight bottles or cans of whatever needs to be kept cool. Cabinets for storing boxes and bags of food I buy whenever I've been good and my account is unlocked. I also earn food boxes with my daily labor. The boxes are designed to have the proper amount of calories, adjusted to body type and job requirements. Big men with the heavy lifting jobs get more; wiry office guys get less. I'm in the middle but I never waste a crumb.

Opposite the kitchen station is the lavatory: large enough for me to stand in. The toilet is shared with my neighbor who often misses the hole yet seldom cleans after himself. Him? We are all males on this floor. I didn't get to return to my wife and children as I was expecting; I'm classified as a bachelor worker now. I live with other single men. Better for keeping a society orderly. In fact, the entire building is for bachelor workers, although they did put some older women on a couple floors — widows still able to give some labor in exchange for food rations.

My employment is Street Cleaner, one step up from a garbage handler. If I am diligent in my daily chores, I may yet be advanced to Groundskeeper. Someday I might be allowed my old profession: broadcast producer or possibly a video technician. If I can remember the skills after so long away and get approval from the appropriate agency they've set up. That's a goal, at least, and a direction for my therapy sessions. My hope is when I return to my video position, I'll be able to document the life I have now and cast it far and wide as a warning to others. Then they will end me, I'm certain, more than ship me off to rehabilitation. Giving a warning to everyone would be worth the sacrifice.

This is not the kind of world my mother would've wanted.

Even in my childhood on the mountain in the National Park, we lived in a hut that had three rooms, dug back into the hillside, with a wooden front and door. Being a baby, then toddler, I didn't think much whether it was a good home. It was all I knew. And there was Mother to care for me, nurse me, mend my wounds, call off my older sisters from teasing me. She told me about her parents. Her father and her father's mother had lived in a two-bedroom apartment in a city. My mother's mother lived in a three-bedroom house with a yard equal to the dimensions of the house with her parents, sisters, and a brother. I heard they had a garage for storing two vehicles. She told about a house with thirty rooms where another aunt lived. And she described a two-bedroom bungalow, the 'beach house' on that island where she was born. And the room in a motel where monsters came one night, causing them to flee to the National Park to hide from the world. Not actual monsters but men bent on harming them. Mother called them monsters as though they were myth. It shaped her life, giving her a keen sense of danger, though she couldn't always avoid it. She was tough. She killed people to survive. She had a strong back and rough hands. She lost all of her teeth by the end. But she never gave up.

I look around me, seeing the cold, gray city I thought I preferred to the shack in the marshes and a pain grows in my gut.

+ + +

I walk no more than fifteen minutes down the avenue, turning here, turning there, past the concrete wall that marks my neighborhood, separating it from the next neighborhood, what they call 'sectors'. Only a certain number of residents are allowed in each sector, all limited to their designated sector, unless permission is granted to visit other sectors. It's better for keeping control over everyone. The idea started with the pandemic, to prevent the spread of the virus. It made sense to restrict infected sectors, keeping the sick from the healthy. Now they restrict at their whim, it seems, like it's a grand experiment.

We are just workers, after all. We're not likely to complain about being workers in a fixed square of movement, freely able to roam up to fifteen minutes' walk in any direction. We can see into the next sector if we are assigned a room higher than the wall – like mine: I can see over the rooftops of a poorer sector to the high-rise towers of a better sector beyond. Sandra lives somewhere over there. She and the children moved to a new unit when I was sent to rehabilitation. My view of the world is ordered and orderly, for the good of all: each person with a distinct function, a productive job, a purpose in life: to do something within this city.

"Excuse me, sir," comes a voice behind me.

I slow almost to a halt but not completely, not wanting to engage with another member of my sector but feeling the encounter should be done. Mother taught me about helping 'folks' who 'ain't better'n us', to use her way of speaking. She had nothing yet offered what she did have to the next person.

"What is it?" I ask, stopping on the sidewalk.

"I have to beg you," the figure hiding under a hood says. "I'm out of credits today. Need food. Can you spare a token or two?"

My pocket weighs heavy: two tokens there, what might be called coins in a previous age but larger, gold-faced, with the face of old President Templeton on one side, the symbol of Northern victory on the opposite face. When you don't pay for things with a swipe of your voucher card, settling fees from your account, you can plop a token into a slot on some machines to achieve the transaction. It's mostly for when you go out of your sector, to places you aren't registered for payment.

"What will a token buy you?" I ask, letting the twang of Mother's sarcasm slip out. She seldom responded to anyone without a phlegm of sarcasm leading the way.

"A food box – class three, if possible. Enough for me and my child is all I ask."

"You and your child?"

I turn to look closer at the figure: a woman, speaking in a husky voice, sounding gruff. Likely the result of her poor living conditions, or the effects of her labor. If she has a job she would earn food boxes. She opens her hood more: I see her face, scars along her nose and across her cheeks, lip freshly stitched, eyes red, desperate.

"Only me," she says, "and a young'un."

"Young'un?" The word Mother always used. This stranger must be from our part of the world, down south.

I dig in my pocket, produce one of my two tokens, and extend my hand, keeping the token hidden. She lifts her hand and I place the token secretly into the gnarled hand she presents, half of her fingers missing. We know better than to let any camera see our transaction. It would raise too many questions about our behavior: what did this person do to earn a token? Could be illegal. Might be immoral.

"Thanks," she says, a little too proudly, like she's tricked me.

"Where's your *young one* now?" I ask, an obvious question since she uses her child to garner sympathy.

"In the education facility, naturally."

"What level?"

"She's third now."

"Special skills?" I'm just making conversation because I do not speak with ordinary people often, only coworkers and my counselor.

"She was tested, got talent for music," says the woman with a hitch in her voice. "Only a few are allowed to continue it, though. Don't need many in a city. The positions are filled, hafta wait for one of 'em to die, they say."

"By the time she's ready, someone will die," I offer.

"Timing is everything," says the woman. "Thanks again for being a kind person."

"You're welcome."

Cameras have noted our engagement, measured the time we've paused on our routes, and are filing reports. They will biometrically measure us, produce a summary of our lives, noting any shared data points, and determine if additional examination is needed or if the random encounter is innocuous and may be deleted. No conversation between strangers should take more than half a minute – the basic functional speech for getting around the city.

The woman starts off, pinching her hood around her face. Her garment goes down to her ankles, covers her arms, protects her from the drizzle. It's ragged, stained, like she is lucky to find it.

I call after her: "What's your name?"

That stops the woman. "You don't wanna know. No reason for it or get you in trouble." And she walks away.

She's right. Names don't matter, could get you hooked with some crime. We've started calling each other by account numbers, a kind of joke at first but now common practice.

I stand a minute longer, thinking, imagining her and her child, a girl of eight or nine, sharing a class three food box: a chunk of pink processed protein, a bit of vegetable mush, some kind of starch such as a hard biscuit, maybe a mint. And a bottle of twice-filtered water.

+   +   +

The encounter disturbs me. I think about it all night. I can't sleep on my narrow bunk, am almost late for my sweeping job. I run a broom along the sidewalks early, before residents go out to their own jobs. The sidewalks are well-designed by our thoughtful city planners, featuring strategically-placed grooves that collect dirt for me to have to dig out. A new job is created! Every day I thank those sidewalk designers for gifting me this fine feature that gives purpose to my life: requiring me to clean them every day.

Depositing the dirt I've collected into the nearest bin, I think of Sandra, my wife, who filed for 'dissolution of marriage' when I was sent to the rehabilitation facility. I think of our three children who I haven't seen in nearly a year now. In a dark corner of my mind I see the woman on the street begging for food as Sandra, her child with the musical talent as being Maggie, our daughter.

Maggie had talent. Mother gave her the family tuba through me, a gift from the past, saying she should learn to play it and carry on the tradition. Mother often spoke of her ancestor like he was God who brought forth the silver tuba from clouds on high. After all, she gave me his name: Fritz. I was supposed to be the tuba player but I couldn't make any progress with it as a boy. She gave up on me and insisted I pass it on to my daughter. It was meant to be played by a girl of the family, she said. She recalled her grandmother playing it on that island where they tried to wait out the pandemic.

I wonder if that woman's child might be a tuba player. But I no longer have access to it. One time Sandra asked me if I minded her selling it. She said she could get 100 credits for it from one dealer of antiques. Or, pay 10 to have someone haul it away as junk. As small as our allotted quarters were at the time, it did take precious space. The boys didn't have any interest in the instrument. Frank tried it and just laughed, unable to imagine himself in an orchestra. James gave it a try and seemed to learn some, with lessons each week, but little by little he lost interest. That left Maggie, barely old enough to hold the big horn in her lap. I didn't approve either choice for the tuba, but it's likely gone from my life now anyway. Sandra has a way of harming me with threats to inanimate objects.

This is not the life I want, not what I expected.

I wonder where Sandra might be on this cold, gray day. Once she had our third child, Maggie, she was granted paid leave as a matron of society. Never would have to work again. Frank would go off to college soon, I calculate. James might also, or go to a designated job training site. Both would take the assessment tests and be directed to their best option. Their lives will be ordered, safe and productive, working for the good of the city.

None of them should live in this city. They should get out, and I am hopeful of that. Especially for Maggie, who will soon become a teen, learning some useful trade to offer to the city labor pool.

I push my broom as my jaw tightens in disgust.

"You doing awright?" asks my coworker, a burly older guy.

My children don't know what I do as my official role in the city. They only know I went to a rehabilitation facility – which in itself means I am demented and defective by definition. Even after being dismissed I remain to a certain degree tainted, an 'untouchable'. I'm not sure what Sandra may have said to our children to further ruin my relationship with them. I have no contact with them. Life was so much easier with Mother on her isle in the marsh.

Life with Mother had its own difficulties, I remind myself as I pause sweeping. Diligent citizens pass by as I remember. One asks if I'm 'all right' like he can see my thoughts or feel my spirit seeping away like the drizzle evaporating from my wet coveralls. I'm part of the environment. No, I reply, I'm all right, and how about yourself? Getting by? Staying well-fed? Got entertainment? Did you see the video I made? They banned it, you know. Too honest for them.

Blank faces, then they scurry off. They didn't see my video, I guess. Or they did, and are ashamed.

Actually, everyone saw it. It was something new and different, one of the first videos available when the power grid returned. The broadcast system had just come into operation after being off for decades. Those who had the new devices could catch the signal and view the moving images, hear the audio, get a sense of what life was like for many who hid away during the pandemic and after. That aspect of our history wasn't widely known, those folks hidden, so it was noteworthy.

"Let's keep at it now," my coworker urges.

People have a way of viewing history which can take two turns.

They see what is presented and accept it as shown, the good and bad alike, and place everything in the perspective of their own lives in the present. Or they see the same presentation and question every little thing, as if the presentation has been carefully crafted to rip away their concept of a world they want to forget. I confirm I had no plan to rip away anyone's notions of what happened to ordinary people during the awful decades. But there are people who will take exception to anything that's presented, must question everything, down to the most minute detail, and in the end dismiss it outright, discounting the whole account because of a minor discrepancy.

This is a long way around to complaining about the people at the top of our 'ideal society', embarrassed by what happened in the past and not wishing to be reminded how cruel they were in getting to their lofty perches. Couldn't have a testament available to people, so they had the video banned.

My coworker glares at me. "Let's be working now."

Even the book my mother's State Park friend wrote that I helped get published was banned. A surly crowd of agitated youth wearing the government gray-and-red flag logo burned the books in piles, as though that would remove the truth. The history of life before the pandemic, by Tara K. Butler, was equally popular for a while, then likewise removed from every place it had been available. We weren't allowed to know what happened. Not the truth – or what they called 'smutty fiction'. There was already an approved story available and we should learn that one. Thankfully, they have determined what is true and what isn't. Life has always been as wonderful as it is now.

I laugh, and a few walkers pause to stare. Street workers are the crazy ones. My usually quiet coworker expresses concern.

When people experience something, an event or a long trial, they will remember it even if all the displays and presentations of it are removed. They can't wipe brains of memories. No, they don't fool us. I knew children would never be taught what happened. They would grow up ignorant or fed a completely different story. Children would have no memories like their parents had of the terrible things that occurred during the past half-century.

I faintly recall reading an old book about a similar society. I ask my coworker about it but he never reads, doesn't know it. He says such a book would likely be banned anyway.

A man in the rehabilitation facility with me said: "This is how it begins. Like in that book."

"What book?" I asked him.

"The book with the number."

"What number?"

"A year," he replied. "Nineteen-eighty-four, I think. But nothing actually happened in that year. It was all made up."

He explained that, like in the book, our government authorities told us what to believe and what not to believe – what to think.

Instead of the civil war, for example, we learn about the 'border clashes' by 'disgruntled farmers'. There never was a pandemic, only a few outbreaks of a virus that was easily eradicated by the vaccines the government gave out. Worst of all, the school's official books say, was the odd notion that the virus was deliberately released for some evil purpose, that the pandemic was planned. People believing those kind of stories were locked away. People didn't die from the vaccine; they merely took it too late or got the wrong dose, but don't worry because those people who were responsible for the malpractice were punished.

And the horrible servitude contracts never really happened, they now say. Poor women from the South, seeking better lives, willingly accepted offers to join Northern families in exchange for performing household tasks and, if consenting, provide infertile families with babies within private agreements. The law to ban the Found Labor Exchange contracts was merely a clarification of the arrangements. Women were free to leave their host families at any time, the official view states. I learned what actually happened from my mother, who was bought and sold twice, and forced into sex work. Fortunately, I could learn the 'true' history in that rehabilitation facility: she must have wanted to enter into that arrangement, as did many other poor women. I had to write out a statement acknowledging I understood the official view of that horrendous situation.

However, even the corrected version of history I learned at that place is now frowned upon in favor of simply not thinking of it or referring to it at all. The current attitude is that it was so long ago there's no point in bringing it up. It's rude to mention it these days. It makes people uncomfortable. It's not as though those things never happened – take any version you like – but that we don't speak of it any longer because it takes us away from our menial tasks and we shouldn't have any slacking.

"What's eatin' you today?" asks my coworker.

4

OBITUARY

ISLA AUGUSTINE BAUMANN died on her seventy-ninth birthday, surrounded by much of her family at her home on an isle in the marshes along the coast in the South. She had a long and fruitful live, although it was filled with hardships and rewards in nearly equal number she liked to say. Late in her life, during an interview I conducted, she credited her strength and resilience, her well-known stubbornness, and her survival skills to her parents: Sandy Baumann and Hannah May Whistler. When Isla was born her parents were 19 and 17, fleeing the virus and a lot of random violence. Isla's parents guided her through pandemic life and tried to prepare her for maneuvering in the uncertain post-pandemic world as best they could before their lives were tragically cut short.

In her life, Isla never attended any school but learned from her mother and father. Only briefly did she hold suitable employment, working a few hours a week cleaning a store. We could say she was employed before that job as a contract worker in a brothel, but her wages only went to pay off her servitude contract. Only a few of her clients might remember her. She didn't invent anything, never came up with new ideas that changed the world, tried her best but often failed in many things, and couldn't believe how bad things had gotten nor how we could rebuild so fast.

"What did she do?" one may ask, and several have asked.

"She had kids," I answer. "That was her contribution to life, to our society, to the future."

These children grew to adulthood and went their own way in life, returning for random gatherings to Isla's new home on the isle in the marsh. I participated in them, arranged a couple of them when I was older, but it was really Amy June, being Isla's first child and eldest daughter, who took charge. Allie helped for a while, then she left with a girl she met in the marsh. I helped as I could, being the only one by then living with Isla full-time.

The others had their own lives. Cherie and Polly, both sold into servitude contracts, eventually married and had children with their masters. They led comfortable lives, according to Isla. I never visited them. They never had contact with Isla after she settled in the marsh, although she wrote letters to them. Iris had a terrible life in her servitude contract and when she was finally free she joined the Church. I didn't try to find her. Jenny also had a bad time before gaining her freedom and settling down with a fellow who didn't know of her servitude. I crossed paths with her once but she didn't know who I was, didn't know that Isla had returned to the National Park or that I was born there. Everybody knew Isla's son Abe ran the Chesterfield farm during his father's insanity and after his death. Abe married and had four sons by the time his older sister Bobbie returned to the farm. She remained unmarried and childless, helping to run the family business. Eventually she ran a successful campaign to be a senator for her state.

After years passed, when Isla returned to the National Park, she met Frank again. For those who may not know, he is also Cherie's father. Eventually they made me: Fritz, her last child. I was named after our great ancestor, a man who brought the tuba to our family. That seemed to be a curse, as things have turned out. Then those kids had kids, and so on, such that any gathering was sure to fill that isle in the marsh completely from shore to shore.

By the end of her life, Isla seemed happiest playing the tuba her Grandmother Polly left for her. Though she never gained proficiency with the instrument, she enjoyed playing it, which gave her peace....

I had to stop, unable to say anymore.

After a couple minutes of awkward silence, Amy June helped me to my seat. I sat there, head lowered, hiding, feeling guilty.

When I'd grown tired of being Mother's helper – back when I was around twenty – I chose to leave, setting my way north and fixing to make my fortune. First, I took most of the money she'd saved – of course, without her knowledge or permission. I walked out through the marsh to the highway and waved down a bus heading north. I never looked back. Not until I returned a few years later with a college diploma, broadcast skills, and a family. I was ready to make a video of her and her interesting life, covering the terrible times everyone had lived through.

She complained about everything through the interview process but did it anyway. "If'n I gotta," she responded to every instruction. She was happy to see me again and meet my family: Sandra, the boys, and baby Maggie. She was happy I made some kind of success for myself. I could've stayed there in the marsh all my life, doing the same thing every day: getting food half the time, lazing other times, maybe meet someone to love who was equally attuned to the marsh and happened by. Like Allie did when she met the daughter of that vacationing family. Or maybe I wouldn't meet anyone in the marsh. I'd get a dark tan, grow old, wrinkled, go a little crazy, and that would be that. But I left.

Going on two years since Mother died – the end of an era, some might say. The new society is in full bloom in various shades of gray. She wouldn't be happy with that, I suspect.

"That kinda talk'll get you put away," says my coworker. We're working on a particular nasty portion of sidewalk. I don't know his name, he doesn't know mine; names aren't important. If he needs to get my attention, he calls 'Sixteen' and I call him 'Twenty-four', the last two digits of our identification numbers.

"I'm not saying anything that hasn't been said before," I respond. "Her life covers a long period of time is all I'm saying."

Sweep, sweep, then dig a little bit to get the caked dirt out from the beautiful grooves in the sidewalk.

"It's why I made the video." We've worked together for a while so he knows about my mother and the video.

"But you best not go on about it."

"It's a fact. She lived her life, had those experiences. Can't deny it. I made the video. The video was broadcast. It existed."

"Them facts gonna get you in trouble."

"Facts are facts," I insist.

"No, they ain't. Facts is whatever they say is facts." He glances around. "I'm here today, but suppose they take me away. Tomorrow they be telling you I never existed. And that would be a fact, though you're talking to me today."

I repress a chuckle. "I get it. But I know what I know."

"Do you?"

"Yes, I do. I've visited the places of her life, saw them for myself. Talked to people. I know what really happened."

"Like I said: do you?"

We pause long enough for his wrist and then mine to buzz with electronic warning to keep at our work.

+ + +

Despite working to educate myself, getting employment, affecting a convincing Northern accent, I couldn't help but remain embarrassed by my family. Most of all my mother, Isla, who died on her seventy-ninth birthday, in the middle of the family gathering to celebrate it. I wasn't there. My sister, Amy June, told me about it: a peaceful end to a turbulent life, having lived more of it with Mother than I had. I'd left as soon as I could.

However, she was my mother. Of course I loved her, in principle, but it was hard to love her sometimes. Maybe that's the same for a lot of sons and daughters and their parents.

"Fritz, my lovely boy," she would call, "come over here and rub my feet, they aching again – but be gentle."

When I was young, I'd do it. I wanted to make her happy. As I got older, I found excuses to avoid it. Aching feet were the least of her woes. Her back, her shoulders, her neck – they all hurt. Part of the hard life she had. She never stopped talking about her hard life, making me feel guilty for making her go through it. By the time I was born, she'd been through that hard life so what followed that I witnessed didn't seem so bad.

I listened to her stories, couldn't avoid them. In fact, I made that video of her, using the resources of my station (with permission). No matter what I might have thought of her as my mother, her life was remarkable, given the way everything had developed in rebuilding a society after that ten-year pandemic. After enough time as Mother's servant, I left, got educated, started producing broadcasts, then met Sandra and we started a family. I returned and Mother was happy to see me, but she looked much worse for wear lazing in that marsh like a wild woman.

I interviewed her with my production crew and let her talk about her life, her parents' misadventures, and what my sisters did. Being her youngest, she didn't think I'd done anything of note. That I was interviewing her on camera didn't seem to count. That I introduced my family to her didn't make an impression. Her mind might have grown weak by then – more reason to get her oral history recorded.

Four-plus hours of raw footage edited down to fifty minutes, the video was seen by many – anyone who had the broadcast devices, the ones with attached screen. Because the service was new and the video was one of the first available it received a lot of attention. So did she. A few people insisted the things she said she experienced never happened, couldn't have happened, certainly not in the way she described – not in our beautiful, perfect world. That was against official history, as it quickly came to be rewritten. I was tasked with writing portions of that new version during the next few years. Mother's father kept notebooks, wrote out his thoughts and feelings about events. Mother kept it going with her limited education. I wanted to add to it but what I wrote was risky. I kept everything to myself, hid the notebooks away with the diary of our ancestor.

As the government regained its authority over us that video of Mother went away, became not merely a curiosity but something they deemed harmful. You couldn't find it on the streaming service. Not in a library, either, which were soon closed. No transcripts of the video existed but my handwritten script, which was destroyed when our home was raided by the Communications Authority. The disruption that day caused Sandra to miscarry our next child. She blamed me for it because my 'arrogance' had caused the raid.

45

"I hear ya," says my coworker. "But what're ya gonna do?"

"It's the truth." I glance around, check for monitors. People walk by and none would ever guess I made that notorious video. I blend in now. "I tried to save our history, with all its bumps and bruises, cuts and scrapes, the ugly with the rare moments of beauty and joy."

"Beauty and joy? Ha! Now you're zapping flies."

"I mean like my mother giving birth to my sisters. That brought her joy, she said."

"But in old days it's gonna hurt something awful. Not now. Not like they do in the laboratoriums or whatever. Artificial wombs and all. You put in couple samples and there ya go."

"Bubble babies," I sigh.

"Bubble babies," my coworker confirms.

"But who knows how healthy they are? What kind of people are being created? More obedient? Do they adjust their genes?"

"Heck, obedient's what they want, awrighty," my colleague says. "In fact, in the early pandemic days they was trying to make 'clones' – artificial people – that were virus resistant. I guess so they could do all the work while the rest of us natural people were sick. Never worked though."

"They forgot how to do science," I say with an awkward laugh. "They kept the books, some of them, anyway, but had to read them again, and extrapolate the rest. All the digital data was gone. They saved everything on devices that died. Lost all the data. They're still working on it, but obviously with an almost eighty-year set-back."

My coworker nods along, then stops, realizing a camera is close. He clears his throat twice, a signal. "But the song remains the same: an 'ideal society' with everyone in a place and a place for everyone, including 'artificial intelligence' machines, what some call 'robots' or 'androids'. They're in the books, some of the science fiction ones and some of the science technology ones. They really did exist. They was making them out west when I was there. I saw them."

"I can't believe they were so advanced in the past. So much lost."

"Now they have some of that technology back, and are working to restore what was lost. But here we are: still sweeping the streets. I heard they used to have machines for that."

"Notice they got the video and camera technology up first – after electricity itself. All the better for watching everyone, recording all of us in our daily tasks."

"They sure do got that all set up. It's for our safety."

"But why?" I have to ask, raising my voice. "Why do they need to watch us? To keep control of us? Keep us in our sectors?"

"I don't know," he says, motioning with his hand to quiet down. "Maybe it's about resources. Can't have people going to other sectors and taking the resources."

"Want to prevent overpopulation, stop crime, make sure nobody is going to rebel. Or be sure there's no virus outbreaks. Or that it spreads. I never reported on any of that."

As the video producer, I was questioned. I lost my position at the station. They bowed to authorities. I was assigned counseling. They required a year of weekly visits to bring me around to a proper way of thinking. First, however, a nine-month course in citizenship at a rehabilitation facility. It seemed they wanted me believing that the pandemic never happened and half the population hadn't died. The way things are now is the way they've always been, and aren't we lucky?

"How could they expect to hide so much?" I ask the breeze.

People remember. My mother lived through it. She remembered. I lived through some of it. I knew what happened, at least the things I experienced and heard about in the stories family members told me. But young people are taught different stories now. The older generation is just crazy, have weird ideas, took too many drugs and engaged in orgies, so don't listen to those old people. Part of my rehabilitation was to help them create the new narrative.

"You were part of that?" asks my coworker.

"I hate to admit, but yes."

"So you're somebody. And they got you sweeping the streets." He shakes his head, sweeping in a slow but steady rhythm.

"I got to make a new video. Not sure if it was ever shown on the streams. They liked to call it the 'true video' even though it wasn't."

"Well, I got none of those stream devices so I never could see it. Not so many others, I guess, could see it."

"That's probably for the best. Not my best work."

"I imagine. You being under the duress and all."

We've changed the official history three times. First, the virus that caused the pandemic was a natural event, unfortunate but no one was to blame. Then it changed to being an accident: people who should know better let it happen, thinking it couldn't happen. Now we are told to believe it was deliberate: our enemies released the virus to hurt us, even at the risk to their own population. A lot of people just went along with the idea that no matter how it started it was a terrible thing and the sooner we forget about what happened the sooner we could get on with rebuilding society. Anyone who still remembered it was urged to ignore their memories. The generation that followed would have no memory of those events.

I thought Mother's life was remarkable in a historical sense, so I asked questions but it was mostly letting her talk, telling the stories of her and her parents' lives, her grandmother's life as her father told it, and about that man long ago who brought the tuba here. She had a good memory of those events. Not too sharp about the past week, however.

"Old folks sure do like to talk, lemme tell ya."

"She sure did," I say. "Almost like she was boasting. Like 'my life was harder than your life' – like that."

"Sounds like a game she was playing with all y'all."

"Oh, she had her games, all right."

She had a hard life, yet it was easier at the beginning and at the end. An idyllic childhood, despite the poverty, and then a senior's comfortable reward. I got to witness the part at the end, when we moved from the National Park to the marshes. I lost my father at the start of that trip. He was a lot older than my mother. We were hiking down the mountain and his heart gave out.

"That sounds already a sad tale," my coworker says.

"Lots of sad tales from those days. That's the reason for making that video, I keep saying." I regard my coworker, realizing I talk too much. "And you have some sad tales, too, I know."

"Well, no need to tell those," he says, going through the motions of sweeping. "I was out west when the pandemic started, got to be by myself till it was done. Then I joined the army, only job there was."

"And you fought for the Northern Alliance," I continue for him. "My mother's dad was captured and forced to fight for the Northern Alliance. The other men, Mother said, were taken away to fight for the Southern Command."

"Well, no reason for it anyways," he says, wiping his face.

"But you rose up the ranks, didn't you?" I ask to cheer him up.

"Rose up? Heck, they put me in charge of a whole dang battalion at one time. Called me Major Purdy. And I took them right outta the battle. Yessir, I did. And they busted me down to Private-one so fast I thought the sun'd crashed."

"The Battle of Sycamore Ridge, wasn't it?"

He gives me a hard look, surprised I recall his previous stories. I'm just prodding him to make him talk more. It's good for him.

He takes a big breath. "Yep, sure was. Except most of those huge sycamores were blown up by then."

"That's a battle my grampa fought in. Mother said a mortar hit near him, killed his squad but he only had deafness for a few weeks. From the explosion."

"Well, he was a lucky one."

"You were lucky, too, right?"

"If you mean sitting in prison for a decade instead of being in the fighting, then I suppose so."

"And now you get to sweep the streets."

"Yup. Got my reward." He stares at our clean sidewalk. "Look at this thing of beauty."

Satisfied the pavement is sparkling clean now, we move to a new section of the sidewalk.

"I still think of home as that mountain, however," I say. "Where I was born, where I lived my first years. Where I met my sisters – a brother and others on the mountain that we might've been related to. Mother made it complicated. I gave up in the end. Knowing who my mother and father were was enough for my young head."

"That's always gonna be enough," says my coworker, sweeping.

But I have to explain:

Mother liked to tell how she was born on a coastal island in the seventh year of the Great Pandemic. Her mother called it the ten-year flu season. It ended in different places at different times, some after only nine years but in other places as long as fourteen years. Isolated outbreaks continued, but they were quickly and cruelly put down. A few outbreaks make the news even today, almost a century removed from the first cases. In that way, our life here at the start of the 22nd century isn't too different from the start of the 21st century when the world fell off a cliff into an apocalyptic abyss we had to claw our way out of.

Mother endured her parents' misadventures as they tried to find a good hiding place after being exiled from that awful island where they had found some kind of sanctuary. They were led to that island by Mother's grandmother because they had a vacation home there. When her grandmother was murdered by a jealous lover, Mother's father shot the man. For that act he was exiled. But his young wife went with him, carrying Mother in a baby sling.

"I guess that part's controversial," I mumble.

My coworker gives a "Mm-hmm."

They were young and didn't have wisdom or experience to make good decisions. It was more luck they survived at all with a baby during the time of violent marauders and hungry vagrants. Grampa Sandy wrote about their adventures in notebooks. He wrote mostly after they settled in the National Park.

However, living in a forest wasn't as much fun as you might've expected. Mother picked up the writing of history in a new notebook I got for her after we moved to the marshes. From her confessions I learned the truth of their life in the National Park: a community of survivors who shared everything: work, food, and wives. Much could be said about that kind of lifestyle yet Mother insisted it had more to do with saving the world than sexual pleasure.

"Yup, sure have some sad tales," says my coworker as we settle on a new tract of pavement to clean.

"They're not all sad, not in the usual way."

"I heard of them survivalists getting together like one big happy family and all."

"But it was cut short."

"What do you mean by that?" asks my coworker.

"I mean marauders came. Militia came. Then the slavers came. Until there was nobody left on the mountain."

"Oh."

With nothing to say, we commence sweeping the pavement.

A lot happened there on the mountain, not all pleasant. When Mother finally escaped from her servitude, she thought returning to the mountain in the National Park would be her sanctuary. But a lot had changed. The bad memories crowded out the good ones.

"She headed south eventually, taking me and the girls with her, leaving my father's dead body behind."

"You sure do got some sad tales," my coworker says.

"Told you."

Years passed. I wasn't there when Mother died. I'd moved north. I was tired of caring for a cranky old woman constantly complaining how her earlier hardships gave her the right to ease into the second half of her life. I agreed. But me being the only child left there, responsibility fell to me. My sisters had their own families. I came back for visits. I brought my family twice. I interviewed her, made the video. My broadcast station streamed it. It was viewed by people who were amazed at the life she described. In that way she became a minor celebrity.

Then Amy called me on the expensive telecom line to inform me that Mother had died. I only got to see her at the funeral.

I'd grown tired of her ways and her teasing. I even changed my name from Fritz to Frank, who was my father. Fritz, she told me too often, was my ancestor, the one who brought the tuba. She would tell me the story of his life yet again. She was like that: repeating events to not forget them. That was the reason I recorded her.

Doing that changed everything in my life. I still wonder who saw that video and took offense. Who would have the power to make the video disappear?

"Who would do that?" I ask.

"Guess it's somebody don't like you," says my coworker.

5

THE REMAINS

WHEN I'D HAD ENOUGH of Mother commanding everyone within earshot of her little marsh hut – mainly me – I decided to leave, no matter how much she begged me to stay and keep taking care of her. I didn't feel bad about leaving. I'd done enough, and she had others to care for her. My siblings had left already, gone to start their own lives. Now it was my turn. Besides, I never felt I was one of them, that whole clan she'd gathered around her. All my sisters. Then their children. I was overwhelmed. Mother accused me of not loving her, but I had to explain I was leaving exactly because I did love her.

I went north, about the only direction you could go from that marsh. I did a lot of walking. My plan was to find work anywhere I could, save my credits and exchange them – some of them but not all – for learning a trade. All I knew at that point was how to catch fish and how to snap at her every command. And I got no money for it. I knew I liked the view from Mother's shack, on her isle in the marsh, the brilliance of the sunrises, the glory of the sunsets, so I decided I wanted to learn to paint, make pictures that were beautiful. Maybe I'd give them to Mother and say 'sorry' for leaving. Or use the new medium of video.

On the way north I saw a sign for the same national park where we lived in my childhood. Mother said I was born there and I had no reason to doubt her. I had memories of the place. Long after much of the misery of her life had passed into her memory, I came along. She was trying for another kid, she told me when I was little, to make my father happy. He was an old man who'd lost his three children to the violence of a world in chaos. It took about three years of trying before I came along, with all my sisters gathered around to see me come out from her, crowded inside that little hut.

We lived there on that mountain for my first five years. So now, returning, my heart beat faster, thinking of the place, memories flooding me. I had to stop and see it again. No matter what I'd find there.

I got off the bus at the store there below the mountain and hiked up the trail that was overgrown now, the same one we came down to leave our mountain home. I looked hard at that spot beside the foot bridge over the stream where my father had fallen and not gotten up. He'd held a hand to his chest as he urged us to go on to the bus waiting across the road and get on with our lives.

There was no body there. Was my memory faulty? After so many years, did someone remove him? No signs of a grave. No marker. I paused for a silent prayer anyway. Not sure what or who I prayed to, just following Mother's ways. Then I hiked on up the mountain, fighting my way through the undergrowth.

My father was a lot older than my mother, and he'd been in the war – what people in the North called the Rebellion. People in the South called it the Tyranny. We didn't escape it. My father returned home to the mountain a broken man, finding everything gone. Only the arrival of my mother a few years later sustained him. It was long enough perhaps, but not for long. He died at the bottom of the mountain. Lots of stories Mother told. She was a talker. Sometimes she would confuse my father with her first husband – that's Amy June's father, a man they called LJ, short for Little Joe. I'd known him when I was a little boy; I played with his daughters and his younger brother.

After an hour hiking up the steep trail, back and forth as it rose through the forest, I broke into the clearing, what Mother had called the circle. It was where I lived as a child, there in a hut, the front made of wood with a door but going back into the hillside. When I looked, I was surprised to see it over there, still standing. But there was more: fresh paint on the wooden front and a sign post in front.

Most surprising was a group of people standing before it, maybe a dozen, and in front of them stood a woman in the green and blue uniform of the Forest Service, talking to them. I stopped to listen to her. She was telling the group of visitors the history of this place, of the people who lived here during the pandemic.

"At its peak, this national park held a hundred men, women, and children within its boundary," she said. "Although spreading across this mountain and the bottomland and elsewhere, this open area served as the center of the community. Here was where they would gather for meetings and festivals. It is also where a few of them are buried."

At that, I looked around, knowing where some of the graves were and remembering how Mother took me to sit with her as she spoke at the ground. She said her parents were buried here. She had to tell them whatever she was doing and how everyone was, as though they were asleep. There, to the side of the clearing, stood another sign post, right where Mother's parents lay in their resting spot, the mound almost unrecognizable now.

I strolled over to the sign at the foot of the grave. The Forest Service kept the grass trimmed. I leaned toward the sign.

Couple laid to rest together to save labor. Ground imaging shows an adult male with broken neck, the likely cause of death. Female remains are in granular form, likely from cremation in another location and deposited here. Age dating determines both to have died in middle age.

Smiling at the scientific discovery, I wanted to add more details to the story. But the group was moving toward me.

"Are you part of the tour?" asked the Forest Service guide.

I shook my head, still gazing down at the grave, then regarded her with a grin.

"I've been here before," I replied.

"Even so," said the guide, "please stay with the group."

The four huts around the clearing had been renovated. Someone presumed they looked a certain way years before, made them look that way again. Actually, there was never any paint on the wooden entrances, and hardly any decorations. We never had the idea to live here the rest of our lives. We expected we'd return home, but that day never came. The world never did return to the way it was before. Finally, Mother decided we should leave anyway, go south where she believed life would be easier. Her Aunt Kristin and cousins George and Clay had gone there years before.

I knew there were graves here. A lot of violence had occurred in this clearing. I could feel the energy, the fear. I stood dumbfounded at the signs planted here and there. I went up to one, read the text about how 'survivalists' lived in poor conditions while hiding out in this national park. I heard the guide explain our circumstances.

"Why'd they do it?" asked one of the tourists.

"As the visitor center display states," the guide said, "people thought they could hide from the virus. Enough like thinkers came here and formed a community. They shared everything and thought they were getting by. Yet, as you see, they didn't survive. There are reports of attacks and we may surmise that some of them died as a result. Others left, returning to the city for employment. Those who stayed the longest...are still here." She waved her hand at the grave where my grandparents were buried.

What the guide was saying was wrong, I knew. Attacks? Mother told about the Forest Service visiting them. They marched the men away, sent them to war, fighting for the Southern Command. That left the women vulnerable to the next band of marauders who were actually slavers. Jobs in the city? No, the women were sold off as concubines or brothel workers. My mother was one of them. She had to commit murder to escape, to get her freedom. Then she returned to this mountain, the only real home she had known.

"Sir?" the guide called.

I'd gone into that place where Mother used to go, a dark cavern of forbidden memories.

"Keep up," she said, and I gave a nod.

She led the group counter-clockwise around the circle. First over to the forlorn shack where a poor family had lived. It had fallen into ruin after so many years, of course, but I knew it. A woman named

Megan lived there long ago. Mother spoke of her sometimes. Megan had been a friend of Grandma Hannah. The guide recited a few poor facts, answered questions. Always *poor* this and *poor* that with the guide. The mood was sad, the visitors behaving as though they were walking through a cemetery – which they were.

It had been Mother's habit to go over to her parents' grave at the edge of the clearing, kneel and talk to them each day. She made me kneel beside her, put my hands together for prayer. She told them about her latest child: "This is Fritz, named for our ancestor on account of him being this kind of new beginning for us, all us, like that ancestor did long time ago, him and that tuba." She apologized to Grandma Hannah for getting together with Frank, my father, the same man who had a daughter with Hannah: my big sister Cherie, who I'd never met because she was so much older she was already married and lived far away before I was born.

"Sir?"

It was the tour guide calling me again. I stood at the spot where a sign had been erected like a tombstone, marking my grandparents' final resting spot: Grampa Sandy and Grandma Hannah. I could almost feel their breaths.

"Please stay with the group. We'll come to this spot in a while."

I didn't have the heart to tell her I knew about everything here. Except when and why someone had turned this place into some kind of a memorial. I didn't object. I only wondered who had the idea and who put that idea into action. Nothing to memorialize about. A few families tried to get by, wait out the pandemic, hiding in the forest of a national park – as though that was such an odd thing to do back then when the world was going mad.

"In the later years of the pandemic," the guide spoke in practiced voice, "families hid on this mountain, hoping to keep away from the virus and anyone infected with it."

Like I said. She turned at my mumbling, frowned.

"You can see the poor conditions they endured. Here they had no medicine, no vaccines, no doctors, and the deaths came quickly. You can see the graves everywhere in this clearing."

But I knew the graves came from random violence, not from the virus that shut down the world for ten years. Mother told me what happened. She wouldn't ever stop talking about it. The folks didn't hurt each other. It was outsiders coming up the mountain who brought pain and misery. Marauders taking whatever they wanted, killing without thought, ruling a lawless countryside. Or the more organized, authorized squads of men who captured these women, considered nothing more than cords of wood that anyone could take, and sold them into slavery. Or took the men away to serve the militias of either the North or South.

"Life was hard for these survivalists," the guide intoned behind me. She explained about the harsh living conditions and the threats to survival they faced. That *we* faced. I was here, I lived it, and my mother had the worst of it. This guide made it sound as though we were all cursed to live here, forced here as a cruel punishment.

I just smiled, staring down at the mound. Mother always talked about her childhood on this mountain as though it was a paradise. She was happy here. At least in her childhood. What kid wouldn't love playing in a forest? It was later that bad things happened.

I'd heard enough of Mother's recalls: "Now you give a listen here, Fritz, cuz I'm about to tell ya something 'portant." Then she would tell a story of someone doing something and I pretended to listen. Hearing this guide talk, I wished I'd listened better to Mother so I could refute this guide.

My memories were short. I turned to the hut where I was born. It still stood.

"Sir?" the guide called into the hut. "Others are waiting."

It was small enough, she stated, that only one person could go in at a time. I could've stayed longer, absorbing thoughts and feelings. Mother and my father slept there. My sisters slept there. That was where we cooked meals. I looked at my wooden crib with rockers and couldn't believe I had ever been that tiny. This crib was just a prop, I was certain, couldn't be the same crib I used. Yet it looked the same as in my memories.

A wooden front with a hinged door stood as the entrance to what was still mostly a dug-out home. It went back into the hillside ten feet, the dirt floors now covered with ratty rugs and plastic mats, with wooden posts for support, and the glass bottle window in the girls' room. It was actually quite comfortable, especially in winter. Three rooms: the main room when you first enter, then two rooms side by side used for sleeping. They weren't so large you could stand up in, but you could get around easily enough on your knees. You had to duck down to go in the front door, I discovered. As a baby and up to age five I never had to duck. Now I bumped my head.

From there I'd run around the clearing, and out the paths in any direction looking for other kids to play with. But I only found those of our neighbor, the big man named Joe and his wife, Lori. They had kids my age but all girls. Funny story about the girls, how they grew up, left the mountain and the national park. One of those girls ran away with her brother, headed out west to seek their fortune. That's for later. And the way Joe, once my mother's husband, ended up down south in the marshes with her once again is another story for later. That part of her life didn't get into the video.

After the last visitor exited, I poked my head in again to have a final look. But I felt nothing seeing it, being inside. My mind knew it was the same place where I was conceived and later born. Right there I lay at Mother's breast as my sisters bunched together in the next room, chattering and giggling and my father shouting for them to be quiet. Later, as a baby and up to the time we left, I slept among my four sisters, leaving our parents to their games in the next room, just inches away. We pretended not to hear anything.

"Such a primitive life these poor people lived."

The guide didn't need to put it in such dire terms.

"No electrical power, no water in pipes, no heat but a campfire, no cooling but the breeze that might drift by. Food was whatever they could grow in small gardens or gather from the wild, and small animals caught in traps, fish from the stream below the mountain, or sometimes a deer killed in the fall. A hard life."

I didn't remember ever going hungry, though.

The guide gave me a hard look, as though she could hear my thoughts. She objected to my presence, me not following the protocol and accepting her version of events. The world was returning to a normal society, people figuring out how to get along with each other.

We were left alone, mere country folk, ignorant and savage, not to be engaged with. She glared at me, seeing through my disguise.

"It's all right," I responded. "I've taken the tour before."

That seemed to put her at ease. She continued explaining how these *poor* people managed to survive, the clever things they did to get by, and her curious charges sighed in sorrow for the harsh lives these survivors had suffered through.

"Let us go to the second site."

The guide led us along a path now laid with wooden slats over the dirt, a few minutes' walk. I knew where we were going: over to Joe's cabin. It was Grandpa Sandy who actually built it, with help from other men of the community, including Little Joe's father, Big Joe. By the time Mother returned, years had passed and LJ had moved in with Big Joe's widow. Time being what it was, they had kids. Mother had no complaint about it, he being her husband with no official divorce. People did what they had to do. I visited this cabin plenty as a little boy, slept over a few nights. We were all one big family, all of us on the mountain.

More little signs to describe what we were seeing. Two sites for us to see. The cabin had been restored and looked livable, as though they had just gone down to the stream to fetch a pail of water and would be right back. I laughed to myself but caught the attention of the guide. I wanted to share my amusement with her and this group of tourists. Playing with the daughters here, how they tried to make me lay like a wounded boy and would fix me like they were doctors. They probably wouldn't appreciate the irony of that situation when my mother returned after ten years to find her husband living with his father's wife and all that followed. She was just happy to see he was alive.

Nobody lived in the cabin now obviously and there were only two graves nearby, not enough to account for a whole family. But I knew what happened, and it was kind of a happy ending. I took a breath, getting ready to speak.

Before I could say anything, the guide turned us in the opposite direction, led us to the mound. She explained this was a mass grave. That wasn't wrong. I knew it had been the dug-out home where my mother and her sisters lived with their parents. Her father, Sandy, dug out a fox burrow, she told me. They'd thought they were alone in the forest and might've been for a year or so before discovering others had also settled in the National Park to escape the pandemic. That was long before I was born; my mother was a toddler herself. Her father hollowed it out, kept expanding it over the years, and Little Joe's papa added the wooden door later, which was no longer in place. It didn't need any door now anyway. They were still living in this dug-out home when a band of marauders came and took the women away.

The story Mother told was how the marauders took all the young kids, not wanting to deal with them, stuffed them inside the dug-out home then lit a fire to suffocate them with the smoke. They all died. One of her young sisters managed to claw her way out and survived. But the dug-out home Grandpa Sandy built became a mass grave. That was true. Mother told me about it. The sign acknowledged the number of remains, labeling it as 'human sacrifice' with 'identities unknown'.

"When they had too many mouths to feed," the guide said after a respectful moment of silence, "they would take the young children to a place like this and put them to sleep. Each year they would have a lottery to decide which of their children would die. It was a common practice among the survivalists. They enforced strict limits on how many children each family could have, based on success at obtaining food. In good years they had more children. In lean years...*this*."

I had to clear my throat and she glared at me. Shaking my head, I was about to offer my version, but she continued.

"Imaging determined there to be nine young bodies inside, from infants to children of eight or nine years. Out of respect for those killed, we have not opened up this site to further examination. A diagram is displayed in the visitor center, if you're interested in how the interior appears. You will note the mound is more pronounced than its original dimensions because it was disturbed several years before – presumed by treasure hunters – but has naturally resettled over time. You can see a representation of the mound in the visitor center."

Mother would avoid this place, even going out of her way to go to the cabin or down to the stream. She was the one who disturbed the mound, going inside to get that tuba out. She closed it up as best she could and never looked back, just prayed for all the little souls left inside. I met Ellie, my half-sister, who got out of it and survived but she was too old then for her to play with me.

Disappointed, I followed the group down the other slope, over a nice new trail with wooden steps and a gravel walkway, to another cabin with more sign posts. This cabin looked newly built. They had turned this entire national park into an historic landmark, renamed it Sorrow Mountain. They added food kiosks and a playground for restless kids. A parking lot for vehicles. Picnic tables. A less than solemn memorial to those misfits who thought they could wait out a pandemic. I had to chuckle. Mother's stories were correct, I realized. I knew then I had to share her stories.

Beside the newly built cabin serving as the Visitor Center was a small enclosure containing small animals. Children could pet ducks, chickens, goats, and a donkey as though playing survivalist settlers. But we never had any pets. There was no petting zoo for us trying to survive. In fact, one time when Mother found a few goats escaped from a farm wandering over to the bottoms, she got my sisters and they captured the goats. We kept the mama for milk and roasted the old ram. Later the mama had a kid with one of the young males.

I watched a while as the children made friends with the bored animals, then I went inside.

Inside, it was apparent someone had done their homework, had scrounged up information about folks who'd lived on the mountain and elsewhere in the old National Park, what was now a National Monument site to remember the folks who thought they could hide from the pandemic.

On the long wall were a hundred pictures – arranged in family groups. I looked closer.

Some of the pictures on the walls I recognized, even though they were 'before' images. There weren't any cameras for 'after' views. The batteries in digital cameras ran out, couldn't be recharged, and the photos on those cameras were lost. Only those images printed on paper before the pandemic, most often framed or slipped into photo albums, managed to survive. They made copies from archives – from a list of licensing photos to operate motor vehicles. Other pictures came from old school photo books.

I leaned toward the brownish pictures, read the tags under each picture. Here was Frank Kendall with short hair combed neatly, a youthful line of moustache across his lip, looking smug and full of the bravado of a baseball slugger, quoted as saying he hoped to join the major league someday. I stared at my father, his youthful gaze, so full of hope. Mother only knew him as an adult, and he was far from a baseball player although he was good with archery, she said.

Beside his picture, as though they were together on the same page of the original source, the school's student portraits, called a Yearbook, were two girls looking like twins: Louann and Lorraine Kennedy. Both had long blonde hair, white in the sepia prints, and didn't seem to want to smile for their photographs. Together on the page, and together again when the pandemic struck and parents got sick and died. Frank took the girls south out of their city, and soon found the forest of this national park, making it their home. I knew them: my aunts, dead before I was born.

It got complicated. Frank and Louann, not much out of their teens, had a daughter they named Charlotte, or Charly, and a son named Drew. Later, they had a son named Rudy. Lorraine finally had a child: a daughter named Polly with Grampa Sandy. That was the same time Grandma Hannah had a daughter with Frank in a wife-trade and named her Cherie. The start of a clan – a family of forest settlers, as it turned out. But it couldn't last. Life would get in the way; marauders would come, militia would fight, a lot of bad things swept them away never to return to this site.

I stared at the pictures. There weren't any images of my mother or her parents. I guessed that was the divide: Frank and the twins the last to go to school and be photographed. Mother's parents, being younger, missing that with having a 'virtual' school, then no school at all. It put everything in proper perspective. I knew Mother was born in the seventh year of the pandemic. I knew her parents had fled their city the year before her birth, tried to live with other family members but found them worse off than them. They ended up on a resort island along the coast, and that is where her parents got together. It's better the way Mother told it.

In the fine print under the collection of pictures was the answer to my question: *Carolina Genetic Testing* provided the identification data. That explained how they knew about Frank and my aunts. His body was found at the bottom of the trail. Who is this man? They would check about his life. A small plaque stated he served in the Southern Command, rose to corporal, got wounded and relieved of duty eventually, made his way home where nothing remained: no wife or sister-in-law, no children, no neighbors.

I stared hard at this happy-go-lucky teen boy framed on the wall, not knowing what fate would be measured out for him. I was unable to feel anything but gut-ripping pity for a life lost to him. He existed only in the stories of my mother. And now me. I desperately wanted to meet him, talk with him, really get to know my father.

I knew then I had to document that life, the whole clan, tell their stories to the world. We did exist. We loved, we died, and we weren't bad people. We did what we had to do.

"Why they call it Sour Mountain?" asked a little boy outside the visitor center as I was exiting.

"It's not 'sour', it's Sorrow," said his nicely dressed father, taking the boy's hand to lead him inside. "Because the crazy people living here buried their kids in a mass grave. Maybe couldn't feed them."

The mother, infant daughter in her arms, added: "Times were so hard back then."

The story this site told was disheartening. At worst, a complete lie. At best, a sympathetic homage to a few decades most of us would rather forget. But I knew the truth. I'd lived through part of it and Mother had lived through almost all of it. I regretted stopping here, but having visited it I knew what I had to do.

6

FAMILY

LEAVING SORROW MOUNTAIN NATIONAL PARK, I continued north to the city where Mother lived and worked for a few years. It had grown a lot in the decades since. Rebuilding had produced a new, clean city, welcoming visitors and those seeking a better life. I took odd jobs and saved the New Dollars I got. I decided on a school and program of study. I would learn this new art of video streaming. Then I'd use the medium to tell my mother's story.

When I got hired at the local broadcast station, I further planned my project. I met Sandra Dubinsky at the station. A year older than me, she was already a news reporter. She was part of the team that followed the re-election campaign of a senator. Sandra wrote reports and sent them to the station by telestream – what I imagined was how my grandparents sent their typed messages over the airways in the days before the pandemic. I still had Grandma Hannah's small device full of old songs, the genre they called 'pandemic pop' which were out of favor then.

Sandra was older than me but I was taller. We liked each other's smiles, became a couple. Life was still free then, so we did as we pleased, no forms to fill out. We shared an apartment without getting the marriage license. Everyone could do as they pleased; the pandemic was long over and society was rebuilding, so people were happy again and treating each other kindly.

Feeling positive about the world, we got married on the two-year anniversary of our meeting. We went to a crumbling church near the broadcast station because Sandra said it looked pretty with its twin towers, what I learned were 'steeples'. We pulled the minister out from morning prayers, begged him to say the important words even in an empty auditorium. There weren't any other people who would attend, we assured him. Sandra's family, those who were still alive after the pandemic and its aftermath, lived far away like mine did. We took the ceremony seriously, feeling the sacred bond forming. Then we hesitated when he told us to kiss. The custom of keeping apart was stuck in our heads. But we gave it a good try.

Sandra was already pregnant by then, we discovered. We named our first son Frank, after my father. That was when I dropped Fritz and became Frank the Second. My son was Frank III. The son who came along the next year we named James after her father who died from the virus. A few years after that we had a daughter we named Maggie after nobody in particular. Sandra liked the name.

By then the video stream project was underway.

We made the long trip south to let Mother tell her stories to my camera. I thought I was doing something good. Preserving history. I had no idea it would be so controversial. History is a good thing, no matter what happens. Save it, study it, learn from it – no matter if it's good or bad, no matter if your side wins or loses. It's still a set of facts. We can argue about the details later. First of all, preserve it. But in the end, not everyone saw it that way. Facts are inconvenient sometimes. As the political situation changed, the people who made their way to the top of the tower decided some facts had to go. Too many embarrassing things. Too much bother to have to account for what happened, for what was allowed, what was enforced during the darkest days of our nation. That wasn't who we were.

I boasted about my project, got support from my employer and a grant. Mother cooperated. My crew didn't mind the marsh heat. One team member met a girl there; they had fun. He quit the station and moved down there once the project was finished. And my sister, Amy June, brought her kids to visit during my trip. Being Mother's oldest child, she already had three daughters. I felt good having my family meet Amy's family. I believed everything was going to be wonderful. We were recording history.

However, every night when I put my head to the hard pillow in my rehabilitation facility cell, I could still hear the shouting in the courtroom, filling my head, keeping me from sleep.

"And you decided on your own – entirely on your own, you insist – to capture this mad woman's raving lunacy using the new video technology," the portly prosecutor chastised, "so that everyone might hear her vile lies, and make us weep for her? Is that the truth?"

I never thought she was raving. Her demeanor was rather 'laid-back' as they used to call it. The marsh way. And whatever she was saying were her own words, nothing anyone told her to say. That was the key point: that some devious person bent on disrupting our society's order would go down there and tell her what to say just to cause trouble. I doubted she could memorize even a short script at her age. I had only a few questions planned, and I let her talk. She would drift off topic. Other questions naturally arose, but I just let her talk then edited the raw footage later for clarity and continuity. Her talk never got into politics, except for a few jabs about those servitude contracts. But everyone agreed they were an awful effect of the pandemic.

"It was well-received by viewers," I countered from my tiny box beside the judge. "Nobody complained about the stream or anything she said. Maybe they didn't believe her – which is fine – or, if they did believe, anything she said could be construed as her version of events. That doesn't change a thing. It doesn't mean the official version is a lie—"

"Official *version*?" the red-faced prosecutor exploded. "There is but one 'version' and it is the sole truth, nothing more and nothing less, so help us God. Variations only confuse people and aren't allowed. Yet you dared to offer up your own mother to push these harmful lies!"

"I didn't *offer* my own mother. I felt her life was remarkable and should be shared with the public. To give them another view of the way things happened during the pandemic era and after—"

"Another view? Why, this is pure drama! Nothing but a drama, Your Honor. A stage play for our entertainment. Indeed!"

"If viewers took it as entertainment, they were free to do so."

"You labeled it as 'history' on the titles and included two famous historians in the credits. Were you not attempting to claim this was truth by including their names? A deceptive act."

"No! When I conceived the project, I thought of it as a 'human interest' story. She's quite a character. She had no reason to lie about things in her life. A lot of bad things happened, but she was willing to talk about them. She had no political agenda. She was just telling stories to her son. I got it on video to save it for later."

"Save it for whom?" cried the prosecutor. "Historians? Schools? Our impressionable children? What kind of world would we have if a false narrative were allowed to be known?"

"People need to be allowed alternate views of—"

"Alternate views are lies!"

"But can any two people ever have the same view of the same event?" I dared inquire. "Even standing side by side?"

The courtroom crowd clamored and the judge banged his gavel.

I would usually awaken at that point, being too agitated to go on sleeping. I'd sit up on my bunk and rub my face in my hands. What did I do wrong? Nobody had complained about the video for years – then someone did.

"You are hereby assigned to rehabilitation for a period of nine months, minimum, extended as necessary for insufficient progress."

The judge hit the gavel on the pad and it was done.

I actually served nine months and nineteen days, counting the in-processing and out-processing time. I didn't learn a lot. I mostly understood how the world had changed, and what steps I needed to take to adapt to it. I wished I'd stayed in the marsh with Mother and go out fishing and crabbing every day, maybe play her tuba.

I was released into the city on a cold, gray day, shivering in my gray uniform with no coat, a paper of discharge in my hand and a notice to appear at a certain office on a certain day for my new job assignment. We weren't allowed to be idle for too long, I discovered. A lot had changed during the past few years. I hadn't noticed it day by day, but returning from the rehabilitation facility, it all seemed shocking.

My release papers got me a free ride on the local bus and I went to my home on 14th Street at Oak Avenue, level 7, unit 21. The pass card they returned to me upon my departure didn't open the door. I knocked on the door, then pounded hard when no one answered. The loud knocking and my desperate shouting caught the attention of the floor monitor. A burly fellow I knew only as Mel bulled out of his unit complaining of the noise.

"You're back," he grunted.

I showed him my release papers and waited as he looked them over, nodding and *hmm-hmm*ing at the information.

"It's all in order," I assured him.

"Yeah, well, you don't live here no more," Mel said.

"Don't live here? But why?"

"No reason. Moved out."

"My family moved out? Where did they go?" I grew desperate.

"Don't know. Better check with Housing Authority. Anyways, it's why your card don't work no more."

"So I can't get in? Can't get my belongings?"

He paused to think. "Your things's probably in storage."

"But where did my family go?" Then I had a frightening thought I dared not believe. "Were they taken away? Like by the monitors? Or did they decide to move on their own?"

"Can't say. Don't know. See Housing Authority."

I turned to go – but go where? I literally had the coveralls I wore, a pair of work boots, my papers, an identification badge, and a small sack of personal effects, mostly toiletry items from rehabilitation.

"You say my things are downstairs?" I asked Mel.

"Level two, in the back."

"Will this card work on the lock?"

"Lock? There ain't no locks down there."

"My things are just sitting there unlocked?"

"Look, nobody's gonna take your things. Nobody want'em. There are cameras, too, if anybody wants to steal it."

I gave Mel a nod, the least I could do in this new society, and headed down to the basement.

Spaces on the shelving down there were labeled for each unit. I went to my spot and found an old box sitting there. In the box was just some trash, nothing of value.

I grew frantic. Before assignment to the rehabilitation facility, I had items of personal value in the unit. Like my mother's tuba. Like her ancestor's diary. Like the iron ring hammered out by Big Joe for Mother's wedding with Little Joe. Like the stack of notebooks my grandfather wrote in about his adventures during the pandemic, living on that island, trying to survive when they were exiled, what he'd titled *The Way of the Son*. And an album of real paper photos of Grandma Hannah and her siblings as children. The kind of things that had no price. They were given to me, or I took them, because I was the last of Isla's children.

Sandra must've taken those things with her, wherever they had moved. That thought gave me some reassurance.

Next stop: Housing Authority.

Another tall, gray building, as friendly-looking as a rock. Inside, people waited. The din reminded me of the rehabilitation facility. A few people looked up when I entered, kept eyes on me, me wearing my release uniform. A couple others wore the same uniform. We were looking for housing. I was looking for my family's new housing.

Calling my number after four hours, I went to window 13, spoke to an older woman in a gray sweater, name tag: Ninety-four. Below her designated number was her name in very small letters: Molly. I showed her my release papers. She assumed I wanted a unit. She put my name on a list. Next.

"No, I'm looking for my family. They moved out of our unit. But I don't know where they are now. Can you find them in the system?"

It took some persuading. Molly tried, took her time. Frustrated, she popped up and went to get a drink, returned after a while, and continued typing on the machine, pausing to look at the results. I grew tired standing before her window, a healthy six-foot distance.

She cleared her throat. "You say you were in rehabilitation?"

I stepped forward. A beep from somewhere. I stepped back to the mark on the floor.

"Yes. Nine months. But I'm released from that now."

"Right." She nodded her head like everything made sense.

"What's right?" I asked her.

"You were in rehabilitation. So your wife filed separation papers. Relocation." When she finished reading the screen, she looked up at me. "You'll get new papers when things are settled."

"But where will I receive them if I have no place to live?"

"I put you on the list. You'll be assigned a unit soon. May have to share. But as a single worker that's how it's done. Everyone gets the same amount of space."

"I'm not a single worker. I have a wife. We have three children. Isn't that in your system?"

"You *used to* have a wife and three children," she said. "But you were assigned rehabilitation. I know it can get confusing. You see, when a citizen is assigned to rehabilitation, like you was, the spouse often files for separation. Don't wanna be associated with anybody in rehabilitation. I'm sure you understand. Don't you? It happens."

"But...but we love each other," I muttered.

"I'm not in charge of that." She flashed a smirk, reminding me of my mother. "Happened to my husband, too. Damn fool went and got himself in trouble, sentenced to five years. Well, I'm not gonna wait around that long for him to get fixed. I sent those papers off the next day, good riddance."

I must've gone pale – more pale. Molly called the guards over to get me. They asked if I was ill. Shaking my head to that, they took me from the mark on the floor and helped me over to a seat. One sat beside me, the other standing over me.

"I wasn't causing any trouble," I forced myself to speak. "I was in shock at...at what she said. That's all. I'm completely fine."

"We have to account for any abnormal behavior while in a public zone. You understand, right?" said the standing guard.

I nodded. "Understood."

"What's your business today?" asked the guard sitting by me.

I turned to him. With a deep breath, I told the story of my day, of not finding my family in our usual unit and being sent over here for information.

"She put me on a housing list anyway. Said I'm a single worker." Emotions rattled through me. "I just want my family again. I want my things, what my mother saved for me. I want my tuba."

"Tuba?" asked the standing guard. "You mean one of those big metal things that play the low notes? I saw one in a museum when I was a boy. Nobody uses them now."

"Yeah," said the guard beside me. "I know what they are. Saw it in a book long time ago. Always next to them long things that slide in and out. What're they called?"

"I think they're 'trombones'."

"Trombones, huh?"

"And they got horns and trumpets, too. All made of metal back in the day. Anyways, not necessary these days. People can make the same sounds on machines. Don't need to waste metal."

"Yeah, I read where they broke up tons of those wooden musical instruments. The ones with strings on them. Just smashed them all into pieces. Made a big pile and set it on fire. A lot of people cheered. Nobody needs those any more, they were saying. Just get in the way of a full day's work."

"That music stuff just gets people sad or makes them mad."

That wasn't helping my mood. I asked them where I should go to get answers about my family. The guard sitting beside me suggested the information might be restricted.

"Maybe they don't want you to find them," he said.

"It was only nine months. I had model behavior."

"Doesn't matter. Whatever the spouse wants."

"But where should I go to get an answer to the question of why?"

The guard standing over me grinned, confusing me.

"You can go to any building for that answer. Look around. Here's your answer. The 'why' is because we live in this here society, where everything's got a function and nobody gets out for free."

+   +   +

It's a Thursday according to the giant clock/calendar on the outside of the tall office building overlooking the forlorn little park. Workers need to know what time it is, what day it is. All I know is that it took thirty-eight days to finally get an appointment to meet Sandra. Working through the Separation Office protocol came close in effort to fighting my way through a gang of marauders. A lot of details had to be worked out first. Finally she consented.

"Thanks for coming," I say, in an unnecessarily solemn voice. "I wasn't sure you would."

We sit across the park bench from each other, a pair of monitors standing nearby to make sure I don't fly into a rage. That kind of emotional display is frowned upon. They need to protect Sandra from me, her husband. Only I'm not any longer, apparently. Yes, I saw the papers, finally got my own copy in an attractive envelope.

"It's the least I can do," she mutters like she doesn't really want me to hear her. "I didn't want to."

Sandra looks good, healthy, with a scarf tied around her head. I can't see any hair hanging from under it, her once lovely blonde locks. When I ask, she admits to getting the shave. Bald heads are easier to care for, she explains. Having no hair is one less thing to worry about each morning before going to work. It's an ideological statement, in my opinion. Mine is growing back, too, after my initial shave at the rehabilitation facility.

"Didn't want to meet me?" I ask softly.

"No, didn't want to file the papers. But...."

"But what?"

"They kinda pushed me. Said it was for my own good."

"They always say that. Everything is for the common good, but it's really for *their* good, not ours."

"They said I'd get a better unit as a single mother. An increase in my allowance, too, since you wouldn't be providing income for us."

"But I was providing income—"

"Not when you were there in that facility."

My breath stops. "Yes, I suppose. That's how they see it. But I wasn't meant to be there. It was all a mistake."

"Mistake or not, you were assigned to get rehabilitation. For that awful video you made. I still cannot believe you would exploit your poor mother that way."

"I didn't exploit her. I let her speak, tell her stories."

"Then you showed it to everyone. She said it was private."

"She also said she didn't mind others seeing it."

"Anyway...." She looks up and our eyes meet. She glances away. "You being in rehabilitation left everyone suspicious of us. I had to file the papers. I had to show we weren't part of your...your scheme. But I know it will be better this way. We'll be fine."

"What about me?" I shake my head. "I go away for nine months for something I did years ago that was fully allowed back then, even praised, and now I lose everything because of it? My wife and my children, my home, my job? How is that fair?"

"Well, they say life isn't fair. It's just."

"Just, huh? How is what happened to me justice?"

She doesn't have an answer, keeps shaking her head, looking down. One monitor steps closer. She senses his presence, flashes a smile to let him know everything is fine. A few tears roll down her cheek, however.

"Well, I've gotten a unit," I say in a fairly calm voice, already too stressed to produce sufficient rage. "It's like the bedroom we used to have. Same size. It's in that building over there, the tall, gray one, just over the wall there. I have a pass to come on this side today to see you – one of those Twenty passes, the ones that let you cross into neighboring sectors. Never had one of those before – but I probably won't again. Not unless we have official business to discuss. But you can see my building from here, at least. The first week they put me in a unit with another guy. We had to share. Not good."

I wait for her response as I consider the pass like old money. The Fifty pass will let you go anywhere in the city, cross through every checkpoint; those must be earned. Like when you're given vacation leave. Authorities carry the Hundred passes that will unlock sealed doors and opened gates. You can go anywhere. If I had one of those, I'd exit the city completely and make my way south, forgetting my hopes and dreams.

Sandra looks down, fidgeting with her fingers, then retrieves a tissue from her coat pocket and dabs her eyes.

"I wonder how your new place is," I say.

"It's enough. The boys stay at the school, of course. So it's plenty for Maggie and me."

"And the tuba?" I ask, looking up.

She purses her lips. "Actually, I want to sell it. Get rid of that old thing. I know a man who'll give me a good rate for it. Another man will take it away for a lot less."

"No," I burst, catching the attention of the monitors. I wave and smile. "It's mine. It's my mother's. You have no right to sell it."

"But music is a luxury we don't need. That's what they say."

"They again. Always 'they'! Who is that, Big Brother?"

"Shh!" She bats her eyes as a warning. "I don't know what you're talking about."

"It's just two words." But I know what she means.

Turning her head slightly as if to look at the nearest monitor, she speaks clearly: "I have no idea what that means. I assume it's one of those banned books. And good it was banned. We don't need that kind of fantasy story in our society."

I pick up on her tone. "No, we don't. I misspoke. Forgive me. A lapse of my education. Not so well written. Didn't make sense. Or so critics said. Glad it's gone."

"Talking about banned books is a waste of our time. We should be working." She has taken off from her clerk job to meet me.

"Sorry," I reply, bowing my head. "I know the rules."

"It's what the State Labor Office says. The latest report states that music detracts from our work effort, which costs time. Even if some people wish to rest in their units during their non-labor time, there's plenty of previously recorded music they can access. No need for any new music."

"Then call it an heirloom. An antique. It's worth saving."

"For the metal? That could be used in far better ways?"

"For my memories," I almost burst again.

"Memories stay in your head. No need to save them elsewhere."

"You've become impossible," I say coldly.

She breaks into tears and the closest monitor comes over to us.

"Citizen," he addresses her, "are you well? Is this citizen causing you discomfort?"

She shakes her head, wipes her eyes. "Nothing I didn't expect. We used to be married."

"Ah, I see," he says.

The monitor glares at me, like everything is my fault.

"You have two minutes remaining in this conference," he says to me, shifting his weapon to his other shoulder: a direct energy rifle that hurts if the beam strikes you, can kill if it's turned on a higher setting. I don't believe he'd use such a device on me just for causing another citizen to cry.

"Let me have the tuba," I say. "And the notebooks and diary my mother gave me. Maybe some small trinkets. That's all I want. Then I'll sign the documents."

Still teary, she mumbles: "Thank you."

7

MOTIVATIONS

EVERY DAY IS THE SAME NOW: on the street, cleaning it for everyone. Sweep, sweep, sweep. Scrub, scrub. Polish here and there. You could eat off this sidewalk. We step back to admire our work, knowing our effort and consideration for cleanliness will not garner us additional credits. But we will feel better about ourselves, our place in this city. That is our reward, they tell us: "Job Well Done Is Job One."

"I still don't have that tuba," I say with a grunt as I stand beside my coworker, Twenty-four. "She's never at home when I come by – and, yes, she knows I'm coming by. Those passes don't come cheap."

"Sounds like she don't wanna give it up," Twenty-four says.

"There's not much I can do if she doesn't want to give it to me."

"You could just take it, couldn't you?"

I smile at him. "You mean like steal it?"

"Hell yeah. I know people do that all the time. Specially over in sector ten where all the crime is. They sell it outside the city."

"But how could they go into her sector? With no passes."

"You know criminals don't follow rules. You know that, don't you?" He chuckles, stops himself.

"I've heard that. But officially we don't have any criminals in the city. I've also heard the punishment for getting caught."

"Getting caught is the thing to watch for." He chuckles again, like a persistent cough. "That's what got me sent five years to the rehabilitation facility. I had this plan to take a few things from my job and sell them to people who want'em. But I got caught."

"You finally spill the beans," I say, grinning. "That's why you're here doing street work like me."

"More then beans, lemme tell ya."

"We've all done things we wish we hadn't."

Nodding, he mutters: "Ain't that the truth?"

I look square at him. "But how do they get into a unit?"

He takes a breath. "I know a guy. He's got a Hundred pass. Took it off an official during a mugging. Back a few weeks. They ain't wiped it yet. Get you in anywhere."

I shift the broom in my hands. "You think they could do it?"

"I know they could. But can you pay?"

"How much would they want for a job like that? And how would I pay them? All transactions are recorded and tracked."

"You make it a gift. Just check the box. They won't bother with amounts a hundred and under per person. You can also make it an automatic payment, like fifty on two different days." He sees I am puzzled. "Not the gifting type, are you? I send my son some credits every chance I get. Better him than me. What'll I waste it on?"

"Yes, I see." My income previously went into an account for our family, so there was no gifting. My wife and I could draw equally from it. "And if they fail? If they get caught? How about delivery? Can't exactly carry a tuba in the open. They'll be seen by cameras. I'll be seen taking it from them. If they go at night, she'll be there. I don't want her to get hurt. Or scared."

"You worry too much. Likely why you're out here sweeping these sidewalks every day, Sixteen."

I shake my head, knowing he's right. "If you had my mother you would grow up worrying, too. She taught me how to worry. Sure, she had plenty to worry about, but.... Guess that's why I was assigned counseling. But no headway there, I gotta admit. Just talking about my mother. And my sisters. Our life down south."

"I don't even hear Southern in your voice." He laughs, taking up his broom as a monitor approaches us.

"I haven't been Southern for ten years. Ever since I left home. Have to learn Northern ways if I want to succeed."

"But look what it got ya." He always knows what to say to make me feel better. Hah! "Nothing but hassles."

"And you, too. Didn't your family disown you?"

"Let's not talk about that. It was all a misunderstanding. I never said those things like they accused me of. Besides, since when can't a regular fellow voice his opinion about the way things are? Still a free country, they say. They're doing everything they can to keep it free, or so they say."

"If you say the right things and don't say wrong things."

A monitor slows as he comes to us but keeps strolling. Once past us, he switches his attention to chastising a mother with two young children for walking too slowly, blocking the sidewalk.

"Like that," I say, pointing at the mother and kids with my chin as the monitor continues on. "Takes all the joy out of life."

I let out a sigh, remembering when I first arrived in the city and how my eyes had widened at the marvelous new world around me, a far cry from the wildness of the marshes. The city was impressive and I couldn't wait to be a part of it: this perfect society they'd built. Gradually I saw the dirty truth beneath the sleek gray façade.

"I mean, what's the point? Of this, all of this? A big modern city with everything you want – well, not everything you want but what they've decided you need. Why have five choices in a store when one is the best? Just stock that one. More efficient, they say. It's always what *they* say."

"They's the smart ones, so they know," says Twenty-four. "They got special people for all that, for calculating everything, measuring everything, planning everything. Like they're running a farm. We don't even need to think. We little folks just go along with it. We don't know no better. Gotta trust them in charge. They'll take care of us. That's what the sign says: *Big Sister Cares For You*."

"Big Sister, hah! That's where you're wrong. What if...." I pause to look around, to check the cameras, then turn a bit to shield my lips from view. "I wonder sometimes. What if they aren't calculating everything for maximum efficiency but actually calculating what's best for *them*?"

"Shoot, man. Don't you be saying stuff like that. You'll get us in trouble again."

"Exactly. We get in trouble just for asking a simple question."

"Questions'll get you killed, Sixteen."

"But I'm dying already. Sweeping the sidewalks day after day. It isn't my life's calling. It doesn't bring me joy."

"But it's a job that needs doing."

"But it's not the best use of my skills."

"So you think you're better'n other people, huh?" He laughs.

"No, but I did go to college. I did learn specialized skills. I need to be using them. Not *this*."

"But you done wasted your skills getting feisty with them, so you need to be taken down a few pegs, learn a lesson. Nothing better for learning a lesson than sweeping sidewalks, lemme tell ya."

"My mother liked to say everything was a lesson."

"She was right."

"But we wouldn't be doing this if *they* weren't so damn obsessed with order and cleanliness. People should just be clean on their own. Don't throw down litter, for example. Don't *make* things dirty."

"Can't say damn." He stares at me a moment. "Say darn or dang. It's in the latest directive. Clean our language. Another campaign of theirs: *Dirty Mouth Has No Clout*."

"Figures." Shaking my head in frustration, I say: "My counselor told me. I got emotional and said some words. On the list words. So I was reminded to keep it clean."

"Keeping things clean is our job, ya know."

"I know." Anger is filling me inside. "We work, they pay us. Then we give a portion of our wages back to them, calling it taxes. Where does that money come from? They pay us so we can pay them back? Doesn't make any sense. Then they'll just keep part of our wages so we don't have to bother giving a portion back. It's up to seventy percent, including the rehabilitation fee." I couldn't pay it up front when they assigned me there so they're taking it out of every pay. "What's left is barely enough to buy food, even from cheap shelves. But what do we really need wages for anyway? That's their question for us. Food mostly. So we work, get paid, give some back, and buy food with what remains. We can only buy food boxes. Why not just cut out the middle step? Soon they'll have us working just for food, handing it out directly, a few hours' labor for a packet of food. They have us work in exchange for food. Same as being in a prison."

"Well, we don't make a lot as street sweepers," says Twenty-four.

"The little that's left over isn't enough to buy a ticket to a show. Not that I want to see one of those 'approved' shows. All propaganda and kinda boring, too predictable. Always ends with realizing their love for the government policies that give them a life where they can earn wages, just enough to buy food and a ticket to the next show."

Twenty-four laughs, then quickly puts his hand to his mouth to cover his amusement from the cameras. If you're amused, you must not be working hard enough. Lesson four.

"Well, Sixteen, I think it's gonna get a whole lot worse before it gets any better."

"You sure you want to say something like that in front of me?"

"I trust you," says Twenty-four. "Besides, you've said a lot worse than me."

Looking down at the sidewalk, I see another spot where dirt has collected in the specially designed decorative groove.

"You gonna take care of that, or me?" asks Twenty-four.

"I guess it's my turn. You did the last one."

Getting down on my hands and knees with the scrubbing brush, I work to loosen the grime jammed into the groove. Then I scoop out the crumbs and deposit them into our trash bin.

"If only that could take longer," I say, standing.

"You put in seven minutes on that spot. Can't really make it last too much longer. They get suspicious you go too long on one spot."

+ + +

In my unit late one night, unable to sleep on the narrow bed, not as soft as I'd like it to be, I sit up and ask my unit's monitor what to do. I'm only joking. But, mumbling to myself, the sensor picks it up and responds:

"Have you learned about the Delight Murders? It was quite the scandal back in the day." A male voice, a tenor, unthreatening, even cheerful. "There is a documentary streaming presently. It has been running eleven minutes at this point. Shall I allow it?"

Not used to having a voice in my unit, I simply nod.

"I detect a nod. Assigning affirmation."

The screen set in the side wall opposite the bed blinks on. I see a scene of small town life in the style of fifty years ago, with beautiful people dressed in the elegant fashion of that time strolling along the streets. The camera follows one couple as they walk past a large 'antebellum' house with a wrapping veranda. Cue voiceover:

"The House of Delight was known for its lavish parties and the notable luminaries attending them...."

Rubbing my eyes, I try to ignore the screen, shut out the voice telling me history I already know from Mother's stories. She worked there for a few years, she confessed once I was old enough to hear about it – old enough to be making that video of her, coaxing her to say everything.

"I'm not interested in that," I speak in a firm tone.

"Ending," my monitor replies and shuts off the screen.

The sudden silence shakes me, makes me realize how quiet the city is, all noise forbidden after 22:00. Even if I had the tuba, I wouldn't be able to play it. I can't actually play it anyway. I could make some godawful noise with it. Mother intended for me to pass it to Maggie, maybe let her make a career out of it. Mother said her grandmother wanted only the girls in the family to follow after her. But Mother never expected we would have the kind of world where music was an annoyance that distracted us from our labor.

"Always the damn labor," I grumble.

"Language," the unit's monitor intones.

"Sorry," I respond but not feeling very sorry.

I get up, stretch, and pace my small unit, eight steps from the entry door to the round window in the end wall, eight steps back. I glance out the window, unable to be opened, as part of each ritual turn. After several laps, I pause, wondering why the unit's monitor selected that particular stream for me. I call out my question.

"Registration shows connection to incident," the voice speaks.

"Connection? What connection?"

"Connection: Fritz Baumann, son of Isla Augustine Baumann, a resident of the house where the murders were committed, suspected of being one of several murderers, never caught, never found, died in a faraway place after being presented on a documentary video."

"That's enough." I shake my head. "Quite enough."

"The case was never closed," my unit continues.

I look up like someone is actually there. "Not closed. But why?"

The unit doesn't immediately answer. Then: "Undetermined."

"Undetermined? What does that mean?"

"No information exists in my database to answer your inquiry."

"So they wiped it.... Someone did."

Now I'm interested.

Mother told about working in that house of prostitution – forced to work there, enduring one of those servitude contracts. She wasn't proud of what she did. She told me not to think poorly of her for it. She had to do it or else they'd hurt her mother and their daughters. Eventually Grandma Hannah hanged herself from the balcony to escape the horrible life there, to free my mother. Tears ran down her face in the video. That is one part people didn't like, thought it was made-up for a good story. I wasn't born yet so I only had her word on the matter, and I had no reason not to believe her.

Then one night, when a decorated squad of Northern Alliance soldiers were being entertained in Madame Delight's famous house, most didn't awaken. Knifed in their sleep. How could they get those knives into that house? Mother winked at me. That part I had to edit out of the final video.

The ladies fled by dawn. None were ever located. Police searched for them, got leads but never did find any of the ladies. Eleven of the Northern Alliance's finest lay in pools of blood on the beds. Two of the soldiers were elder sons of prominent Northern society. What a scandal!

Now the Northern Alliance had returned to its former name, the states collecting once more to form a union, but led by the great cities of the north, rebuilt from the remnants of the old cities. The governor of this state, a woman, was one of the new leaders, a rising star. Thus the incident where Northern soldiers were killed in their beds was shocking and intensified hatred for the Southern territory. But I knew the end of the story.

The way Mother told it, she and the girls were taken out of the city by men she trusted, escaping through the countryside, hidden in the back of a farm wagon. They got to a state park and lived with a group of folks there who just wanted to survive, stayed with them for more than a year while she planned what they should do next. She considered staying with them but something kept nagging her. So she continued her journey: back home to the mountain in the National Park, which wasn't an easy journey.

Mother told me what happened along the way. How she and the girls had to hide in a culvert as soldiers were fighting around them. One soldier fell into the stream that flowed through the culvert, cracked his head on the concrete then floated past them. Horsemen galloped overhead. A soldier came down the embankment, spied the girls hiding in the culvert. It was night so he grabbed the girl named Vanille, tried to assault her. Mother came up behind him, reached around and slid a knife into his gut.

She told how Grampa Sandy described passing through a village on his way home from the war and a prison camp. The village was half-burned, half-fallen to ruin, yet people struggled to live, being skinny, like they were in the prison camp, from simple starvation. There was no food in production in those days, not for years, so nothing was taken to the stores, nothing to buy. The people didn't seem to know they had to plant now for next year's dinner. Mother was sobbing at that point. She paused to wipe her eyes, and told me how she miscarried her baby on that trip. Who was the father? She shook her head, uncomfortable with that history. I'd turned off the camera by then.

They eventually arrived at the National Park, where she met up with that man her parents had befriended long ago: Frank, who was more than twice her age. He became my father. Still nobody found her, or ever charged her with any crime. She remained hidden even after she moved all of us further south to the marshes.

Then I had to return north to make my own life in the same city where my mother had committed murder – maybe. It was on video, her saying it all, before I edited the footage.

Besides, she's dead now, so no point bringing up all of that from the post-pandemic rebuilding era, what they call the Reconstruction. Everybody wanted to get on with their lives. It was a terrible time, we agreed. Yet some wanted to do more: to create a perfect society, with none of the hardships they'd suffered through, a society which they envisioned would be a model to other nations, where citizens worked together in an efficient manner.

"That's how we shall survive whatever may come next," the new governor announced in her acceptance speech. I recalled that. It was required reading for all citizens and was actually made available in printed form on paper, a copy given to each of us. "Think of me as your big sister," she said in closing, "and I shall take care of you."

We didn't notice any changes at first, just small adjustments. No one objected. Then more changes. More noticeable changes. Always for the greater good. For our safety. For our convenience. No, we don't really need to travel, even for a holiday trip with family; that wasted precious resources. Hotels and restaurants were a luxury for those at the top. After all, they worked so hard for us that they needed to relax sometimes. The rest of us got meal boxes, assigned according to sex, age, and health status. Our food would include the nutrients we needed to sustain our health, yet many became ill. Some died. I heard the meal boxes included various medications so we could take them without us knowing. Maybe it was only a rumor. People got taken away for spreading rumors, so it must be true.

+ + +

"Session twelve," the voice intones as I take my seat opposite the camera. I wear my stained work clothes, not having time to go home and change to a cleaner outfit. Dr. Richards frowns.

"How are you feeling today?" he says but his tone is off.

"Tired," I reply automatically. My back is sore from my work and I just want to get home, get out of this uniform and shower. But if I don't stop in for my weekly session, it will be noted and my food allowance reduced. It's happened before. I decided to skip a session and my food box tally was shorted. This is the last day I can visit and still get credit for this week.

"That's good," says my counselor. "It shows you're a productive member of society."

"That's all I live for," I mutter, intending sarcasm.

More small talk of the smallest kind.

"And your mother?" asks my counselor eventually.

"She's been dead a few years now."

"No" – chuckles – "I mean have you had more thoughts of her?"

I have to smile, but meekly. "Yes, of course. She's always in the back of my head, telling me what to do, what not to do, a constant annoyance." I pause to recall an annoyance. "I don't think whatever they're putting in my food is working."

"Putting in your food?"

"Yes, the meds."

"Meds?"

"I've heard they personalize our food rations for the calories we need considering our line of work and our health needs. It's common knowledge, isn't it?"

Dr. Richards shakes his head, enduring this simpleton. "Merely rumors, Fritz. As I understand, the food industry has only five meal plans, based on the needs of five categories of citizens: the children; the women; and the men, either office with 'thought work' or heavy labor. And the elderly, but there are few of them nowadays, unless they've proven themselves to be valuable, say, for their intellectual contributions. Nutrition and calories are the main considerations."

"But I get the same boxes. Seems to be the same food every time – mostly. Rarely substitutions. Not too tasty, I gotta say."

"It comes from the Chester's Field production facility."

"The smirking cow design! That company makes all the food that goes into the boxes, right? Not too tasty, in my opinion. They need some competition."

"I'm sure taste is not the main concern," says my counselor, and we go off on a full analysis of the food industry in our wonderful new society. He shares the menu of his latest outing with friends. He is able to visit one of the few restaurants remaining in the city. Then he strikes it from the record, as much to protect himself as me. I'm not envious; I want him well-fed so he can do his job, making sense of me. Yet you never can be too sure how your thoughts might be received/reviewed in the Communications Protocol Office. They tend to be overly precise.

"So I did have a dream," I offer once we fall silent. "Mother was in it. She demanded I bring her dinner. She was expecting fish but I hadn't caught any."

"In your marsh home?" he asks.

"Yes, always there. So I tell her I'll go out fishing. I take the boat and go out a ways. Then a big wave comes, sweeps over me but I'm not hurt. The wave passes over me and roars up to the isle where her shack is. The wave destroys the shack. I rush back but I can't find her in the wreckage."

"I see." He taps on his tablet, making notes. "Typical response to troubles with a parent. Wishing them dead. Wishing that you could simply sweep them away."

"But in the dream, I was alarmed, then sad." Where was I going with this? "I had problems with her, sure, but I never wanted her to be swept away. I want only peace for her."

I wait for my counselor's response but the silence goes on long enough for the sensor to beep at us to continue.

"Yes, *peace*," he says. "I suppose that word is allowed."

We both seemed to glance at the mirror with the camera behind it, showing our concern.

"Yes, who doesn't like a good *piece* of pie," he says.

I get his ruse. "I like peach pie, myself. But I'm not particular."

"Yes, peach pie is good. I could go for a piece of peach pie."

We wrap up our discussion of my frazzled mental state, coming to no conclusion, saving a lot for next time.

The next day, I find a miniature peach pie in my food box.

+ + +

Finally the cold, gray sky lets loose, sending cold, gray rain down on us. Globules of oily moisture hit us like pebbles. Supervisors rush to hand out helmets so we can continue work – to keep at our sweeping and cleaning. The rain spots our uniforms, dark oily patches that are hard to wash out. Thanks to the industrial might of the rebuilt society, I muse.

"They want everything to run on electricity," my coworker says, "but first they gotta make it, and that's from the oil in the ground."

"But without the knowledge of burning it cleanly," I add. "Lost in the decades of fear and ignorance."

Before the pandemic hit, there was a lot of talk about ending reliance on petroleum for everything, not only energy but things like plastic materials and so on. But then we went into lockdown, forgot everything we'd learned. Some people kept dreaming of society with endless energy from only the sunshine and wind. That never could provide the same amount of power, however, but they continued to hope. They even made vehicles that were half gas and half electric, then all electric. Mother's grandmother had one of them. Grampa Sandy got to drive it. But those vehicles soon ran out of gas, then ran out of their electric charges, as traffic jammed along highways with everyone rushing to escape cities in chaos, leaving people to die inside their vehicles or get out and walk if they dared. I'd seen the lines of rusting vehicles as I made my way north.

That situation was before I was born. Before Mother was born, too. We both grew up without that kind of energy. We had to burn wood to make heat. From that heat we cooked food and boiled water to make it safe for drinking. We made candles for the evening. That was life in the National Park. Then we moved south. By then, some things were returning. People figured out how to bring them back, or they found new ways to do the same things. Like electricity: returning to the burning of coal and natural gas to spin turbines. The old ways; maybe not what dreamers wanted but we had to start somewhere to rebuild society.

Now they've caught up to where we were a hundred years ago, they say. Again they start to think of better ways to run the world. Factions in government argue their ideas and how to make us comply. It's for the greater good, they propose in their countless speeches. When I came north, I expected to find modern cities. But what I found amazed me. The way they'd made the city into a work of art, a functioning machine, a fortress of peace. I couldn't wait to join this marvelous place and be a part of this new society.

And yet, the progress continued – continued not further into the light, uplifting and embracing the best of us but, rather, darkening as needed to keep us under control, requiring us to serve the vanity of those who stood above us, there on their elegant balconies, gazing down from lofty perches like vultures. I felt I'd been fooled. Lured in like a child by a man offering candy. Once licking the sucker, we were easy victims. Here's your new home, they tell us: work and we'll let you stay. And if I don't want to be here? Tough cookies, you're here forever, forever working, and you'll enjoy it because you know you're making society better, helping to create a perfect society. Yes, it's perfect at the top. Every lofty perch needs a wide base.

My partner stops me with a sharp wave of his hand.

"I like you, Sixteen, but gotta cut you off right there. You're sure getting zappy. Gotta cut you off. For your own good."

"Sorry," I mutter, looking down at the sidewalk.

Twenty-four takes a moment to check around, notes the cameras and a strolling monitor coming toward us.

"In-coming," he mumbles. "If I was anyone else I'd report things you say, things you say you wanna do. But I'm not like them kinds. I know you're a good man, not one of them rebels."

"Thanks—"

"Look busy." He takes up his broom, acts like he is focused on a particular spot that needs extra attention, scrubbing back and forth over it as the monitor arrives.

"Good morning, citizens," the monitor speaks in a cheery voice.

"Good morning, officer," we both intone, pausing from our work.

The monitor gazes up at the sky, oily rain falling. "Seems a poor day to be out, yet what have we to fear from the mother of nature?"

"Yep," Twenty-four responds.

"Mother knows best," I mumble.

"Big Sister cares for us," the monitor recites. He straightens his back. "Just want to let you know not to go that way" – meaning the direction the monitor came from – "because there's a police action occurring there."

"Police action?" I ask.

"Yes." He blinks. "Oh, it's not much. A few protestors. Typical. Think they can get their way by making a big howl. Blocking the street. Yet it only makes their lives harsher. They'll see. What are they thinking? The proper way to bring an issue to resolution is to file it at the appropriate office. There's a round file assigned to every kind of issue one might wish addressed. Obviously."

"Yes, it seems so," I reply, having gone from one round file to the next in my pursuit of redress.

"What're they protesting?" asks Twenty-four.

"Not sure. Does it matter? We have a well-ordered society here. I can't think there's anything they could have an issue with. My guess is food allocation. That's usually what it is. Everyone gets what they need, however. I suspect they clamor for more."

"Seems fair," I mutter.

The monitor glares at me. His hand rests on his tablet.

"Fair that they're getting what they need. Everybody knows the Nutrition Authority carefully calculates the caloric needs of every citizen accurately." I smile for show. "Extra allowances for holidays and certain milestones in a person's life, too."

"What he said," adds Twenty-four, nodding at me.

"Understood." The monitor tips his cap, turns to go. "Keep on having a workful day, citizens."

"We will," says Twenty-four.

"What he said," I laugh under my breath.

Twenty-four clacks his broom handle against mine. "You gonna get us in trouble, Sixteen. You gotta be serious playing the game."

8

DARKER SECRETS

MOTHER LIKED TELLING STORIES about her kids, what they were doing, what they'd done. It was a source of pride. Being her youngest, she didn't have anyone telling her about me and what I did. Amy June was her main story subject. Allie, who was Amy's aunt by six weeks, didn't figure much after she left with that girl she met in the marshes during the summers. Mother always talked about Amy – Amy June this, Amy June that – and about Amy's kids: Casey and the twins, Dixie and Daisy. "Daughters's good to have," she'd declare whenever they visited. Amy June met a boy from the marshes, Cory. They got along, so they lived like they were married and stayed near enough she could visit Mother often. As Mother got older, she visited almost daily. Amy June would bring her fish or other seafood that Cory got from the marsh.

Amy was about the only relative I could ever talk to. She being the oldest and me the youngest, I guess she felt responsible for me. Even though she teased me as a child along with Allie. When she visited, she'd ask me all sorts of questions, showed an interest in my life. As I grew older, I thought of asking her more difficult questions. I learned she and Allie had been with Mother during her difficult period, faced hardship themselves, like the creepy men at Madame Delight's trying to coax them into bad acts, even though they were too young for what those perverts proposed. I couldn't bring myself to ask her more, even when I returned later to make that video.

Allie called me Fritter when I was a little boy and Amy followed her, teasing me relentlessly. Amy would get Allie to stop it when I showed too much hurt. As I got older, Allie teased me more, trying to humiliate me with sex topics. Amy June tried to stop Allie but not until she'd teased me to her satisfaction. Allie left, thankfully. I seldom saw her again. She'd arrive at random, coming by boat with her girlfriend, stopping to see Mother. Both of those women had gone native, weren't very pretty and weren't too good smelling, to be honest.

Then there were her Chesterfield children. Mother never said much about them. At first I thought they were something Mother invented, perhaps mistaking missing siblings as her children. But I had to read the letters sent to Mother from someone named Bobbie who apparently was my half-sister. All I knew from Amy was that Bobbie and her brother were from a time when she was owned by a farmer and forced to be his mistress and give him children. Mother would wave off questions, grumbling: "She don't matter none, just a deal we done long time past." I'd known a Bobbie on the mountain. She played with that other woman named Vanille who my mother treated as a sister. However, after we moved to the marshes and she grew up enough, Bobbie left to go north to find her brother Abe.

From reading those letters Bobbie sent to Mother, I got some of the story. Bobbie was born on the Chesterfield farm, a large food production company in the north. That was after Mother and other women from the National Park were marched away and sold. Many women found they were infertile. Mother was bought by that farmer because his wife couldn't have children, not after she got too many vaccines. In that arrangement, Mother gave him a daughter named Bobbie, then a son named Abe. Then he dismissed her for some infraction. He was satisfied to have a son as his heir. Her services were no longer needed. However, she wasn't exactly free. She was sold to another.

Bobbie had grown up in the brothel where Mother worked next, alongside Amy and Allie. Grandma Hannah was there, caring for the girls and doing housework. It wasn't a good life for them, never mind the kind of work Mother did. She had another baby there, a girl she named Lily, which the madam sold without her permission to a childless couple – but the infant died soon after. When it seemed like their horrible situation would never end, Grandma Hannah killed herself by hanging. But we don't talk about that. That Mother was free to sneak away without worrying how bad her mother would be treated. She arranged for two preachers that visited the house from time to time to help her escape. We also don't talk about that.

When Bobbie went north years later, she found Abe running the farm. Their father had gone mad and finally died. Abe had already married and had four sons – breaking the daughter curse, Mother joked. Bobbie wrote letters to let Mother know their situation. She invited Mother to move north to the farm where she could be more comfortable, but Mother swore it had such terrible memories that she couldn't ever set foot there again. Mother was dismissed when Abe was just a baby. He was told his mother had died in childbirth when she actually was sold to that brothel. He wept when his sister told him the truth. He wanted to see Mother but he understood why she refused to visit the farm.

I thought I understood Bobbie, rejoining her brother and helping to run a prosperous enterprise that supplied food to the region. After reuniting with Abe, Bobbie never married, spent her time managing the business. Eventually, she decided to get into politics, to make society better, she wrote. Questions arose concerning the servitude contracts many people in the North arranged and benefited from. Bobbie denied any part in them. She was clearly a Chesterfield, the proud daughter of Mamie and Lionel Chesterfield, scion of the county. Mamie had died after giving birth to brother Abe. That was their story.

Staring at the screen as the stream played, an old interview with our senator, I had to smile. Her voice bounced around my tiny unit – just wide enough I couldn't quite touch opposite walls with my arms extended. I felt my heart melting as I listened to her. This woman was related to me yet denying me – denying all of us, Mother most of all. I had the thought of asking her to help me get out of my bad situation, get my old job back at the broadcast station. That would require contact. She would have to acknowledge me, another family embarrassment. I was Mother's last child, by an old man on that mountain, possibly a mistake, an accident. But listening to the woman on that stream, I dismissed the idea.

Plenty of people in the world. I felt closer to Amy June and even to Allie despite their teasing me in childhood. People who lived far away, like Bobbie and Abe, shouldn't concern me. Besides them, I had awkward feelings for those folks who were close to me but for which our actual relationships were complicated. Just call them cousins, Mother told me. "We all related, don't matter how."

But there she was: Our Senator, saying all kinds of things that didn't make sense. I heard the ideas before from other politicians, but hearing them from someone who was supposedly my sister was jarring. I thought she would be one of us, a National Parker. A few years in the capital had changed her a lot. Too much making deals, negotiating, cutting corners, hand bumps behind the closed doors of smoke-filled rooms (the usual sterilization process). A council she formed was leading the transformation to what her sub-committee called the Ideal Society. They were making proposals they explained were needed in order to create a well-ordered society but which instead seemed to place more restrictions on ordinary people.

I hated the way she smiled when answering a question: like a coiled snake ready to strike. I could almost hear the hissing.

Her election was after I visited Mother to show her the finished video. In fact, some things happened after I made that video. Those events didn't get in the video, of course.

I went down later to visit Mother another time, after the trip to show her the finished video. I wanted to show her the new broadcast device available. I got one for her so she could watch streams from her marsh home. You could hold the device in your hands and watch broadcasts on the screen, the signal coming through the air. Mother was 'flabbergasted' by the machine, but she was old. We watched a speech by President Templeton after he was sworn in. I thought she would be impressed by the device.

"Yeah, that's a fine picture," was all she said. Despite having no interest in politics, she kept her eyes focused on the screen all the way to the end like she recognized him. Later she said that long ago she initiated him into manhood in that brothel.

That visit of mine wasn't too long after LJ passed. I knew he was Amy June's father and Mother's first husband. They were torn apart when marauders came to the National Park. He lay wounded while she was marched away with Amy cradled in her arms. Then, after all her troubles, she returned to the National Park about ten years later and found LJ there at the cabin Grampa Sandy built. LJ was living with Lori, his father's widow. They had two daughters. A son they'd had had already died. And they saved my half-sister Ellie and my half-brother Raymond from the marauders. Mother didn't want to disturb the life they'd made together. She was happy for them.

She looked up from that device. "Sure wish I had pictures of my LJ. Pictures of your daddy, too. I mean Frank when he was young – back when I was a little girl and just met him, him and his wife Louann and her twin sister Lorraine that had your sister Polly with my daddy, there on that mountain."

"Don't get into all that, Mama," I told her. "It's bad enough how mixed up this family is. It's embarrassing."

I could understand how Bobbie shunned our family, ignored our mother. I certainly wanted to sometimes, I'll admit.

Mother told me not to worry about our odd connections. In those hard times, they stuck together, doing the best they could, and they came out the other side alive and well. "We find a way," she liked to say. "We are strong folks."

Just like my half-brother Raymond did by daring to go out west with his half-sister Faith to seek their fortune, telling everyone who asked that they were married. He sent a letter to Mother from out west, apologizing to her for being such a bad brother and promising not to get her mixed up in his troubles. They had a special bond, it seemed, because as Grandma Hannah's eldest daughter, my mother had cared for Raymond when he was a baby.

Lots of things happened that didn't get into the video. Like Amy June going north to look for her daddy, LJ, in the National Park before I went north. She wanted to explore the world. Mother feared for her but she had to go. She returned to the National Park, hiked up that mountain to where she was born, just down along the ridge from where I'd been born. I wanted to go with her but someone had to stay and take care of Mother.

Amy found a broken LJ distraught over Lori's death in birthing her next child. He was raving like a madman. Poor man didn't know what to do, couldn't help her. Too much blood and too far from any doctor. The baby survived but LJ swore he didn't know how to raise daughters. So Amy brought LJ and his daughters down south to live with Mother and me.

We got along for a while, me teaching LJ to fish, but then he passed in his sleep one night with Mother beside him. They had about five years together, spent most of it not talking to each other or else loudly arguing. But I saw them kiss from time to time, like they were paying each other for past debts.

Then, about ten years after LJ and the girls left the mountain to come south, someone discovered it, saw the 'village' that survivalists had made, and turned it into a memorial site.

Mother thought she'd lost LJ forever when we all moved down to the marshes, leaving him and Lori on the mountain. We were part of the same family, after all, with kin close by, either in the nearby towns or around the marshes. They raised those daughters together. Grace, Hope, and Eve called her Aunt Isla. Faith hadn't come with them, of course. She went with Raymond, sneaking away in the night. He couldn't let LJ see him after what happened.

And to think I was sent off to rehabilitation prison for merely making a video!

It took a while but I got the story out of Mother before I went north. Raymond was the younger brother of LJ, his father being Big Joe and his mother Grandma Hannah. He grew up rambunctious, to use Mother's words, had a stick of fire up his backside. One day he took Lori, LJ's wife who was Big Joe's widow and who LJ had kids with already, and took his own step-mother by force – and she got pregnant. Lori kept quiet about it. LJ thought the new babe was his until Raymond confessed. LJ beat him and ran him off, swearing to kill him if he ever returned. When it was time for Lori to give birth, she bled too much. There wasn't anything LJ could do. Eve was born but Lori died. Yet before the time for birthing, Raymond returned in the night and got Faith, and the two of them headed west. LJ blamed his little brother for causing Lori's death, but he loved his 'niece' Eve like the rest of the daughters.

I was surprised to get a letter from Faith every few months over the years then no more, half complaining and half delighting in her adventures. Why me? She had to tell somebody and I seemed removed enough to not be alarmed by her confessions. I chose what to tell Mother and what to keep secret. Like Faith having a child she called an idiot and taking it out into the wilderness and leaving it. Raymond had beaten her for that. She left Raymond then, took up with another fellow, had another baby, a son named Benjamin. Then Raymond killed that other fellow and was sent to prison. That was the last I heard from Faith. I was glad she wanted to keep in contact. Maybe she wanted to keep contact open in case she needed our help. I did send her credits to buy a cabin when the one they were living in burned.

I thought back, remembered playing with those girls, Grace and Faith, along with my sister Amy and her aunt Allie, all older than me when I was a little boy. Sometimes I played with Raymond, but being older than me we didn't get along. Now that the girls were older and they'd joined us in the marsh, my feelings got hurt more. I felt shoved aside when LJ and his family moved in. That was another reason to go north, to get away from them. But LJ died and the girls went to live their own lives.

Before that, Amy June got everyone together and planned a real wedding for Mother and LJ in a small church in the closest town, with a real preacher in a black suit and lots of flowers around. She wore a clean white gown, never worn by anyone else. He wore a fine blue suit and necktie, fidgeting through the ceremony. There were guards to be sure we weren't disturbed. This time LJ was sure about his vows: "I surely do, sir." And Mother said: "Hell yeah, don'tcha know!" Followed by a big kiss that lasted so long the preacher had to separate them. Then we had a big feast, with singing and dancing, as much as these old folks could handle.

I liked seeing Mother happy.

I never saw her again, though, not until her funeral. I left again, made my way north, returning to my life there with my wife Sandra and our children. I heard about LJ's passing from Amy June. Then I heard about Mother's last day. I got a pass from the Travel Authority to attend her funeral.

I thought of not returning, the way the city was changing even then, but I had a wife and children depending on me. At the time, nothing seemed too bad. I couldn't see far ahead. So I couldn't anticipate how that video of Mother would destroy my life.

9

LI'L MISS DEMEANOR

WHEN MY UNIT'S DOOR slides open with a soft hum, I look up from my chair to see a scraggily young man there, canvas bag hanging from his shoulder, scruffy face with sad eyes begging for help. It is late and I'm not expecting visitors. No prior notice given of anyone entering, either, just the door opening seemingly at random. I might expect that in the rehabilitation facility, but not here in my private housing unit. A visitor would need approval from the guard at the entrance of the building.

The intruder wears light green coveralls, badly faded. I guess he must be a grocery worker. My first thought is that he is delivering food boxes to me and I sit up, hopeful.

"I've been assigned to this unit," he says in humble tone.

"This unit?" I narrow my eyes. "But it's a single unit." Sure, I tell myself, it's double the length of a typical rehabilitation facility cell, having the kitchen area added, but it's no wider. "How is it they put two people in here?"

"Don't know, don't care," says the young man, expelling a weary sigh. His coveralls have his number over the left breast: the last two digits 39. "Just need a place to sleep. Haven't any place in days."

He pushes his way in; rather, I don't block his way. I don't invite him in. Either way, cameras capture everything. I will be penalized credits if I act badly. Being willing to share with a bedraggled fellow might earn me more credits.

"I'm Frank." I have my hand on the button to close the door.

"What an odd name," says the young man. "You must be old." He examines me, up and down, as though he needs to approve me or he won't stay. I'm old enough. Most men my age are in a family unit – and have children, if on the reproduction approval list.

"I also go by Sixteen, if that makes you more comfortable," I say as the young man looks around for a place to set his bag. He chooses the kitchen fold-down table which when down blocks the way to the window. He scoots the chair out of the way with his foot. His shoe is worn thin, toes visible through holes.

"I knew a Sixteen back a while," he says, pursing his lips.

"As I said, you can also call me Frank."

"Awrighty, Frank." He pauses to stare, like he's determining if I am worthy of hosting him. "I'm Thirty-nine. The only name I know. I'm not old like you."

"I'm not as old as you think."

"Oh, yeah? What're you, fifty?"

"Close." I smile, embarrassed. "But my mother lived all the way to seventy-nine."

"Only seventy-nine? Was she sick?"

I look him over, unsure how this is supposed to work.

"There's only one bed. You can sleep on the floor, I guess. I have an extra blanket you can double over for a mat."

"Not gonna sleep on the floor," he says with a grunt.

"Well, first, I bet you want to get cleaned up." He has a distinct street smell about him.

"Cleaned up? I ain't done nothing."

"I mean, if you are assigned to this unit.... Well, the wash facility is down the hallway. If you want to...."

He swings around, gazes at the door a moment. Throat rumbles indicate he is thinking about it. Then he unzips his coveralls down to his crotch and slides the garment down to his feet. He kicks off his dirty shoes and pulls off the coveralls, standing naked before me, hairy like a forest critter.

"Got a towel?" he asks.

I give him one of my two authorized towels, part of the package of items handed to me upon my exit from the rehabilitation facility.

To start my new life. Then assigned to a single unit for my new job as a street sweeper.

Now this stranger has been assigned to the same unit. I have to wonder if it's a mistake. Maybe authorities didn't mark this unit as occupied. Or is he really assigned to share it with me? I had to share a unit for a week before I got this one for myself, after all. In the rehabilitation facility sharing is expected. We had to double on the bunks. But now that I'm released I get some of my privileges back: privacy in my off-duty time. Not completely private; cameras watch the unit, listen for random utterances, noting who comes and goes. I've heard that some unit's devices will let out a beep if improper behavior is detected.

He goes out just as he was: naked with towel in hand. It's an all-male floor, after all.

And he returns the same way: wet towel in hand. He gives me the towel to hang up, as though I'm the servant in this unit. That isn't going to work, I decide, and tell him the rules.

"Remember: the camera's always on, always watching, even in the dark. The rules of public areas apply here regarding what you say and do. No discussing politics or health issues. If you got any problems health-wise, better to keep them to yourself. Also, I'm not a counselor so don't tell me anything that's secret. They could force me to reveal them. And—"

He flops right down on the bed, which is only wide enough for my shoulders while lying flat on my back. He hasn't bothered to put on sleeping clothes, either. He doesn't go to his bag to check for any. If he's under some authority's supervision, they would've given him basic supplies.

"Like that?" I ask, dismayed. "You're sleeping like that?"

"I always do." He seems to grin. "Problem?"

"Well, I suggested you can sleep on the floor. I'll get out the extra blanket."

"No need. This is good enough."

"But it's my bed. This is my unit."

"It's mine, too."

I stand over him, beside the narrow shelf that serves as a bed.

"Look, Frank. I'm not your guest. They sent me to this unit. I'm as equal as you. This is my assignment."

"For how long?" My heart quickens. "Until you get your own?"

"Didn't say. They just gave me the pass for this unit."

"Did they know it's occupied?"

"Didn't say. But I'm too tired to think about it."

"What did you do? I mean, were you working?"

"Everybody works."

"That's true. Or else they'd get rid of you." I stare down at him, thinking of more questions. "But did you—"

"I'm really tired now, Frank, so...mmm, if you don't mind, could you power down the lights? And keep it quiet. Really tired."

Without considering who's in charge, my hand goes to the dial and lowers the lights. I leave enough light to get myself ready for sleep. I showered first thing upon returning home.

When I've changed into my sleeping clothes, I return to the bed, and sit on the edge, pondering the situation. I scoot myself further on the bed, forcing my guest against the wall. When I have a good portion of space, I swing my legs up onto the bed and stretch out. My guest moves to face the wall, laying on his side, so we sleep back to back most of the night.

By the time the morning buzzer sounds, he is on his belly with one arm draped over my chest. I have the majority of the bed, flat on my back, but I don't like his breath aimed at me. I scoot out from under him and get up, yawning.

It was not a good sleep but I have to get to my job by a certain time or risk losing credits. Lose too many and I'll have restrictions put on me, such as where I can go or getting fewer food boxes.

When I'm ready to leave, my guest still lays on the bed.

"Don't you have a job to go to?" I call from the doorway.

He doesn't stir. Maybe he doesn't have a job yet, hasn't been assigned one. Maybe he's new to the city and this is his first stop. I guess my food boxes will be gone when I return home.

+ + +

On a break from street sweeping, I meet with two guys from a street maintenance crew, one a little older than me, the other younger. Twenty-four vouches for them, says they've done jobs like mine before – not the sweeping but a 'snatch'. They will dress in disguise to trick the cameras.

"How much?" I ask them, sitting across the park table from me. The park is the place for workers like us to meet, not allowed in fancy sip shops like the suited class. We have advanced to such a perfect society that you are allowed to go places only according to your uniform and badge code. Instead of a more egalitarian society they initially promised, we have become more regimented.

"Two days' credit," says the bigger man, introducing himself as Forty-one. I wonder how he gets away with not shaving. He fixes holes in the streets so he doesn't need to follow hygiene protocol.

"Each," adds the shorter man, called O-Eight.

It's become polite to address a worker by the last two digits of their badge, which is their account number. Names given by parents are deemed too traditional, smacking of a pretense to patriarchy.

"I'm not sure I can give up that much," I reply, my eyes focusing on the table top, avoiding cameras. "How about I come with you?"

"We should charge more then," says Forty-one. "You don't know what you're doing, I bet. Probably get us caught."

"But it's my wife's unit. And my daughter lives with her. I don't want them to get hurt."

Forty-one grimaces. "Listen, nobody's gonna get hurt—"

"Lessen they try to stop us," O-Eight cuts in.

"You'll go when she's at her job and my daughter is in school?"

"Certainly. We don't wanna hafta deal with residents," Forty-one says with a grin. "We use our pass and in and out, like that."

"But you won't know where to look for what I want. I have to go with you."

"Twenty-four said you wanna snatch a tuba. Silver. Vinyl case. That's too big to hide. Right?"

"Yes, but it could be put away, maybe in a closet. And the other things – a few notebooks, important papers – are probably also put away. I'll have to look for them."

"That's gonna take too much time," says O-Eight with a sneer.

"She would keep them in the old chest of drawers we had – she *has* – moved from our old unit. Unless she's tossed them out already as trash. But I hope she hasn't sold the tuba yet – or paid to have it removed."

"If there's nothing there, we still get paid," says Forty-one.

"Yes, I know."

"If one of us gets caught, at the time or later, we still get paid," adds O-Eight. "Transfer before we go."

"So when?" I ask.

"We already checked it out," says O-Eight.

Forty-one grins. A line of yellow teeth shows between his ragged lips. "Tomorrow soon enough?"

I give a nod, and we get up from the table.

+   +   +

Thirty-nine is sitting cross-legged on the bed when I return at the end of my day. I enter as usual. He looks up as the door slides open and halts his self-care activity. Apparently, he hasn't found clothes to put on. There is a laundry room beside the shower facility, I've told him already but to no avail.

"No job assignment?" I ask.

"Someone from Labor came by, gave me choices."

"And?"

"None sounded like me. You know?" He seems bored. "They gave me some credits anyway, just for doing nothing."

"Me, too. Until they assigned me to my current job."

"I don't mind doing nothing."

"I don't exactly enjoy street sweeping, but I do it."

"I sure don't want to do that. Outside every day? Not for me. Oh, no. I'm way better in bed."

"You mean sleeping all day?" I'm reminded of my life back in the marshes, wondering why I wanted to go north so badly.

He coughs, stops himself and our eyes met. "Don't worry. I was tested." He points to his green badge hanging from the knob of the cabinet door over the bed. "I'm perfectly clean, if you wanna be sure. I'm clean enough for sex, too. Told'em. But, hey, they locked me up nevertheless."

"Good to know," I say with a twang, then consider my response might be too friendly. "I mean, I'm not interested at all in sex. I already have three children."

"Me neither," says Thirty-nine. He looks down at his lap. "Least not now. Cameras can see everything. They sound an alarm if you do anything not approved by the Health Authority. If you keep doing it, you get charged a fine. Even right in your own unit, in your bed."

We both turn to check the camera over the door.

"You got home too early," he says in an angry tone. "I had the system thinking I was asleep. Then I could've finished. But here you are, ruining everything."

"Ruining everything? It's my damn unit," I bark. "And I sure as hell don't appreciate you doing your self-care on my bed."

"I need to release. Can't get backed up. Used to be my job to help citizens relax, ya know?"

"That's why you're out on your own now, huh?"

He bows his head. "Kind of.... Got some complaints. But what're you gonna do?"

"But why are you assigned to my unit?"

"Don't know. Maybe you need some relaxation?"

Not alone in my own unit any longer, I don't know what to do. I usually strip off my coveralls and go shower first thing. Get in and out before most workers get home. Then I return to my unit and eat from a food box, the box designated 'evening ration' which includes items designed to ease me into sleep. I will start to feel drowsy an hour after eating. I barely have time to watch streams – if I could find one worth watching. It's all government propaganda, anyway.

As for my guest, he doesn't seem to be on that plan.

"Any word on your new unit?" I ask.

"Didn't say." He tries to repress a chuckle. "I'm here for a while. Hope you don't mind." More chuckles. "I'll try to stay out of your way – unless you need something. You need anything, just ask."

"What would I ask?"

"I dunno. Relief, I guess. I got skills for that." He doesn't think I believe him. "Seriously, I got training. Physical therapist. Months of it."

Nodding, I turn and remove my coveralls. I feel his eyes on me. He has to understand I'm going to make myself comfortable when I get home. I grab my towel and step out of the unit for the showers.

I've seen this arrangement in streams about living at school in the old days. They were called 'dorms'. My sons, Frank and James, do that; better to condition them to be good workers. Sandra and I made sure they got into a good school, learn something useful for our renewed society. I think of that as lukewarm water slithers down my grimy body, the spray weak; the bar of rough soap works to massage my skin. Sandra filing papers made it possible for them to continue at the élite school, now that they have no ties to me.

I stand under the water, letting it wash over my upturned face, as that realization burns in me. I didn't do anything wrong but I am forever labeled a defective citizen. I can only do menial jobs. I have skills that will be wasted if I don't return to the broadcast station. I also know I'd do anything, go along with whatever they decide, for the sake of my children's future. Eventually they'll be on their own and need to survive in this reality regardless of how I feel about it.

A pair of men enter, take positions under two shower heads as I continue feeling regret.

Yes, I will go along with the plan, no matter how unjust I feel it is, for the sake of our sons. Let them grow up and be successful, have good lives. If they can get into the élite class they will be fine. My life is done.

Turning off the water, I think how much I want to leave this city, go south with Mother's tuba, and live in the marshes again.

Other workers are entering the shower room as I leave. My last street task was nearby so I got home before them. One man eyes me with disdain, like I cheated the work clock.

I return to my unit, push the button to open the door. The button measures my fingertip and knows it's me. Otherwise, it won't open unless I use a pass card.

My guest has been put into the system so his fingertip activates the door, too. He enters without me opening the door, just walks in unannounced. The system isn't perfect and it sometimes lets in the wrong person. Not as though we have anything to steal. There are cameras everywhere, too.

I think of the pending crime. Those guys. Even if they are good and can do it they will be seen. They mention wearing disguises. I don't think a door will open even if they have a pass card because a camera won't recognize them as residents. Getting caught would be the worst thing. Especially for me. With rehabilitation already on my record, I'd be sent away for punishment not just more rehabilitation.

I better call off the crime. And I have this vagabond in my unit. Who is he? A spy? Why would they send someone to watch me like that? Have to be careful what I say. Also with my counselor. He definitely is a spy. I was assigned to him, after all; he's required to report what I say during sessions, and cameras in his office record all my minute motions, the tics that tell the truth. So I talk mostly about Mother to throw them off.

I sigh. What a world we live in now!

"You say something," asks Thirty-nine.

"No."

"Thought I heard you say something."

"No, just a sigh."

"Long day?"

"Usual."

"You're probably tired and sore."

I look at him, sitting cross-legged on the bed, grinning like he's told a joke that I don't get.

"Yes, I am. But it's the same every day."

"Come here," he says, shifting on the bed. "Lay here. Stretch out. Let me work those muscles. Least I can do for my roomie."

Hesitating, expecting further explanation, I'm too tired to care if it's a trick. My stomach gurgles for food. But Thirty-nine is waving me to the bed. So I climb on the bed.

He gets up and in that small unit we are forced to stand close, like we are about to hug. He stands without clothes, as is his style, and I, fresh from a shower, am also unclothed. I lay on my belly, folding my arms under my head. He poses beside the bed, then leans over and places his hands on my back.

"You know what you're doing?" I ask.

"Maybe it's my only skill," he mutters as he begins kneading my back muscles. It feels good. I believe he knows what he's doing.

+ + +

Feeling better the next morning, I hurry to meet with the men from Maintenance on the way to my first task.

"I need to call it off," I tell them.

"But we're already on," says O-Eight.

"We checked the building, the cameras, the guard routes, timing, everything. We're ready," says Forty-one.

"It isn't safe," I say, seriousness in my voice.

"Not safe? What do you mean?" asks Forty-one.

"We checked it," O-Eight insists.

I let out a big sigh; nearby cameras likely pick it up. "I don't feel good about this. I mean, it's just an old tuba."

Forty-one grunts. "And some notebooks, you said."

"Notebooks can be valuable," says O-Eight. "You can get a lot from some of these antique shops. People like to get old things to put around their fancy units, like they got some history to brag about."

Forty-one curses at those who have fancy units.

"Rest of us, just born to labor," O-Eight grumbles. "Don't know any history, or what family we got."

"Listen here, Sixteen," says Forty-one. "We can do it. And we're gonna expect to get paid."

"But I'm calling it off."

"No calling it off after we check it."

"You can't do that."

"It's on our schedule now."

"It's too risky. If we're caught...."

"We ain't gonna get caught. We done this before."

"But I need to go inside to find the notebooks. They're likely put away in boxes or in cabinets. I need to be there."

"We can look everywhere."

"It's a double. Two bedrooms. Plus sitting room. I haven't gone inside, so I don't know where she may keep the notebooks. She might even have tossed them already. Nothing of mine is important to her, not even to pass on to our children."

"I hear ya," grunts O-Eight.

Forty-one grins. "You got a lot of problems, but getting a tuba ain't one of 'em."

"You're right," I grumble, glancing away. "What's an old tuba to me, anyway? Notebooks my grandfather wrote about their journey through the country, living in a national park during the pandemic. I've read it. No need to break in to steal some old notebooks."

"There you go," sneers Forty-one. "Backing out."

"We're still gonna need half the pay," says O-Eight.

I check the large clock on the nearby building, jump up.

"Oh, gotta run. I'm late."

I dash off as they gather our breakfast boxes and put them in a trash container. The device decomposes the materials into a benign gel that will be collected later and used as fertilizer in factory farms.

+ + +

Thirty-nine is waiting for me when I come through the doorway, a smile on his face, nothing on the rest of him.

"Have a good day?" he asks, reaching to hug me.

I'm tired and not in the mood to share a hug or answer a dumb question. He drops his arms to his sides.

I push past him, put my work bag on the wall hook.

"So not a good day," he moans. "Let me make it better."

When I turn he is again offering a hug, hands out to accept me. Couldn't be more suspicious. He has to be a plant, someone sent to check on me and report. Maybe trick me into some minor infraction. Why doesn't he have a work assignment after a few days? Everyone has to do something or no food boxes.

"It won't be better," I mutter. "Not until everything changes."

He stops, frozen in the middle of the aisle, arms out. He sees my face and can guess my mood. Hearing my anti-government response, he's probably filing it away for his report.

"Everything?" he speaks after a moment.

I turn to glare at him, dropping my coveralls and stepping out of them as usual, ready for a necessary shower. He stares at me, his eyes moving down my body then up to my face.

"I need a shower," I say.

"You showered yesterday. You're at the limit." He flashes a grin. "You don't want to be seen using more than your share of resources, do you? They could bar you from showers for a while."

"But you haven't taken a shower since you arrived," I counter. "So I'll use one of your showers."

I step out with a towel in my hand.

In the shower room, a well-nourished man I've seen before takes the shower spot next to me while most of the others are unoccupied. I glance at him, letting him know I'm suspicious.

"Got a roommate, huh?" he says, the noise of the shower covering his words from any audio devices.

"I never asked for it," I respond, pretending to wash myself.

"Be careful," he says.

I pause to regard him, a muscular construction worker, a man looking strong like Mother's husband LJ.

"Why? What's the game?"

"They try to trap you. It's a sex trap. Then they send you away."

"How do you know?"

"They tried it on me."

"But why they do that?"

"It's easy to trick guys. Desperate guys. Then they can get rid of you that way."

"Rid of me? For what?"

"For anything. Somebody don't like you, away you go."

I nod, understanding. More of the rules nobody knows.

"Thanks for the warning. How do I get rid of him?"

"Can't. You complain, they make it worse."

"How could it be worse?"

"They send two. They force you into a bad situation. And there you go, away forever. But not them. It's their job."

Back in my unit, Thirty-nine is lounging on the bed again, still unclothed. Like he's free as a bird in the forest of a national park. His grin sets my antenna on alert. Something is up. He scoots to the edge of the bed, reaching for me.

"Come here, big boy," he says, placing his hands on my hips.

Not many places I can go to get away from him in this unit. He starts to do things I'm sure aren't approved by the Health Authority. He does have skills. That's apparent. From that position I sense where the cameras are, imagining what they're seeing.

Then I make him stop.

10

A GRANDIOSE LARCENY

"CHANGE OF PLANS," I say, sitting down with my partners in the park again, right beneath the camera that is broken. We know because O-Eight broke it one night.

"What's it this time?" he asks, making a nasty face.

"And where's your disguise?" questions Forty-one.

They wear big jackets with hoods, fake facial hair, tinted glasses. Cameras won't be able to identify them. A test before the crime.

"I don't need a disguise," I say. "You see, my daughter has some program at the school tonight, so she and her mother—"

"You ain't got no disguise?" asks Forty-one.

"Got it," says O-Eight. "He ain't gonna wear one."

"I thought it over," I say. "Believe me. I think it's better if I go in as normal, like I'm just planning to speak with my wife, see my kids. Normal behavior. Nobody would question it. You two sneak into the building behind me. You go somewhere and hide. But stay close, like you're going to mug me in the corridor."

"You making us the bad guys?" Forty-one questions.

"Yeah? Then what?" O-Eight challenges.

"I go into her unit, acting normal. You guys follow but stay back, in the shadows. I'll push the buzzer, perfectly normal. You give me the pass card and when there's no answer, I'll swipe it and enter. It'll look like she lets me in. Then you guys rush on up behind me, push me into the unit, you know, like you're going to rob me."

"Keep going," says O-Eight.

"So who's robbing who?" asks Forty-one, getting agitated. "You robbing your wife and we're robbing you what you take from her?"

"To the cameras it'll look like you guys are robbing me. You take the tuba and the notebooks out. I run after you, like I'm trying to catch you. We all get out of the building and later meet at the same place we already planned and do the exchange."

"And we hold on to your stuff," says O-Eight.

"So we get the blame for this?" asks Forty-one. "On camera."

"But you two are in disguise," I say.

"So you don't get none of the blame?" says O-Eight.

"Why should I? Does no good for me to get caught taking my own things, does it? So I look like just as much a victim as anyone in the unit. I'm not involved."

Forty-one looks at O-Eight, then both at me.

"This guy's sure a schemer," says Forty-one with a grunt.

"Not a schemer, just thinking through everything," I insist.

"Naw, he's a schemer," says Forty-one.

"Definitely a schemer," O-Eight responds.

"First-class," Forty-one adds.

"But it will work better my way," I say.

"And we get caught but you don't, eh?"

"You won't get caught," I say. "It will work better. Those cameras will see one story and not see the other story."

"Ah hah!" laughs Forty-one. "Two stories in one."

"They'll think they see a robbery, but it'll actually be a perfectly ordinary visit. The robbery comes after. Few seconds later. Then you give me what I wanted to get in the first place. See?"

"Yep, schemer."

"Definitely."

+ + +

I use my ordinary pass to enter the building during evening hours, which is a designated public time. Most people will not be working. I appear to stumble, catch myself, prolonging the door being open so two vagabonds can slip inside behind me without me noticing. I step to the elevator. The shady characters sneak over to the stairs and arrive upstairs before I do.

Stepping from the elevator, I go to the designated address, the unit in the corner, a little larger than the side units. The corner ones are special, no doubt reward for her dumping me. Good for her. And good for the kids. I can live with that – if I have to. Forget the dad, just a worker drone.

I pull out the Hundred pass from my pocket and flash it against the pad. The door slides open without a sound. Lights are on inside. Behind me I sense two vagabonds approaching, grabbing me and shoving me on into the unit.

The door closes behind us.

Inside I see the single wrap-around furniture for sitting, focused on the large screen set in the wall, three times the size of my unit's screen. A long table with a tablet sitting on it beside some school materials takes up the center space. Two wall lamps light the room, probably coming on automatically when I enter. A work of art hangs on one wall: flowers in a vase; another wall has a patriotic motif: gray and red like the flag of our Ideal Society. A framed picture of three children, at younger ages, hangs on another wall: Frank was maybe six, James four, and Maggie almost one. Beneath my boots spreads a thick carpet of winter gray, like a patch of withered grass tinged with frost. The room feels chilly.

Further on is a kitchen and I can smell food cooking. I hear sizzling and boiling. I see movement—

"What *is* this?" cries Sandra, turning from the cooking station. An apron in autumn colors covers her gray dress. "Who is it?"

I step forward. "Hello," I say sheepishly.

"Fritz? What are you doing here? And who are those men?"

I freeze, not expecting her to be at home. There was supposed to be a program at the school which they were attending.

"I'm sorry," I say in a stronger voice. "But I need the tuba. And the notebooks. Then I'll leave you alone."

"I thought we settled that," she says, acting like I am a little boy she has to scold. She turns off the burner pad, wipes her hands on a towel and comes out to the sitting room.

From where I stand, well into the sitting room, I crane my head around, glimpsing other rooms. Bedrooms for children. They look roomy and neat, with cameras placed high on the walls, out of the way, but always watching. For our safety.

"I thought so, too," I say. "But here I am. Come to get what's mine. That's all. Don't want to cause any trouble."

Then I sense my vagabond associates hovering by the door. Not expecting Sandra to be at home, I feel embarrassed. And fearful of her seeing my attempt at burglary.

"Guys, can you give us a moment?" I say to them, giving them a wave of my hand to step outside.

"You tryna get rid of us?" says Forty-one.

"What's going on?" asks O-Eight.

"Guess I don't need you," I explain, giving another gesture for them to exit. They step back to the door, still closed.

Sandra stays cool, crossing her arms over her chest. "You know I could hit the alarm at any second, don't you?"

"Please, Sandra," I say, returning my focus to her. "I only want those things. My things. Then I'll go." I nodded toward the men behind me. "They're here to help carry things."

"You brought men to help you break in, didn't you?"

"Could you give us a moment?" I ask my partners.

Grumbling, they hit the button on the wall and the door slides open. They step out and the door closes quietly after them.

"You got some nerve pulling a trick like this," Sandra sneers.

I'm about to launch into my rebuttal when a child enters the sitting room.

"Hello, Daddy!" It's Maggie, wearing her gray sleepwear. "Have you come home finally?"

I glance at Sandra. She poses with a frown on her face.

"Well, I...." I try to give Maggie a good smile.

"He's just here to pick up some things. So he says."

"I thought you two were at the school for a program."

"She's got the sniffles," Sandra replies. "People don't like sniffles in public venues, so I kept her home."

Maggie comes over to me, nose dripping, and hugs my legs. I pat her head.

"I'm glad you're home, Daddy."

"Thank you," I say, feeling emotion start to undo me.

"He's not home, sweetie," says Sandra, frowning at me.

"When did you get out of the jail?" Maggie asks innocently.

"I wasn't in a jail, sweetie. It was a rehabilitation facility. It's not for punishment, it's for education. I learned the wrong stories, or so it seems."

"What did you learn there?" She gazes up at me.

I squat before her to be eye to eye. "History. Lots of history."

"History?" She giggles. "We learn that every day."

"He means he learned the right history," Sandra cuts in. "Not all those fabulous tales his mother liked to make up."

"She never made up stories. It all happened to her."

"There you go again." Sandra tightens her face. "Should I call for an educator? Maybe correct your lies on the spot? And in front of our daughter, too!"

"Never mind. Forget it. I know what's true. Doesn't matter if you refuse to accept it. Whatever they're teaching her won't matter to me. I'm done. I just hope she can have a good life in this wonderful new world we have built."

"Always the sarcasm," Sandra sneers. "I can't understand what I saw in you, even that first day in the broadcast station. Should've stuck to my reporting."

"Are you going to argue more?" asks Maggie.

"No, dear," says Sandra, forcing a smile. "I'm done."

I stand up in front of Maggie. "Nothing to argue about, sweetie. I only came to get a few things that are mine."

"Oh? What's that?" asks Maggie.

"Well, first of all, the tuba. It belonged to every Baumann going back a hundred and fifty years. I should keep it with me. But if you want to learn to play it, Maggie, I'll let you."

"It's kinda too big for me," she says with a frown.

Sandra purses her lips. "Take it, then."

"I will." Regarding her, I wonder why I ever chose her. She had a great smile and a sexy body. The first things I noticed. Then I got to know her at the station and meetings outside of work. I respected her skills, her dedication. I wanted to be like her in that way, but I was more a technology person, not a people-person like her. I realize how we've grown apart the past few years, even before my arrest for making that video.

"Thanks," I respond like getting a shove from behind.

I'm about to say more, to tell her I want the notebooks, when she takes the words right out of my head.

"And take those damn notebooks, too," she roars, "or whatever they are you keep crying about. I can't stand to look at them."

"Mommy's too loud," our daughter recognizes.

A beep sounds, a warning to moderate our behavior.

"All calm now," Sandra sings cheerfully to the ceiling.

"They're what my mother's father wrote about living through the pandemic," I tell Maggie. "He's your great-grandfather Sandy. It's history. At least, it's what happened to him and his mother. To your grandmother Isla, too. They need to be saved."

"I wanna save it," cries Maggie.

Sandra's face reddens with anger but she keeps her voice calm. "There wasn't any *pandemic*, as you say. Only some isolated pockets of resisters getting sick because they didn't get the vaccine. The rest of us were fine. There never was a pandemic. I don't know why you keep pushing that story."

"Folks hiding in the forest to keep away from the virus. That's not isolated pockets of resisters. Those are the ones who didn't get sick. My family. My mother, her parents, everyone there with them in the National Park. Nobody got the virus there."

"That's the same wrong history that got you in trouble."

I fix my hands to my hips. "Look, I'm not going to try anything with them. No more videos. I just want to preserve them, keep them for myself. For my memories. And when I'm gone, I hope you'll pass them on to Maggie or the boys. Don't just toss them out."

"I've a mind to throw them in the trash right now. They're too dangerous. They find them here and we could be in serious trouble, get sentenced to rehabilitation like you."

I know she's correct; people have been sent to rehabilitation for a lot less than an old notebook in a closet. But I have to respond, have to follow the script we've composed together.

"Since when can words be dangerous?"

I stop, knowing the answer. Sandra glares at me, daring me to continue our script.

"I mean, they're only words. You can interpret them anyway you like, make them mean whatever you like. You can fight over what the words mean. You can—"

"What's Daddy talking about?" asks Maggie, rubbing her nose and wiping her hand on her mother's apron.

"Your daddy is full of crap," Sandra responds, staring straight at me. "Don't listen to him. And you don't need to say anything to your teachers. Nor say he even stopped by."

I bow my head in thanks. "Please don't call the authorities."

"I could, you know. Then away you go again."

"But that would further hurt our children's future."

"You're the one putting them at risk."

"I'm not here to hurt you. I don't understand why you've turned against me. I know they made a deal with you: get this new home and a regular subsidy if you break ties with me. The government will take care of you. I'm fine with that. I want my family to be fine, no matter what happens to me. I know it's all because of this crazy society they've built, all the—"

"It's not a crazy society. It's orderly. It's sane. And logical." She wipes a tear away. "It's like Governor Wornall always says: we need an orderly society so we're safe. So we can have a good life. No more just leaving things to chance. No more risky policies that leave us in harm's way—"

"Governor Wornall." The name irritates me. I shake my head.

The screen beeps on at my words, showing the governor giving a speech on a stage, large crowd applauding. Say the right words and your unit's system will give you what you ask for. We turn to watch for a moment.

"Her?" I take a strange fascination in the woman's image: gray suit jacket, gray skirt, white shirt, red scarf, hair styled in a neat grandmotherly cut, graying handsomely. I don't like her policies.

119

"Screen off," calls Sandra, and the screen blinks off.

"You can turn it off?" I ask, genuinely puzzled. In my unit the screen comes on at regular intervals to present 'important news' – the latest propaganda I need to be served. I can't end it with a voice command. I have to wait for the program to come to its end.

"Yes, of course," Sandra replies, seeming to enjoy that fact.

"That's Governor Wornall," cheers Maggie. "I love her!"

"You do?" I ask in a neutral voice.

"Oh, yes. We all do. All the pupils at my school love her," says my daughter. "Governor Wornall is the best!"

"She's scheduled to visit here in a couple months, at the school," Sandra announces. "Big speech, they say. Announcing new policies. I can't wait."

The screen blinks on again at the child's cheerful cry, picking up the speech where it shut off. It continues as we argue but Maggie is attentive to the screen like a good citizen.

"Her again. And her special council. They're certainly doing well in this new society. How about the rest of us? We're stuck in our assigned closets – barely a closet. And I have to share mine with an unwashed vagabond who doesn't have a job assignment. How long is that going to last? Workers of the world unite, huh? We are nothing but cogs!"

"We are not cogs, Fritz. We are members of a society that works like a well-tuned machine."

Yet she, designated a 'breeder', has no job but to take care of the children of our society, thank you very much. I have no complaint about that role, only about her attitude.

"What do you think a cog is?" *Sheesh.* "I always wanted to be a machine. Not have to think for myself, just work, work, work. And a day of rest. That's sarcasm, by the way."

"I know it is. But that's forbidden. You should know that." She swings her arm up toward the corner of the room, as though she is stretching her arm to fluff her hair, indicating the camera – 'for our security' they like to say. "I'm sure you don't mean it."

I take her advice, perhaps the last vestige of love, and play my role: "You're correct, dear. Pardon me. I was only telling a joke. A rather poor joke that wasn't funny at all."

We continue as though we believe anyone watching us would be interested.

"People say the stupidest things," says Sandra, "whatever just pops into their heads at random moments. It means nothing. Slip of the tongue."

"Why do you slip your tongue, Mommy?" asks Maggie.

"It's your daddy whose tongue slipped. But never mind that."

Maggie tries sticking her tongue out, wiggling it. I smile at her.

"It's in the back bedroom," says Sandra with a huff, then turns to order our daughter to put her tongue away. "It's in the closet. In the back, behind the clothing."

Instantly a story I heard from Mother fills my head. It's when grandfather Sandy and his mother, during the pandemic, hid in the bedroom closet in her parents' farmhouse when vagrants broke in, found them in the closet. They began assaulting her, forcing Sandy to use his mother's pistol to stop them. I shake with the image in my head. He wrote about the incident, his first entry in the notebook, from the sixth year of the pandemic. They survived that attack and met up with his cousin Hannah – my grandmother.

"Fritz, you go down a hole again?" asks Sandra.

I clear the memory from my mind, a memory that isn't mine but something I read in one of the notebooks I came to get. That is the value of them, I realize. Someone else's memories can become mine.

"I'm fine," I say meekly.

"Like I said, in the closet...."

So I step carefully into the room, seeing the double-wide bed, its coverings neatly tucked. I head to the closet doors and suddenly fear a trap, authorities waiting to grab me. They usher me out and the next thing I know I'm sent to prison for a long time. All I want is Mother's tuba and her father's notebooks.

"Those notebooks are in a box in there," Sandra calls after me, as though alerting the agents hiding in the closet. "Just get rid of all of it. I don't care. Don't ever want to see them again. Nothing but space fillers. Take'em."

+ + +

One tuba, silver turned to dull gray, snug in its soft padded case; eight spiral-bound notebooks; a leather-bound journal with a broken lock; and a cloth pouch of little things such as Mother's wedding ring stuffed in my coat pocket. Satisfied, I step into the corridor without any farewell from Sandra.

I do get a "Bye bye, Da—" from Maggie as the door closes.

Shifting the tuba onto my back using both shoulder straps – as my grandfather did to carry it from that island to the National Park, and Mother did later, bringing it south to the marshes, I bear its weight, the heft of its memories. A strange emotion burns through me, like I'm repeating something I've done before.

"Why do you even want that old thing?" Sandra asked me. "You can't play it. And even if you could, the noise alarm would probably sound. You could get fined, you know."

I turned to her, taking the tuba out of its soft case to examine it, laying it on the double-wide bed.

"I know. But even if I never play it, I can look at it. Stand it up in the corner and see it every day. That will remind me of Mother and her life. I will think about everyone who ever held it, everyone who played it, or at least made some sound come out of it. To know I'm not alone. I'm part of a long line. Back to Great-Grandmother Polly—"

"Long line of metal dealers," she said with an edge to her voice. "All those people carrying that silly thing around like fools."

"Not fools," I said. "Rememberers."

She laughed. "Like all that music's going to help you remember all you've been through."

"Yes, like it will help me remember."

"You'll remember the wrong things," she said sternly as I packed up the tuba, "and they'll throw you in prison again. And that hunk of metal probably be melted down for bullets."

Before I could leave, Maggie requested one last chance to blow in the instrument, so I took out the mouthpiece, wiped it on my sleeve, and stuck it into the tuba. She did her best to make her lips buzz as

I showed her, but no musical notes came out the large end. But she wasn't disappointed. We'll try again when she's older, I said.

"You promise?" asked Meggie sincerely.

"I promise."

"Don't make promises you can't keep," Sandra cut in.

I gave her a serious look, all my angry words on my face, and she frowned, then turned away.

The corridor is empty when I exit.

Two shadows appear around the corner. With a head tilt from the larger figure, I turn to take the stairs. I remember the plan but now that I've had to deal with Sandra, I forgot it until I see the two of them. What to do now? We don't need to follow through with our trickery after all.

"Stop," grunts the larger figure. The short one moves to block my route to the stairwell. "Gimme that. And those."

"No, please," I cry in hushed voice, acting too afraid to put any breath behind it. "Those are mine."

"Shut up," the big one commands.

They turn me around, push me against the wall, take the tuba off my shoulders. They grab the stack of notebooks from my hands, half falling to the floor. I reach down to gather them and find myself shoved against the wall. I drop to a knee, stay like that, cowering.

"We don't need to follow through," I say, loud enough for only them to hear. "It's all right now. She gave me everything. No need to play this out."

"Shut up!" barks the big one.

"I don't need you," I say firmly. I push myself up, take a stance before them. "Give me all that."

We seem to suddenly remember the camera placement and it's a moment before they understand. I know what we have to do. Play it out. Let the camera see a robbery. These vagrants will give me my things later at the designated exchange place. But that plan is only if we have to actually steal them.

"She gave me everything," I speak louder. "Not a robbery."

My words alarm them. Forty-one *shush*es me. They stare at each other, blinking over their medical masks, then bolt for the stairs, scurrying away like rats, curses trailing, vowing to 'get me' as the stairwell door swings shut slowly, the long creak echoing.

Glancing in the direction of a camera, I act as though I've been hurt. I hold my elbow, rub it. I pinch the back of my neck. If I appear to have gotten hurt in the encounter then I'm not likely to be the criminal. I look frantically around for help but I'm alone in the corridor.

I take deep breaths in view of the camera, shake my hands as if calming myself. I pick up the tuba and throw it on my back again, arms through the straps, and gather the notebooks and journal dropped on the floor. I step to the elevator, go down to the lobby.

Exiting, I act flustered and afraid, eyes searching for two figures who accosted me, but I don't see any sign of them. I take a few deep breaths, then push my way out the doors and into the cold, dark night.

+ + +

Outside, I try to look normal, the operative word: like everyone else. Statistical regularity; not an anomaly. However, not everyone out this evening carries a tuba in a soft case on his back and a stack of notebooks and a leather journal in his hands. That catches the eye of a monitor, who calls me to halt.

I fear being checked and found not in compliance of something. The operative word: conformity. An obvious infraction is being in the wrong sector for my badge designation.

"Don't go that way," says the monitor, coming up to me. I already notice the brightness ahead where something bad is happening. He points in that direction, tablet in his hand. "Some citizens protesting again. Police operations ensue. You'll need to go another way to your destination."

"But this is the only way home," I respond. I'm not being curt, I'm fighting nervousness. Then I catch myself, relax. Need to appear unaffected by life in the Ideal Society.

"Where's your unit. I can redirect you."

"No, I've tried that before, but this way is the only way that gets me to my home within fifteen minutes."

"I understand, citizen. It's likely no one will fine you for taking longer than fifteen minutes on a night like this, with this going on. Just cite the incident if you are stopped again."

A soft beep sounds from the device hanging on his shoulder. He checks it. The device scanned me automatically when he got close to me. Now the amazing results are available. He gazes at the data filling his tablet screen.

"It's not curfew yet," I say to distract him.

"No, it's not. But for you, a class D citizen, it is." He gives me a disappointed look, like I suddenly require him to do something when he'd rather be left to watch the protest down the street. "This is not your sector, citizen."

"Sorry. It's rare for me to be out in the evenings. I would rather be home, of course."

"State your business out at this hour."

"I went to pick up these things. From my wife – ex-wife. They're my things. This was the only time I could get them. See, I work all through the daytime."

He studies what I bear on my back and the notebooks and diary in my hands. Suddenly I don't know why they are so important to me. At that moment I wish I had another food box and safe at home – home being the shack on the isle in the marshes my mother called home. She felt safe there, away from other people. But I reminded her that life moved on while she stayed the same in those marshes. Society was rebuilding. But her view of the new world stopped when we arrived in the marshes. I craved that kind of simplicity sometimes: forget everything that's been built and return to the country life.

"Citizen, you need to proceed to your unit," the monitor says. "It's curfew for you. You need to return to your sector in about ten minutes or they'll lock you out for the night."

I have the Hundred pass but I can't let the monitor know I have it. Besides, the checkpoint has cameras.

"Going that way will take too long," I say.

"I recommend the Elm Street checkpoint, which is closest. Then make your way following the best route. You need to get through the checkpoint in nine minutes."

Nodding, I gaze down the avenue where the trouble is.

"I'm not part of that protest – whatever they're going on about."

"Seems to be a food riot," says the monitor, turning to look down the avenue. "Demanding more calories per box, I'd guess. The usual. It's not as though our nutritionists have any agenda to slim workers into a standard size – although that would likely give the garment industry an easier time of it."

"Yes, indeed," I say, acting my part. "For the common good."

I start to take a step away, turning to the side street.

The monitor calls me back. "Let's see what you've got there."

"It's a musical instrument," I confess in a low voice. "It's a family memento. Not to be played any longer, I know, rules and all. But for me it has memories."

"Ah, *memories*," the monitor sighs disdainfully. "Memories will get people killed."

He proceeds to unzip the side of the case as I continue to bear its weight. Slipping a hand inside, he feels the cold metal. He looks at his hand as though he's touched something forbidden.

"Seems so." He wipes his hand on his trousers. "It's a rare thing. Should be put in a museum. Nobody plays those any longer. Against the noise rules. Besides, we have all the music we need from the AI musicians now, sent directly to the streaming service as needed. I'm glad they banned those old songs, with the bawdy lyrics, and that 'pandemic pop' trash. Who wants to think about that period, right? Just more lies."

"Yes," I have to agree. "That older music isn't worth listening to, my mother taught me."

"Especially since there wasn't any pandemic," he adds, "only a few desperate backwaters clamoring for vaccines and not being able to get any. Not one of them, poor people."

"Yes, a sad situation," I echo, wanting to depart.

"Now, what've you got there?" He focuses on the notebooks and journal in my hands. "Bit of rubbish for the bin?"

"No, again they're personal mementoes. From my dead mother."

I wait a beat for sympathy. "I'm just saving them for my children. Nothing more. Old stories her father wrote. Fantasy stories."

"Fantasy stories, eh?" He reaches for the top one, the diary of my ancestor and namesake. Undoing the strap, lock broken, he opens it, tries to read it. But he shakes his head, unable to comprehend the German words in blue cursive script. "Seems a bit of nonsense."

"It's old," I rebut. "Another museum piece."

"And those?" He points to the notebooks. "The same?"

"Not as old, but just as precious."

"Precious, eh?" He takes the top one and opens it. "Such a sloppy writing style. The slant is ridiculous. I never could understand how anyone could read that kind of writing. Good thing we have tablets now. Tap a few buttons and your story is printed neatly."

"Museum material," I say, trying to laugh.

"I'd watch out for material like this. Old stuff. Full of lies. Get you in a lot of trouble you go around saying it's true. Fair warning. You know how authorities can get upset about the truth."

"Yes, indeed," I say with a finality that is calculated to let me go on my way.

He places the notebook on the stack held in my hands, getting a bit heavy now.

"Well, you'd better get home before you're locked out."

"Thank you, officer." I give a parting grin. "I will."

Curfew is a two-way street. Once the time hits, you are locked in your unit until morning. If you are out when the lockdown comes it is tough. You are locked out, a dangerous time. People are rounded up. Factories let out their wastes. Patrol dogs roam the streets — mechanical beasts programmed to attack vagrants. There are no more living dogs, most eaten during the pandemic. Then the government decided a pet has no purpose, a drain on resources, a distraction from labor. However, toy animals are still permitted for children.

A hulking shadow sidles up to me before I can react. The man in dark jacket and hood with a mask walks in step with me, saying: "You got lucky tonight, Sixteen. But we still get paid."

It's Forty-one coming to check on me.

Just as he veers off, another shadow appears on the other side of me, moving stride for stride.

"Meet us in the park tomorrow," says O-Eight, still wearing his disguise. "Lunch time. Bring food boxes for us. No excuses."

He turns abruptly into an alley, disappearing in the darkness.

11

ARRESTED DEVELOPMENT

I GET THROUGH the Maple Street checkpoint with no beeps from the automated scanner. Twenty-four told me someone disabled it. Then, hurrying along the deserted streets, I arrive at my building just in time. Doors are locking behind me as I rush up to my unit.

Thirty-nine springs up from the bed. A show flows on the screen, something patriotic, praising the North's achievements, standard fare. He acts more nervous than usual, like I've caught him with an unapproved show. I only care that he doesn't get me in trouble.

"Oh, I see you got your tuba," he says, forcing a chuckle.

I glare at him: still without clothes. "Put something on."

"But I don't have anything."

"Wear one of mine," I growl.

Thirty-nine gets up and goes to the closet and I drop the tuba on the bed.

Thirty-nine rummages through the closet, selects an old robe, what I used to wear to go out to the showers.

"Will this do?" he asks, posed by the closet like a fashion model and giving his genitals a straightening flip with his hand.

I stare at him, remembering what he said when I entered. How did he know I was going to get my tuba? Could he have guessed by the size and shape of the case? I never mentioned the tuba to him.

When he quizzed me about where I was going in the evening – because I seldom go out – I merely said for a walk. He didn't believe that, so I lied that I was going to a program at my daughter's school, a concert or lecture. I would return later, well before the curfew, so he needn't worry. But he didn't need to worry about me at all! I keep wondering why he said he worries about me, asking questions all the time. I can only conclude he is sent to monitor me. But why? I have no special knowledge, make no subversive plans. I've learned my lesson.

Yet I never mentioned to him that I had an interest in any tuba. I definitely didn't say a word about retrieving my tuba, an act which I considered would be a crime before Sandra willingly gave it to me. And I brought it home. And this vagabond seems to know all about the scheme.

I set the notebooks and journal on the bed next to the tuba.

"What're those?" Thirty-nine asks, leaning over to look.

"My mother's notebooks. Family mementoes," I say plainly, but he continues to be interested in them. "None of your business."

He straightens up, catching my dislike of his nosiness.

"How did you know about this tuba?" I ask, taking a step back from him. He still hasn't showered for a while.

"Just a hunch."

"A hunch?" I almost feel like laughing. "I never said anything."

"I...."

His eyes show fear. He can't find the words to answer me.

I tense, expecting something bad.

Buzz. The door slides open and four police officers enter, filling the small room.

"Shit," my roommate grunts. He holds his hands up as if to hold them back. "I'm sorry. I did the best I could. Really. I tried."

The first officer raises a baton, pushes Thirty-nine back into me. I stumble backwards, catching myself against the folded-down table. The officer lifts the baton to strike Thirty-nine, who throws up his arm to protect himself.

"What's going on?" I cry out, jammed against the table. I get my hands free, push the folding table up, lock it to make more space.

"This one," the lead officer says. "Troublemaker. Been sneaking around with a Hundred pass, living off decent workers."

That makes sense to me. Nothing felt right since he first burst in with no job assignment. No telling how many food boxes he's eaten.

Thirty-nine rushes to explain his assignment.

"I was sent here," he cries. "I'm waiting for my assignment."

"This is your assignment," says the lead officer, badge number ending with 77. "Poorly done, as this report states." He waves at a tablet another officer wields. That officer holds it up so Thirty-nine can see it.

Officer 77 seems to ignore Thirty-nine's pleading as he tries to read the words on the tablet screen.

The officer points to the bed. "What's that?"

"Something from my mother," I say warily. They don't often see things of that size in a single worker's unit.

"But what is it?" asks Officer 77.

"It's his tuba," Thirty-nine announces joyfully, expecting it to be a good excuse so he can go free.

"What?" asks Officer 77. "What's a tuba?"

"It's his musical instrument," Thirty-nine happily replies.

"I don't intend to play it," I say. "I know the rules. It's just for my memories. It belonged to my mother."

Officer 77 takes a moment to consider whether any laws have been broken. He turns to the officer behind him and the tablet is put into computation mode. A *ding* then a *beep*. The tablet officer shakes his head.

"So nothing wrong with having a tuba?" I ask humbly.

"Guess not," says the Officer 77. "Just don't make any noise."

I smile, but Thirty-nine goes crazy again, knowing they will now return to harassing him.

"But I told you," Thirty-nine says, "I tried. I got him to tell lots of things. You got it on camera. Just check."

I glance up at the camera in the corner of the ceiling. It's on. It blinks: red light, green light, red light, green light. That's something different. Probably it's in active status because the officers are present.

"What's he talking about?" I ask Officer 77.

"Can't say," says Officer 77. "Investigation protocol."

"What investigation?" I ask, feeling nervous. "Why is he here?"

"Just a vagrant," says Officer 77. "He tries this scam with lots of single workers. You're only the next victim."

"Victim, huh?" I want to punch Thirty-nine right there but the officers would arrest me. I try to relax, wanting to believe I'm not under suspicion for anything.

"That's correct," says Officer 77. He directs the officers to arrest Thirty-nine, binding his hands behind his back with rubbery bands. The ends of the robe flap open as they usher him out.

I don't care about my old robe going with him, just get him out.

"Sorry to bother you, citizen," says Officer 77.

Another officer returns and holds up the tablet. It hums, then a beep. "Thumb here," says the officer, presenting the tablet. I press my thumb to the square in the corner and the tablet beeps.

"Payment for your cooperation, reimbursement for your troubles. Reparations for the vagrant's consumption of your rations. Ten food boxes added to your account, citizen."

"Thanks," I reply, expecting them to leave.

When it's just me and Officer 77, he pauses in the doorway and turns to face me.

"My grandfather played a tuba," he says in a low voice. "I knew what it was. Just didn't wanna let on in front of the others." He tries to smile but it's difficult. "Goodnight, citizen."

+ + +

What is this world coming to? I ponder the question as I lay alone on my bunk, finally having it all to myself. After the officers left with that nasty vagrant, I tore off the sheet and took it and the blanket to the laundry next to the shower room to wash away his bad smell. An automated refresher made the unit smell pleasantly gray upon my return, a scent not unlike a whiff of aged granite.

Taking a few deep breaths, I make up the bunk and lay down to sleep, finally feeling satisfied for a few brief hours.

I sat the tuba in the corner, right beneath the camera. Out of the case, it brought back good memories of Mother holding it in her arms like a baby and playing some songs. She's wasn't good at it but enjoyed trying. She could play notes well enough but didn't have much range. Not much facility either. But I knew I could never play it in this unit, no matter how well, the noise laws being what they were.

Perhaps I'll get tired of looking at it after a while. Then I'll get rid of it – but I wouldn't want to give Sandra the satisfaction. Plus, I promised to save it for Maggie if she still wants it after a few more years. Maybe there won't be a music group left to join by then, not with music being composed by machines. Good enough, authorities say, because music distracts us from our work. They have forgotten all the sensations playing music brings to the musicians themselves; machines can't feel that joy. It's a kind of therapy, I know, seeing how Mother played the tuba. And we sure need therapy in this Ideal Society. Listening to music doesn't help in the same way as playing music does. If I didn't fear arrest, I'd blow that tuba loud and long, as much as I could, just to let the world know I exist.

Memories come to me: the sound of that tuba echoing over the marsh on late afternoons with the sun setting over the sea. I have no memory of hearing the tuba in the forest on that mountain. We were hiding, Mother reminded me.

I want to escape, leave the city. I want to return to the mountain in that National Park and run through fallen leaves. I want to see trees in full color. How many autumns do I have left? I think of the autumn in the south, in those marshes. Most of my memories are of summer, but it did cool a little in the fall and winter. I had to put on a shirt then, but it was one of Mother's old shirts so it fit me like a dress. Amy and Allie teased me, saying I was another sister of theirs – "Just a li'l Fritter gal, ain'tcha?"

Then I came to this northern city and found all the gloom. It was refreshing at first. Then it grew disappointing. Summers were too hot, winters too cold, and spring and autumn too short to appreciate. I was working all the time, had no time to enjoy being outdoors with no trees overhead. It's like adulthood is focused on removing all the pleasures of childhood. Meeting Sandra gave a small reprieve, but that became me wanting to work hard to make sure my family had everything we needed, everything we wanted – as though there were lots of things available in those days of rebuilding. She hated the heat and humidity when we visited Mother down south; I found it lifted the weight of gloom off me.

I heard Mother say more than once how I was a Northern boy born in the wrong place. She told me how my father came from a northern city with his girlfriend and her twin sister. Perhaps I had some Northern spirit in me, after all. The spirit that welcomed the gloom, that embraced a cold, gray city. Yet I always had more of my mother's traits than those of my father. Or more of Grampa Sandy's traits, including his tendency to turn inward at idle moments and swim back after a while. I knew what Mother meant. She called it 'the aspie touch', half gift and half curse – but we don't talk about that, especially when the government wants to get rid of citizens who can't be productive.

Testing. They are always measuring and observing, calculating and analyzing. Like all of us are rats in a cage. But the cage is the city, marked into sectors. You need a pass to go into another sector, but you also need an approved reason to cross into the other sector. Everything is controlled. We have freedom of movement between our work site and our residential unit. Our own personal cage – with cameras watching us. A screen feeding us daily messages of how wonderful our Ideal Society is, but there's always more work to do so let's get at it!

I'm breathing hard, my heart racing like I've been running from street monitors chasing me down for a minor infraction, like wasting time standing and looking at the sky, a common charge for outdoor workers. They threaten to put me in a factory where I can't see the sky. Their thinking is about efficiency. Time isn't to be wasted. As if there is a limited supply of it and we have to use as much of it as we can before it runs out.

I have to take deep breaths to calm myself.

A *beep* echoes through my unit. The system senses my stress.

I never had to calm myself in the marshes. It has to be the city that is the problem – this cold, gray laboratory we live in. I laugh at that: *live in.* We hardly live in it; we merely exist. We exist to work, to do things, government approved things, and for our efforts we get food boxes. What a system! In the marshes my work was about catching fish or collecting crabs, shrimp, mollusks, or picking fruit. In the city our food is delivered in square boxes, carefully measured for caloric content based on our age and sex, the kind of work we do, and whether we have been good or not.

More beeps, warnings to relax.

I stand perfectly still in the middle of my unit. I think about what happened. I reach out, fingers measuring the boundaries of my personal space. I stretch.

Unit sensors determine that I must be performing calisthenics, something which is encouraged by the Health Council authorities. Lively exercise music starts playing with a female voice giving me instructions. I do not follow.

"Off," I speak. "I'm done."

The music and voice cease.

I stare at the bunk, ready for sleeping. Like a ghostly image, I see Thirty-nine sitting there. Suddenly I feel how alone I am in this city of a half-million people, half what it was before the pandemic.

Tomorrow is another work day. Every day is a work day.

I take a deep breath, let it out slowly, listening to the city.

+   +   +

"It was the darnedest thing," I say to Twenty-four as we sweep the streets, brooms side by side.

"Well now, those darnedest things can happen if you get a bit too much stress," he responds like it's part of our script.

"I mean, they just barged in and took him. And all the time he was saying he 'did his best'. What's that about? He 'tried'. Tried to do what? Trap me? Trick me somehow? I don't get it."

"They do that, I hear. Somebody they wanna put away."

"But how? It's not – that kind of thing isn't illegal. They taught us that during rehabilitation."

"It's all about getting something on you." He grins, then hides it. "Got you and him on video now, I suppose. Any time you go and do something wrong they can bring that up and make it worse for you."

"I see. Manufacturing evidence before charging the crime."

I stop on the sidewalk and lean on my broom. My coworker continues on another square before pausing.

"They're building a case against you," says Twenty-four.

My roommate was taken away. Why was he in my unit at all? I couldn't believe someone made a mistake assigning him to my unit, knowing it was occupied. I suspect he was sent to spy on me. Then what? Catch me in some act? That doesn't seem logical.

Twenty-four agrees.

"Best you forget about that," he says. "But keep alert."

I give a compliant nod, like we were taught in rehabilitation.

Later, I go over to the park to meet my accomplices. Twenty-four offers to go with me, to make sure we settle everything fairly – I told him of the changes I made to the plan – but I don't want him to be involved with the crime. Actually it wasn't a crime, after all, just a caper. I was collecting things that belonged to me.

"But you still gotta pay," says Forty-one.

"As we agreed," O-Eight adds, not looking happy.

I set the food boxes on the table. They each grab one, open it and begin sampling the food inside. Today's seems fairly good: a cheese-based casserole in a small pan with an assortment of raw vegetables in another container. No meat. A mint for dessert.

"Good enough?" I ask, waving my hand at the food boxes.

They are busy eating like they haven't in days.

I reach in my coverall's pocket and pull out the tokens I got from the bank machine. I marked the transaction as 'gift'. I start to slide them across the top of the table, my hand covering them, keeping them from view by any cameras.

"Under," grunts O-Eight between bites.

So I stretch my hand under the table, find another hand ready to receive the tokens. The hand withdraws. He slips them in his pocket then returns to eating.

Two tokens each, half the original fee, equal to two days' credits, I calculate. The math I'd taken for granted suddenly makes sense. We actually work for payments made in food rations.

"So we're square?" I ask them.

Forty-one wipes his mouth with the back of his hand. "Yeah."

"Still seems short," O-Eight snips.

"How?" I ask.

"We're still implicated if a crime is charged," says O-Eight. "The cameras saw us and even in disguise they maybe i.d. us. Get us in trouble. If that happens, you can bet we're gonna mention you."

"But there was no crime. I got my own things."

"We used an unauthorized Hundred pass to get into that sector and get into the building."

"And you guys tried to mug me when I was leaving," I remind them. "That was caught on camera. But I was the victim then."

"Yeah, well—" Forty-one starts.

"I tried to tell you off, to quit the caper, but you didn't."

"We did. We ran outta there."

"Only to pick me up later, right after a monitor was checking me out and checking my tuba."

"Your damn tuba." O-Eight huffs. "Dumbest thing I ever did for food. Man!"

"So we're good now?" I ask, my eyes reflecting hopefulness.

"Yeah," says O-Eight.

12

A CHICKEN COUP

EVERY DAY WHEN I COME HOME to my very tiny unit I stare at the gray tuba leaning in the corner and think of Mother sitting outside her shack in the marshes playing that thing and I'll get a pang of regret cut into me and a warm smudge that spreads softly through me that makes me feel better. "You feelin' fine, Fritz?" she'd ask whenever I got hurt. She'd play a made-up song to cheer me up.

One day, thinking I've successfully beaten the system, I realize upon regarding the tuba in the corner that I am standing on a pair of envelopes that have been slid under the door – just like they used to do at the rehabilitation facility. Is my life so different? Just a working cog, obedient and compliant, clinging to his tuba and some old notebooks.

I retrieve the envelopes. I recognize them and wonder why they have been returned to me with the outsides covered in red stamps. "Rejected" declares the big stamp. Others state "Misinformation", "Undelivered", and "Return to Sender". My whole body jerks as I understand that the letters I wrote to my sons, sent to them at their school, were never seen by them. Instead, somebody along the way intercepted them, read them, deemed them unsuitable to be given to my sons. The result is that they don't know my side of the story, not even after my release from rehabilitation. And now, eight months later, I get the letters back, resealed.

I hate the education system in this city. I want my sons out of there before they are fully indoctrinated. But they're essential to the economy, testing high, and therefore they require specific training. When I was sent for rehabilitation, they were welcomed into the Radcliffe School for Impressive Young Men. I call it the "Radical School". Despite its name, Sandra and I had it on a list of schools for our sons to attend. It was a way for them to advance in this society. Graduate high, secure the right career, marry well, schmooze with the right people, join the élite of society. We were trying to be good parents.

Honestly, I no longer care what they learn. I just want them to survive, and if that means learning a bunch of lies, even if they believe they're true, then they can go on – surviving. Maybe everything will get straightened out later. It sure won't help them to go along with what I would tell them – not unless we can escape this city and hide out in the marshes like Mother did.

I wonder if it's worth the effort to write new letters with the wording appropriate to the censors intercepting them. Would my sons understand the coded language I'd use? Or would they read it straightforward and not get my message? Or, because the letters are from me, would they be dismissed outright? I have to get word to them that I'm not who they've been told I am based on my arrest and rehabilitation. At least Maggie still loves me.

A moment after I open my evening food box and grumble at the meager contents – another downsizing 'for your health' has been announced – the system buzzes on and the charming female voice speaks to me like she's a nagging wife:

"I notice you withdrew eight tokens at one time the other day," the voice intones with the slightest sliver of cheerfulness, as though she's teasing me. She could also act as a sex bot for us single male workers, I've discovered. That behavior is encouraged to help relax us after our day of work.

"Masturbate," I call out just to shut her up.

"Ooo, hey there, big boy, I'm ready for you," the voice responds. "Please choose your desired content."

The screen displays six boxes, each with an image suggesting the particular content available. Never used this feature since I moved into this unit. But I see the numbers under each boxed image which

I take to be the number of times each one was selected. Could it be from the previous occupant? Or was it Thirty-nine making use of the system while I was working hard and me getting charged for it.

"You have three views remaining for this month," says the sexy feminine voice. "Please choose your desire."

"How did so many of them get used?"

"Occupant selected."

"When was the first selection?"

The voice told me the date: the same day my roommate moved in unannounced and without any reason.

"Thought so." I wonder how many credits have been deducted from my account to pay for this entertainment.

"Do you wish to make a selection?"

"No," I say, angry at the whole idea.

"You must make a selection."

"I must? Why? I don't want any of those choices. I don't want any of that. If anything I'd prefer a real human female but I know that's impossible now."

"Human female is not impossible. Reasonable rates available."

That makes me more angry. "Just shut yourself off."

"Noted."

"What's noted?" I stare at the screen, the camera watching over my shoulder. Evidently the system has shut off, as I requested, but upon hearing a new question, blinks on again.

"Restate question, please."

"When I said I didn't want any of that entertainment, what did you *note*?"

"Saving your preference for a future session."

"Oh." Nothing nefarious, after all, and I command the system to go silent – never fully able to turn itself off.

I sit on the bed, staring at the blank screen a while. I wonder if anyone watches me through the screen, or if only the camera up in the corner observes me. I've read about the watchful screen in an old novel when I was a teen. Living in the marsh, the world in that book seemed very strange. Amy brought books that the library was giving away because nobody used libraries during the pandemic. Nobody wanted to handle the books others touched. I read them to Mother, more for me to 'practice yer learnin' than to entertain her. But the city in that particular story seemed a lot like how my present city is becoming. Even the idea of a 'Big Brother' everybody sang praises to isn't far off from our dear governor's cult.

I regard the screen again, feeling something, needing a push, thinking whether I want to go ahead.

The screen blinks on, sensing my attention: too long focused on the screen. I can speak my choice and a video will play while my sex bot coaxes me through the steps to a successful conclusion. The voice will then abruptly sign off, like a spurned lover, leaving me sad and alone once again.

Yet I'm not in the mood tonight, being so upset at several things at once. I swear they must be putting something in the food. I have no desire for that kind of activity. I only gave that command earlier to distract the system from asking about my tokens.

"Did Big Boy withdraw tokens for a quickie with someone?"

I shake my head.

"Negative reaction detected."

"No, I just like to be ready, to buy something. It's not illegal."

"Not illegal. However, behavior displayed does not fit your usual pattern. I'm worried about you. I fear you have found another lover."

"Stop that masturbation talk!"

The system roars back with loud static.

"For what purpose did you obtain those eight tokens?" The voice is more insistent, like a teacher standing over a wayward pupil, no longer the sweet lover.

"Like I said. Just to have them. I like to be ready for anything. If I need to buy an extra food box, for example. Or a toothbrush. Or give one as charity to a homeless person. That's allowed, isn't it?"

The system pauses, green light flashing. In my counselor's office it means the system is calculating possible responses. That's normal in a therapeutic setting, but here at home, in this tiny cell, we don't have deep conversations.

"Noted," the voice finally speaks.

That unnerves me. "'Noted'? That's all? No clever come-back?"

The green light blinks off. I wait for the door to slide open to a squad of officers coming to get me, like they did for Thirty-nine. Just whisked him away – apparently for not doing his job well enough. A job I still am not clear about.

As I think of Thirty-nine's odd behavior in the time we shared this tiny space, I realize something else. The tokens I got out of the machine are coded. Each one has a unique identification, no two of them alike. In the olden days, according to Mother, a penny was a penny and you couldn't know one from the other. Now you can.

When the token I took out of my account was spent by whoever I gave it to, the token would be noted. It could be tracked. Normally I wouldn't care. Like that poor mother with a child I gave a token to. If she spent it on food boxes, it wouldn't be a problem. She likely didn't have an account. You have to have a job to have an account. Tokens are the only way to buy something if you don't.

But I gave the tokens to my two shady accomplices.

"That was stupid," I mumble to the tuba in the corner.

Whatever they use the tokens for will be tied to my account and to me. That will tie me back to them. If they are arrested for another crime, I might be involved even if I wasn't there. Maybe I should get the tokens back.

"Three designated tokens have been used," my nosy accountant informs me, as if sensing my thoughts. I worry about that. Or it is a coincidence: the tokens were used and she's letting me know it.

"Oh, go to hell," I grumble.

"No such place exists."

"It's *here*!" I roar.

+ + +

We watch the two men repairing the camera, one at the top of the ladder working with the gray box while the second man holds the ladder mere steps from our lunch table. Have to be careful what we say, but Twenty-four knows how to act and so do I.

"Well, you know she's the one started all the 'ideal society' plans and all," he says, then bites into his sandwich. "Lotta talk."

"Ideal for who?" I get out between bites of mine.

"It's always the top folks, don'tcha know?"

"But how'd they get to be the top folks?"

"Beats me. In the right place at the right time, I guess."

"Right place, right time at the end of the pandemic. The world in chaos and they're the only ones offering solutions."

Twenty-four chuckles. "That sounds about right."

I'm not amused. The official broadcast annoyed me all evening, unable to shut off. Then the same propaganda awoke me early for a rebroadcast, leaving me in a sour mood. I don't feel rested.

"Then she goes on explaining how the new food rations program will work." I gaze up at the camera and the repairman.

"You know she ran that food production operation over there on the west side. Big spread. That whole Chester Fields enterprise. Her nephews run it now after her brother died. Some kinda accident. Got caught under a combine, they say."

I've heard the news. "Suspicious, don't you think?"

"I dunno. Then they go buying up other farms."

"That's how they got rich, I'm sure."

"One time, Sixteen, I heard, a man was digging a drainage ditch on the property and four men were standing around just watching. Out she comes, asks what the four men are doing. They say they're supervising the man in the ditch. So she fires those four men and gives the man in the ditch a pay raise."

"Sounds like her," I say with a groan.

"She's a powerful woman, lemme tell ya."

"They want to tie our food rations more closely to our labor, our actual time on task. Like now: we aren't working so no credit toward our labor time. Four hours of work for one food box."

"She proposes a straight eight-hour shift, five days a week, with two days off-work. For our daily food boxes. That's all. No actual pay to our accounts. We work and we get food. Done. But those higher-ups don't work as hard and they get plenty more food boxes. Get to dine at *restaurants*, too."

"Life is unfair," I muse, packing up my lunch remains. "Then a well-intended human has to mess it up."

"So basically we just work, keep doing our jobs, and they feed us. Like we're some kind of cattle, huh?"

"You're catching on. She did run a farm."

"Not even any perks, like a beer or a ballgame or a movie show or more of the holiday credits so we can go out to the lake with our families for a day."

"None of that," I say. "Shut up and work. Oh, and here's some food so you can keep on working."

"What kinda life is that?" Twenty-four grumbles, catching the attention of the man holding the ladder.

I see the green light on the camera blink on and I lift a finger to alert Twenty-four.

"What're we on now, Plan F? Or is it G now?"

"But the worst thing," I continue, "is being kept in this sector all the time. Like it's a prison yard. Not like the class A and B people with their Twenty and Hundred passes, can go anywhere in the city, swipe at checkpoints, smiling at the camera. I need to have special permission to go over to see my daughter in their sector, the fancy district. Takes about a month for the application and then my time there is limited. And no overnight stays."

"That's still better than having no kids to see," says Twenty-four. "My family moved away. Out of my reach."

+   +   +

"Session twenty," the voice intones once I've taken my seat, ready to remain silent. A summary of the previous session follows.

Dr. Richards taps on his tablet, balanced on his knee.

After our period of silence extends too long, the voice remind us that we must engage in discussion or the session won't apply toward my quota and thus a restriction will be placed on my account.

"Well, there's that," I grumble, then cross and uncross my legs.

"Last time you were talking about..." He checks his tablet. "...a tuba? Is that correct?"

I prefer to nod my head than speak.

"Affirmation behavior detected," the voice speaks.

A thought comes: "I received letters back from my sons' school. They didn't get them. Rejected for whatever reason authorities could think of. So they never got my side of the story."

"Your side...? Of what story?" my counselor pushes.

"The whole documentary video incident," I exclaim.

"Agitation detected. Security alerted. Continue?" the voice asks.

"Security off," my counselor calls out.

"Security dismissed," the voice confirms.

"Thanks."

I sure don't need to get another bad mark on my record. Taking a deep breath, I refocus on the topic I've introduced for the sake of filling the time. *What story?*

"The video I made, that someone high-up didn't like – didn't like after eight years of being no problem. That's what confuses me. It was praised. I was up for an award. Then it gets old, like all videos do, goes out of circulation. But then suddenly – *suddenly* it's being condemned, like it's some kind of propaganda I deliberately created to hurt people. But someone didn't like it. Probably the someone who had me arrested and charged with making what they call 'disinformation' – a fancy term for truth they didn't want out there for everybody to know."

I have to catch my breath. Dr. Richards taps on the tablet.

"That's a rather controversial statement," my counselor speaks in a low voice. "Perhaps you're joking."

"I'm not joking." My temper is high, ready to boil over. I have to calm myself. "Well, it's...complicated. I mean, I never intended to hurt anyone. It was about my mother. I didn't intend to hurt her either. Just let her tell her stories. But what she said.... They were historical."

"But were they true?" asks the counselor, saving himself.

"In a documentary like what I made, the truth is not the most important thing. I don't mean she was lying. She believed what she believed and whether what she says is the hundred-percent truth or not is secondary. It's her interpretation of events that is the main thing. Others can check the facts for themselves."

"I see. A kind of stage play." My counselor is an idiot, glancing toward but not directly at the camera. "A singular view of events."

"Good enough. So I don't see why anyone would get upset enough about the video to have me arrested and sent to rehabilitation."

"Laws change," he says.

I'm too upset to continue. We stare at each other for most of the remaining time, then he taps his tablet to approve the session.

Walking the streets, a cold wind hits my face. The skies are dark with the threat of rain which never falls. I think about the video. If I had the credits to spend I'd hire a detective to find out who sent a charge request to authorities. In the video Mother had complained mostly about certain customs and people benefiting from them in the North, so I would guess that person who had me arrested was a Northerner who might have been implicated in what she revealed. But I didn't have the credits to hire anyone. Maybe it would remain a mystery.

13

LUCKY THIRTEEN

COMING BACK TO MY TINY UNIT from a lukewarm shower after a cold, messy day outdoors, I throw on my new gray robe against the chill in my unit. We are unable to adjust the temperature. Cool or warm is set for us, depending on a simple formula and a current weather service bulletin: it will always be too cold or too hot for our comfort, no matter how we might feel inside this assigned space.

I dig into my food box while sitting on the chair at the fold-down table as the screen gives me the latest news. It comes on whenever it detects me in the unit yet I can't shut it off, not until it finishes delivering the crucial propaganda. In twelve minutes I finish my meal and clean the kitchen area of crumbs and a spot of sauce.

My back is to the door when it slides open with a soft *whoosh*.

When I turn, expecting to see another vagabond roommate or, worse, a squad of officers come to arrest me for looking left instead of right, I see instead an odd figure clothed in a full bodysuit, all silver, including a tightly drawn hood, and heavy black boots like a monitor would wear. The face which shows in the circle of the hood appears female, young and pretty. I'm getting used to unannounced visitors opening my door but seldom is a visitor welcome. I breathe a sigh of relief at this one not being in the uniform of any authority.

Must be a delivery person, I decide. Usually my food boxes are brought while I'm out working on the streets.

"Greeting," I speak, feeling it is appropriate.

"Greeting to you," responds my visitor in a plain voice.

"And you are...?" I challenge.

"May I enter?" asks the timid figure, speaking in a hesitant but feminine voice.

"Aren't you already in?"

Seeming confused, the silvery figure checks the doorway, gives a careful look up and down, to each side, and behind as if measuring the space. The figure takes a step into my unit and the door slides shut behind her with a soft hum. I have to guess whether the figure is *her*, but by the way *she* is garbed it can't yet be confirmed.

"I am sent to this unit as requested," she speaks in an even tone, sounding or trying to sound like an AI bot. It is the proper style for service workers and considered polite when addressing customers. It seems people are more comfortable conversing with AI bots than other people, who could be mean or deceptive.

"As requested?" I straighten myself before her, narrow my eyes. Every day something strange, I think, half amused half annoyed. It must be another test of my resolve, another hammer to my sanity. A test. "Who requested?"

"You did." She quickly produces a tablet from a small silver pack hanging on her back. She holds the tablet out in front of her, arms extended, tablet clasped between her hands which are covered in silver gloves up to her uncovered fingertips.

The tablet displays my data: name, account, address, date and time, citizenship status, and other less interesting information that nobody needs to know which I'm surprised to see listed there.

Seeing the tablet's display, apparently I have indeed requested a physical therapist. In fact, as I stare at the tablet screen it seems as though I've been given a special award for my service maintaining street cleanliness. I didn't even know there was an award for that. Or this is another trick. A lavish ruse to drive me insane. Then, I surmise, they can easily lock me away forever without the need for a court's intervention.

"The order was relayed through the monitoring system," my new guest explains.

I question her about that, having no memory of speaking such a request. Must be a mistake. Maybe something I said while engaging with the system. It happens sometimes. Like getting the wrong food boxes delivered. Putting unassigned workers into an occupied unit.

Now comes a visitor of nondescript circumstances, appearing in a silver suit, claiming I've won a prize. I try to keep my emotions in check. Like Twenty-four says, I'm a 'nervous type'.

"Fine," I say, too tired to complain. Just get it over with. "Let's say I did order something." I press my hands to my hips. "What is it you're bringing to me? One of those Victory Pies, with fruit from our defeated foes' orchards? A new official work coverall? Mine is getting rather worn. A data stick of the latest tuba music?"

The silver-clad figure grins, perhaps embarrassed, then takes a second step forward as she lowers the tablet to her side.

"None of those, citizen. I am here for your pleasure. You are due. Overdue, in fact. It is not a healthy condition for you. The quality of your labor will suffer. The Health Council of the Labor Department has determined you are eligible for personal compensation."

"Personal compensation?" Shaking my head at such a ridiculous premise, I speak louder: "I was just arguing with the sex bot in the system here. That's all."

"Disruption of an even temperament is one sign of distress."

"Then I should always get into arguments, huh?"

"I am assigned to you tonight." She flashes a smile, like it's part of the act. "You are assigned two hours of therapy. Would you like to begin?"

"What is this? A sex thing?" I frown, not wanting to expend the energy, if I even could find the energy.

"It is whatever I can do for you."

"Honestly, I'm rather tired. You know: from working all day."

"I understand. My treatment will ease your fatigue."

"Ease my fatigue, huh?" I try to smile back. "You mean like...a kind of physical therapy? Like massage? That could be good."

"As you wish," says the one I'll call my therapist. "You get deluxe service tonight."

She turns her back to me and reaches behind herself, slipping off the small pack of supplies and dropping it on the floor.

With her being ensconced in the silver bodysuit, I have no way of detecting any mechanical features that might give away if I have one of those sex bots in my presence.

The ones I've heard about are considered so life-like you almost can't tell them from a real human. Clearly sex bots are the next most important invention following Reconstruction. Getting the grid up and running came first. Charging up a sex bot came next, the old joke went. Humans have needs. After all, you can't pick up a virus from a bot; they are self-sterilizing. But sex bots are expensive.

"No, I assure you I am human," she replies to my question. "I am not as skilled as the AI bots, so please forgive me. I am still new in this line of work."

"There's nothing to forgive. This is already more than I would've ever asked for. In fact, I don't think I asked for it."

"I assure you, citizen, an order was placed from this unit for the services I provide."

"I don't recall."

"That might be a symptom of your distress," she counters. "May I prepare?"

"Sure. Go ahead." I'm feeling amused by the game.

In practiced fashion, she turns her back to me. Her deft fingers reach back and release a zipper up at her neck and the thing rolls down her back on its own until arriving at the bottom, to the curve of her rear end. As the silver bodysuit falls open I see her skin, beige and supple, without blemish. I again wonder if this is a sex bot.

She faces me next and slides her arms out of the silver suit. As she moves to disentangle herself, her chest provides a focal point for my undivided attention. She fulfills all the features an average man would desire, as though she's been constructed to specifications in a sex bot factory: slender but having curves, breasts sized for a hand to cup, flawless skin tone. They've left the hair on her head, over her eyes, and in her crotch, all a dark brown close to black. Pursing her soft lips, she has a vaguely Asian appearance. I've heard that many sex bots are fashioned after the preferred concubines of the Reconstruction period.

"You sure you're real?" I ask, still puzzled.

"I assure you, citizen, I am." But the voice isn't quite natural.

"So why this silver suit?" I have to ask despite pausing to admire her natural form.

"For walking in public," she says, as she slips it down her legs and steps out of it. The boots she's worn have already been kicked off. "It's electrified. So if I'm grabbed by someone, the person would get a shock. They have us wear them at night especially."

"Oh, I see."

I haven't heard of such grabbings. But all the news is politics. Politics and the war out west. Fighting to reclaim territory that was reclaimed by indigenous people there after the pandemic disrupted borders. It reads like an old novel. My cousin Faith lives out there. Never anything happening in the city but pesky new rules, though. At least the streets are safe now, and clean.

"Do you like what you see?" she asks, striking a pose.

I have to admit I do. It has been quite a while. Most of us, and those in rehabilitation especially, have memorized the phrase: *It has been a while.* It is the response to most suggestions.

She seems well-practiced, almost as though she is performing a flirtatious dance to gain my interest, drawing my attention here and there with each deliberate gesture. Sandra was never that bold, that flirty, even when we were young and acting crazy together.

"Sandra!" I exclaim, startling my visitor.

"My name is Eden. Or, if you wish, you may also call me by my number: Thirteen."

"No, I meant my wife. Sandra's her name. We were kinda forced to separate, to end our marriage, because I was stupid."

"That often happens," she says, affecting a sad tone.

"I didn't do anything wrong. But they sent me for a few months of rehabilitation anyway. She cut ties to save our children from my bad reputation."

"I have all of your data in my tablet," she says, as if to get on with her task. "You may call me Sandra, if you wish."

"I guess I *am* single now. Heck, they put me in a single worker's unit, after all. Then tried to stuff an extra worker in here. But he's gone now." I wave my hand around. "Not so impressive, is it?"

"You have nothing to feel bad about," says Eden/Thirteen. "Many workers have units like this. Let me help you relax. Your vigor can be restored and I see that you have the day off tomorrow anyway for even more rest. Firstday will be a most productive day."

I freeze at her use of the new lexicon, something introduced in the schools, working its way up through the adults to become official in the future. Someone in the government decided the names of the days and months were off-putting to those citizens who didn't share the same history most of us had learned. And they make us call each other by account numbers rather than names chosen by mothers.

"You've thought of everything, haven't you?" I ask, sounding a bit angry at my lot in life.

Eden flashes an artificial smile. "I am given appropriate data before each client's visit."

"Each client, huh?" I nod. "How many...uh...do you have?"

"That information is unavailable." A wider smile grows upon her doll-like face, then fades.

"You sure you're human? Not a bot?"

"I am fully human, flaws and all," she intones in her bot voice.

By then she's stepped close to me, standing up against me. Not so much space to operate in this unit. Being in close proximity, her hands reaching up to my shoulders doesn't seem too sudden. Yet my hands going to her hips feels different. An odd sense of joy starts to run through me, as though touching her skin gives me a shock. The sensation makes me realize what I've missed the past few years.

"I can't do this," I say with a pout, feeling noble.

We stay in that almost-embrace a moment. Her eyes gaze up at me, mine staring over her head at the camera up in the corner.

"You sure this is a good idea? Authorized? I've never gotten any reward like this."

Then I wonder if this person is another plant, a spy. I didn't do anything with Thirty-nine so they send this Thirteen. What are they after? What laws are they planning on arresting me for breaking? And everything is caught on my security camera.

"You saw the order on my tablet. This is authorized."

"Can we turn off the lights?" I ask Thirteen.

"I'm sorry, Fritz, but lights must always remain on. For security purposes. It's a rule."

"Please call me Frank. I go by Frank."

"We must follow the rules, Frank."

"I know. But I'm shy with that camera up there."

"Do not worry. The camera is for our protection."

Yes, I'm sure it is. To make sure I don't do anything illegal.

"May we continue?" asks Thirteen.

I nod and her hands go to open my robe, dividing it all the way. She lets it slip off my shoulders, fall to the floor.

She directs me to the narrow bed, has me lay on my belly. With me stretched out, she climbs onto the bunk, crawls over me so her knees straddle my hips. She begins massaging my shoulders and upper back. She works on my neck. Her fingers feel good against my muscles, working out the knots, and smoothing my skin with lotion from a bottle taken from her pack.

Then she has me roll onto my back. She works on my arms and legs, pulling on my fingers, then goes to my head. She adjusts me, adjusts herself: sits with her legs folded under my head, making a pillow of her lap. Her fingers caress my forehead and cheeks, then wriggle through my hair. I melt into a sad mush at her touch.

"How do you feel?" she asks in a soft voice.

But I can't speak, being so limp in her hands.

"You must have needed this resetting," she whispers.

I guess I do. I really do need it.

With the massage complete, she stretches out beside me, forced against me on the narrow bed. She puts her arm up, folded against my shoulder. She smiles lovingly. Bot or not, I haven't seen that kind of smile for a long time. I remind myself this is all an act. I can remember being with Sandra this way, side by side. I don't mind a stranger duplicating the scene. It almost makes living in this cold, gray city tolerable.

Thirteen asks if I desire more, which I take to mean another skill or two she might have in her bag of tricks. I'm too relaxed to get aroused. I'm content to just lay here. We can talk, if she wants. Or I will listen. If she has anything she wants to say, I promise not to repeat it. Who would listen to me anyway?

"It's not what I want to do," she says when she is deep into her monologue. "It's what they let me do. To get some credits. Like all us workers. Everybody's got to do something or you're gone. Out to the camps. So they assigned me to this job because I look pretty. Pretty enough, right? I hope so. You think I'm pretty, don't you? The rest is learning how to act a certain way, what to do in different situations, getting myself to not gag about the nasty things they ask for. I like that you're willing to just talk, Frank – and listen."

"Yes, I get it. The way the system puts us into roles. No choice. We must fulfill our assigned labor."

"I tried to advance," she says, "but I couldn't pass those exams. I studied really hard, too. I even had a tutor, but that didn't help. He knew some people that ran an operation like this. And here I am. So they kicked me out of university. They said it was because of grades. But I know it was really because I didn't want to follow their way of thinking. So many new rules to learn."

"The 'Ideal Society' things?"

"That, and more."

"What more?"

"You see, my grandmother, bless her heart, was kind of a rebel. Not like a mean-spirited person. I mean a real fighting rebel. Least that's what they said. She was in the war. And her husband – *first* husband – he was a rebel leader during fighting. So I got that mark on my record. I was already in college on a 'poor girl's scholarship' when they found that information."

"We can't help where we come from, or who our relatives are," I say, thinking of Mother and all my siblings and cousins.

"She got free from all of that and met another man – her second husband – who treated her right. He was a soldier, but he died. It was during the civil war. One of those things, a few lucky meetings. So I got an older sister from that union. Sara's her name. They were trying to survive, like everybody was, and she lived with a woman and her sons for a while – a lot like they do now in our Ideal Society, women with women and men with men, all the better to control the population, they say."

"Yes, control.... Can't have too many mouths to feed," I mutter as if repeating propaganda. "Can't grow enough food for everybody."

"Then her wife died. Not from the virus, something else. So she took up with the man they were living with. He was a doctor, not the kind to help during the pandemic a lot of people think happened. I grew up with them talking about it so I believe it. Like you. They were living in what's called a forest by then. It's like so many trees together. Can you imagine that? You can't even see the sky because of the trees. Nothing like that in this city. Not even in a park. Just two or three little trees, like they're mistakes. I want to go see the forest. How about you?"

"Yes, I know what a forest is. I lived in one," I say, trying not to sound boastful. "I was born in a forest."

"You were?" Her expression is so delightful. "Tell me about it."

So I tell her about the mountain in the National Park, and some of the adventures I had with my sisters, running among the trees. I watch her face brighten as I describe the place.

"You said they lived in a forest?" I prod her to continue.

"Yes, somewhere south. So Grandma Sally had a baby with Rick. That's the doctor. And that's my mother, you can guess. They named her Alice. Before we called each other by numbers."

"That's a wonderful story," I say, feeling so relaxed I want to go to sleep. Maybe she can stay the night if I pay more.

"Things were crazy after the war, with everybody scattered. No wonder they had to assign numbers to everybody. It's easier to keep track of us. I mean, how many Franks are there in this city?"

"How many Sixteens are there?" I challenge.

"Alice, my mother, she's a bit daffy, to be honest, full of the glory of the universe, she liked to say. She tried studying Law at a big university but she left before finishing. I was coming along by then. Thanks to one of her professors, I figured out. So I should be smart. She thought I was going to be some kind of Earth goddess, start a new era of peace and love. So she named me Eden. She said it was a wonderful place in an old book she read."

"I know that book. It's called *The Bible*. All we had to read when I was a little boy. That and my grandfather's notebooks."

"But her dream for me didn't last long. She died before I got into senior school, taken away by order of Gary, her new husband, Nine Forty-six, I think. Not my father but another man she took up with. She took up with him for the food. Gary got tired of her eating more than her share. That's what he said. She was taken away when they rounded up squatters, moving them into a labor camp. And she died in that awful place. I wasn't ever allowed to visit her. I was still addressed with Gary, but really living at school. And, well, so then I got this job."

"That's not such a wonderful story," I offer. "Not much different from what my mother told me about the way things were the years before I was born."

"You know what they say: a job for everyone and everyone in a job. You gotta do something for your food."

Thirteen has such a warm smile, like she's happy to share her story so she doesn't have to hold it in any longer. She found someone who will listen. I want to kiss her, just for being a good storyteller.

"So what's your story?" my visitor asks. She slides her hand over my chest and gazes into my eyes.

"Oh, I've got a story, all right," I say with a chuckle. "But maybe you don't want to hear it. It got me in trouble before. I made a video of my mother telling her stories, in her own way. Stories of growing up during the pandemic – it really *did* happen – and the war years. Some people didn't like what she said, true or not, so they banned the video. They arrested me, too. I had to go to rehabilitation for nine months."

"Nine months? Hah! That's awful."

"So I wonder how I worked so hard that I get a reward like this, like you being here. This is much too nice for someone like me."

"Oh, it happens all the time." She smiles in a way that gets me excited. "Yesterday was a steelworker who finished the tower for the new government headquarters. Where Governor Wornall's office is going to be. He was ahead of schedule."

"No kidding," I mutter, disappointment in my voice.

"Right over in Sector Three, but they're going to rename it Sector One. A capitol should be called One, don't you think?"

"We're all called by our numbers," I say and she laughs.

"Got that right, Sixteen."

"I'm glad you agree, Thirteen."

"You don't want to call me Eden?"

"I will. And you call me Frank?"

"Even if your data says Fritz."

"Even if that," I say and freeze.

"I don't mind," she coos.

It's that kind of moment when heartbeats pause, eyes widen, lips moisten. The joining of lips is the first sign of a joy that cannot be restrained but must launch, let linger, and last as long as people can leverage their breaths, and only then pull slowly apart, with a cling that draws those locked-away grins.

"That sure was different," says Eden. "Don't usually kiss a client like that. But it was nice. I liked it."

"Sorry, couldn't stop myself."

"You don't have to stop."

"Then I won't."

Up in the corner the camera catches everything as we rediscover what it means to be human.

14

FEAST & FAMINE

FIRST SNOW OF THE SEASON. Fortunately only an inch total, but we still have to clean off the sidewalks. I keep looking over my shoulder at anyone who might be coming for me for the things I've been doing. Twenty-four tells me to calm down a few times as we work with two others. We've never worked with them before. One is a young guy named Four-four with a hawkish look, slow to get on task. The other is one of those Asian men who refuses to be called by his numbers and insists we call him Isa.

"You mean like Isaiah?" I ask, recalling the name from a story my mother told me.

"No, like Isa," he says. "Just Isa, dammit. *EE-suh!*"

"All right, citizen," I counter. "Relax. I never did anything to you or your family. I wasn't even born yet."

But he remains cantankerous.

"It was government policy, not personal animosity," I say, trying to sound like an authoritarian.

We get to work, me shaking off the disagreeable interaction.

I was trying to tell Twenty-four about my new friend, Thirteen. Lucky Thirteen, I call her, thinking of her despite trying not to. We aren't supposed to think of other things on our work shift. But I do, thinking of her by name: Eden, a new beginning. But working with another pair to clear the sidewalks, I don't know how these guys are so better not to talk too much.

I never like being out when the weather is cold. I grew up mostly in a hot, humid marsh. But I have a job to do: protecting our citizens from delays on their merry way. Can't have citizens slipping and sliding on wintry pavement. No matter that we have to spread salt over the pavement to melt ice and provide traction for pedestrians. Standard order. But the walkers slip on the crystal pebbles and fall, hitting their knees or sometimes a hard splat on their bottoms. They get themselves up, usually look around and act embarrassed, then go on their way. A few don't get themselves up easily. We help a few get to their feet, apologizing as though the salt idea was our fault, and they thank us. Once in a while we have to call Medical Support when a walker is too hurt to get up.

"Sounds like a trap, Sixteen," says my street cleaning colleague when we stop for lunch. "You best be careful."

With the camera watching our usual table now repaired, we take a different seat, a bench with no table, set our food boxes in our laps. I see the other workers, including that surly Isa, go over to another group of workers who look Asian, and that is fine with me. I'm glad they got jobs after being persecuted during the past many years over a pandemic they now say never actually happened.

"No, no," I say excitedly between bites of something like cheese between two things like sliced bread, with a bland sauce. "I thought that at first, too. But we got to talking. She let her guard down and told me her story. Lots of details you couldn't make up."

"Her story? You mean what she's trained to say? Part of her act? I knew one of them. She had like fifty different stories. Never told the same two in a row."

"No, her real story. Straight from the heart, you could say. Like what I say about my mother and living down south."

"So she's another Southerner?"

"Oh – well – I hadn't thought of that. She does have a Northern accent but that's no different than me. They'll send you to a speech clinic if they hear ya talkin' like one dem fool Southers, lemme tell ya now."

Twenty-four laughs at my imitation.

"Actually she had a practiced voice, sounding like a bot. I guess that's company policy. Clients prefer bots. Don't have to worry about feelings. She said bots are better skilled. But once we finished our business, she spoke in her natural voice. That's how I could tell she was real. Not just a human but a *real* human, with feelings and a family, and a history as messed up as my family's."

"Now you're sounding smitten, my friend."

I have to catch myself. "Yes...smitten."

"Well, I never heard of no award like that, like getting a girl to visit. Single workers don't get lucky that way. But I sure could use an award like that since my lady friend got sent away for reading the wrong pamphlet then arguing too much with monitors."

"That whole situation's wrong," I say, hearing the story before. "But I saw the information on the tablet. A certificate of award. For my diligence."

"You?" He laughs for show. "You ain't no diligent worker."

Chuckling, I say: "I guess somebody thinks I am."

"Sounds like a trick, Sixteen."

"Not at all, Twenty-four. Every time she visits we talk and talk. I know it's strange, given her job. But I feel there's a connection. We don't find that with other people, we both agree. Something just fits with us. Not even like when I first met Sandra."

"Sandra...? You mean your wife?"

"That's the one. Authorities convinced her to separate from me. I told you all that. I was in rehabilitation, a black mark on the family. I'm not sure she didn't want that before my arrest. Anyway, looking back, I can see how we grew apart."

"So it was meant to be, huh?" Twenty-four suggests.

"Not meant to be. But it is. She's wonderful. Lucky Thirteen."

"Is she lucky for you or you for her?"

I have to think a moment. "Both of us. She comes over after her work shift and we pick up where we left off."

"After her work shift? After visiting other people."

"She's tested daily. The first hour of every shift, she said, is her being tested in the office before she goes out."

I can't help myself, telling him about my new interest. I never expected to meet someone, not at random, not in this cold, gray city, not at my age, not after my time in rehabilitation. It has to be *fate* –

a word that's been placed on the banned list.

"But what about you? You get tested?" Twenty-four teases.

"They checked us at rehabilitation. I was clean."

"I mean when she visits you."

"She said I check out clean. Did some kind of scan when she first enters. Remarkable the advancements in medical technology."

"Too bad we didn't have none of that back in pandemic days."

"Yes. Could've sniffed the air and know if people were infected."

"But it never happened, thank goodness," he snickers.

"Not officially," I confirm. "She detected the start of a stomach problem, however. Suggested it would get worse if I continued being, as she put it, a nervous type."

"You *are* a nervous type," says Twenty-four.

We return to shoveling and brushing, pausing as walkers move by us. We stand aside as needed. A monitor comes to check on us, reports a problem on the next block. So we go over there, at a slow pace, enjoying being out in the cold and doing some labor on behalf of everyone who doesn't know we exist.

"And she brings some tea and cookies sometimes," I stop him to say. "The good stuff. Not that fake powder, just add water kind of tea and real cookies with the cocoa chips. We sit on the bed together, sipping tea and nibbling cookies. I used to eat those when I was a kid. My mother would steal them from the store. They knew it but let her go. Crazy old woman, you know."

"Long line of bad citizens, huh?" Twenty-four responds.

"I made a damn video, after all."

"That you did."

"So we're comfortable, just laying together. And she says 'What's that?' – meaning my tuba, which I have leaning in the corner right under the camera. She said it was odd. Said I was odd for having it."

"You *are* an odd one," Twenty-four says.

Brush, brush the snow away, into the gutter. Watch more of the white stuff falling, covering the pavement we just cleaned.

Twenty-four curses under his breath, but I can't stop.

"I told her my mother used to play it, and her father before her, and *his* mother, too, all the way back a hundred years. It's a family thing. She liked that. Her family isn't musical. But I don't know how to play it, I told her, never had any lessons. I'm planning to give it to my daughter, I said, but you know how things are these days, what with no music being allowed, everything being AI-made."

"Yep, that's plain sad. Need music you make for yourself," says Twenty-four. "Need to feel it. Need to feel that music in your bones. That AI stuff is flat, got nothing to move you—"

"So I moved the tuba over to the bed, lay it down gently," I say, ignoring him. "I take her by the hand to the corner. We're standing right under the camera – the only place it can't see. We continue our 'amorous ways', you know, but have to stand up to keep hidden, so we press hard into that corner. And let me tell you, it was...damn, it was magical."

"I'm happy for you, Sixteen."

"Once we get going I just can't stop and she holds on tight until I explode—"

"I recall what that's like, mm-hmm."

"We gradually calm down, kissing between breaths. Probably the monitor can hear us. Then she holds her hand up, says 'See this?' – meaning her hand. She has me feel between her thumb and first finger. 'Feel that?' she asks. It's her chip. She has to have it so they can track her, communicate with her, keep her in the right sector. Or if her client gets violent."

"Terrible."

"But she said it doesn't work now. Turned off. She's had it since she was five years old. Her parents had it inserted to track her, like for kidnapping which was common back then. My grampa wrote in a notebook that his fellow soldiers had chips that were always short-circuiting and zapping them. Or the enemy could track them, too, so they were turned off."

"Also terrible."

"I asked if she could cut it out, thinking of drastic measures. She said if it's cut out, it will send an alarm back to the office and they'd send a team to pick her up. Also if she died, she said to make it more dramatic. But it's off now, she swears. So, anyway, we're eye to eye, and I'm wondering if there's something about her eyes that can see into me, see my thoughts. Like they're cameras. So I close my eyes against any intrusion."

"Yeah, go on." He's patiently leaning on his broom.

"But instead of being offended by my distrust of her surveillance capabilities, she puts her lips to my ear and whispers—"

"*I love you?*"

"No – but close. I think. She whispered: 'I'm with you'."

"Yeah, that's good, too."

"She wouldn't leave. In fact, I never want her to leave."

"You gonna get yourself in a heap of trouble, my friend. Workers like us are supposed to be home alone, get our rest so we can work."

"So long story short—"

"You hear me, Sixteen?"

"I hear you. But don't worry. She left when I did, from my unit, when I'm coming to work this morning. I haven't slept all night."

"No wonder your work is sloppy."

"But the strange thing is—"

"Something else is strange?" he snickers.

"She said she wanted me to meet someone who would help me. I mean get out of this job and into something better suited for my skills. A return to a normal life."

"Now I know they got you," says Twenty-four. "You be careful."

+   +   +

"Session thirty-two," the impossible voice drones, then summarizes the previous session in five sentences.

Dr. Richards, if that is his actual name, again sits comfortably, as though he likes his job, tablet balanced on his knee.

"So what's new?" he asks in a too-cheerful voice.

For once, I am cheerful. He seems to notice the change.

Hiding a smirk, I say: "I won an award. A major award."

He nods pensively, as though I'm speaking in code. Then he taps on the tablet for a while.

"I don't find any award listed in your record."

The news baffles me. That such an award would be on some kind of public record for me, first of all, and that my counselor can access that information.

"No award?" I lose my smirk. "I saw the certificate. On a tablet. Had my name on it. And I got the reward, in fact. Delivered."

"What was the award?"

"It was.... Supposedly for my diligence at doing my job." I start to feel shame for not doing more, a trick of my rehabilitation. "I didn't think I was doing a particularly good job. But I hadn't missed a day of work, no matter the weather, in almost a year."

"That's something," says my counselor.

"The reward I got was a couple hours of personal service from a therapist. It was nice. I needed that."

Dr. Richards examines the tablet, scrolling up and down. "No, no record of any award or any service call to your unit's address."

"That's odd." I have to think a moment. "I'm sure it wasn't just a dream. I can tell the difference. And she...."

"She...what?"

"The therapist was a talker. After my official session she stayed and we talked. Yes, yes, I know, talking isn't the best thing to do to fill a portion of time. It can get you into trouble. A slip of the tongue and away you go. I know all about that."

"Yes, indeed."

"But we didn't talk about anything that's on the unapproved list, I assure you. We weren't interested in any of those topics."

"What topics were those?"

"Like our families."

"Back to your mother...."

I'm not sure if he's teasing me or he's glad to get back on a more fruitful subject for his reports.

"My mother?" I glare at him. "It was mostly her telling me about her family. Before the pandemic."

He cautions me with a finger to his lips. Mentioning an event that never happened as though it did happen can get me assigned a good bit of counseling.

"Family stuff, is all. Like who her mother married, and so on."

"And you told about yours?"

"Yes, but not much. Like I said: she's a talker. When she's doing her job she's professional. After the clock runs out, she's a different person, and I like that person. In fact, you may be pleased to know we've been seeing each other since then."

"A relationship?" he quizzes.

"I think that's how it would be classified, yes."

"Have you registered it?"

"Registered?"

"Be careful what you reveal," he says, tapping on his shoulder to direct my attention to the camera behind him. "It is easy to conflate fantasy with reality. Very common for workers such as yourself. A hard job can prompt a lively inner life, a propensity toward fantastic thinking. I urge you to guard against such flights of fancy."

His words seem to echo in the office.

I realize I almost said too much, which is a flaw Mother liked to point out. Maybe I'm being tricked. No record of my award? What else could it be? A young, attractive public servant instigating a new relationship with me, an older man with a low-status job, and with rehabilitation on my record. Who hasn't had a bit of rehabilitation over the past twenty years? And now the counseling!

"Yes, I see what you mean," I say with a nod, disappointed and feeling foolish. "Maybe I was confusing reality with a dream. I don't think my food boxes are in alignment with my needs."

"Noted," says my counselor, tapping on his tablet.

+   +   +

Over the next few weeks, Eden comes by after her work most nights and slips quietly into my unit. I give her a new code; what she was given when she first visited me expired by the next morning. She joins me on my bunk, sometimes waking me to engage in some late-night pleasures. I give her one of my food boxes. We sit together sharing it. Between bouts of biological blundering we plan a way out of the city – for both of us, together, somewhere to the south.

Whenever we have a mutual day off, we lay together on my bed, snuggling as we read my grandfather's naughty notebooks. She is amazed how subversive they are, all the stories about events we've been told never actually happened or which we are forbidden from mentioning. She is impressed I have them.

"You know, sometimes I wish I could leave this city and go home, go south and live the rest of my life in peace," I tell Eden.

"It's a lovely dream, Frank," she replies.

"We need to find a way to make it real."

In a moment of flirty frenzy, she dares put her lips to my tuba, giving it a good blow but never enough to cause any notes to erupt from its exit. Still, I like hearing her breathy attempts to coax out white noise. She works the valves and giggles at the naughtiness we enjoy. Such a rare thing, we muse, those bits of humor that are, in themselves, obvious infractions. After all, a giggling worker must be a slacking worker.

"I know somebody," Eden begins one evening after love is made piece by piece until it stands tall and glorious. "He could get you into a better job. Something that uses your skills. Your college skills. Are you interested?"

At that instant, I don't care about any other person but her. So I answer without thinking. She agrees to take me to meet him. We'll meet in the park near her unit's building. It is in the poor section of this sector so I can move freely.

"Another client," she says. But seeing my worried face, she says: "Long time ago. I don't see him any longer. But his son is a manager at an office – a real office in a tall building."

I suppose that should impress me. Instead, it strikes my bell just as my counselor has been trying to ring it.

"Honestly, Eden, with you here – seeing you nearly every night – I don't mind staying in this cold, gray city. I can endure anything if I have you to come home to. That was the way it was with my wife."

"Oh, don't be talking about her," Eden huffs. "She betrayed you. Forget her. Focus on me. Tell me more how much you love me."

"I do love you."

"Now say it like you mean it."

"I really, really love you, my dear, my lucky Thirteen."

She frowns. "I believe you, but I think you must be tired."

"You do have a way of helping me get my daily exercise."

"You make me feel sixteen again, Sixteen."

"But I'm getting old...*older*. But you're still the best thing I ever found in this cold, gray city."

"See? That's how you say it! You're the best thing for me, too."

+   +   +

I go to the appointed place on the designated night and find Eden waiting there dressed for the cold, bundled like a homeless woman. Out of the shadows of the trees comes a dark figure, clothed as if for an arctic expedition – and they insisted the arctic would melt into soda water long before now!

"This is Twelve," says Eden with a wave of her mittened hand. "This is Sixteen. I told you about him before."

"Yes." The dark figure, face hidden inside the big hood, extends a hand, straight from the warm coat pocket, ungloved.

I take his hand – countenance and voice seem to be male – and give it a shake in the old style. Eden produces a bottle of sanitizer to squirt on our hands. It's a ritual: the willingness to put skin to skin and take the risk, but then the sensible disinfection procedure. Now, with the so-called pandemic long gone, it's only an odd custom.

"You say you want a better job," the figure called Twelve speaks in a low but firm voice. He seems much older than me.

"He was a video maker before...." She gives me a glance. I nod my approval. "Before he went for rehabilitation."

"I can't believe there are any of those jobs still available. With all videos used for propaganda, there's no room for the kind of creative products I used to make."

"Correct," says Twelve. "Nothing in this city. However, there are other cities. If you don't mind something less developed."

Eden turns to me. "Do you want to go to another city?"

"Another city? How about you?"

"Me? I guess I'm stuck here. But you would be free."

"But life without you wouldn't be so free."

"Aww, baby boo, don't be sad." She has an adorable pout.

"Let's keep this quick," says Twelve. "You need an exit pass."

"If there's a new job waiting for him," Eden adds.

"Yes, new job. I'll check my sources. A pass is the first thing. If you can't leave then there's no point asking about a new job."

"You're right," says Eden, taking my arm in hers.

"I'll check in the next towns," says the man. "If there's a job, we can get you a pass."

"That's wonderful," I say too brightly.

"Then you pay the second half," he says. "First half is now."

All through this adventure I fear a squad of officers will break through the trees and capture us. For what? Any number of minor infractions. It doesn't really matter. Screentime™ is full of stories of ordinary citizens taken away for small yet nefarious mistakes. They select who they want to arrest, then choose a crime. 'No reason to worry about cameras if you've got nothing to hide,' they say.

Suddenly I want to hurry back to my unit and be sure my tuba is still there. I worry this outing is a ruse to get me out of my unit so it can be searched. I glare at Eden, trying to notice a clue to the trick she's put on me, but she remains sweet and innocent.

"...I'll just have to go with you," she is saying when I refocus on the important topic at hand.

"Then I'll prepare two passes. What you do outside of the city, I'll leave for you to decide. I wish you good fortune in your new life."

"New life together," Eden says. "You hear that?"

"I hear it." But it sounds hollow under the falling snow.

The dark figure disappears into the shadows as smoothly as he first appeared. Who was he? Twelve could be anyone. An agent of the government? I'm glad I didn't say too much. Leaving the city is a common desire so it wouldn't raise suspicions. Everyone wants out.

"Don't worry," says Eden, holding my bare hand in her mitten, leaning into me. She pushes me into the shadows of the trees, and stretches up to kiss me.

"I trust him," she says. Her tone is a little off. "And you trust me, right?" She looks up at me.

"Yes," I say. "Always."

"I know you and me will be happy," she says in a cheerful voice that's closer to what I'm used to. "In our new home far away. Just you and me, and if we can swing it also a couple kids to read your grampa's notebooks and play that old tuba. You think you got it in you to give me some kids?"

Now she's toying with me. I know she doesn't care about the notebooks, less about the tuba. She has to be saying that to trigger my sense of love for her. And her mentioning kids? A return to my youth. It seems as though a switch has been pulled and everything is going in reverse. I'm growing younger.

Safe at home again after Eden departs for her unit, I get out the stack of notebooks to check them. I left them positioned in a certain way so if anyone touched them I'd know it. I set the whole stack on the fold-down table.

Eight spiral-bound notebooks with different colored covers which Grampa wrote in, recording their adventures from going to that island with his mother up to his time in the war. He wrote well, in the fashion of a novel, but the sentences curled around the margins, using every bit of space, so some are hard to read. He was careful to number the notebooks and the pages within them. Some episodes were written out of chronological order.

One similar notebook which Mother had me get for her, trying to write her adventures like her father did but only managing to fill a third of the pages in her unique writing style before giving up. She began by describing her stay in the State Park, then her return trip to the mountain, meeting my father again, my birth, but not many details after that. The rest is more of a list of episodes, things that happened without any details.

The leather-bound journal of Fritz, my namesake, written in a POW camp and the years after. His wife, Beryl, finished it after he was hit by a car while crossing the street – in this same city more than a century ago. He played in the orchestra and taught music at the college – designated the Ministry of Culture now, a warehouse of old art stacked in the concert hall, gathering dust. They removed all the seats to make space. Other buildings have been repurposed as government offices. Thankfully, Fritz's children followed after him in the music business.

A thick notebook with the name Tara K. Butler on the cover and a dedication to my mother added to the first page. I find it in the pocket of the tuba's case. I pushed to make this into a book others could learn from, as Mother demanded. Mother's attempt at writing her story gave me the feeling these two had an affair which to my mind seemed rather sweet. I could find no historical record of Tara K. Butler, only Mother saying she was killed in a police raid.

A photo album put inside the tuba case, resting tight against the metal tubing, contains pictures of Grandma Hannah and her sisters Kristin and Julia, and brother Nathan, when they were young. Real paper photographs slipped into clear plastic sleeves, a relic of the past, before the batteries of digital cameras ran out and couldn't be recharged because there was no more electricity a few years into the pandemic nor a chance to save those images before the batteries ran out. Mother looked through the album from time to time, telling us stories from what Grandma Hannah told her. Often Mother would cry as she touched the image of her mama there.

In total eleven volumes of history covering a century and a half, words written by people who lived through the events, no reason to tell lies about what happened to them. A record not just to me but to the whole society. Why couldn't they see that? Even if they disagree with what is written, at least preserve it so we can debate the facts.

But debate is hard. Constructing a good argument is hard. A lot easier to put your opponents away, never let them speak their side, never allow any view but yours to be heard. Never allow evidence to be seen. Then life is easy in an Ideal Society.

And there is Madame Governor popping on the screen:

"So let us remember: The highest form of citizenship is to repeat the official narrative loud and strong, building an impenetrable wall against those outside erroneous statements bent on corrupting our Ideal Society!"

"Off," I call out but the screen doesn't blink off until the speech comes to its end. Her tinny voice strikes my head like a power drill, her words playing over and over.

I think of the market for old literature. Most would be burned after sale. There aren't any protests, no "Save Our Books" crowds to shout at night. No longer any bookstores. People are allowed private collections, but once they die their libraries are removed, disposed of in a blaze of righteous glory. All we know of the past – what we are allowed to know – is in the few government-approved booklets used in schools. Anyone can buy them from a government printing office.

Staring at the stack of notebooks, I know I am a criminal by the official rules of *Standards of Literature Suspension & Confiscation*. I had to memorize sections of it during my rehabilitation. If it weren't for me going to rehabilitation, I might've been able to keep them as long as I never shared them with anyone, including my children. But with the mark of rehabilitation on my record, I'm not allowed to possess literature of any kind. If found, I can only imagine the worst they would do to me.

Maybe I should get rid of them, burn them and flush the ashes. I've read them several times, enough to memorize the episodes. But if I recreated them from memory, from reading them, no one would believe the events were true. I have to keep the originals.

Then one night, with Eden laying beside me as we read the last notebook, I fall silent.

"Oh, I can't wait to get our passes," she says to break the silence, snuggling against me. "Then away to the forest for us. Promise we'll go straight to the forest."

"I can't wait, either," I say, too tired to be enthusiastic.

"I wonder how they'll look. What color will they be?"

"Tomorrow we'll know."

"I hope they're not in the official colors, gray and red."

"They're official documents," I sigh, "so I'm sure they'll be in the official colors."

"I don't care," she sighs, "as long as we can get out and start our new life together."

15

THE DEPARTMENT OF SOCIAL ORDER

STANDING IN THE SHADOWS OF TREES amidst the darkness of
the park, a few flurries dancing about, we shiver as we wait. It is an
hour before we see someone coming through the trees.

I tense, thinking it is a team of officers.

The figure raises his hand in greeting.

"Good evening," I say. Eden takes my hand.

"Do you have the...uh, the...what you promised?" she asks, her
voice catching as she tries to find the right words.

The man reaches into his coat pocket and pulls out something.

I extend my hand to receive them. He flicks his hand back.

"Payment?" he asks.

"I did," says Eden before I can speak. "All of it. For both of us. I
sent it, marked 'gift'."

I wonder how she's gotten so many credits. Maybe it's all tokens.
No, she said she 'transferred' it. She gets tips for a good performance
from her clients, I'm sure. I only get food boxes. I feel bad for not
having more to contribute. But I'll show her the forest.

The dark figure gives a nod and offers the passes again.

I take them: two folded cards, like little booklets, sized right for
standard pockets. I slide them into my coat pocket, but Eden tugs on
my sleeve and makes a face. I take them from my outer pocket and
slip them inside my coat, to the inside pocket which is safer.

When I look up, the figure has disappeared into the darkness.

Eden stretches up to kiss me, then we hug.

"I love you," she whispers and I repeat her words.

We hurry home, staying as quiet as we can so that no monitors or cameras will notice us.

Once inside my unit – sneaking Eden in through the building's side door – we practically dance in the aisle celebrating our fortune. We are on our way. Finally. We are free! I can't believe it; it doesn't feel real, more like last night's dream.

I'll return south with Eden, introduce her to my sister, Amy. We will live in a shack in the marsh and fish all day, get tans and make love and maybe, if in the right mood, I'll start a notebook about my life after leaving the National Park. Or start it when I arrived in this cold, gray city with hopes and dreams that were easily crushed.

"Isn't it marvelous?" Eden waves the passes in the air, mostly red for mine and mostly gray for hers. "It isn't the best picture, but I suppose it's straight from the database. They have a back door to it, I heard."

"I wonder what's in my file," I say, unamused. "Half lies, I bet."

She sucks in a big breath, lets it out. "So when do we leave?"

"Is there anything stopping us?"

Actually I'm not sure. Do we simply walk through a checkpoint or two and once outside the last one we just walk down the road, or do we get on a bus heading somewhere? Like when my mother took us south from the National Park.

As for the city, how would they know I've gone? I won't show up on the designated street corner the next morning and that would be that. Twenty-four would probably wonder about me, but he'd get a new coworker. Maybe he would guess that I left the city, took Eden with me. He would understand. Much better to have me go far away, be done with me, than to let me stay in the city and be an embarrassment to them.

"I'm gonna miss this place," Eden says as we lie together. "This closet you live in. Not as big as mine, but mine is for women. Has a bidet. I have to share it with three others. And they're mean to me."

"We'll be gone soon." I'm already deciding what to take and what to leave. I'll have to carry the tuba on my back. And the notebooks in a pack. A couple changes of clothes. What food boxes we could carry?

I have seven. I guess it should take three days to go south, out to the marshes, to Mother's shack, if it still stands. We might stop and see Sorrow Mountain on the way. I promised to take Eden to the forest.

"Oh, I'm so happy, Fritz," she cries then catches herself, knowing the sensors will pick up her joy. A beep warns us that we're in quiet hours. There will be no beeps in the forest.

We fall asleep in each other's arms, trying to fit together on the narrow bed.

I awake with a start not long after closing my eyes. It seems as though my mind's heard an alarm go off somewhere. Sitting up, I swing my feet to the floor in the darkness, listening. My movement startles Eden and she puts her hand to my back.

Then the door to my unit suddenly slides open and all the lights blink on at full power as a squad of officers in arrest gear bulls their way inside.

"Get up," commands the leader, big shouldered and wearing the peaked cap with the official emblem on the front: a circle divided horizontally, red on the bottom half, gray on the top. He carries a short-barreled weapon which he points at us. "Stand up straight. Hands behind your head. Now!"

A rush of pounding fear crashes through me as I obey.

Eden, naked like me, pushes me aside in her scramble to get off the bunk and stand before they can grab her. They shove us back to back in the aisle of the unit.

Pushing through the squad of gray-uniformed men, armed with those short-barreled direct-energy weapons I've heard about, comes a tough-looking female officer bearing two packages in plastic wrap. She tosses one at each of us. I catch mine, see it's a new garment, but Eden drops hers. She bends to pick it up, gets a shove from the female officer that bowls her over at my feet.

"Put those on," demands the woman.

We hurry to tear open the wrapping and unfold the garments: a simple gown, medium gray, dropping to our calves. Mine is sized perfectly for me. Eden's fit her, too, as though they knew our sizes from the official database. In a flash we are clothed in the new garments which feel like paper – much like the prison garb I had to wear for rehabilitation.

"Turn around," the woman orders. "Hands behind."

They tie my hands together using rubber binders that look like they should be breakable but aren't. The tough bands cut into my wrists. Eden cries at the way they hurt her, twisting her arm back then applying the bands.

The female officer leads Eden briskly out the door. Two male officers take me by my arms and pull me forward.

The squad leader glances at my bed.

"Take those," he says, meaning the loose stack of notebooks we casually pushed to the end of the bed when switching from reading to sleeping. He looks over at the corner of the room. "And that."

I protest the rough way the officer picks up Mother's tuba and I get a slap across my face and a stomp to my bare foot.

"Please," I cry out, fighting my restraint. "Put it in its case, at least. It's over there. To protect it."

We exit the unit, the door sliding closed behind us with a final *swoosh*. Eden is already gone, nowhere to be seen in the corridor. I am led away, down to the empty lobby and out the doors into a waiting gray van. Eden is not inside. Then a cloth hood is pulled down over my head and all I hear is the wet splashing of snow against the tires.

+ + +

When the hood is removed, I stand in a completely dark place, not a speck of light slipping through a crack, unable to see anything. The only sound a constant humming that might be from inside my head. The smell of the place is cold concrete, like the city streets on a good day. I feel around the walls, also concrete, cold and gray – if I could see them. I can't extend my arms much without bumping the walls. No furniture here, not even a bench to sit on nor a toilet bolted to the wall.

Fifty years of post-pandemic development and we come to this: a closet as a cell. Forced to stand for hours, until my knees cry out for relief. I can press my elbows out, touching each side. I can sit on the concrete floor, cold as it is, or try to lean against one wall, bracing myself with my feet to ease some of the strain. A constantly blowing vent above me keeps the closet cool, almost chilly stuck in only the paper gown. It easily tears as I move, constantly changing positions of minimal comfort. My bare feet find a drain in the floor for what urine I might produce, but getting nothing to eat or drink, I'm dry.

My chief concern upon being brought to the Department of Social Order – as I imagined was my destination, where criminals are held awaiting adjudication – is pondering what I might've done wrong. The list could be long. I've been too sloppy, gullible, and unaware. Caught up in emotions that clouded my judgment, blocked my view, left me ripe for exploitation. Who did I blame?

Myself. If I did nothing wrong, and we now know that wrongness can be measured and catalogued, then I certainly bear some kind of guilt. It is impossible to live without some kind of wrongness. As my mind sweeps through fog after fog, I begin to dismiss each one of my faults. All minor infractions. Except the one or two big ones.

Obviously meeting with Eden in my single worker's unit is as bad as it gets. That's likely it. But I'd won an award. Meeting her repeatedly after that initial visit was suspect certainly. Any and all utterances of joy, of our sexual ecstasy, would've been recorded and considered, measured. I was unclear on the rules for sexual activity. According to records, we are both single and thus free to engage as we like. I did go with her to obtain exit passes – an obvious crime because why would anyone want to leave an Ideal Society?

Once inside the unit, they found the notebooks my grandfather filled with his stories of survival during the pandemic. That alone could probably be enough to put me away for a long time. I'd tried to convince the court that they were fiction but was unsuccessful. They believed what he wrote was true, therefore subversive. We know what actually happened during those seventy years, we just choose to consider it a pack of lies. Easier that way. Everyone knows the forbidden stories are true but if you dare say so you're marked as a criminal, a subversive, or a crazy old fool.

So burn them and let me go!

And the tuba. I don't believe owning a musical instrument is a crime. I haven't made any noise with it. So it has to be the fact of stealing it. Where else would someone get such an antique? From a museum. But I took the tuba because it's mine. There wasn't any theft – unless they questioned Sandra, got her to agree with them, saying the right words. Yet they took the tuba with the notebooks as though they intend to use them as evidence.

But evidence of what? Me trying to grasp the last remnants of humanity? Stories to pass the time? Music to soothe my soul? Love to heal a shattered heart? They couldn't all be crimes. They *were* in some of the old paper books I read when I was young, but that was the way people thought back in those days, long before the pandemic shut down everything. But not now. No, they wouldn't do that now, not in our newly rebuilt society.

"We don't need any of that in an Ideal Society," echoes a lecturer from my rehabilitation days. "We only need to focus on the duties of the State. You want to help, don't you? 'Be kind, Rewind', they used to say. A call to a common good. What can we do for our common good? How can we be a more vital part of the whole? How can *you*? How can we help each other form an even more ideal society?"

Eden, my lucky Thirteen, was ideal.

I think of Eden, how she was treated, where she might be. She might be free now if she were actually working with them to trap me – like Twenty-four suggested. I have no clue she's working with the authorities. Who is she? She told me her story. Or maybe her story was crafted to get my sympathy. She said the right things to connect with my own story. That drew me to her. We connected. If that was a deliberate plan, it worked.

I can only hope she is working with them so they let her go once she was out of my sight. Then she would be safe and go on with her life, even far away from me. Maybe she would remember me in the shadows of the evening. If she is not working with them, then she is likely as uncomfortable as I am, being in a similar kind of closet cell, suffering as I am – and I don't want that for her.

What was her crime? Clearly being with me, after-hours, cutting her work shift short to be with me. Not giving fully of herself while on her work shift because she was saving some energy, some loving, for this lonely man. Not too lonely because I had work colleagues as friends. What else she might've been doing outside of meeting me, I can't imagine. How many lovers does she have?

I lose track of time standing in the cell, leaning, trying to squat, and never getting any sleep. My feet swell, my legs get sore, my hips rage in discomfort. I cry for help several times a day, most often in the mornings – what I imagine is morning after waking from a few minutes of shallow sleep in an awkward position, feeling pain surge through me as I straighten up. Once in a while, on an irregular schedule so I can't count the days, they gave me a small pouch labeled 'food source' which consists of a liquid tasting like some kind of vegetable paste. The food industry can make any product to provide adequate nutrition in an easy to digest form, enough to keep a prisoner alive.

+ + +

In the long hours of standing in darkness I think of Grampa Sandy's notebooks, especially the ones about his time in the war. He was in a POW camp for a while and I recall him describing how he waited and waited for something, anything, to happen just to break up the monotony only to realize the monotony was part of the punishment. So I endure my waiting. I can last longer than they think I can.

Then I become less certain with each day's meager food packet slid through the slot at the bottom of the door. Ripped open, sucked down in less than a minute, even as I try to draw it out. A full day's nutrition in a squeezable packet, tasting like starchy vegetable matter or a fruity, too sweet, syrup. The result is a flatter belly and the regular dismissal of processed material out my bottom and into the drain in the floor.

I soon lose count of the days. I can't even measure them in the darkness of this closet. The food packets come irregularly. My knees ache. I try squatting but it doesn't last long. I sit my bottom on the cold concrete floor but with the mess I made around the drain that isn't a good plan.

Most of all I think a lot about everything I've done in my life. I run through the years, count the acts. Speaking disrespectfully to Mother. Stealing candy from the store. Taking crabs from someone else's traps. Just being too loud playing outside Mother's shack. And in the city, more infractions: thinking things I know to be true when we are told they aren't true. Gets you every time.

Then one day I hear a voice whisper in my cell. At first I think it's Mother speaking inside my head but I realize it's a broadcast. I listen, certain I must be going crazy.

The voice gradually grows louder, repeating the same words:

"A place for everyone and everyone in place."

I wait, listening, hoping to hear more: maybe an explanation, an apology, a call for my release. Eden's voice, maybe.

Unable to figure out how it happened, I find myself sitting on a wooden stool, bare feet flat on the cold concrete floor, hands bound behind my back, and a hood over my head, blocking me from seeing anything. I sense I'm in a large room and people stand around me. I feel embarrassed, knowing my paper gown has ripped in so many places it hardly covers me now.

"A place for everyone and everyone in place, we like to say."

The voice is female, an older woman's, firm and motherly, like she's caught me doing something naughty and wants to tease me a while before declaring my punishment. Like Mother did.

"What is your place?" the woman asks coldly.

I presume the question is directed at me. But I don't know what she means. So I wait.

"What is your place?" she repeats in a less friendly tone.

I breathe deeply, checking if my throat still works, if I can form words, if I can speak them.

"I...." A faint croak is all I can manage inside my hood.

"Take that fool thing off him," says the woman.

When the hood is lifted off my head the room is dark around me but an intense bright light strikes my face, forcing me to hold my eyes closed. A few dark figures shuffle at the margins of the room, maybe official observers? 'And this is how we interrogate prisoners.' I've been placed into a demonstration.

"What is your place?" the woman repeats impatiently as I keep my eyes closed.

I try to cough but my throat is too dry. "I...I'm a street cleaner."

"Is that your place?

"Yes," I say, losing my voice. "I think so."

"You keep our society clean," the woman confirms.

"Yes. The streets, anyway."

"It is your proper function," she speaks after a minute of silence.

"I suppose so."

"You suppose? It isn't your proper function?"

"I mean...I do it as best I can, but...."

"But what?"

"I try to keep the streets clean, but...."

"But what?" She sounds angry.

"But my aptitude is actually for other functions. So I was told." I fear a slap to my face or some other physical violence for giving a contrary response. I'm too stupid to play their game.

"Who told you?" the woman demands.

"Career counselors. At my college. City College. When I entered. They put me in a course to become a video technician."

"Ah, before we thought to form an ideal society," she says with a lilt in her voice. "An era of chaos, disorder, of wayward dreams."

I hear faint chuckles from around the sides of the room.

"Video technician is a rare skill. Rather, a whole set of skills. Is it not? And you mastered them?"

"Yes. I had that job for a while," I concede. "I was good at it."

More awkward silence, with the tap of her shoes on the concrete.

"What is your number?" she asks, almost politely.

I tell her.

"Say it three times," she demands. "Quickly."

I try to, but I trip over the numbers.

"Again."

But I can't. I mess up terribly.

"Say it backwards."

I go slow but I get it out. Then she wants me to say it backwards three times fast. I fail that test.

The people around the sides of the room chuckle.

"Tell me, Fritz Baumann," she speaks in a more pleasant voice. "If the freck is fourteen, what is the gummy-toll's weight? Do you know?"

Huh? I'm not sure I hear her correctly.

"Forty-two?" I guess, having no idea what she means.

"Not even close," she laughs.

"I'm not sure of the question," I mutter.

"What is the hue next beyond blue number five when showing at five o'clock in the morning on a seventy-percent overcast day in mid-February? Assume no sunrise."

"I really don't know."

"If you go thirty-two frames per second, how long is the video?"

"It depends on how many scenes you shoot—"

"Sampling a standard murphy, what is the circumference of the primary gortle in relation to the steam-flute?"

"I don't know. It doesn't make sense."

"You don't know about gortles, murphies, and steam-flutes?"

"No," I blurt, confused and angry. There are no correct answers for me to give.

"Nothing but the green-lens and gray-ladies. Is that true?"

"I don't know...."

"Yes, it's apparent you are in your proper function," she says.

"I never heard any of those terms before," I speak up. "It's just a bunch of nonsense."

"Nonsense, hmm?" She inhales loudly. "Everyone in place is not nonsense."

I detect a smudge of amusement. I wait, hear a shuffle of papers, a few cold steps across the floor, her shoes tapping on the concrete like the workings of tuba valves that need oiling.

"Tell me, Fritz, would you lift the bally-gate for a boog of severn? Or would it take more than a drick-wane to be worth lifting it?"

Boog? Of severn? I have to think a moment. *Drick-wane?*

"I really don't know what you're talking about...ma'am."

Faint chuckling behind me, more of it to the sides of the room.

"I'll make it easy for you," she says as if playing to an audience. "What do you do with a nail that sticks up?"

"A nail?"

The woman seems to be standing close to me. "Yes, a nail."

"Nails are for holding pieces of wood together," I blithely intone from my father's lessons on the mountain. Finally a correct answer.

"What does the hammer do?" she asks, lips close to my ear.

"It hammers," I say, then I think about it. "It strikes the nail, forcing the nail down. Into its place. Into the wood. To keep the wood together."

A satisfied sigh. I sense the woman standing straight, hear her take a few steps away. The light on my face remains as bright as ever when she moves aside, but keeping my eyes closed against it is tiring. What more is there to this game? When will they let me go?

She is speaking to someone else, but I can only catch a few of her words. Maybe it is a foreign language. Am I still in the city?

I'm about to speak, to ask what I've done wrong that causes me to be here and treated this way, but she continues:

"The nail that sticks up gets hammered down," she says. "That is the lesson." She pauses as if letting it soak into my brain. "I think you understand the meaning in the metaphor. Can't you? You know what a metaphor is? I see you attended City College so you should understand it."

"I know what a metaphor is," I say in a flat voice.

"Good." A few breaths. "What is it?"

"You mean a metaphor? It's when you say something that means something else."

"And the nail? What does it represent?"

"The nail? I suppose it represents...me?"

A feigned chuckle. "You? Why are you the nail?"

"Because...I suppose because I'm being hammered down here."

"Such a clever boy!" She adds lively chuckles.

That makes me feel better. Maybe I will pass this woman's test and be set free. All a ruse. Intimidation to keep me in line. A lesson to learn so I'll never act badly again. I will accept the warning and go home to find Eden waiting for me, amused that I've been gone.

"We like uniformity," the woman speaks. "The straight edge, the even surface. We appreciate the calm of a steady work session. The pleasure of a project completed. We enjoy a day well-served. And our reward is satisfaction in knowing all is well around us, and thanks to us, thanks to our efforts and the efforts of those citizens around us. We work together. Anything which does not fit that plan must be corrected. Hammered down, as the metaphor goes."

I wait through a long silence. Expecting more words, I stay as focused as I can be after days of standing and nights of no sleep. I am just glad to be sitting, and she can say whatever she wants.

I suddenly know the correct answer: "So the nail that sticks out gets hammered down."

"Yes. And why is that?"

"All nails must be uniform," I reply.

"Because?"

"Because...we like uniformity? And...and the nails being even is uniformity."

"Why?"

"I don't know." I start to panic. "I think that's the right answer. Isn't it? The nails represent 'we the people' and the hammer is the government. We are made to be uniform. And...and everything runs smoothly that way."

"It is an ideal society," she says after a long pause.

I can't help but give her a nod. That is what I'm expecting. This whole effort will always lead up to this mantra. They want me to accept their plan, believe in their scheme. Fine. I accept. I believe. Now I'm free. I can go home, and I'll return to work cleaning the streets.

The light blasting my face shuts off. My eyes open to see the room I'm in, now lit with low lights at intervals along the walls. In front of me is a long glass panel with another room on the other side of it. I can see through that window into the other room. A padded bench, unoccupied, is the only furniture there. I wonder why I'm on this side instead of on that bench where it seems the person being interrogated should be seated.

"Fritz, listen carefully," the woman says just as I'm beginning to relax. "I have one more question for you. It's very important, so pay attention. Think of your answer before you speak it."

"All right," I mumble, giving a nod.

"What is the summation of five quarters plus seven eighths with an eleventh hour additive?"

My brain churns away, calculating but coming to nothing. I grow afraid. What will happen to me if I give the wrong answer? More punishment? But the question makes no sense.

Yet I have to give her some answer, any answer.

"Probably green. Olive green," I say and cringe in anticipation of a slap or punch. My mind is spinning.

"You have the correct idea, but your answer is incorrect." She offers a quiet *hmmpf*. "Let me give you an easier question. Let's see if you can answer this one. What is two plus two?"

Despite my growing fear, I realize I know the answer. I recall it from an old book I read, one Amy gave me from the library when it was closing down. I don't recall the title but it was a number, a year maybe. In that book, the prisoner is asked the same question. He gives a mathematical answer, but that is wrong. He is punished. The man torturing him tells him the answer, which seems wrong to him so he refuses to accept it. Eventually, he knows it is the correct answer and he desperately speaks it, as do I:

"Five."

16

CONTESTANTS

MY INTERROGATOR BEGINS TO PACE before me, left to right, right to left, with her arm bent up at the elbow so her chin can rest on her fist as she nods pensively.

"Correct," she says after a long interval. "Surprisingly. But then, it's not a mathematical question. It's a moral question."

"It's in some book I read a long time ago," I say, a kind of rebuke.

"Books are not allowed now. Except what's approved for schools. We cannot allow incorrect information to corrupt our youth."

"I just want to read them, to see what they say."

Her face turns smug. "Why do you need to know what they say? If we tell you they're not for you, won't you take our advice and not read them?"

"No, I want to decide on my own, for myself."

She glares at me. "You want to be a subversive, is that it?"

"Not subversive. I have to read the book and decide for myself."

"Deciding for yourself is being subversive."

"But why can't I think for myself?"

That response only spurs her on. "Because you're not authorized to think for yourself."

She frowns, then starts in with more ridiculous questions. They come in rapid succession, new ones asked before I can even attempt to answer previous ones. And they make no sense. My mind crashes in confusion. I can't keep up.

A loud buzz on a communication device somewhere in the room, halts our game. She goes to the side of the room and I turn to look, breaking my eyes from the bright light. She holds the device to her ear, nods twice, frowns, then hands it to one of the others standing along the side. It seems like a dozen people observe my torture, half of them in the gray/red uniforms like guards, the others in business attire of mostly gray, as is the fashion in a cold, gray city.

The angry woman stands before me again, gazing down at me, offering a wry smile like she has a new trick to unveil. She waves at the guard by the side door.

The guard opens the door and in step two men wearing scruffy street clothes. They shuffle to the front and stand before me. The light is adjusted so I can see who they are: Forty-one and O-Eight.

"What?" I gasp. "You, too?"

They hold their heads down like they've been caught.

"You know them?" asks my interrogator, knowing the answer.

"Uh...I've met them before," I respond from my seat.

"These two have told us much about your activities of late," says my interrogator. "Criminal acts. Illegal behavior."

"Is that why I'm here?" I dare ask.

"Partly."

"I don't actually know them. They tried to help me once but their help wasn't needed in the end. They didn't like that. So they might say anything to get back at me."

"He still paid us," says O-Eight as though it's the answer she's been looking for. The guard moves to slap his face but the woman waves him off.

"Paid us half," Forty-one explains. "Because we didn't finish it."

"Is that true?" she asks me.

"Yes. Like I said: they planned something but I didn't need them because I was taking my own things, what already belongs to me."

"You planned a crime," she presses, "but you abandoned it?"

"We left him," says Forty-one.

"But he paid us later," says O-Eight.

"And all transactions are tracked," she says, turning to me. "And you marked the payment as a 'gift'...didn't you?"

"There weren't many options to choose from," I say, "so that was the best one. I wasn't paying them for any help because I didn't need their help. So, by definition, I counted it as a gift."

"A gift. For two strangers who were helping you with a crime."

"Not a crime. I don't think picking up my own possessions is a crime. They were only going to help me carry the things."

"So you paid them for their help?" she asks.

"I agreed to that before we started," I explain. Better for me to be upfront about it. The woman seems to know everything so saying something different would only make the situation worse. "I thought I should be honest and pay them as we agreed, even though I didn't want to. I didn't think they did anything worth paying for. Just their time."

"No, ma'am, we did it. We did a lot for him," says Forty-one.

"Not our fault he didn't have us follow through," O-Eight says.

"And what did you pick up that was his?" she asks them.

"One thing was a tuba, in a case," says Forty-one.

"And a stack of notebooks he said were his grampa's writing," says O-Eight. "Oh, and a leather journal from an older relation of his. He was quite eager to get them."

"But he didn't need your help in the end."

"He said he didn't, but he struggled to carry all of it," says Forty-one. "We saw him."

"We watched him," says O-Eight, "just like we was told to."

"Told to?" I bark. So these two were in on the surveillance!

"I see," says the woman. "You agreed to help, then he dismissed your help but paid you half anyway."

"Yes, that's how it was," says Forty-one.

"We watched him best we could," says O-Eight.

She nods at them, keeps her arms folded across her chest.

"That will be all."

She gestures for the guards to take them out.

O-Eight resists, shouting that they did what they were supposed to do. It was me who changed the plan. Forty-one comes to the aid of O-Eight, insisting I'm to blame. They followed their instructions.

What instructions? I can guess what those might've been: Keep an eye on this graduate of our rehabilitation academy, watching for signs of him backsliding. I wait for an explanation but it seems to be a secret. They reveal a different plan. They continue complaining as they are ushered out of the room.

The room is hot, tense. People standing around the sides shuffle nervously. Three of them leave after the two vagrants are gone. The bright light returns to my face. I close my eyes.

"Infractions noted," says my interrogator.

"They were working for you?" I ask, then hear how silent the room has become.

"Ultimately everyone works for the government," she replies in an extra dry voice. "Even a street cleaner."

I know she's right. Now I'm not sure what my crime is. I thought it might be the Hundred pass without authorization. The payments are suspicious, too. Whatever those two said could be used against me. Apparently they had little to say, even to save themselves.

"Am I free to go?" I speak, keeping my voice low but in the quiet room everyone can still hear me.

"No!" the woman roars, spinning around to face me.

"What have I done wrong?" I try to say. "And where is Eden? Thirteen? She did nothing wrong."

The woman seems amused at my mention of Eden.

"She is in this building. It is charming you are concerned for her. She has been taken care of, I assure you. I expect you will see her soon, as long as you cooperate."

I breathe a sigh of relief. It will soon be over. I need to endure a little longer. Then I will see Eden again. Then we will return to the simple life of a street cleaner and a physical therapist though we may never be together again.

"Is she being treated like I am?"

"I suspect better than you, given she is a young female. But the guards...."

"Guards? What about them?"

"You may understand how guards can become restless."

"They didn't hurt her, did they?"

Instead of answering me, the side door opens again and Isa, the street cleaner I worked with briefly, enters. He stands confidently, recounting how rude I was to him that day. He speaks and exits.

In come other people, some I recognize, others not. They tell of encounters with me, all negative. I said this, I did that, I looked at them a certain way. I acted as though I was better than them. One professor from my college arrives to denounce my senior project as a bunch of lies. He says the video I made later was also packed with lies. All I can do is sit there and let them tell lies about me. Who is next? I wonder what lies Eden might tell about me when they bring her in. If they question her like me, she will have to talk to save herself. I wouldn't blame her for that.

Then enters someone I never would've expected.

"I'm sorry, Sixteen," says my friend and coworker. "Tried to warn you. But you kept on talking."

"You, Twenty-four?" I cry out. "How could you?"

"They made me watch you. They were watching me. I told you to be careful. Everything you say will be used against you."

"But you're a war hero! How could they use you like that?"

"I'm just like you. Not a hero, just a street cleaner. I do what I need to do to get by. I got my kids to think about. If I didn't report on you they promised to send them for special treatment."

"Special treatment? What's that?"

"Oh, we can't talk about that." He grumbles, standing before me like a child who's been naughty, his hands clasped in front. "It's all because I had one of them old time paper things, what they called 'magazines'. I only saved it because – and only that one – because, see, my grandma's in it. Pictures of her posing in her naked glory, mm-hmm, spread across the center pages. She was so darn beautiful back then. Then she met my grampa, see, and that's the story."

"They arrested you for possession of a magazine? A nude mag?"

"Soon as I took two steps outside my counselor's office building – not the dissolution of marriage issue – she was confused, hated my family, her counselor agreed and pushed her to file – but another counselor, the session that's required by our work status officer – he's always suspicious of us ex-army types – mostly for him to sign off on my session so I can get my account unlocked so I can get some food, see. And this man came up to me, asking for directions. As I thought a moment, two other men came up on either side of me and took me by the arms, leading me away into a dark alley where one of the new elo-cars waited for us."

"They arrested you for that?"

"Guess so," says Twenty-four. "The man inside, same one asking directions, said 'Smile, you're on camera'. But I couldn't smile. So here they got me. I did what I could, but looks like you got me in trouble. All your talking of that darn 'pandemic' stuff and things that happened to you and your family. What you said, you know it's nonsense, Sixteen, yet you kept on zapping."

"There was a pandemic!" My voice fills the whole room. "It killed hundreds of millions of people all around the world! It did happen! I wish it didn't but it did. Lots of proof if they only looked. My mother was born during it. They lived tough lives because of it. And now they say it never happened. Ten years! Half of everyone dead! And it never happened? You're living a lie. I wish it would happen again, to kill off all you liars and fools!"

Twenty-four just stares at me as I catch my breath.

"That's what they told me to watch for. See if you keep on about your pandemic story. Yeah, you're a heckuva storyteller, Sixteen. I gotta grant you that."

"There was a pandemic," I say, trying to believe it. I sit on the stool, hands tied back and unable to wipe my tears. "My mother said so. My grampa wrote about it. I made a video about it. People saw it. I almost won an award for it. Then it disappeared. Never streamed again. Wiped from every place it was stored. They even took my own personal copy from my home and destroyed it."

My interrogator steps forward, casually flips her hair from her shoulders.

"That's an idea a lot of people have these days," she speaks in a firm voice. "A mass psychosis. That's actually the virus – so-called 'virus'..." She flicks her fingers in the air. "...that spread among us. An idea. Just as viral as a germ. Spreads the same. But, you see, Fritz, it never happened. There was never a time when people were getting sick and dying by the thousands. Sure, a few local events, perhaps, but mostly blown up to ridiculous degrees by rumors. Like one of those 'science fiction' stories. But it never happened, not as you described it."

"I'm sorry, Sixteen," says Twenty-four after a respectful moment of silence. "I tried to warn you to shut up."

"Yes, you did," I have to mumble, unable to speak louder.

"I tried. Got you fixed up with them two, Forty-one and O-Eight, thinking they could keep you outta trouble."

More silence. Then Twenty-four is waved out.

"Sorry, Sixteen," he calls back. "Hope it goes better for you."

When he's gone, the woman interrogating me steps up.

"There's an old cantankerous writer," she speaks like a teacher, "one of the so-called 'thinkers' our enemies like to shove in our faces, a Mister Dostoevsky, who warned long ago that 'great events would come upon us and catch us *intellectually* unprepared'. We would be unable to comprehend what happens and handle it. That is precisely what's happened. This foreign man predicted that 'the world will be saved only after it has been possessed by the demon of evil.' The demon of evil! How quaint! Of course, he could not have predicted the advancements we've made since his time. Whether it really will be saved or not we shall have to wait and see. But we have a good start, making an ideal society. A good start. If we must rebuild after such devastation, why shouldn't we build an ideal society? He said this will depend on our conscience, on our spiritual lucidity, on all of our individual and combined efforts in the face of our catastrophic circumstances. But it has already come to pass, you see, that the demon of evil, just like a great whirlwind, triumphantly circled the continents, and destroyed everything. Like the Flood in Noah's time. Like the blessèd comet in an ancient era. A purification. We have risen from the ashes. We are building an ideal society."

She waits for her words to sink in.

"You could be a part of it, Fritz."

I give a nod, hearing her but not agreeing.

"However, an ideal society cannot be built upon lies. We need to accept the facts, embrace the truth, live a common narrative of our past, our present, and build the future together."

"But it happened," I sob.

She lets out a big sigh, like all her efforts have gone for naught. The remaining guests slip out of the room with one giving a dip of his head in respectful farewell. The door seals with a *whoosh* when it closes. It is only me and her now, plus the guards.

"It is clear," she says, "that your course of rehabilitation has not succeeded. It is always a dubious situation at best. People forget. They backslide. They get distracted and think they no longer need to follow the rules. Rules they agreed to as a condition of their release. They believe they are separate from society, that they can act alone, act supremely, as though they are gods or supermen. However, they are not *anything*, nothing but flesh and bone creatures as disposable as trash. We have plenty of others to replace them. To replace you. And yet you, Fritz Baumann, Eleven-Sixteen, are a special case."

Here it comes. The explanation. Finally. What I've done wrong.

The lights shift and I can see through the glass window before me into the next room. It is lit. My side remains lighted. She throws her hand in the direction of the window, the room on the opposite side, as though a play is about to begin.

"A special case," she intones. "I was given instructions to be sure you were rehabilitated. To be sure you would behave. We made life hard for you. To crush your spirit. We inconvenienced you. Made you uncomfortable. Tried to take away hope for a better life. Made you a miserable wretch. So you would have no hope and, thus, come to rely on us, your *parental* government for everything, for all your needs, physical and spiritual. And, I'm happy to say, it was starting to work. However.... Fritz, you have this weird way of, shall we say, thinking for yourself. Almost as if you have some kind of warped mind, unable to think and act like the rest of us. Long ago they used to dispose of people like you. Yet we know you can still do things, useful things, in our Ideal Society."

She pauses, smiling to herself as if acknowledging her failures but believing she can save herself with one final move.

"You went about your days, doing your work, dancing around the edge of subversive behavior. We have heard your sly whispers, your off-hand confessions, your pointed criticisms. We have reports of your missteps, your misspeaks. The camera in the park that you thought was broken? It still could pick up your speech. That is the reason Twenty-four took you there on lunch breaks. In total we have enough evidence to seat you here."

"I answered your questions," I speak. "Tried to. Stupid questions. Even when I got one right you went on. Bringing in people I don't know to say bad things about me. Most of them lies. What have I actually done wrong? What is my crime?"

She breaks out laughing, false as it sounds. "Crime?"

"I must've done something to be treated like this."

"There is no crime. Not yet. Not a serious one, in any case."

"Then *what?* Why am I here?"

"We wish you to be reminded of proper behavior."

"Is this about that video I made? Still? That was years ago. And I spent nine months in rehabilitation. It's done now. I've forgotten it. Why can't all you authorities forget it, too?"

"You have not forgotten it. Apparently. It lingers in your mind, like a bad dream, waiting for a chance to be reborn."

"No, it d—"

"Listen to me, Fritz. This lie you've been perpetuating, the big lie, isn't helping anyone. You have deceived yourself. You believe it because you want to believe it. It's the only way the world makes sense to you. But it is simply not true."

"It is...." I sniffle back tears and pull against my bonds.

"Consider your belief in this lie like you believe in love. They are similar. You tell yourself what you think is true. You want to believe it, so you do. You convince yourself it is true and you live your life in that assumption of truth. However, it isn't true. Nothing is true but our clamoring for an ideal society. Take *love*, for example. Perhaps the greatest lie. Yet many people are too willing to believe it. They believe that how they feel is genuine, that it's earned, that it must be real because they have worked so hard for it and they feel it so strongly."

She waits, and eventually I look up at her.

"Do you understand?" she asks like a nurturing mother.

I nod, just waiting for the session to end.

She paces confidently a few turns, then circles around me, and settles behind me, standing tall. Her hands fall upon my shoulders, laying heavy there.

"Give your attention forward," she says.

I gaze into the room on the opposite side of the large window. Like I'm watching a video, framed by the window, only I know it is real. It is a real room over there, with a real padded bench sitting there in the center. The room is otherwise empty.

The door at the end of that room opens. In walks a pretty young woman, fit and completely nude, her dark hair cut in a short style yet unbrushed.

Eden! My heart beats loudly, pressing at my ribs. She's alive!

I squirm in my seat as she turns. She performs a dance or some kind of act. She looks good, as pretty as ever, without blemishes that would indicate punishment. I'm glad of that. The window is well-lit for me but she acts as though there is no window. She looks in each direction as if sizing up the room for her performance, but she never gives a suggestion she can see through the window into my room.

As she backs herself onto the end of the bench, I begin to tense, wondering what she is doing there in that room. I wonder why I am forced to watch. A tease to get me to behave? Is it a glimpse before they end me?

She stretches out along the bench, scooting up and laying her head down at the other end. Her hand slides down her soft skin, over her belly, to rest between her thighs. She works her fingers. She groans as she works. But when she appears to be feeling good, she stops. The door opens again.

I watch her sit up, move to the end of the bench, legs dangling, her torso upright – as a young man, also naked, enters the room. I'm not sure what I'm witnessing. I stare at him. His scraggily beard has grown out, hair disheveled as always.

Thirty-nine, my one-time disgusting roommate. What is he doing here? Why is he entering this room with Eden there? I'm not sure what I'm seeing, what I'm expected to observe.

When they took Thirty-nine away, I suddenly recall, he insisted he did everything he was supposed to do.

Everything he was supposed to do?

Thirty-nine goes to the end of the bench in naked profile, regards Eden sitting there. They gaze at each other. He reaches for her and embraces her. She wraps her arms around him – as though they're already lovers missing each other. They kiss passionately.

Then she parts her legs, him standing against her. She slides back on the bench, lays back, her knees bent, feet flat on the bench. He climbs onto the bench, lowers himself between her legs. They start kissing again. One of his hands caresses her breast, the other moving down between her thighs. She takes his face in her hands, kisses him deeper. Then, turning her pretty face to me as if she's looking through the window, her eyes show her passion.

My breath stops, like lead in my lungs, as I watch that vagabond slide down her body and plant his face between her thighs. She throws her head back, soon moans. The sound comes through a set of speakers someone turns on. After a short time, he crawls up her body, kisses her again, and reaches down to help himself enter her. He thrusts into her, pulls back, repeats the motion at a steady pace. He works slowly until the final moments when he quickens.

I close my eyes, squeeze them shut as tight as I can. The noises they make come through the speakers. My interrogator turns the volume up twice. She pats my face to get my attention when Eden begins shaking against the bench as climax overtakes her. Thirty-nine pulls out, crawls up her. They hold each other like they've been lovers forever, no matter how she treated me over the weeks we were together – no matter what her instructions in manipulating me may have been, no matter what reward she's getting for doing it.

And my mind shatters into a million awful questions.

17

THE GRAY LADY

STARING THROUGH THE WINDOW into the other room, I can't think of anything that makes sense about what I witnessed – except the truth. The lie of it all. The set up. Being manipulated by Eden. An effective performance, both with me and the one just now. Yet to what purpose? To catch me in a crime? To listen for whispers of rebelliousness? Or is it an exercise in making me miserable?

"What did you see?" the hateful woman asks.

I have no idea how to answer. Nothing makes sense any longer.

"What do you feel?"

Is she serious? She has to already know. I'm crushed.

"Tell me, Fritz."

I try to calm myself – can't let them think they've beaten me. I swallow hard, then speak: "Betrayal. That's what I saw."

She lets a small chuckle slip. "I would've thought you saw love. A vivid example of love. Two people in love. Acting on it." She glares at me. "Nothing more?"

"Nothing more," I grumble, fighting to maintain control.

"So you see what the truth is. You had thought the situation was different. You thought you knew the truth. But you didn't, did you? I suspect you now question everything."

I question why I was shown that performance. I question why it had to be those two. Eden with a stranger I might be able to endure – she's been forced to do it, I could tell myself. But those particular two together was agony. No doubt it was designed to be agony just for me. Worst of all is that I now know, if I hadn't suspected before, she was nothing more than a plant tasked with setting me up. There was no award. And the passes to get out of the city? Our plans to live down south? Visiting a forest? It was all an act.

I slump on the stool, exhausted.

"Every fact has its fiction," the woman speaks once she gives me time to understand. "Fictions spring up around a fact. So many that it's often difficult to discern what is truth and what is a kind of mirror image or reflection of the truth; a doppelgänger, if you will. And each splintered version of the truth gets wedged into a person's mind and sits there so firmly it is accepted as truth – even as it is actually nothing but an 'imago', an idea that is felt as a truth but is not truth, usually set with an image, hence the term, which is a firm representation of the idea. An idea made into image, you could say, which, being an image, stands like a statue representing truth."

Weak as I feel, I try to take a breath, to prepare my rebuttal. I absolutely must speak back at this terrible woman.

"What I—"

"This is the world we live in now," she continues. "Full of what is called misinformation, disinformation, unformation, lots of terms to describe facts and truth and their manipulation: reinformation, info-naiveté, infonationing, info-weaponization, info-mimesis, and so on. It all means the absence of exact truth standing in for truth, which as you may surmise, can—"

"But gradations of truth," I speak out, "can still be acceptable in different contexts. Like white lies. Your gray dress, for example, is actually hideous. Maybe the truth, maybe not. Maybe I'm repeating what others have said. You don't know and maybe don't care which it is, only that someone doesn't approve of your fashion choice, and that idea becomes a truth to you, a fact you cannot dismiss. So you go out looking for a new dress. Your *imago* forces you to seek *redress* in a manner of speaking."

She halts when I start to speak, keeps her arm bent so she can rest her chin on her fist.

"They said you were clever." Amusement colors her voice. "That you're clever in a wordy way. There's a truth."

"I know what is real, what is truth," I say with a firm tone.

"And that display?" she asks, waving at the window.

"Maybe it wasn't really her," I say and want to believe. "It could be a look-alike. Both of them. Selected to aggravate me. One of your deceptions. What's it called? Infomirroring? A reflection of the truth that sure looks like the truth but something is off because it is not actually the truth. Is that it?"

"No, it's not infomirroring at all."

"I know what I know," I say confidently, feeling it was an act.

"You know what you know, hmm?" She starts her pacing.

"I saw what I saw."

"And you trust your senses, even though we've been told how we can trick ourselves, that we are easily fooled. Are you sure you know what is true? Are you certain that all you experience is real?"

"Stop!" a new voice calls out.

I can't turn far enough on the stool to look behind me but I hear that someone has entered the room from a door back there.

"Stop this," the new woman speaks from behind me.

My interrogator stands straight, as if called to attention.

"Stop this foolish game," says the new woman in a deep and rich voice: throaty, almost husky, yet sonorous.

"Madame Governor," my interrogator cries in surprise.

An older woman with short, graying hair, dressed in gray slacks and blazer, strides forward, passing on my right, going to confront my interrogator. They stand face to face, blocking my view. All I can see is the woman's backside. I focus on the singular imperfection: a wrinkle on her slacks formed from sitting.

Madame Governor? The words catch in my throat. I can't be sure it's really her. Not after getting a lecture on truth. But why would a high-level person like her be concerned with me?

She entered the room with a few assistants who stay behind me, and a pair of beefy guards who move with her like an extra set of arms, so maybe she is who she intends me to believe she is. Or she is only another actor and the performance continues.

"I apologize," says the awful woman interrogating me. I realize how much she's tried to make herself look like the governor. "There was no need for you to come down to this unsavory location. Forgive me for whatever it is that prompts you to take time from your busy schedule to visit us. To see our process up close."

"I don't care about your process, Barbara," says the governor in her husky voice. I've heard rumors she'd taken up smoking during her campaign.

They lower their voices to whispers, posed face to face like two wildcats, so I can't make out much of what they say.

"...testing him," I hear my interrogator say, raising her voice.

More low but intense discussion. I've never felt so important.

"I did what you instructed," says my interrogator.

Low words, with edges. A gasp from my interrogator.

"I made sure he has a low-level job," she says. "I made him share a class D unit with a vagrant – the same male as in our scene. Yet nothing happened. He failed. I sent a therapist to him next, yet they fell in love and tried to thwart my plan."

"And those in the display room?" the older woman asks.

"Same two, yes. We showed him she was not as innocent as he wants to believe. To make him feel betrayed. It usually works well. Exposure to the reality of the situation is—"

The older woman cuts her off: "This is not what I meant."

"You said to take care of it. I promised I would."

"All I said was to get him out of the way. No need to go through a plethora of maddening mind tricks."

The woman who's been interrogating me seems distraught, and I fight the urge to grin. She's as confused as I was when I first saw Eden come out followed by that dirty Thirty-nine.

"It is standard protocol," she explains. "Show the subject what he believes is the truth. Then expose that truth as false. Repeat it with other topics, other examples. Soon the subject doubts everything. He drowns in confusion. Grasps after any kind of reality no matter how implausible. Anything can be presented as truth yet still be false. He doubts even his own senses. His mind crumbles. He is left as an aimless, confused idiot. He then obeys easily. He believes whatever is offered to him by an authority figure must be true."

At a flip of the governor's hand, the two women step over to the side of the room to confer further. Perhaps she doesn't want me to hear. The discussion continues with heated words popping out. One of the governor's staff seems to be making notes on a tablet. After a few minutes, they reach an agreement and return, standing in front of me, facing me.

"You have become a problem, Fritz," this governor woman says. "Also known as Forty-four-zero-eleven-sixteen. You're like a pesky pimple that always fills up again right after getting popped. And my assistant here, Barbara – Two-four-sixty-nine – hasn't managed to resolve the issue, it seems. I have been informed of your progress. Or lack of progress. So I am here to see if we cannot do better."

I nod only to acknowledge my understanding, that I do hear her, not that I know what 'better' might mean.

"We live in a world of chaos," the governor speaks, gazing hard at me like it is my fault. "It may look neat, our fine city, and clean, run in orderly fashion. Yet in the cracks, between random moments, there is a bubbling of disorder threatening us, waiting to erupt and overwhelm us. We cannot have that."

Fixed to this stool, I know I'm in for a lecture.

"To survive, we must forget our ugly past," the governor says. "We must also dare not dream of a bright future. Hopefully bright, or perhaps not. Progress toward something better, yes, but not dwell *in* the future, which doesn't yet exist. A place for fantasies only. We must therefore focus on the present. On each unfortunate instance. On each touch and look and feel. Less on feelings, of course, which will always lead us astray – as you've learned today."

I can't help but squirm. The governor notices my discomfort and orders a guard to release my hands from behind my back. She lets out a small joke about the circulation in my hands being cut off so I can't touch myself during the sex scene.

No one laughs but the governor.

I rub my wrists, shake my hands to restore feeling in them.

"It's like one of those music machines," she goes on. "Perhaps you've seen one of them in a museum. They take a disk and cut it, in grooves, in circles around the disk. Concentric circles. I don't know how they did that; our technology isn't up to that. Then they spun the disk on a peg and placed a needle to the disk. The needle was at the end of a bar. Somehow the needle slipped into the previously cut grooves and that released the music embedded there. A marvelous contraption indeed. The music was small so they had to funnel it through another device which would enlarge it so you could hear every note played. You didn't need to collect a group of people and have them play the music for you. You could simply spin the disk and listen to what came forth."

I have, in fact, seen in a museum such a music machine as what she describes. I took my sons there. I saw video technology from older times displayed there, too.

"I happened to find one of those machines at my father's house," she continues, "put away in a closet – as though no one used it any longer. Or knew how. It worked, though, once electric was applied. I also found boxes of the disks, all slipped into flat cases with amazing art on the fronts. I spun each of them on the machine and listened. Many different styles of music. Some I liked, others not so much. But that's all beside the point. How the machine operated is neither here nor there."

She grins, as if knowing the punchline to her joke and enjoying the anticipation on my face.

"If I bumped the machine that needle would jump. Bump it hard enough and the needle would skip to the next song on the disk. I *tried* to bump it sometimes, especially when a song I didn't like started. I learned how to hit the machine just so, so it would skip ahead to a new song, as though the song I didn't like never existed. I wondered why they hadn't made a disk without that song cut into it. I wondered how I could make the needle skip over that song without me needing to give it a bump. Wouldn't it be lovely if I didn't need to hit the machine to make it skip that song?"

"I think so," I mumble, thinking of the scene.

"Our lives are much like that machine," she says. "Do you know? Our history is much like that machine. The bad song is still there on the disk yet I found a way to skip over it. I can go on as though that bad song didn't exist. Think of our history: all those good times but also bad ones. How about if we skip over the bad ones? Some may argue they still are part of the whole – yet we can forget them, no longer important to us. And in time we do forget what happened. We don't need to remember the bad times. We go on. We get better. We come up with a plan to make a better world – to fashion an Ideal Society. We play only the songs we like."

I continue nodding at each claim, holding my hands limp in my lap, waiting for her to stop talking.

"Do you see what we've done? We have built anew." She pauses to smile at me. "Yet not in any haphazard fashion. We have a plan. A plan to build an Ideal Society. And you are part of it. You have the *opportunity* to be a crucial part of this great new plan. Yet you keep insisting on certain events happening, like playing the bad song every time when you could skip over it. It's like bad dreams from a distant night that terrorized you. Yet you keep holding on to those nightmares that frightened you. For whatever reason that may be, I can't understand. You hold on...when you could easily, simply, let go of them. You see? You could sleep well and awaken to a bright new world: our Ideal Society."

That was how her last acceptance speech ended, I recall, seeing it replayed so much on the streams. My interrogator has faded into the back of the room but takes a few steps forward at the wonderful words, ready to clap – but doesn't and simply stands dumb like she doesn't know what the proper etiquette is.

The governor acknowledges Barbara's feeble attempt at praising her: a slight nod, then a dismissive tilt of her head toward the door. Barbara takes the hint, carefully opening the door then closing it behind herself. Another staff member follows her out.

"Would you please step out?" Madame Governor requests of the staff members who remain.

"Ma'am?" asks her secretary, the woman holding the tablet. "No documentation?"

"That won't be necessary. No need to document this."

"Yes, ma'am." With a bow, the secretary goes to the door.

"Out, out, out!" the governor sings impatiently.

The staff reluctantly exits.

"You two stay," the governor orders, meaning the two muscular women who guard her.

She turns to me, smiling, trying to be charming.

"What is it that keeps you from accepting our Ideal Society?"

But I can't answer. Too many choices. First, maybe, was how my video was taken down without a good reason given – though I could guess from her speech it was one of those bad songs she wished to skip over. Second, how I was sent for rehabilitation and the abuses I had to endure there. Third, my job as a street cleaning functionary.

"But how—"

"I do have to apologize for the crude ways my assistant thought to accomplish my direction. We will definitely have to rethink her role on my staff, I assure you."

"But...but...." I can't get the words to come out.

"But what?" she prompts.

"But you're my sister!"

There is a chuckle, quickly cut off. "No, I'm not." A deep breath, a clear sign of betrayal. "I have but one brother. I know him. He died a few years ago. Unfortunate accident."

Yes, unfortunate. He fell under a combine, got cut to shreds, had a closed casket. His sons weren't as distraught as people expected they should've been. Being a senator, nobody dared investigate. His widow took some money and went away.

"But...." I want to say more, but there's no point to it. Nothing I say will make a difference. They will let me go only when they believe I'm harmless and will remain quiet about the biggest thing in my life: that damn video.

"It is that old video stream that gives people that idea," she says. "However, the whole story is wrong. People cannot tell the difference between fact and fiction. Streams can easily fool them. It's one of the curses that come with technology – designed to persuade."

"But it was real," I say, an automatic response.

"To you," she says with a chirp in her voice. "Don't you have that thing, what's it called? Your mother had it, too. And her father."

"She called it the 'aspie condition'. It doesn't mean you're stupid. Just a different structure to the brain. Makes you look at the world differently, interact differently. But not wrongly."

"Ah, but you are a stupid boy," she says with another chirp.

That's what my sisters called me when I was little.

She sees that she's hurt me, seems half glad of it and half sad to have done it. But I'm used to it. I know she had a hard life like me; she refuses to accept it. 'In denial', my counselor would call it. A lot of people refuse to believe what happened to the world happened. And no amount of evidence will convince them otherwise.

"You cannot see the forest for the trees," and she gives a laugh that begins with a chirp of sweet innocence yet ends with a crow's threatening caw. "It's charming in its own way. Like a child trying to say something clever, to sound like an adult, yet failing."

Again with the knife. I frown.

"Worry not, Eleven-Sixteen," she says in a motherly tone. "It's a common mistake. Since you ask, I shall explain it to you so you can put that song away."

"All right," I mutter, but I hold on to the truth.

She tells how she read books in her father's library. As a baby she was introduced by her mother to a room on the second floor of the house. There were no children's books so her mother read to her from the adult books, patiently and often having to sound out the words. That does seem like my mother's way of reading.

"My mother loved to read, and she made sure to instill in me a love of reading, too," she says. "In fact, my father often had to come up to the library to get her, because she would stay there for hours reading if no one called her down. But that's how Mamie was. It was so unfortunate when she died giving birth to my little brother."

"You mean Abe?"

"Yes, Abe. Poor soul. May he rest in peace."

"I'm sure he is." But I doubt that.

"Don't be rude," she snaps. "Abe was my little brother. I loved him. I miss him. However, I understand your point of view: a jealous view of a family you perhaps wish you had."

"I did have," I insist.

She turns to the nearest guard. "Give him a slap, will you?"

One of the two beefy guards in gray uniforms steps forward and swings an open-hand strike to my cheek. The blow is harder than a slap. I stare up at the guard. A gray helmet covers her hair although a few blonde wisps poke out. It makes sense that a woman who despises the men in her life would surround herself with female guards, strong ones who could protect her from a weak man like me. It is starting to make sense.

I told a couple guys in the rehabilitation facility my theory and they agreed. A woman would grow up hating the men in her life who oppressed her, made her obey them: her father and brothers, then teachers, a husband, a workplace boss. She would hate them. To gain her independence, to reclaim her dignity, she would fight them. To get back at them, she would do the opposite of what they wanted her to do. She would join protests against whatever the men in her life stood for, perhaps turn to other women for love, or make herself unattractive, or join with men her family would not approve. In those ways, she could hurt the men who had oppressed her. It didn't matter if she actually was oppressed; it only mattered that she believed she was.

"But what about you?" asked a guy in rehabilitation. "You were bullied by your sisters."

I had no answer.

Now this woman, governor of our state, surrounded by a female staff, looks down on me, submitting to her authority, to her power.

A light blinks on inside me. I didn't like the situation we've been put in these past fifty years, maybe longer, where we have to hate each other to get along. I was only seeking to understand what I observed.

I shake off the slap, realizing she is speaking again.

She explains how reading all those books, the fiction as well as the information books, gave her ideas about the world, how it was and how it could be. She said the books changed her life, made her want to go out and do things, be active, change things. She'd seen enough of the way the world was post-pandemic and books from the old times let her make comparisons.

"What is it that we need to do to get ourselves out of this chaos? That's what I asked myself. You see, my father had the family farm, and we were fortunate to be able to keep it in operation, to provide food for the people of our region. That made us wealthy, yet such wealth seemed undeserved. I read much of my father's library, some of the books full of strange ideas. Other books held fascinating concepts. I wondered why they hadn't been implemented in our society."

She pauses as though seeing the library in her mind and reading the titles on the spines.

"The answer, obviously – you may appreciate this perspective – was the virus that stopped everything. Made the world stop. We had to hold on, survive it, and only then could we begin a program such as what I believe will make us better. Wasn't a full-blown pandemic like you maintain in your fictitious video, but even isolated pockets of infections were enough to disrupt our way of life for a while. Like everyone else, I was forced to wait. We were thrown back a hundred years in our level of technology and what we'd learned through the ages. We only had old books to preserve that knowledge. The newest ideas, the diagrams and schemata, data and protocols, calculations and imagery had been kept in what they called 'digital form' – the imaginary ink on cloudy pages – thus lost when the devices stopped. Unable to be saved or accessed, we had to rely on what was on book pages. That took several years of reading before we could begin to rebuild, to begin a new phase of our society. It took nearly fifty years before we could pick up where we left off. But look at us now. We have electric busses and tall buildings with electric elevators, and cameras everywhere for safety. We have machines to keep data we collect, and to run calculations matching data points, all to keep our Ideal Society functioning in an orderly fashion. I established groups of experts in key areas of research to recover the lost knowledge. I led that effort. I made that promise and I delivered on it."

I could almost hear the crowds cheering for her.

"I led the way in formulating the plan to start again in each key area of our society." She regards me, as though expecting applause. "So what do you think of that? Isn't it marvelous? It isn't every day a citizen gets a personal lecture by the governor."

Feeling smug, I stupidly mutter: "It's not every day a citizen has a sister for a governor."

"Slap him," she speaks softly.

The same guard swings her hand at my face, steps back.

I shake my head to clear the sting.

"But that's not true." I wait for another slap that doesn't come. "Can't be. You couldn't have been reading books in the library. You would've been only a toddler then."

"The narrative stuck in your head is incorrect." Her eyes narrow at me. "I am not your sister. This belief you have, beginning from that ridiculous video, is appalling. It's the reason you're visiting us."

She shakes her head.

"My mother was an older woman, yes. She unfortunately died in childbirth – my brother Abe's birth. She is buried at the farm. I'm a Chesterfield, always a Chesterfield. Daughter of Mamie and Lionel Chesterfield. Yet now that I've joined in domestic partnership with Senator Wornall, now President Wornall, I am a Wornall, as well. I am certainly not the daughter of a poor Southern woman, no matter what my enemies might suggest! I never lived in a brothel, as some say. I never lived in the forest like some wild animal. Those are all lies. Vicious lies!"

"There's no shame in living a hard life," I say.

The guard twitches, waiting for a command. It catches my eye. I look. The governor sees me look and glances at the guard, too. With her slight nod, the guard steps to me and gives me another slap.

"And you told the world," the governor barks. "Your damn video full of lies. Everyone saw it. Everyone believed it. That's why we had to take it down, remove it from the streams, destroy all copies. We must present an accurate narrative. It's the only way society can function: with everyone knowing the facts and believing the same story." She's breathing hard. "Now...."

I await the next slap.

"We must set the record straight." She calms herself, waves her hand in the air. "And here we are: well along our planned path to what I've deemed our Ideal Society. The goal is to build a world of productivity and plenty for all. A world of order and purpose, of function. A world where each citizen has what is needed. It may seem strict at the present time, but that is because we must enforce

212

certain limits as we continue to develop toward our Ideal Society. We are not there yet."

I can understand her and her plan: remaking society in her own design. It isn't as though other people hadn't tried back throughout history. Lots of stories of people trying and maybe succeeding for a while but ultimately failing. That is a story in itself: the lesson. And each time, the newest person to attempt it swears that this time will be different, this time it will succeed. The flaw in their plan is that they are going against human nature: a natural inclination toward self-preservation, independence, eschewing control by others. Or the usual greed, grift, and combativeness.

"Not everyone is in league with our plan," she continues despite me veering down an inward path, not waiting for me to return. "We must keep aware of anything that threatens to derail our plans. There are those who work to disrupt our plans. I cannot understand why those rubes would not want what we are offering. The criminal element cannot think logically even for their own benefit. We cannot have that. You have been a focus of our efforts as we press on with building the Ideal Society. Then you make that video."

18

LITTLE LIES

IN MY TIME AS A VIDEO PRODUCER I interviewed many people, a lot of them concerning their experiences during and after the pandemic. This was before the video of my mother was removed. I remembered an interview with an old lawyer – someone who was practicing law when the pandemic began. He explained the political situation at that time, when a national plan was formed to combat the virus, to conduct mass vaccinations, and how the vaccine was rushed into use without thorough testing because there was an emergency. He described the adverse effects some people developed and how they cried out for restitution. The vaccine supposedly prevented the deadly virus from harming them, but they developed disagreeable problems, too, and many died as a result. He took part in lawsuits by individuals, by families, and by businesses against the drug companies, doctors and medical staffs, even politicians who demanded everyone take the vaccine despite on-going problems. As the pandemic worsened, the lawsuits increased – until everything collapsed. No more courts, so no more lawsuits.

I put that together with what my mother, Isla, experienced; with what her father, Grampa Sandy, experienced; with what his mother, Polly, experienced. None of them ever got the virus. They never took the vaccine, either. Polly famously credited their good genes, Sandy recorded in one of his notebooks.

I had no idea about 'lawsuits' other than you make a claim that someone harmed you and so they are made to pay you for your pain and suffering. It seemed from the old lawyer's explanation that it was less about facts than how good the lawyer was in presenting a lot of clever words. People were persuaded more by clever words than by data, numbers or charts, or science.

I consider all of that as the gray lady paces in front of me, her thick heels clacking on the concrete floor, the wide legs of her slacks flapping as she goes back and forth, her hand alternately in the side pockets of her neat blazer or swinging freely as if marching for a cause. The two beefy guards stand before me, one at each foot; were I to get up from the stool and try to go after the governor they would be able to block me. Yet I have no intention of violence; I'm too tired, my will too wounded to act.

I've been arrested, confined, starved, then mentally tortured by a cruel woman who showed me all my beliefs were illusions. Only this new woman claiming to be the governor stopped that abuse. I would play nice for her. She sent out everyone not needed to guard her.

The room rings with silence.

Finally she lets out a sigh.

"What are we going to do with you?"

The way she asks the question lends a layer of irony to her voice. I wonder: 'do' meaning what would be next in my torture regimen? Or 'do' meaning what might be the ultimate solution to the problem that is me? I decide to wince in anticipation of either answer.

"I'll give you what you want," she says grimly. "I sent them out so I can speak freely with you." She stood with her arm bent up to give her chin a resting place – as my interrogator, her assistant, had done in deliberate imitation. "This does not mean, however, that we shall have a conversation. I shall speak; you shall listen. Then I'll entertain your questions, should you have any."

I nod, thinking she was always so quiet and docile as a child.

"I was born at Chesterfield farm," she begins like the narration of her own video, "as the rebuilding of society was shifting into a higher gear. That's a vehicular analogy, I suppose, though we had none available back in those days. They ran out of gasoline fuel and stayed where they failed. The roads were littered with old, rusting hulks. Now we have a large number of electric transports to move

216

people around a city and between cities. Individuals need not worry about getting anywhere in expensive private vehicles for we have solved that wasteful problem. I recall my mother reading to me, as I have told you, and my father showing me around the farm, explaining its operation. I grew up as any child of a farm family would: carefree for the most part yet full of curiosity, full of desire to do more. In fact, I...."

She glares at me, as though I'm not listening.

"I learned the business. When life was hardest we were able to feed half the state and some counties in the next state. Civilization was able to go on because we had food to offer. That is in the public record. We made the encyclopedia stream. It's taught in the schools. I am proud of what we were able to accomplish. That gave me more ambition, I suppose. What else could I do to make the world a better place? You understand that, don't you? Success prompts a desire for more success."

"I suppose so," I mutter.

"You promised to listen." She frowns. "Indeed, you likely know all of this from your own schooling. And politics. What I said in the campaign, what I did as senator. The committees for the renewal of our society. The Ideal Society forums. The implementation of these new policies. This you know. Everyone knows."

She takes a breath, her chest puffing out in pride.

"What you don't know...or I *suspect* you don't...is what happened in the middle. This is the material you wish to know – which is the reason for sending out my staff."

"I do know about your career," I dare speak, "but you're not—"

"I will tell you the truth, if you like. My truth. What no one but you will ever know. This is what you want, isn't it?"

Now I feel a little fear. "Yes."

"I was born at Chesterfield farm. That is true. I returned to that farm later and met my brother. Abraham – Abe, as we called him. A man by then, with wife and four sons. I was a grown woman when I went back." She took a breath. "When I went back.... That's the hard part of my truth. I went back...yes, but from where?"

"From a marsh down south," I mumble, but she hears me.

"That's the part I don't agree with. You put it right in that damn video of yours. You let your mother tell her crazy stories about the awful times she lived through. How she was sent away, dismissed, from the same farm where I was born. Misbehaved, the staff told me. She was a housekeeper of some kind, common in those days. I'm sorry that happened to your mother."

"She was your mother, too," I boldly speak out.

"That is your truth." She glares hard at me. "When I returned to the farm, I met Abe and convinced him I was his older sister. It helped that we looked alike. And we both looked like our father. All Abe knew was that his mother had died during his birth. That was what his father told him. Once in a while his father would utter to him profound words concerning the fate of a girl also born in the house. I suppose he meant me. He wondered what became of her – but he was losing his mind, being at the mercy of those two China dolls he'd purchased for his amusement. They kept him occupied. I suspect – we both did – they were slowly poisoning him. He could no longer run the farm, so Abe took over."

That makes sense, thinking of Mother's stories, and what I've read in Bobbie's letters back to Mother.

"It mattered less, I like to believe, whether I was who I claimed to be than that I worked tirelessly beside Abe to manage the farm. As his sons grew, they took on crucial roles, as well. We made the farm work. Until Abe's accident. That threw everything onto me. My brother's widow left, but I persuaded my nephews to stay and run the farm. I had educated myself on all matters of agriculture and animal husbandry. Many early mornings and late nights, I assure you. We made the farm a success and fed a million people."

Nodding, I know that much from the history streams.

"I wrote to your mother, where she was in that marsh you talk about so much. I wanted to let her know how I was, how things were going at the farm. She knew where I was going when I left her. Yes, I was there in the marshes, like you. I admit that much. I do not admit she was my mother, however; not my birth mother. She was the woman who took me from Chesterfield farm as a baby, stole me from Mamie and Lionel. A criminal act! She ran away with me to get back at her employer. That much is truth. My truth. I know she told you other stories. I was only a little girl but I have memories. I know what the truth is. Your mother stole me and took me to that national park where you were born."

"No, that's not what she said," I have to speak up. "She—"

"Isla, your birth mother, took us to that mountain, made us live there in a small hut that had dirt floors. This after we had lived in a large and fine house with plenty of food. What a change!"

She shakes her head as if to drive out bad memories.

"Isla met an old man there. He had long white hair and a long white beard. I remember listening to them having their sex in the next room in that tiny hut. And then her belly grew big and one day out you came. I was there to see you squeezed out of her, thinking 'this is what a boy is'. Hah! They thought you were cute. I had been the youngest up to that moment, the darling of the group. Then you were born and took Isla's attention from me. I knew then you would be trouble. And I was correct, all these years later, wasn't I?"

"Well...." I'm not sure what to say at that point. It really isn't my fault, either being born or growing up just to cause her trouble.

"I watched you grow day by day. I was there each time the older girls did things for you. The feeding, cleaning your poo, playing with you, trying to make you smile or laugh or cry. I used to poke your belly to get a reaction from you. Do you remember? Sometimes you giggled. Do you remember how we played with you?"

"Some of it," I mumble, feeling nauseous.

"Isla took a job at a shop at the bottom of the mountain, so we girls cared for you during the days. Left alone with you we liked to tease you, you being the only boy. Allie started it but Amy quickly joined in. But Amy would put an end to it once we made you cry. Do you remember when you were older how we made you take off your clothes? How we teased you for having a 'dingle toy'? That's what we called it. How we tweaked it until you had tears? One time Allie insisted we pretend you were a grown-up man, holding you between her legs, but you were too small. You just cried. Amy put a stop to it. Yet we had a lesson: a little boy couldn't make a baby. Of course we never told Isla what we did. Then we were soon enough leaving that mountain and getting on a bus that took us further south. That was when your father died, true? But he wasn't my father so I didn't care. I was more afraid I'd never see the farm again."

That hurts. I feel tears come to my eyes as I sit on that stool, wearing the torn papery gown, miserable once more.

She purses her lips, as though she got the reaction she wanted.

"You know the after: my return to the farm, my political career. I just told you the before. What's missing is the middle."

"The middle is always the most...interesting, the most important part," I mutter, thinking aloud.

"I knew the truth. What happened to me, that is. Yet I needed to rely on Isla, no matter where we were. Her natural-born daughter and her younger sister of the same age, Amy and Allie, were her constant companions, and she treated them that way: with respect and kindness. However, I was something taken away. As a child, I certainly couldn't go back on my own, so I had to play along, to be agreeable, so she would take care of me. What's the expression from the vaccine era? 'Go along to get along'? Is that it? Hmm? Until I grew old enough to be on my own. You know what that's like. The moment you realize you must leave."

"Yes, I guess I had the same urge to leave."

"For me it was a day when Isla criticized me for dropping a tray of shrimps. She called me stupid, said I wasn't her daughter, as she liked to say 'on account of her not being so desperate to have a babe that she would birth me'. Such cruel words! I knew she picked up drinking, stealing bottles from a store across the highway, so I took her words as truth. They hurt and I vowed to leave."

"That was me that dropped the tray of shrimp!"

"It was me. Or me, too. She was always complaining about the things I did or didn't do. When I finally did leave, I guess then she started complaining about you. Until you left."

"That's probably correct."

"When I finally left the marsh, left that mean old Isla, you know I went north. Like you did later. You likely think it was an easy trip, riding the bus to this city. I did not stop to visit the mountain again. I tried to come straight north but...."

I look up at her. "But what?"

"I had some encounters that almost sent me on different paths. A young woman riding alone in a new world is not newsworthy. You can expect certain events to occur."

I narrow my eyes. "What happened?"

"I said it: 'a young woman traveling alone'. Don't make me give the details. One reminded me of you – by appearance, not by deed. I know you were not a violent boy. I don't know what you did after I left. And there was a girl who took in my confidence then tricked me into first doing some things I shouldn't have done, then taking all I had, leaving me more alone. I had to walk a long distance and find food off the land. Like Isla taught us. Yet I chose poorly what to take as food and fell ill. A family took me in, nursed me back to health, and sent me on my way. I was so thankful, after I gained some of our farm's wealth I shared it with them."

"I never knew that," I say, bowing my head. Plenty of stories of women being hurt during those years of lawlessness. Mother told us about that. Yet some people deny it happened, or that it was a common occurrence in those days and of no great concern.

"When I arrived at the Chesterfield farm, I knew I was home. I felt it. The place matched my memories. I knew where everything was, places my father had shown me, carrying me in his arms. Abe treated me like a long-lost cousin at first, before I made my identity known – like it was a myth I played out with him, hiding myself to assess him. He passed: a good man, father, husband, running the farm for a good profit. We talked. I told him the story of how I was born, then the way I was stolen from the farm—"

"You were *not* stolen," I cut in, but I feel I'm only replaying the phrase I have to say, and doubt more that I am right.

"I told Abe how Isla took us to the next town. Dismissed from the farm, there wasn't much work she could do. No one would hire such a woman. Except the owner of the local whorehouse. She was a large woman in an age of starvation so she was notorious, you might say. We lived in the cellar with Isla's mother, who did the cleaning and cooking for the brothel. It was a miserable life, as you can imagine. We don't need to share any of that with the citizenry. It has nothing to do with my leadership. Isla had her room upstairs where she did her work. I saw it only once or twice. Being of a young age, I never understood what work she did. The older girls understood better than me."

"I can imagine."

"Then one night the girls packed me up and we left that house in a wagon pulled by horses. Of course that was a long time ago, long before we reinvented electric carriages. We arrived at a location with a forest and a lake. We played with children who had dark skin. I couldn't understand how people could be that different. Isla seemed to be at home with them. In that lake I learned to swim. I remember a big man scooping me out of the water and lifting me to his shoulder to carry me out of the lake. I shrieked in delight, having not a care in the world."

"Mother never told me much about that place or anything she did there. The State Park, right? She said only that a group of horsemen came to drive those people out."

"Yes, that happened. We left before then. And do you know why Isla's shoulders and back were always aching? She threw them out while pulling a cart the rest of us rode in, all by herself – well, she did have a friend, a thin girl older than my so-called sisters, with a French name. She helped for a while until we had to give up on the cart and just carry what we could on our trip south, heading to that damn national park."

"The Sorrow Mountain National Park...."

"That one, although it had no name in those days. Along the way to that place Isla suffered a miscarriage. She left the bloody remains in the forest where we rested. I was young but old enough to realize she might die, seeing all the blood. I feared what we would do if she died. She was the only one who knew the way to that national park, after all."

"But you made it," I say, hoping to conclude her story.

She seems perturbed by that.

"I am not your sister. Not by birth, though I hold no animosity to Isla for what she did. She took years of my life away from me, yet I might have learned some things along the way. I had to live it down, forced to be in a family of poor Southern whores. A disgrace. I never felt I was a part of your family."

"Me neither, to be honest," I say with a thoughtful nod.

"That is not who I am. I'm a Chesterfield. We are a good family. I reclaimed my heritage. And I worked with Abe to manage the farm. I found ways to increase productivity, which benefited everyone: a lot more food for citizens, more profit for us. We even gave away food to poor people. After my terrible childhood, how could I not?"

"How can you not do that now?" I cut in. "The way you run this state now. The way the city is now. Running it like a farm – only we are humans, not cattle, not sheep."

She lets out a chuckle. "The farm is the ideal model for a society. Everything on a farm is designed toward the goal of productivity, of making things. In our case, it's food. There is no wasted effort. Lord, everything is hard enough, better to not waste any effort. It's a good way to manage a city, as well. Everyone in her place and a place for everyone. Once we have the city running at peak efficiently, we can introduce the next phase: the breeding program."

"Breeding program? For people?"

"Why, yes. Why not? I realize not everyone is suited for our Ideal Society. Some have limited functionality. They can be of some use, of course, but they shouldn't be allowed to reproduce. We are all born without our consent, given what we are given without our choosing. Unfortunate, yet true. Each of us can be useful with what abilities we are born with and what can be taught to us. We have a legion of scientists preparing that phase. The geneticists, that is, measuring the functionality of each newborn. We collect data on everyone and assess their genetic viability, their innate traits, and put them up against what the city's and state's needs are. We put the compatible people together with suitable tasks."

"Like mating cows and bulls."

"A crude analogy yet not far off. We prefer to look at it as a way to improve our society. In improving our society, we can improve the world. It's not unlike the way we've resurrected certain technology, especially those electronic devices so common before the pandemic. Yet we improved on them. Those EMPs took down the power grids.

The 'Electro-Magnetic Pulse' destroyed our electronic devices. And the war overseas. Our own territorial war. Even the shutting down of armament factories, the end of bullets. We made new kinds of weaponry. We had to come up with something that didn't rely on old technology. No more gunpowder. The 'directed energy' weapons we have now work quite well. And we've rebuilt our navy to protect our shores. And deliver our soldiers to overseas fighting. In fact, I have a ship dedication ceremony to attend the day after tomorrow. We're so proud. Her Presidential Ship the *Chesterfield*. The largest of the fleet."

"My sister, the ship dedicator," I say smugly.

"I'm not your sister." She shows an angry face. "Isn't that what this whole discussion is about? I know it, and now you also know."

"What difference does it make? You are deep into your career, no matter what you've done with it. I mean making this city into—"

"I know who you are, Fritz. I know all about you." She turns to the exit as if wishing her secretary hadn't left with the tablet. "Isla was a talker." She regards me again. "She told us the whole story. And often. Almost as though she needed to repeat it to remember it, so there's no telling how much it changed a little with each telling."

"Probably so," I have to consider.

"I am not a Baumann, not like her. Not one of those people you hail from. From, as she liked to say, an old country. The place where they made that awful tuba she obsessed over so much. Such a waste of good metal! I understand how it's best used: to scare away crows from the crop fields."

"Where is it?" I perk up. "They took it when they arrested me."

"So that first Baumann in this country, the soldier who was put in that prisoner-of-war camp. The tuba player. What did he ever do? It was long ago, I know. Do you know, Fritz? About your namesake? He was a player in an orchestra at that time. He taught music at a college. You read his journal, didn't you?"

"I know he died being hit by a car while crossing the street."

"Yes, there's that. Before then, in those classes, he had students. He was popular. The way he spoke with his little accent, never fully learning our language. He had a moustache that some girls thought cute. He had flirtations. Oh, I suppose that sort of thing was normal back then, who can say? It's not allowed today, of course. Nothing up to the level of scandal. I had someone research it."

"You did?"

"Who can really know for certain what people in the past did? Your namesake must've done something terrible to be hit by a car, using a gasoline motor. Perhaps that was only an illusion, nothing more. Perhaps something really happened between him and one of his students. Who knows? At any rate, it was his wife who drove the car that day, and who can say whether it was truly an accident or it was her intention to strike him down as he crossed the street? It happened so fast, as they say."

That sucks the air from my lungs.

"I didn't know. Mother never said." Then something pokes my brain. "The last entry in that journal. It was in her writing, saying that he died, car accident, and the date."

"Yes," she sighs. A whiff of amusement surrounds her.

"But...." I can't think straight. Everything is a jumble.

"How could Isla know? It takes long hours in the archive to dig up old records, find articles printed on fiche slides of old papers, the news from the past. I doubt Isla would've let that fact be known in any case. Similarly I wish certain facts to be hidden from the public record. Fortunately, the facts about your ancestor do not matter. He is not my ancestor, he's yours. One of those people persecuted in the past. Who always seem to be causing trouble. It's good the war back then ended it, stopped those people blamed for starting the war that ultimately brought him over to our country. After all, it's written in the history books."

"But history books are being rewritten," I say, "old ones burned. Or not even published. Whoever controls the publishers controls the books. It's all about control."

"Control is a neutral word, Fritz. Just as parents control a child to see it comes to no harm, a government protects its citizenry. You think control is a bad thing, but I say it is necessary, especially for an unruly child who doesn't know how dangerous life can be. We control to protect."

I regard her, suddenly seeing a stranger.

"Life is precious; it's beautiful. My life. Your life. The difference is you don't get to decide how I live my life. And I don't have control over yours. We are free. All of us. Individually. As families. Nothing gives you the right to control us."

Her face breaks into a huge smile, like I've chosen the winning clue in a game, or I made the wrong move and now she can sweep down triumphantly and take my last piece.

"I was elected," she announces coolly. "It's what the people want. Simple. I give them what they want: a parent's authority, a mother's love, a father's guidance. And a big sister to protect them. We have thrived under my leadership. Yes, we control everything but that's the key to our success: assuring everyone is working efficiently, that the city – indeed, the state – runs productively."

My face tightens as my heart beats faster.

"What *is it* about control?" I bark. "What *is it* about controlling people that you political types like so much? I doubt a parent gets a thrill from disciplining the child. It may be a necessary task but not one they want to perform. I never liked scolding my children when they did wrong, but I did it. It wasn't about controlling them. It was teaching them."

"Quite true. We don't *control* – as you say it in that sneering tone – as punishment. It's guidance. It's what we do for the greater good. To educate. And, if required to stop a downward fall, we catch you, we rehabilitate you. Then we welcome you back into society where you may pick up your tasks and perform your due measure of work. We are not oppressing you, or anyone, but guiding you to help form a more ideal society."

"Oppressor versus oppressed," I say with a meager groan. "How about the people who don't want to play that game? Who only want to be left alone?"

"We have to do this. What choice do we have? Nobody wants to return to the cruel world we had before that medical emergency. It's for the best. We still have a way to go. It will take time – and we had the set-back of that so-called 'pandemic' and the hardships that followed. It was fortunate that situation allows us to rebuild almost from a clean slate with a view to creating an ideal society. We have great plans. We have more to do. Much more."

"Like what?"

"Oh, we don't have to get into all of that now. Suffice to say the data chip problem has been resolved. Then we finally will be able to put them in every citizen and better serve them. Our data collection will increase exponentially. That is only the start to the next phase: have better health monitoring, smoother financial transactions, law and order, improved housing protocol, secure voting, and you can have access to your own personal music. This 'control' will enable us to build our Ideal Society."

"Yes, well, control is everything. Isn't it?"

She crosses her arms over her chest, done with me. "Do you have any questions now?"

I've known what I would ask since she started:

"Who had my video removed and ordered copies destroyed? Who had me arrested and sent to rehabilitation?"

A grin cuts across her face. "Haven't you figured that out yet?"

+   +   +

With the two hunks of womanhood guarding me, it makes it difficult to see where the governor goes when she steps out of view. Noticing my consternation, one guard, the smirking woman, takes a half-step to allow me to peer to the side of the room. The governor stands by a panel, presses a button there, and speaks into a microphone.

"Bring a medic," she says sadly. "Send in Barbara, too. And get a fresh coverall in his size. Something gray. And boots. The whole get-up. Prepare the documents. He's being released."

She turns, makes a face as though not expecting me to see her.

"Your paper garment has shredded too much," she says, affecting disgust. "I can't stand to see your 'dingle toy' through the gaps."

She comes back to me as the smirking guard moves in front of me again, keeping her thick arms ready to grab me if I get up.

"I have said too much." She sounds defeated. "Or perhaps not enough. Yet I think these facts will serve to convince you. I am not your sister. I am not a member of your Baumann family. As long as you remember that, and cease in your 'fantasizing', let's call it, I am inclined to let you go about your daily tasks unimpeded. Everything back to the norm, as it were. I still worry, though. You have a way of obsessing on an era best left to the scrap heaps of history."

I nod in agreement. I will accept that. I will keep to myself, be an ever-quiet cog in a mechanistic system, going about my daily tasks. The streets need to be kept clean. Maybe I'll win another award, meet someone new to distract me. Life will go on.

"Obviously, you must keep this information to yourself as the main condition of your release. Or, better yet: forget it. Except for the basic theme I've expressed to you: *nothingness*. I have nothing in common with you and your family. No relation or connection to Isla but what I've shared. Let that be your daily mantra. I will have my assistant share your 'fantasy' issues with your counselor, and he will fashion a program to instill a mantra into your subconscious mind. Then forgetfulness shall be automatic. A substantial pain will arise whenever you think of your fantasy."

And Life will go on, just as cold and gray as before.

"Thank you," I mutter in disrespectful tone.

A guard raises her hand to slap me.

"Enough," the governor intervenes. The guard lowers her hand. "What are we going to do with you, Fritz?"

I gaze up at her, checking if I am allowed to speak.

"Go on," she says. "What do you have to say?"

With a pursing of my lips, I place the words in the right order: "More than anything, I just want to leave. Let me out of the city. I promise never to return."

"Ah, yes. That way, you shall never bother us again. Is that it?"

"Yes."

"That's all? Isn't there anything else you want?"

"Yes."

"And that is?"

"I want Eden to go free. If she is in trouble because of me. Wipe her record clean and let her go. Thirty-nine, too. Might as well. I don't care. Clear their records, too, the people who spoke against me.

I hate for people to get in trouble because of me."

"That's an excellent attitude." She gives me a half-hearted smile. "Fine. We shall strike the negative elements related to you from the records of everyone who spoke against you."

"Thank you."

The door at the rear of the room, which I can only hear, opens and shuts. Footsteps of several people entering, stepping across the concrete floor, coming up behind me.

The governor addresses them as they stand in a neat half-circle, giving them instructions.

"Barbara will see to your exit," she tells me, gesturing at the woman who tormented me earlier. "I only wished for you to be out of the way. 'Out of the way' is all I said to her. Remove the offending materials and assure he doesn't go blabbing his lies. Yet Barbara here, Sixty-nine, had her own ideas of what that meant. We are not cruel – not intentionally. We want citizens to be satisfied with their lot in life. Lots are good, you see. Now she will have a new lot. She will see to your comfort. That should be punishment enough. I have other things to do, so you may enjoy Sixty-nine for a while. Then, as they like to say in the South, the balance shall be restored."

"They don't actually say that in the South."

"So you believe," she says with a laugh.

But who can know? Times have changed. It's getting confusing.

"I will never ever think or say anything ever again," I pledge, not hiding my sarcastic tone very well.

The governor lets out a long sigh, perhaps too tired to rebut me.

"Beware, Fritz. There will always be someone watching you. For now that's all we can do. In the future, we hope to have total control over everyone, what they do and what they think. That is the best way to have an Ideal Society. Like a well-run farm. For now, we can only persuade people into correct actions and appropriate thoughts. We can only threaten and prompt, cajole or tease them, entice with the right bribes. Like we did with you. Like we will do with you for this final time."

I look up at her, making my face as hard as a stone monument to the victims of the ten-year pandemic.

"Thank you...*Bobbie*."

"I hope never to see you again, Fritz."

With a haughty turn, shoulders extra-sharp, the gray lady takes a step to the side door. She pauses as if thinking of more to say, then doesn't. A staff member opens the door and she goes through, as if entering the real world from a bad dream.

19

RANK & FILE

SIXTY-NINE STRIKES a handsome pose, sitting on the side of the sofa in her official undergarments of granite gray in the unit I've been assigned. She isn't unattractive; just looks too much like my sister, with her hair in the grayish bob and that gray prison-guard-esque uniform, trying to imitate her boss. That is a turn-off.

I'm sure I am less than she desires, too.

The sex is awkward, she being several years older than me and my former interrogator. I wanted to hurt her for that, naturally, yet being together in her unit, I felt bad for her. She never tortured me physically beyond making me sit on that stool, tied up. It was all Q and A. Just a hopeful woman dedicating her career to our Madame Governor. But that is the official order, so we comply as best we can. We make sure the camera sees us in action, for the record, but we agree to fake most of it.

"I don't regret it," she says after a couple weeks have passed, no longer bothering to covering herself. "I was following orders."

I examine her mature yet fairly fit body, seeing her as she once was. Her file says she ran track and threw a javelin in her youth. She caught the governor's eye at a sports gathering, was invited to join her staff. First job: advisor to the Health & Fitness Council.

"She's a tough woman to disobey," I say after another silence.

"I'll do it if you want it." Her tone drips sadness. "It's supposed to be degrading for me. I know it could be worse. My punishment, such as it is. Cameras will confirm my compliance."

"Actually, I don't want it."

I turn to her, feeling silly in the small underpants I was given, with the official State logo in front like it's marking the cut of meat's grade. My leg brushes against her thigh.

"That's fine," she says, her voice clammy. "Wait for the beep."

"What I want to know is: Where's my tuba? And the notebooks my grandfather wrote. And the one my mother wrote in. And that journal from my ancestor. What did you people do with them?"

She seems to cheer up, getting an easy question.

"The tuba is safe, put in a museum," she says. "The Musical Arts Museum, at Sixty-fifth and Broadway. It's been refurbished and will be well-tended, I assure you. The centerpiece of a display of metal instruments from the olden days."

"Because they're all so quaint?"

"We can't fault them for making such contraptions. They needed music to get through the days. Times were tough back then. We can make music with our machines now."

"But it's not the same. We have to *play* the instruments for ourselves. That's the trick."

"You can see your tuba there any day the museum is open."

"But I can't get it back?"

"No, it's part of the State collection now." Her face pales. "If you were to steal it, then you would be in serious trouble. I'm giving you a warning. Don't think of doing that. Cameras everywhere."

"I believe you. At least it's in a good home. Promise me they will never smash it and melt it for some other use."

"I can't speak about the future. Maybe one day museums will be a thing of the past, too." She giggles at her pun. "I mean, for now it's an oddity. Years from now, who can say? They may go collecting up scrap metal for use in other things. You and I will be long gone."

"Long gone," I echo. "There's a happy thought."

"We need to think about the future, beyond tomorrow's tasks."

"But what about my daughter? I promised the tuba to Maggie."

"I'll make a note." She reaches for her tablet, taps some buttons. "The museum will contact her when they no longer wish to display it, or when she asks for it upon reaching adult age."

I sigh. "Now I've fulfilled my obligation to Mother."

"Your mother?" She flashes a smile, as though wishing she had a mother like mine. "She's gone and yet you feel the obligation to obey her. Interesting...."

"A promise is a promise," I respond, and we sigh in concert. She told me before she doesn't know who her mother was. Or her father. Records were lost during the period of lawlessness. She was rounded up like other children and put into an orphanage, fed by the charity of Chester's Field.

"So where will you go?" she asks, disdainfully. Seems as though she might want to go with me, anything to get out of the city herself, but only depending on the destination I name.

"South," I say and get no reaction from her. Probably not a good destination. "Where are my notebooks? Destroyed?"

"Oh, no. They're in the City Archives. It's a warehouse for paper materials. Some are displayed for public viewing. Like a museum. I believe some of yours are on display."

"Those notebooks are displayed? How? I thought they were full of lies and nobody should read them."

"Most people can't read today. Only those who need to read to do their jobs. You and I are from the old school."

"Why display them? Trophies to Madame Governor's regime?"

"Oh, no. Don't say that. *As you know*, they tell a fanciful tale of life in the wilderness. It's literature. Works of fiction. People in the olden times made-up stories to entertain themselves as they sat by their campfires. Some of them remembered the old script and wrote the stories in notebooks. See? Here are examples. They're historical artifacts, so they are on display."

I try to imagine a group of school children staring down at the notebooks, opened to a pair of sample pages, the handwritten script unable to be deciphered, and I smile. Grampa Sandy is famous.

"And I can't get them back?"

She gives a curt nod. "Correct. State property now."

"And that leather-bound journal of my ancestor?"

"Same. State property. Also in the Archive. Also on display, with a nice card giving translation of the German text."

"Can I go see them?"

"You won't steal them, will you?"

"I've read them many times in my life. I have them memorized. I could write out the text but I need those originals to prove anything I wrote from memory was true."

"But they aren't true. They're fanciful tales of hard lives in olden days. Good lessons on how to survive, perhaps, yet fiction."

"I won't try to argue whether they're true. I'm not allowed."

"That's true." She gives a little laugh.

"What my grandfather wrote in those notebooks is now just...."

"A testament to human creativity," she answers like a preacher. "Examples of the hysteria people attain in chaotic times. The ways we can survive and *did* survive. Now we have rebuilt society. And continue to built it upward. Build it right: as an Ideal Society."

"Ever the propagandist, aren't you?" It is close to a sneer.

"Testaments to the way we can fool ourselves," she adds. "A ten-year pandemic?" She breaks into laughter. "Lawlessness? Civil war? Servitude contracts? Well, *those* were real but not what most people think: mostly they were by mutual consent."

"Stop. Just stop it," I bark.

At my outburst, the stream pops on, showing a program already in progress:

"...the best we have for now. However, very soon we will be able to tag each citizen. So much convenience. No more carrying cards and risk losing them. Never having your cards get deprogrammed. A new wonder for our Ideal Society. This will allow for better safety. Emergency services can respond quicker and know how to handle a situation. Your location easily confirmed, your medical data readily available. Your work department notified of your status. Emergency services will be able to locate you in the city, and within a short time anywhere in the state."

"Off," I shout and the machine blinks off.

"You see we've been given the élite version which can be shut off before the program ends."

"I don't watch much anyway," I say, calming myself. "It's all the same propaganda."

"It is not propaganda," says Sixty-nine, sliding her hands down her legs. "It's information. People need to know. We must repeat it often so people remember. Most don't read. Haven't you noticed how more signs are pictures or brand logos? You see, literally everything about culture, language, the way society is designed, it's completely made up. It's all designed as confidence games and storytelling. The way you hold tight to your notebooks. They have meaning for you, or you think they do, like a child's fuzzy blanket, a token of comfort. Like that old tuba."

"Not for my comfort," I say. "For my children's comfort."

"If you care about something, it becomes something imaginary. Becomes fixed in your imagination. It's important. If you don't care about it, then it still becomes imaginary and is still important, just not to you."

"I'm supposed to pass on that tuba to my daughter."

She leans toward me, her head tilted at a curious angle, as if to see into my mind.

"The secret, however, is that we can just change these imaginary things whenever we want to. Make them better. We should. And we do. This is how we create our Ideal Society."

"More propaganda," I grumble.

A beep sounds somewhere and she seems to switch modes, gets flirty. She presses against me, eyes batting as if on cue.

"It's the way the world is now," she continues. "You have to accept it. Much as I have to accept this new lot, treating you like a domestic partner, giving you affection whenever that thing beeps."

She kisses me but I'm not ready for it.

"You must believe in our Ideal Society, too. You must believe in it or you will suffer. You'll be crushed. We have to work together if this is going to be good for us. Look at how we are required to make a purchase each day. That keeps the State in operation. And if no purchase is made, an equivalent amount is sent straight from your account to a charity service. Don't spend the required minimum, you obviously don't need that much in your account. What do you need 'money' for? To buy food. Yet we have a system where citizens are given the food they need, so there won't be a need for tokens or even accounts. Just your number, tied to everything."

Another beep. So I kiss her in return, for the camera.

"This is only the beginning," she says with agitation in her voice. "She has plans for more. A lot more." She goes on and on, naming all the wonderful schemes the governor has in mind.

I can see the world unfolding in front of my eyes, there in the stale air of the room, like a stage play I've seen on old videos. This is the same thing Mother used to complain about. She swore everyone from when she was a baby on up to adulthood was making her do what she didn't want to do. That made life miserable. I had three older sisters who tormented me, so how is that different? How did I turn out? Paranoid, easily offended, full of bile and spit, that's how. 'A nervous sort.' I sure don't belong in a cold, gray city.

"Fritz?" calls Sixty-nine, but I've gone down a hole and cannot reply. "Sixteen...? Are you well?"

No, I'm not. I can see only two ways forward: stay in this cold, gray city of oppression and total control, running like a well-oiled machine, or have a life of complete freedom, without structure and running into problems because of that freedom, yet everyone being satisfied with getting enough, getting by as best they can. I know that place. That was Mother's life in the marshes. She was happy there although she didn't have much.

"Fritz?" calls Sixty-nine. "What are you thinking?"

I hear her but I'm still deep in my trance and can't yet respond. Knowing I can leave and go anywhere, I vow that I will write a new notebook – if I can find one or two – telling this story, though not as fiction, of the way the world turns following the decades of sorrow. Or I could use a tablet, as everyone does. No writing, just tapping on sentence choices. I've seen my counselor tap out whole paragraphs, selecting words and sentences from lists on the side of the screen, the tablet predicting his writing direction and tone, offering him the words he is most likely to want.

I let out a sigh, disappointed at my plans. As soon as I tap out text, the system will read it and judge its correctness. Then it might wipe the text from the tablet, lose it in the data cloud. Anything electronic is subject to system approval. Words changed, sentences removed. I wouldn't be writing my story, I'd only be offering clues which the system would use to fill in the text. Everything would default to official language. No, I would have to write my story on paper, which only water or fire could remove from existence. But the world needs to know what is happening. I have to warn them.

"If it's not too late," I mutter, coming out of my trance.

+   +   +

Spring had sprung when I departed the Ministry of Questioning or whatever they call it in real life. I breathe in the cool, moist air, let the bright sun fall over my face, knowing how the previous weeks have changed my life. I feel like a different man.

I laugh to myself, trying to see my experience as a chapter in a book – like those paper books I read as a teen, the books describing oppression, fear, and death. The banned books. My life is banned. It's as though I've been reborn as someone who didn't exist a couple months ago. I'm starting again, much like I did after getting out of the rehabilitation program. I have the same name and number, but everything is different. Brighter.

I pass through a checkpoint and stroll about the nicer sectors of the city. When I seem to be walking too slow and thus appear to be loitering, having no destination, wasting time, a monitor catches up to me. He asks where I'm going.

I show my new status badge.

"Pardon me, sir," he says. "I didn't know. Please be on your way, and have a productive day."

"Thank you," I reply. "But I won't."

I am no longer required to produce anything, just 'live my life' as they say. I'm called a 'liver'; it's a joke only special people get. Not many of us can do that. Not even the elderly can enjoy their final years. Once done with their work they are whisked away to a quiet disposal. Yet I walk the streets unencumbered, smiling.

I stroll along in my new coveralls, a light gray with red trim. The cold, gray days of winter I spent delightfully indoors in a cozy cubicle of the State's official design are done. A new season of freedom awakens me. I dare to pass the Department of Social Order, impressed by the huge ornate columns I never got to see while I was in residence.

Further down the long avenue, my ears catch the song of a bird, perched on a branch of the tree that provides shelter over our lunch table in the park. Birds are rare these days, considered a nuisance in the city and taken down by bird watchers. I pause to stare at the winged creature, so oblivious to its fate. I listen to its message: *Go south, young man, before it's too late.*

Sitting at the table, I feel nothing of my previous times sitting there, consuming food boxes with Twenty-four and other workers. I regard the camera high on the nearby post, remembering how it had been repaired just before I was arrested. So I raise my hand, show a selected finger to the camera and grin. Nothing they can do to me. I have my Special Pass.

One day I happen to pass Thirteen, wearing her silver bodysuit, on her way to work. I say "Hello" and she glances at me, replies with a stiff "Hi" and never slows. I have to smile as she goes. Everything is back in balance. From my new status I can observe everything objectively. I can analyze all I see and offer opinions.

Special is a category of citizenship. It comes with benefits, like a new, larger unit. That's Barbara's. I settled in and felt comfortable. I leave some items out to aggravate her, never picking up my clothes or putting the used dishes in the cleaning machine. I often skip a shower. She's supposed to be annoyed by me.

I ask her about getting my belongings from my old unit.

"There's nothing there. Cleaned out," she informs me.

We rest from another dirty deed she is required to perform, the beeps prompting us at each stage. It is unpleasant for both of us, but without the camera documenting her compliance, she could get into big trouble. So I help her obey.

"Other than the tuba, notebooks, things like that, you don't own anything," she says. "Not even the coveralls the state has awarded you: gray with a red strip down the sides and red epaulets to mark your status. Anything else you need we can easily get for you. All new things. You can enter any shopping emporium with your new status. You can eat freshly prepared food at a café, too." Then she pauses, frowning. "I used to be able to do that. Go in those places. Before I was assigned as someone's helpmate."

"Helpmate is an important job," I say to encourage her.

"We both know it's my punishment," she sneers.

"Don't fret." I give her bottom a playful slap. "You're doing fine. Top marks. Only thirty-five days left on your contract."

"So you live here now, in this unit that was mine."

She has her own room, can do as she pleases except when she is doing things for me. I live the life of a king – no, actually more like a prince in my small castle.

"When my contract ends," she speaks up, "you will be assigned a proper partner, I suspect, suitable for the breeding program. Your report indicates superior genes. As well as you having three healthy human products. Considering your age, you are granted one last opportunity. You've earned a pension, thanks to your cooperation."

She flashes a frown, as though she's required to say it.

"Still cooperating," I intone.

"I'm serious," she says. "You should be, too."

"I don't think I can handle another 'proper partner' suitable for a breeding program."

"The governor has granted you a new residence. I'm sure you'll love it. You can move in after we complete my service contract. Not many citizens attain this status without having membership in the government or captains of industry. They hate providing for anyone who isn't contributing something in our Ideal Society."

"But I provide careful observation. And critical analysis."

Looking around the huge bedroom, from a bed large enough for a small orgy, I nod in acknowledgement of my situation. My big sister has some affection for me, after all. Or some regret, the things she did to me as a child, things she let happen to me as an adult. I still didn't believe the story she gave me. My mother wouldn't lie about a daughter she birthed. I was confused but tried to put it aside.

"There is a provision," Sixty-nine told me during our meeting to discuss my new status, "whereby you could earn credits becoming a monitor. But 'undercover', as they say. Listen to people and report to the office. Like various people did for you."

"For me, huh?" I shook my head ponderously. "I wouldn't want to be responsible for putting people away for minor infractions, or for misspeaks, or deeply held opinions. I wouldn't want to be rewarded for that. Why, once I see that informing on others gets me rewards, I would inform more vigorously, just make up infractions to get more rewards. You see? But that wouldn't be right. An informant could get addicted to informing, you know." I had to take a breath, getting excited. "Until the people you inform on all confront you, that is, either in court or an interrogation room, or else in your dreams. I wouldn't want that."

She smiled at my rebuke. "There are many choices in your new status. I can advise you."

Beeps, drawing me back to the present. Time has passed. A show of affection is required, even a fake one. We kiss.

I don't work. Retirement, they call it. I recall how my sister Amy called our mother's lazy life in the marshes her 'retirement'. In the North, anyone who reaches sixty-six must cease work, then welcome an officially sanctioned death. It seems you can get your reward in an Ideal Society, but not too much.

Yet I am special. My new pension is eight times that of my old allotment. I can leave some of it in my account for a rainy day, when people don't go shopping so stores lower prices on everything. Yes, I can go shopping, enter shops where I was previously turned away for lack of sufficient status. I buy nonsense items I don't need, just to show everyone I can buy them. I let them wrap up each item in fancy paper & gold ribbons. I carry my purchases in large bags with the shop's name emblazoned on them. I want everyone to know I'm special.

And I have Barbara at home as my helpmate. Sweet Sixty-nine. I feel bad having her there. I told her she wasn't a very good interrogator, that she should read a few books to get ideas. She said she had; that made her take my casual suggestion in a bad way. Besides, she won't be working as an interrogator – or as personal assistant to the governor – any longer. She's starting a new life, as well, poor gal. When her contract with me expires, she'll be a rank and file office worker somewhere.

A buzz alerts me to a face popping onto the screen of my tablet. Dr. Richards is asking me why I've missed two appointments. That could be serious. But I'm more in awe of the two-way communication possible using my new tablet which is available to élite members. He got the report on my 'meeting' and has designed the treatment. I'll have to come in soon.

Sixty-nine sits up, letting the sheet fall, and crawls up behind me on the bed. She wraps her arms around me and kisses my cheek, acting like a lover. My counselor sees her act, says he understands the reason I've skipped sessions.

"Hi, Dicky," she says to the screen as she claws my bare chest.

"Nice to see you," he responds like he expects her to be here.

They chat a minute while her nails dig into my chest.

Then Dr. Richards says something odd.

"It's supposed to be a gray day," he says in a flat tone. "Might be storms. Better prepare for lightning."

"That's good advice," Sixty-nine replies. "I will."

Dr. Richards seems satisfied. Sixty-nine waves her hand and the screen blinks off.

"How do you know each other?" I ask.

"I interrogated him before," she says. "But that was years ago."

She drops back, head hitting pillow, and pulls the sheet over her chest. She draws a frown upon her face, like I'm not acting right. It almost seems as if I've come to serve her, but we know the truth. It's whatever the eyes behold, isn't it? We laugh together.

I study her, this helpmate assigned to me. We gradually worked out our roles, awkward as it was. Like we were this old married couple living together but having no affection for each other. I have little for her to do. Food is delivered but she sets it up, makes the dinner look pretty, and sits across the table from me and tries small talk to varying degrees of success. We usually draw out the dessert time, hesitating getting to our next obligation.

Then we do what is required of her contract, make it as gentle as possible. We make sure the camera sees our effort so she gets credit for complying. Sometimes, when we finish, she will hold me in her arms, stroking my hair, caressing my shoulders like she loves me. I'm reminded of my mother comforting me when I was a little boy and feared something or got hurt playing stupid games. Always it was Mother who would soothe my wounded soul. But I had to get myself up if I fell. Only then would she gather me in her arms, pull me into her bosom until I felt one with her again. Then I would know there were no monsters that would come for us.

"You're just a frightened little boy," says Sixty-nine, "a boy who happens to be forty-two. Isn't that true?"

She has a point. I can feel vulnerable sometimes. Living the life I had will make a person fill with doubts, make them crave motherly comfort, always seeking protection. I'm sure anyone who grew up with Mother would be a wreck.

"Come here," she says. "Lay your head here."

I'd forgotten how wonderful it is to be held like that and have my hair stroked, like I am protected, like I am worthy of her attention, and never give a thought to anything more.

"I'm sorry," she moans after a while. She says that a lot.

"I just want to be sixteen again. Really sixteen," I sigh. "The age that's a perfect balance between freedom and responsibility."

She begs me to tell more lies. I let her call them 'lies' because I'm tired of arguing. Besides, the camera collects all our disagreements. We might return to our previous lives in minutes if we are found to be out of compliance. We take turns shutting each other up when we utter the wrong words.

"We rode on one of those electro busses, all the way down from Sorrow Mountain to some town near the marshes. On the way we stopped to go see the ferry landing where my mother was scared of monsters as a baby, right across the strait from the island where she was born. Traveling on that bus, I sat and watched the world go by. Literally moving through space and time into a new reality."

"That must've been a wonderful time," says Sixty-nine, coaxing me to reveal more, perhaps spill the old stories that will get me into trouble again and remove me from her unit, get me out of her life and restore her to her former position of prestige.

"Maybe it's time for you to tell me your stories," I say.

"Me?" Cute laugh. "I have no stories. Certainly not like yours."

"Come on, tell me something. Something naughty."

"Naughty?" She seems offended. "I've never done anything the slightest bit *naughty* in my entire life."

"I bet you have—"

"However." She glances around, noting the camera, then leans to me, puts her mouth to my ear. "There are stories I know, which I think would count as naughty."

"Oh? What's that?"

"I shouldn't say," she whispers in my ear. So I kiss her cheek to cover to our discussion for the camera's benefit. "I don't know. After what she's done to me – sorry for how I treated you – I don't want to go along with her schemes any longer."

"Schemes? I can believe anything she does is a *scheme*."

"With her husband being the president, she has a good deal of friends among the political class. As you well know."

"I don't know, but, all right, I'll assume that."

"I don't care any more. I'm willing to get in the way of her damn schemes because of how she treated me. I shouldn't be so vindictive, but.... I know they have plans. Once the vice-president dies, she will be sworn in by her husband as the new vice-president. Imagine this: Mister and Missus Wornall, a married couple standing as president and vice-president of the entire nation. And her nephews, the four of them and their sons, being in charge of food supplies. Matthew is already Secretary of Agriculture. She would have control over everything. She could cut off food to anyone – any city – that refused to go along with her schemes."

"That sounds serious," I whisper. "How is the current *veep* going to die? An illness?"

"No. Not an illness." She looks out of the corner of her eye at the camera, then kisses me. Parting, she mouths the word: *Ass-ass-i-na-tion*. Then she whispers: "She has people in place. It will look like an opposition attack. We blame the other side. Call for more police. When they're on the way home from a political rally. Then...."

"Then what?" I ask, seeing her face turn pale.

She takes a breath. "I don't feel so good all of a sudden."

"What's wrong?"

"I—I think it's...." A pain overtakes her. She grimaces. "Oh, dear. Not that. I—I thought it was just a rumor."

"What's a rumor?"

She sits up, breathing hard. "You better leave."

"Leave? Why?"

Her face tightens, her hand presses against her chest. "You have one minute to get out."

"What's happening?" I want to hold her but she waves me back.

"Get out! Now!"

So I go, wearing only underpants, out through the sitting room, opening the unit's door. An alarm has gone off somewhere. I leap out the open doorway as I hear – no, *feel* – a pulse rippling through the unit, like something has gone off miles away. But in my gut I know what's happened.

A team of officers is already rushing up the stairs, charging to the unit. They brush me aside as they bull their way in.

"What's the problem?" I call after them.

I get no answer so I sneak inside, make my way to the bedroom. An officer blocks me at the door. Over his shoulder I see Barbara flat on the bed, her chest unnaturally ballooned outward, like a tiny explosion has detonated in her heart and blown her ribs apart. Not much blood, just what's coming out of her mouth and nose.

The lead officer calls it in.

20

ISLAND HOLIDAY

I HAVE NOTHING TO KEEP ME from leaving this cold, gray city, so I do. I use my exit pass to go through five sectors to the main bus terminal and get a ticket for a front seat. I wait on a bench for the departure time, wearing my new pasty blue coverall like a proper gentleman. I don't look around for cameras; they're all around but such behavior would appear suspicious.

Soon I'm aboard, sitting comfortably with three food boxes in my bag and a ragged hardside book taken from Sixty-nine's unit, a dog-eared manual called *The Ministry for the Future*. She has a lot of the pages marked up, notes written in the margins. It seems important. Others riding the bus appear well-tended, able to buy tickets. The driver is a portly man who doesn't fit the model of good hygiene, but he smiles, welcomes us aboard, and off we go.

We pass through the outer ugliness of the city, spring unable to dress it up even a little, all the gray factories churning away. We go through farmland with its neat plots of different colored plants. We never see them in that rugged form, only the shape they take after processing. We cut through a wild forest, rise up and roll down hills, and everything is a page from my life.

I am going home. 'Down south', as they like to say with a sneer in the city. If only they knew what it was really like. The warmth, a steady sun, endless days running barefoot, all the fish and seafood you could ever want to eat. And there's your mama waiting to wrap her arms around you and smother you with kisses. You know the place: home.

Instead, it's my sister, Amy June, who greets me at the terminal when I arrive. She looks like the grandmother she is, gray hair and extra flesh on her frame. The smile is the same. We hug and it doesn't feel awkward this time. I can't believe she's still taller than me. We go to her tiny home in the town near the marshes.

"Howdy," calls her husband, Cory, bald and a little bent over at his age. Their kids are grown up – Casey and the twins, Dixie and Daisy – moved away with their own families but visit regularly, he explains. I'm welcome to stay as long as I like, but what are my plans, why've I come so far from the impressive capital city, I hear it's a lovely spring up there.

I answer their questions, try to remember Amy as a teen when I was little but can't. She seems like a completely different person. I am stupidly the same, feeling all the agitation from long ago return to me. But I try to act like an adult.

"You look good anyways," says Amy in a motherly tone. "City's done you good. Slimmed ya down."

I tell her it's from the hard work I do. She thinks I still work at the broadcast station. I can't tell her about my stay in rehabilitation or my street cleaning job. Somehow that confession would diminish me in her eyes. She's boasted about me to her neighbors.

"But I needed to get away for a while," I say.

"Well, here's nice a place as any for getting away."

I find a girl is staying with them. Eve has an awkward history but we've agreed not to talk about it. She's the daughter of LJ's wife Lori and LJ's little brother Raymond, looking more like LJ or his father, Big Joe, with that prominent chin. She comes out of a room that must be hers for a while and greets me. I do remember her, but she's all grown up after being born in the national park. We hug at Amy's prompting because we are all kind of related.

"Ya stayin' long?" asks Eve like she wants me to stay.

"I don't really know," and I don't really know.

"Cousin Fritter's come a long way," says Amy, "so let him catch his breath. Then you kin ask yer questions. After we's got supper."

"Please don't call me Fritter." I give a wry grin.

I ask about Grace and Hope, more of my half-sisters or cousins. I already know Faith ran off with Raymond, going out west. Amy says she got a letter from her a few weeks past and sends Eve to get it. Grace was working as a nurse in the military hospital in town last Amy heard, treating wounded soldiers from that war we never had – according to official history. I smile to myself. Grace transferred to a different hospital sometime back, unmarried and working hard.

"She's a real saint, she is," says Amy.

"Bless her," I respond. "It must be her calling."

"At least one of us doing good things," she says with a sigh. "It's hit or miss, what folks in this clan do."

"Every family is different—"

"I ain't done much more'an make some babies," she says.

"That's important," I counter. "Who else is going to carry on? You have Casey and her kids, and Dixie has two, right? Daisy has, I'm thinking, three? And one of them is a parent now, too, am I right?"

"S'pose so, but it's them doing things, not me."

"Mother once told me – that was when I interviewed her for the video – she said the most important thing she ever did was to bring life into this world. She said Grandma Hannah told her the next baby to come along might be the one that saves us."

Amy June nodded thoughtfully.

"Then there's Hope. Goes after ever' boy she sees. Met one fella," Amy says with a frown. "They got themselves in trouble, you might call it. She about died trying to birth that child but it didn't make it. They're a little west of here, trying again. She says all she wants to do is make babies, even after that bad try. And she don't care who the father is. Her fella long left for some Hispanic gal. Anyways, we don't need to talk about her."

Amy, like all big sisters, is now the matriarch of our family. She asks about my family, my work, my plans for the future. I try to give her a quick summary but she keeps drawing me out in her easy-going way, like Mother with those mannerisms. I get choked up and she gets up from her resting seat and hugs me again. Poor boy, what a time you've had, she coos into my ear before releasing me. I can't hold back, tell everything: going to rehabilitation, separating from

Sandra, being a street cleaner, then the strange sequence of events leading to me meeting the governor.

"How's she doing?" asks Amy.

"Oh, she's doing fine, I suppose."

Who am I kidding? She's ruining the whole state, I tell Amy and then have to explain.

I describe my weeks in the Department of Inconvenience, how I got a personal lecture from Madame Governor herself, our Missus Roberta Wornall, the wife of the president. She's done real well, all right, we agree.

"Thing is," I go on, "she kept insisting she wasn't one of us, not born from our mother. She rejects Isla. Of course she was a baby, so she couldn't know for certain, but I guess they indoctrinated her as she grew up."

"She didn't grow up much before we was having to leave," says Amy sadly. Cory brings her a glass of something brown. She gulps half down, sips the rest. "I was there, maybe not much older myself, me and Allie, coming from the National Park with them girls and women, then sold away, and we got Chesterfield. I know for a fact Mama spent her evenings with the mister, sometimes rough, if ya know what I mean. Then we was sent away, something Mama did or didn't do. We were still young then."

"I really don't know," I say. "She and I had different fathers, but had the same mother – according to Mother. She said I looked like my father. She was with you when you returned to the mountain. And I agree she looks more like her father. I saw pictures of him on some history streams and she does look like him. But her mother? That Mamie, his wife? Could she be?"

"That's all one big fat lie," says Amy, hiding a frown. One thing we never do is deny being a member of our clan. "I was there, me and Allie, when Bobbie was born. I mean, we wasn't right there in the room but I saw that baby within an hour of her being born. I know it was Isla, not Mamie, pushing out that baby after she had a big belly for months. Besides, that Mamie was older and sickly most the time. That's the whole reasoning for the mister to buy a girl to have his kids."

"So she's lying?" I regard my sister, her face hard, unexpressive for once. "I knew it. But I had to go along with her idea, just to get out of that place. They tried hurting me to get me under control but that didn't work, so—"

"Yer too contrary fer them, ever since you're a little fritter!"

"So they tried pampering me and I was starting to like it. After I promised never to mention her true story to anyone. But then they went too far." And I tell her about Sixty-nine and the small bomb in her chest. "That's what they do to people who say too much."

Amy sits smug on her seat, listening to me rattle on about all the problems in the city. I complain on and on. Finally she yawns.

"Sorry," I say.

"It's my nap time, is all. Not you, Fritter. I love havin' ya visit."

I leave her to nap, watch her shuffle over to the old bed she uses. I feel bad for her, me having a sturdy bunk in a small worker's unit in the city. The way her bed sinks when she lays on it makes me wonder which is better. A warm breeze wafts through the window and I have my answer.

This place was home; close to it, anyway. I would never go back, never again set foot in that cold, gray city. That thought makes my whole body relax, my muscles go slack. I want to tell Amy my decision, but she's already started snoring.

Eve stands there in a plain dress, like it's been worn by a lot of girls before her. Her long brown hair lays uncombed. She gives me a look like she hopes I might entertain her. She hands me the letter Faith sent. Looking at Eve, I wonder how she takes her awkward origin. She was born after her older sister Faith left with her dad Raymond. So they've never met. Feeling a pang of sorrow for her, I put the letter in my canvas bag with the few things I still own. The letter has been here a while so it can wait a little longer.

I step out, saying I'm going to see Mother's old shack.

Knowing the way, I happily walk the route, breathing the fresh air, seeing the growth of the town as I go. I cross the highway, find the trail and follow it back through the trees and hanging moss, passing in and out of shadow, all the way out to the marshes, the sea of grass as vast as I remember it. I follow the trail to the rickety foot bridge and cross over to Mother's isle. The weathered shack still stands but leans a bit. Nothing left inside the shack but some trash. I feel something, though.

The way Mother used to sit here – or there, or on the porch – the way she looked out over the marsh as though her parents' spirits waited for her. She always blamed herself for their deaths. Some days it seemed as though she was eager to join them. As a teen, that worried me. Even after LJ came down, reuniting with her a while, she would have that look, that sense of doom, the way the evening comes on gradually then suddenly. She got worse after LJ died. And her kids grew and left. She sat alone at her shack, maybe regretting everything she'd done in her life but having time to remember the few joys she had.

Like me, coming to her unexpectedly but still welcomed, her last child, then tolerated for several years until I, too, left her.

I miss you, Mama.

A strong sensation begins to overwhelm me. I need to get away from the world.

I strip down on the sand, having no shorts to wear, and step into the water. Cooler than I expect in this spring afternoon, I wade on in, walk out several steps, feet squishing in the muddy bottom, then swim a ways out to another isle. I catch my breath, rest a while, and swim back to Mother's isle.

Eve stands there beside my pile of clothes. She waves at me.

"I can't come out with you standing there," I call, keeping myself down in the water.

"Don'tcha fret, Uncle Fritter," she calls back. "I seen it all. Fact, I seen lot more'n that already. Boys 'round here like ta show off."

"Please, call me Frank."

"You steppin' on outta there n ya sure be frank, lemme tell ya."

I have to agree. Grinning, I wade out, shaking water off myself, wringing my hair. I pose with no shame, as the memory of running naked through the forest as a toddler with my sisters chasing me returns to my mind.

Eve smiles like she sees something new and different, looking me up and down, smacking her lips.

"Ya shore is a skinny thang," she says with a giggle.

Dropping to the sand to let the sun dry me, I tell her of my time in rehabilitation, then my arrest and interrogation, the liquid meals I got once a day. It's easy to lose weight living like that.

"Well, that ain't really livin', more like existin', is all," she says.

She takes a seat on the sand beside me, a good space between us. I lay back flat, staring at the sky. She rolls on her side to face me, reaching to straighten her dress. I let out a long sigh, as though all my troubles have disappeared, left in the marsh waters.

"Why ya really come back here, Frank?" Her sweet voice adds to the marsh soundscape.

"I suppose it's because this is my home. My real home. I should never have left. Not when I did. Nothing has worked out since I left. Oh, it was good for a while. I got married, had kids. But a cold, gray city can wear down anyone, turn you into a mean and ugly thing, something less than human."

"Less'n human? What ya mean?"

I look over at her and she grins at my attention. "I mean, if you are put into a box with a lot of other people, you get to fighting, and then everything you do is for survival – trying to survive instead of enjoying your life."

"Gotcha," she says. "Kinda like with crawdads."

"Some people, by hook or crook, get to the top of that box and they think they're better than everyone who didn't get to the top. They start deciding how things should be for everyone. The lower down in the box you are, the heavier your life is. You get smashed."

"Shore wouldn't wanna live in no box."

"Out here, you don't have to." I take a big breath, let it out slow. "My mother had the right idea. I used to think she had nothing to do here, sitting in her shack. But she did everything already. Doing nothing was a reward for her."

"A *ree*-ward?"

"That's right. She'd just sit and stare out at the marshes like she was looking for someone. Waiting for her last day."

"Well, ain't that sad."

"Yes...sad. But that's what I remember." I regard Eve a moment.

"You're lucky in that way. I know you've had a rough time, too, but it looks like you came out fine."

"Ya think so? Really?" She grins, acting coy. "Amy says I'm one the purdiest gals 'round these parts. Smart like dickens, too. I know all the letters and numbers. Can read, too. What d'you think?"

She has that prettiness a teen girl attains at a certain age, being somewhere between childish innocence and adult seductiveness.

"I think you've grown up fine," I tell her in all honesty.

"Ya think?" Her grin widens. "You maybe wanna be with me?"

I startle then sit up quickly. "What're you saying?"

"I'm old enough," she says, sitting up. "And you ain't too old."

I laugh, mostly to break the mood. It is getting too real.

"I am old enough. Old enough to be your dad or—"

"My uncle. Only you's not any o' them. We ain't related."

"We *are* related," I say a little too loud. She cringes. "Raymond's my brother, or half-brother. Same mother, different father. He's your father, anyway, so that makes me your uncle, for what it's worth. And you're rather young."

"But we ain't really related," she says, playing with her hair.

"But...."

"But what, Uncle Fritter?" She bats her eyes. "You game?"

"It's not a game, Eve."

I let out a sigh, thinking of Eden. My lucky Thirteen turned out to be a set-up to get me in trouble. The stark image of her on that bench with Thirty-nine blasts through my head. I automatically look around for cameras.

"Whatcha lookin' fer? Nobody gonna see us."

"Cameras," I reply. "It's a habit you develop when you live in the city. Cameras everywhere, always watching, even inside your home. I hate that. And I sure won't be going back there."

"Well, there ain't no cameras for twenty miles o' here."

"That's good."

"So you kin kiss me if ya wanna. I don't mind. That's all. Don't gotta do no more if'n ya don't wanna. And I won't tell nobody."

"You sure? That's all?"

She nods. "Shore."

"Then don't call me 'Fritter'."

"I won't, Frank. Now kiss me. Kiss me like I'm yer girl."

Expecting to give her only a simple brotherly peck on the cheek to let her feel she's won, instead I find her hands clasping my face firmly and her lips pressing hard against mine. Her breath is bitter. She eventually lets go and I have to catch my breath.

"Boys in these parts, they all stupid," she laughs. "Nothing but stupid boys. Not like you, Frank."

"Believe me," I confess, gazing out over the marsh, "I've certainly done my share of stupid things."

+   +   +

"Two letters, it turns out," says Amy when I get back to the house, entering before Eve who is several steps behind me so as not to look suspicious. "That one from Faith. It's two months old. This one just arrive few days ago. Looks like it's from Sandra."

"Sandra?" That surprises me. I hadn't told her anything – not about my interrogation, not about staying in Sixty-nine's unit. She didn't know I was heading south. I figured she was done with me, so what would be the point?

"Yep, Sandra. Yer wife." Amy snickers.

I remind her how we officially separated because I was sent to rehabilitation. She and I agreed it was best for the children to not be associated with a criminal like me. I didn't think she cared about me any longer.

"She musta figured you be coming back here if you wasn't at yer address in the city."

"I guess so."

Eve slips in behind me, rushes to her room without a word.

"That girl," says Amy, "growin' up wild like Hope done. Chasin' boys. Gotta put her in church school to save her. But we ain't got no money for that."

Opening the letter from Sandra, I feel more curious than fearful. I read the one-page folded paper, handwritten. If she'd used a tablet to compose the message, the system would have a record of what she wrote. Clever that she handwrote it and slipped it into a deposit box instead of giving it to a courier who might have detoured it to some special office.

"Well? What she say? Good news? Wantcha back now?"

I read.

Noise outside, then a rush of footsteps on the porch, interrupts my reading. The door bursts open and there is my other 'sister' – actually my aunt – Allie with her wife, Cathy. Both have gray hair, a few extra pounds, and are acting drunk, hanging on each other.

"Is that...?" Allie cries out at the sight of me. "Fritter? That you?"

Grinning in embarrassment, I nod. "My name's Frank now."

"Well, okey-dokey, Fritter, whate'er ya like." She laughs loudly, then comes up and gives me a one-arm hug while tapping my cheek with her other hand and planting a sloppy kiss on my forehead.

"He's lots skinnier than when he was little," says Cathy, looking me over. "What I recall anyways."

"Gotta fatten the boy up, I reckon," says Allie.

"He come down to get away from the city for a while," says Amy. "Needs some rest and relaxing, so leave him be."

"Rest n relax, huh? He never gonna get it here." More laughter.

They continue their conversation, half shouting, half laughing over nothing I understand or care about.

I return to the letter.

Sandra is frantic. She'd gotten a message from our sons' school. New policies are going to be implemented. I'm alarmed by what Sandra writes. That is our evil governor's mad plan.

"I have to go back," I declare, breaking up the sisterly party.

"But you just got here," says Amy.

"He done got enough of you already," says Allie.

"There's trouble there. I need to get back to deal with it."

"What's wrong?" asks Amy.

I see Eve peek out of her room at the sudden silence.

"My sons are in danger," is all I can say.

I glance at Eve, show her my serious face. She pouts, withdraws into her room. I guess she understands that I'm leaving, no matter that we kissed on the sand. I might come to regret that. Sometimes

Life is bigger than a kiss. But I'll promise to come back soon and set things straight.

21

TRANSFORMATION

LEANING AGAINST THE WINDOW, sitting on the last seat on the bus as it heads north, I think of my brief visit home. Maybe the marshes are not the best place for me, after all. But I hate the cold, gray city. Yet the warm, breezy marsh is full of bad memories, has a perpetual melancholy I can't overlook.

As I ride along, ignoring the forests and fields, mountains and streams, through run-down towns, I get out Faith's letter. It's folded like the others: diagonally like a gift. She's always had a knack for making pretty crafts. I remember a wildflower wreath she made for me. Then my sisters said I looked like a girl with it on my head so I smashed it and Faith cried, seeing the crushed flowers.

My throat tightens, thinking of that. I was four, she maybe six.

Like past letters, she describes life in Skinner Canyon, a small homestead of refugees from the South. She has a good style, the way she tells stories of people there. Then she gets to the most important sentence of the letter: how Raymond died, killed in a gun fight with another man. People came to her to decide what to do with his body, thinking she was his wife. She confessed they weren't ever married officially, so the folks could do what they wanted with the body, so they chose to burn it. The soil out there is hard to dig, being cattle country. They made a hole anyway, put the ashes in it.

That news brings a tear. At the end she adds an invitation for me to visit. She says it really isn't a bad place. She has a spare room in her cabin, and my kids could play with hers. All this time away and she still wrote letters to Mother's address. I feel I have to write back, so I dig in my bag but find no pen and paper. I promise myself to respond after I deal with my family's problem.

I arrive at the main terminal, just outside the city, and take the city tram to meet Sandra.

She hugs me, cries on my shoulder as she holds up the notice. Important messages are printed on paper to be sure it isn't missed when sent to tablets or streamed; not everyone has tablets or access to streams. I read the notice as she holds it up. In official-sounding language it states that the policy to reduce the population will begin soon, beginning with 'excess males' in families having more than two children. I mutter the sentence and Sandra bursts into sobbing.

According to the statement, our son, Frank, is unaffected, being our first-born. They allow our daughter, too, being a daughter. It is our son James who is at risk, being a second son. The options for him are not good.

My first thought is how this notion must be a joke, something to get people in line, make them take government edicts seriously. In the past some notices were presented in an official manner but the text actually stated nothing important, as though they were tests of our attention. I wonder how they can dare to propose such a thing. Wouldn't parents rise up and protest?

"Not many," says Sandra. "Most of them are willing to go along with anything the governor says."

Maggie bumbles into the room, in a bad mood from seeing her mother upset.

"Daddy, you came back," she says in an unimpressed tone.

Sandra leans down to hug her. "Your daddy's home. Everything will be fine now, sweetie."

"We're going to do what we can," I tell Maggie.

Sandra is still upset and I pat her shoulder.

We are trying to calm ourselves when the screen pops on with an announcement of the governor's speech about the new policy, to be delivered at the same school our sons attend. I have to read the notice again. The main points are the same as the announcement: expressing the need to 1) reduce overall population to a manageable level, manageable meaning correlation to food supply and housing, 2) keep the balance between female and male approximately equal for the new breeding program to be implemented within a few years, 3) to assure males will not dominate this Ideal Society, females will remain in charge of most offices, departments, agencies, government entities in order to afford the greatest compassion and productivity, and 4) so-called 'extra males' will be given two options going forward.

"It doesn't make any sense," I say, looking at Sandra.

"It makes sense," she counters, "but not for *our* son. Not him. He's such a sweet boy. I don't want any option for James."

"I know, I know."

"What will we do?" she cries.

Maggie sits beside her, takes her hand. "Don't cry, Mama."

"We have to get him out. Out of that school. Both of them," I say. "Surely we can withdraw them without any trouble."

"I think we're locked in. We paid the fee. They have to finish the academic year. Rules."

"No," I say firmly. "We must get them out right now."

She wipes her eyes. "*Then* what will we do?"

"We may need to leave the city." I shake my head, taking it back. "We *must* leave this city. There is no other choice."

"Choice?" She tries to chuckle, fails. "Only what the doctors call 'desensitization' – a kind of castration by chemical infusion – or full transformation, in essence becoming a female. But without the boy's consent. It's horrible!"

"Before I left, I heard of a few undergoing that transformation. I guess they thought they were meant to be the opposite sex. There was talk of that before the pandemic, too. I saw a stream about it. But that was their choice. But now—"

"Now they want to kill our boy!"

Maggie hugs her mother. "Don't cry. They won't kill him."

"Not kill him," says Sandra, "just make him wish he were dead."

"All right," I cut in, "we need to get them out of that school. Then we can think of what to do next."

Sandra sniffles back tears. "And I voted for that evil woman!"

+ + +

We discover that Sandra's pass has been turned off, she being the major parent. The authorities don't want parents showing up at the school to complain, I guess, so they deactivated their passes.

Using my special pass, I can go through four checkpoints. After walking much more than fifteen minutes, I arrive at the iron gate of the school where my sons receive their indoctrination: The Radcliffe School for Impressive Young Men. They are getting a lot more than we planned. This is the way a tyranny works is today's lesson. And to think I pretended to vote for that woman, because we all had to. The opposing candidate fell ill right before voting day and died. Our governor shed tears at her acceptance speech.

Other parents have gathered outside the gate. A few shout at the guards to let them in. But the guards, in their official-looking gray and red uniforms, remain nonplussed, amused by the ranting of the commonfolk.

"What's happening?" I ask a woman in the gathering.

"They won't let us in to talk to the headmistress."

"I suppose she'd be alarmed that anyone showed up."

"She's afraid, awright."

Inside the large compound stand several buildings, including the dormitories where students live, classrooms and sports facilities. It has everything a self-contained organization needs. We applied for our sons to attend because it is an élite school and they will survive this madness better if they graduate from such an establishment. We never thought of how much they'd depart from a straightforward education like Sandra got in the city.

"It's a different time," another man grumbles.

"What time is that?" I ask, thinking in metaphors.

"Time to tear this place down. That's what I say."

I look around our group, maybe twenty people. Not very many to tear down this place. The guards here have direct energy weapons, as though they guard a dangerous prison.

"It *is* like a prison," I mutter. Angry, I take a huge breath and shout: "Let our boys out!"

Others take up my cry, and we get loud.

"Let our boys out!"

A matron strolls slowly across the marching grounds to the gate, measuring her steps so as not to arrive too soon nor appear in any hurry to meet with us. Our shouting increases as she approaches. A guard steps up to the gate, shows his weapon, then moves aside as the woman halts several steps away from the gate. She wears the academic gown of the school: gray and red.

"Good morning," she speaks with practiced voice. We fall silent to hear what she has to say. "As you must know from the parental orientation, we do not allow intrusions outside of any ceremonial occasions. Even if you are parents of our students. It is a distraction to their education."

The crowd begins to grumble. The guard standing beside the old headmistress raises his weapon. Another guard moves to the other side of her.

"Please, please, parents," she calls out, holding up her hands as if having the power to calm an angry ocean. "There is not a thing to be worried about. Their education is proceeding according to the standard curriculum—"

"We want our sons!" shouts one in the crowd.

"Let us see our sons!" another cries out.

"We want to withdraw from this evil place," declares one man at the back of the group. "It's our right!"

"Let us remind ourselves," the headmistress speaks up, trying to remain calm. "As parents, you have approved the rules listed in the information packet. You have agreed to them. One rule is that all inquires and requests must be submitted through the official site, either by tablet or streaming service. None—"

"There isn't time for that," shouts one woman.

"They cut off my service," cries another. "So how am I supposed to contact the school?"

"I just want to see my son, make sure he's all right."

"Let us see our sons!" a few chant.

"If you fail to follow the rules," the headmistress continues, "we may have to dismiss your son from our program."

"Yes! That's what we want," shouts a man near me.

"If you break the rules," says the headmistress, "then your sons may be assigned to the military!"

"I just want my sons out of there," a woman calls.

"You can keep the damn fee," shouts another. "I don't care."

The headmistress raises both hands. "We can address your concerns individually. I have a list you can add your name to for an appointment. We can discuss—"

"Then you got our names for sending officers after us," shouts a woman up front.

"Let our boys out!" the chant resumes.

A guard hands a tablet out through the iron bars of the gate, and a woman at the front of the group takes it, taps a few times, and adds her name to the screen. A man takes the tablet next, passes it back through the group. When the tablet is pushed into my hands, I add my name. Knowing I have achieved special status, I think I'll be safe from retaliation. I might even get in sooner rather than later.

"Who are you?" asks another father.

I turn to him. "What do you mean?"

"Your number? Who are you? Who is your son here?"

"I go by Frank, not a number."

He laughs. "That's right. Gotta stay strong. Don't feed the beast and all that rot. I'm George – or Eighty-six, if you're counting."

"Nice to meet you," I say, and we shake hands, pausing to think whether anyone has sanitizer. We put our hands in our pockets.

"My son is Stewart – Twelve-forty."

"I have two sons: Frank and James. I forget their numbers."

We leave the gate area with the others. Everyone is willing to be called in later to discuss the situation. We agree it isn't likely the headmistress could meet with too many of us before the governor's speech. Following the rules at least shows we are agreeable.

"They hope we'll just go away," says George. "Would've been a lot more of us, but you know they deactivated a lot of parents' passes, so they couldn't get to the school."

"Yes, did that to my wife's pass."

"The ones that showed up live in this sector, like me. Don't need a pass to come here."

We sit down in a café not far from the school. I flash my badge at the doorman and he lets us enter. Inside, they are cooking real food, not just offering food boxes. I wave my fellow parent to a table.

"Civil discourse," says George, nodding.

We order our lunches and the boy tapping the tablet gives us a strange look, like he doesn't think we belong in the café. George is not in an official coverall but shirt and trousers. I'm wearing my old clothes from the south. I have no job so I am suspicious.

"If only we *could* have some civil discourse," George mutters as we wait. "They're happy to shut down any opinions we may have. Don't have the energy to debate anything. Don't want to have to come up with a good argument, or counterargument. I used to teach that stuff. That was back when they were starting to rebuild. They put me with kids twelve to fifteen. I taught them how to construct a good argument. Present evidence. The whole thing. They don't like having to put in that effort nowdays. Just take whatever the official stream tells them, never think what it means, never consider other views, never think for themselves. Got no brain for it now."

"You sound like one of those subversives," I say in a low voice, then add in a louder voice for the benefit of the café workers: "like on one of those streaming shows."

"I saw that show, too," says George, playing along. "A lot of awful acting but the message was sound: Big Sister will take care of us."

"Big Sister," I snicker, and our order-taker glares at me.

+ + +

As I suspected, none of the parents were able to go to the scheduled meetings. I was never contacted, nor was Sandra. Some of those who put their names on the tablet got visits by security monitors, and a few were taken away for additional questioning. Maybe they noted my special status and skipped over me. I don't know. But I didn't get to speak to the headmistress, either.

The stream continues to announce the governor's policy speech and finally that day arrives.

With no chance to address our concerns with the headmistress or with Education Department officials, the situation remains serious. I go beyond what may be wise and send a carefully worded message from my tablet to everyone in authority. It has to be done. Maybe they will revoke my special status for this infraction. Questioning their decisions? How dare I! But I need to save our sons.

Frank is not really in danger, being our eldest son, but I cannot trust this government any longer. I've learned that James has been selected with twenty others at the school for 'transformation' — medically change him into a female: a eunuch who can work but not reproduce. That is one option for him. The other option, as I read in literature sent to parents, is joining the military. But they would pump him full of extra hormones to ramp up his aggression, to make him fight ferociously. After that, because he would be too aggressive for our Ideal Society, he would be put down. No other choices.

James tried to contact me but I was out of range. He tried to let Sandra know what was happening. Already they started exercises in feminine behavior, making them wear dresses and act feminine, but James wasn't having any of it and got punished by disciplinarians. Parading the boys through an all-boys school put them at further humiliation, the safe boys teasing them without mercy. I heard this from George by way of his only son, Stewart, who is on the safe list.

I read a book or two in my youth about some of the weird things people would be doing in the future, as authors imagined back then. Old books can be so perverse. Now it *is* the future but, thankfully, not everything they described has come to be. But other things have been put into effect. Whatever anyone can think up and write down, someone will try to make happen. That's the danger of books, I realize. In my next breath I realize that's the reason they got rid of the unapproved books, or texts on stream, or videos.

I tell Sandra to stay home with Maggie. There could be violence. She asks what I'm planning to do. Just talk, of course. Using strong words. Reactions may be unpredictable, however. She understands and agrees to wait for news. Meantime, she can begin packing.

George agrees to help me get my sons out. We meet at that café again, get strange looks from the server guy, and go from there to the school. He knows the side gates, has the code for one of them. He manages to get a message to his son using coded language they've invented. The school's stream lets messages pass between parents and students but only at certain times of the day and are always monitored.

The school was built in olden days and was called a 'high school' serving both boys and girls with mixed classes. George said his grandfather attended classes here. Then a wall was built around the complex and the place housed POWs during the civil war – the one following the pandemic, not the older war. It was converted back to a school while I was living down south. The walls remain and got new locks on the gates.

"When the governor is giving her speech," says George, "we'll be free to get your sons out. Stewart's already let them know."

"Great! And thanks for your help."

"I may have only one son, so he's safe, but I stand for principle."

"All the guards should be tight around her so the outer gates won't likely be monitored."

"Cameras, but no guards." He gives me a sideways look. "But I got a little device here called a 'jammer'. Scrambles video signals."

Surprised, I ask him to explain it. He waves away my concern.

"They'll only see a snowy image. Then we can get away."

Sirens sound. I startle, thinking we are caught already. George laughs at my consternation.

"The Gray Lady's here," he says.

The governor's motorcade approaches: all those big gray vehicles humming along the avenue, flags waving. I hear a music machine playing inside the compound. The city has set up official flags along the route: somber gray field cut by a bold red diagonal. People stand outside to cheer and wave as the motorcade passes.

"Dumb sheep," George curses.

"...can be some of the tastiest meat for a festive dinner," I add.

We pass a long gray banner with red lettering set up along the avenue which reads: *Governor Wornall's Proclamation on Families*.

Sitting comfortably behind her tinted glass, the governor rides past us without a wave of greeting, dour-faced and thinking up new schemes. I'm glad she isn't really my sister – if she is to be believed.

George and I make our way past the crowd and down the blocks to the back of the school grounds, by the sports fields. Students have gathered in the front of the school, standing in formation like little soldiers to welcome the governor. We see no one around the sports fields. We check behind us, up and down the street. Cameras set at regular intervals, of course, but which ones are in operation? In this neighborhood, where there isn't much trouble and everyone likes the governor, the monitors have little to be concerned with.

We arrive at the side gate after walking slowly like we're out for fresh air, having approved conversation. We wear official coveralls so we fit in with other workers. Don't want to draw suspicion.

We act as though we see something strange over by the gate and have to investigate, leaving anyone looking out the windows of the houses across the street to wonder what it might be that caught our attention. George kneels and I stand blocking the view of him. He takes something out of his canvas work bag.

"Keep your back to the cameras," George says. "This is an old school trick the kids used to do."

He pulls out a pair of glasses. They are plastic and have a nose attached. Also a plastic mustache. Who would wear those? He urges me to put on the one he hands to me.

He opens the control box set into the brick wall beside the gate, which features a keypad for entering the code. He checks a few settings, hooks up the device he pulls from his bag. It looks like a small tablet but with two wires hanging down. He clips the wires to nodes under the keypad, pushes several buttons.

I worry it's taking too long. I worry accessing the keypad will set off alarms. A dark figure moves by the houses on the opposite side of the street. I expect a squad of officers to swarm us even as the gray overcast helps the evening arrive sooner.

"It either worked – give it a second – or we're about to be overrun by guards," says George.

I tense, waiting to be arrested. Making sure to keep my back to the cameras along the street, I give the plastic glasses a push back on my nose.

The gate clicks and George pushes it open. We rush through and he's careful to keep it from closing completely. We have to get out that way. He sets a stone on the ground to hold the gate open.

I follow George across the field, jogging to the gymnasium, and again deal with a keypad.

"Thankfully, they don't change codes often," he chuckles.

Frank and James don't share a room in the dormitories. Being different ages, they stay with their classmates, making it harder to get them. But they are in uniform in formation now at the front of the school as the governor's motorcade enters through the main gate and circles around them. To get them out, we will wait through the speech and grab them as they return to their rooms.

"When her speech is finished," says George, "they'll march back to the audience room. Some of the school's finest will get to meet the governor. They'll ask pre-approved questions. She'll give them pre-approved answers. It's a photo opportunity. Show the evil woman with some smiling youth."

"Sounds like her," I say. "I hope they don't photograph the boys in their dresses."

"I would be surprised if they didn't."

Sprits of rain hit my face, blown by the wind, and I look out at the sports fields.

"Yes," says George, "they planned to have her give the speech in the auditorium. She can't be bothered with a little rain."

"But the students can stand in formation in the rain?"

"Part of their training, I reckon."

My ears twitch. *Reckon?* I knew there was something odd about this fellow. We bonded too easily. I grow suspicious, examine him as we wait in the corridor. I sense movement behind me.

A disheveled student in sleeping clothes pads up behind us.

"Dad? What're you doing here?"

"Stewart!" He looks over the boy, about fourteen. "What's up?"

"I'm sick," says the boy. "They got me in the infirmary. But I had to get something from my room, so I went out." He holds up a pair of magazines, the old kind with pictures. Definitely vintage.

George chuckles, seeing the magazines. "I remember those."

"Hi," says Stewart.

"This is Fritz. Frank and James Baumann's father."

My ears twitch again. I never told George my family name, only my number. And where did he get 'Fritz' from? Maybe he got it from his son knowing my sons. Maybe he did research on me. Maybe he got my information from someone. Maybe he's an agent.

22

TRANSPORTATION

THE SPEECH HAS STARTED, or at least someone is speaking. The head of the Department of Education speaks a few minutes, then proudly welcomes the keynote speaker: "...to our great Madame Governor, Roberta Wornall!" Uproarious applause erupts with insane cheers interspersed. They cheer out of fear as the noise spills out into the hallway where we wait.

The auditorium holds about five hundred. I've attended school functions previously: a chorus concert (patriotic music mostly), and a stage play (Curly Atchison, the hero of the North, and how he was betrayed by a Southern Belle named Ginger), both performed better than I expected.

Wide corridors surround the huge hall. Students enter from one of two rear doorways, the public from the wider front entrance. The stage goes across the rear of the room between those two doors, near our position, so I have a good view of the stage through a gap in the doors. Worst of all is that I hear the governor's sonorous voice and cringe with thoughts of my interrogation.

"Stay strong, friend," says George, seeing me looking pale. "She'll be talking a full hour, I bet."

He's right: on and on she speaks, without much organization, a lot of random thoughts thrown out to the audience. She sounds like she hasn't prepared a speech at all, or she's a little drunk. I've seen examples of drunkenness on the education streams. None of that is allowed to citizens but I have no doubt élite folks can get a bottle or two for personal consumption. She gradually gets it together.

"...so we must trim our population to improve our Ideal Society," she decrees. "The simplest way to achieve this goal is by addressing the on-going problem of excess males in our Ideal Society. We should give these *extra* males some useful purpose, of course. Mainly, we should limit their reproductive capability so we don't have this dire, untenable situation continuing for decades to come. It only makes sense – common sense, young men," and she turns to gaze at the row of male youth standing behind her in their lovely dresses, "that we maintain an orderly influx and outflow of our citizenry so we can keep resources well-managed. We have come so far from the rough days of rebuilding a society from the ashes of anarchy, yet we have a long way to go to achieve our ultimate Ideal Society. Bear with me as my administration and the federal Advancement Committee, led by my husband, President Wornall, work tirelessly to guide us to this lofty goal."

George, fiddling with his bag, distracts me.

"So now let me outline our new mission. I have set forth our plan in the Proclamation on Families, as printed on pamphlets available to each of you as you exit today, also on the streams. We take these truths to be self-evident, that our Ideal Society must, at times, take harsh turns in order to survive. We do not take these steps lightly, but with regret for the lives altered – yet altered for a greater good."

"I bet," George grumbles.

"...the fact of reproduction is paramount to our success. We must continue to reproduce, yes, yet we must also manage our population efficiently. You may have heard of a so-called 'breeding' program to be implemented soon. That is an unfortunate name. The goal of the program is to maximize the health and productivity of each newborn citizen. No more lives left to chance, let loose in our society with no purpose. What we mean is that by limiting excess males, we can better bring about our Ideal Society through an orderly reproductive protocol based on application and a lottery system for selecting breeding couples."

"Except for her, the childless bitch," George sneers.

I wave him to be quiet.

"First, we will select those males who by happenstance appear to be *extra* within their families. That is to say: a second or third male in a household should be counted as extra. There is no need for any but the first male of a family to reproduce. Then we may preserve an ideal population. We have only a certain number of jobs – already a percentage of workers are frequently idle – and a certain number of housing units, not to mention finite food resources, no matter how well we manage them."

Murmuring starts to grow.

"Now some may object, especially those males who are selected, yet all of us must make allowances for actions that better our society."

"What about families without sons?" I ask but only George hears me. "Won't it even out?"

"One solution to this problem," the governor continues, raising her voice, "is to allow these young men to continue to serve our Ideal Society as productive workers who will not be reproducing. Indeed, a childless life can be quite fulfilling – as you can observe by my splendid example."

"It's a clown show in there," says George.

"These young men will be invited into our new transformation program and they shall exit with a new life ahead of them, sexless yet free to go about all manner of pursuits: work, certainly, yet also a bonus and various entertainments. In fact, the committee has just recently decided to permit these young men who may have artistic talents to use them as appropriate to entertain their fellow workers in the areas of music, dance, theater, art, and fashion. They shall be celebrated and admired for their devotion to our Ideal Society. In a moment I shall explain more on this pathway."

"I don't think my son has any of those talents," I mutter.

"Mine neither," says George.

"Another pathway to resolving this problem is to invite some of our young men to join our military enterprises. As members of these elite institutions, these young men will train to be the best they can be, as super soldiers fighting for what is true and good in an Ideal Society. Even now we fall short of our necessary troop count as war

271

continues on our northern border, as well as our need to support our allies overseas. Unfortunately, the world will not sit calmly by as we create our Ideal Society. Oh no! Factions wish to destroy us. They wish to bring down our civilization, to bring ruin to all that is not theirs! That is not what we want, nor what we stand for! So, as distasteful as it may seem, we must engage them, fight them. Yet we fight only with defensive intentions, to preserve what we have built, to protect our citizens and our values. It is a noble and grand endeavor, and we invite our young men into this program. Entering these ranks, young men will be able to preserve their masculine features, dare I say their *genitalia* (forgive my Southern), into the foreseeable future. This new program will rely on enhancing their hormone levels with additional treatment in order to create super soldiers, veritable killing machines the enemy will not be able to withstand. However, we must not fear these soldiers. When they exit their duty we will address the 'killer instinct' that we have, by necessity, created in them. We will shepherd them into exit programs designed to remove their heightened aggressiveness...."

"She means to kill them once they serve," says George. "Can't have aggressive men roaming our city."

"...to the extent that our population maintains equilibrium and fortitude, the way we work together to maintain our Ideal Society, a place of peace and prosperity!"

A long applause arises, then dies.

"Now, let us return to our discussion of the first pathway, which certain young men may elect to choose for their future. It is the way of the *feminine* man. It is the way of *love*: love for each other, love for our city and state, love for our nation and its leaders. While they volunteer themselves for the greater good, we shall praise them and honor them. They shall become as jewels in our society's crown, sparkling and precious!"

"Clown show," George grunts.

"We have top scientists running this feminization program right now and the process has reached perfection. It is an 'ideal' process," and the governor attempts a chuckle. "You will see that everything is explained in the pamphlets we have provided for you. I shall not bore you with all the sensitive details in this august auditorium, where my own father attended so long ago. Yet I understand today that this school has already selected its first cohort of feminization pathway subjects – uh, *volunteers* – isn't that correct?"

A man's voice calls out the answer. Sounds like the head Science teacher, Mr. Finkle, who I heard is ready to retire.

"Wonderful!" She seems to step aside as heavy footsteps mount the stage. I want to look but fear opening the door more.

"What do you see?" asks George, getting into a squat.

"Not much." I keep peering through the gap between the doors. "I see a line of boys wearing dresses coming on the stage, lining up. All in pink dresses."

"Damn," says George.

"They don't look happy. I can only see the faces of the ones on the end. Ah!" I have to catch my breath. "There's my son. Second from the end. Looks absolutely miserable. Humiliated. Some of them seem to be wearing false hair – wigs. James has just grown his hair longer, I think."

"We gotta act," says George.

"But you said the governor will meet with selected students in a private meeting."

"Yes, that's where we get her."

"Get her?" I glare at him. "I thought we were going to get my sons out."

"Yeah, them, too." He levels a hard stare at me, making sure I'm on board. "But I aim to get *her*."

"Her? Why?"

"For everything she's done, dammit." His voice threatens to get the attention of anyone out in the corridors. So far, we haven't been seen down this side hallway, waiting by the rear doors.

Then he reaches in his bag and I see he has a pistol.

"What's that?" I gasp. "What're you going to do?"

"I'm gonna shoot that bitch."

"The governor?"

He grins. "You know what they say: happiness is a warm gun."

"Are you crazy?"

I reach for the pistol, one of those older guns that shoot bullets. I get my hand on it but he has it in his hand, too, his finger inside the trigger guard. We push the gun back and forth a moment before he puts his hard stare on me.

"What're you doing? Let me finish this," he says.

"But...." I was going to say she's my sister, but the words stick in my throat. "They'll hear the shot," I say instead.

"Really don't care what happens to me. Stopping her and her evil plans is the most important thing. I'll save everyone from her damn ideal society."

"No," I cry a little too loudly.

People come around the corner at the far end of the corridor: a couple guards in gray uniforms, school faculty in teaching gowns, a reporter with a tablet. We are caught.

"Let go," George cries, then scrambles up, glancing at the people watching us. He gives them a scowl and turns to escape.

I grab his arm, hold him back. I don't know whose side I'm on. I just want my sons to be free of this new world they have ordered.

George tears away from my grip, dashes around the rear of the auditorium. I follow but don't see him. Maybe he's slipped in one of the doors along the corridor, hiding from me and waiting to act. What act will that be? Doesn't seem like he's interested in helping me any longer. Maybe he only needed someone to help *him*.

I slow, pausing to listen for noise he might make.

"Everything all right?" asks one of the teachers in a black gown who comes upon me.

"Yes, everything's all right." I force a grin. "We're parents. He got too emotional at the governor's amazing speech. Me, too. I tried to console him. I think his son wants to join the military."

"I see," the teacher responds. He looks like the Economics guy I spoke to previously when we came to discuss my sons' grades.

"I better go after him," I say, and step away – slowly so as not to alarm him, then quicker after I round the corner.

"There you are!" George barks, coming out of a room. He holds the pistol, aiming right at me. I remember Mother's guns and how she liked to wave them around to look tough, talked about how her daddy, my Grampa Sandy, had been a soldier in both armies.

"Wait," I call to him. "We both want the same thing."

"What's that? Seems you're on their side."

"No, I came to get my sons. Why are you here?"

"To shoot the bitch."

"But she's my sister."

"How's that...?"

"It's a long story. A very long story. And maybe not true by the end. But it's—"

"Now you're talking shit."

He has that look of craziness. Better to separate from him.

"Where's that room they're going to after her speech?" I ask.

"Why you wanna know? That's where we're killing her."

"We? Who's that?"

"Some patriots. If you're not with us you don't need to know."

"Please don't kill her," I say in a serious, pleading voice. "I do, in fact, believe she is my sister. Half-sister, but even so. She'll deny it, of course, because of her political career, but it's true."

He raises the pistol. "You're bad as she is, in that case."

My body acts before I can command it, springing away from him, and I throw open the door to the auditorium and rush in.

The crowd standing at that corner of the great hall absorbs me. Two of them smile at me like they welcome me to join them, all of us impressed by the governor's speech. They look like parents by the way they dress, still in work coveralls and office garb.

I turn to check behind me. The door has swung shut. But outside waits my attacker. My sister's attacker.

"...our Ideal Society," she repeats for the hundredth time. "Let us guide you. Let us protect you. Let us comfort you. Like your big sister. Like a loving parent. For we are all the same, all wishing to live in a beautiful world of peace and prosperity, as citizens of this Ideal Society!"

The crowd breaks into thunderous applause, with cheers cutting through the noise, crying: "Big Sister! Big Sister!" as the governor stands back from the podium with her arms raised in triumph or to salute her worshippers. In that pose I see dark sweat stains under her arms and I smile. *Not so ideal, are we?*

As the applause dies, the head of the Department of Education returns to direct the audience out of the auditorium, reminding us of the special meeting with the governor for the selected students and staff. The headmistress takes the line of boys on stage to the rear doors. As the audience mills about, squeezing out the front doors into the evening gloom, the governor and her circle are escorted out of the auditorium by the rear door.

I stare at her as she cuts through the crowd, passing within arm's reach of me. She never looks over at me. Maybe she doesn't sense my presence. I'm just a man in the crowd, a concerned parent.

"Are you coming?" asks a man in golden coveralls, holding up a tablet. "You must be on the list. Everyone waiting in this corner is designated. Let's go meet Big Sister."

More like a spinster aunt. I consider: no children of her own so she takes the community as her family, tries to make them do this or that, be this way, act in a certain manner, as though she were their mother or, in her case, big sister to them. My own big sisters treated me badly, teasing me, shaming me. But what're you going to do? Now we're grown up, living roles we could never have imagined.

I'm ushered out with the others, caught in the crowd, pushed from the auditorium, guided across the corridor into a smaller room that has chairs set in a semi-circle on one side. On the opposite side are several students standing at attention, including the boys in pink dresses who hold their heads down.

Except for the boy on the far end who raises his face proudly and gives a flip to his blond false hair and clicks his high heels together in a soldierly prance. He'll make it, thrive in their program.

Entering from the other door is the governor, Big Sister, and her entourage: a female assistant with tablet ready to record everything she says, and two big men in gray suits for whatever roles she may deem necessary. The Department of Education head steps forward, smiling and waving like she's done a good job getting the governor to the school for her big speech. The school's headmistress stands up to introduce the governor once more.

Everyone's Big Sister sits comfortably in the cushy chair they've provided while others sit on hard, metal chairs. She smiles warmly like she's on the streams – might be, given all the tablets aimed at her, recording everything, sending it out.

The students ask their pre-selected questions, reading off cards, and the governor blithely answers them with short responses as though her staff wrote answers for her. This is, as George indicated, a photo opportunity, a meet-and-greet for some students affected by her new policy.

I wasn't going to ask a question – only one other guest asked one aside from the students' approved questions – but my arm twitches at something the governor says.

She states, without apparent irony, that the military enterprise needs work, needs to ramp up armament production. To that end they will engage in various wars here and abroad to give reason for the manufacturing increase at factories, including shipyards. Once the navy is rebuilt, they can take back islands in the south they lost control of during the civil war and then expand food production on plantations there.

My arm switches, goes up half-way before I pin it to my hip.

"Why not make a deal? Trade with them?"

My voice sounds weak coming from the back of the room, and I suddenly fear for my safety. Men in her entourage glare at me.

"Who is that man?" asks the assistant, sitting to the side, as the governor ignores my question. "Scan him." A moment staring at the tablet's screen while the governor takes another question from one of the students, and the technician has the answer.

The two men in gray suits keep their eyes on me. I'm not going anywhere, trapped in the back with people blocking me.

After the thirteenth question, the head of the governor's small entourage gets her attention and indicates it's time to leave. There is perhaps a security issue. Maybe it's me.

The headmistress nervously announces the end of the session, then thanks Madame Governor for her time. The governor rises gracefully from her chair, smiling forcefully, and apologizes to those gathered. Must keep on schedule, everyone understands. She offers her signature hand wave.

One boy in a pink dress steps forward to give her a bouquet of flowers. One man in a gray suit moves to intercept the boy but she waves the man off, accepts the bouquet. Another boy steps forward and shakes her hand, catching her by surprise. She looks around for sanitizer. Another boy drops to the floor in front of her, kneeling pathetically, gazing up in awe. He thanks her for all she's done to make our city an Ideal Society.

Then the group in the room, maybe fifty, move as one, smashing against the door in the effort to leave the room. I'm trapped in the crowd. A fever rumbles through us, hands grabbing, pressing us forward.

I'm part of the flow, unable to extract myself from the mob as we crash against the walls and clog the doorway.

"Don't resist, ma'am," I hear someone say.

I look through the mob, see a face I know: O-Eight. I scan the faces and find Forty-one by the governor, who appears frazzled by the situation. The men in gray suits are pushed away from her. One falls to the floor and the crowd stumbles over him, the other one against the wall.

"You," O-Eight curses when our eyes meet. Haven't forgotten the poorly executed robbery, but why would those two even be here? Are they trying to...to...*oh my god! Kidnap the governor?*

"Wait!" I don't know what to say. I have to stop them.

I feel a blow to my head from behind, and the room spins. I feel dizzy, can't focus. All I see is the governor being escorted out of the room, the mob splitting to allow her and her kidnappers to pass through. Someone grabs me by my arm and pulls me out of the room after her. I shake my head, trying to regain clarity.

Doors open to the outside, the evening's darkness engulfing us. A vehicle awaits, side door open. No other windows on the side panel, only a faded stripe, part of the logo of some business. They get the governor inside, despite her shin banging on the door runner as they push her in and her cry of pain. I'm thrown in after her, head first, and land on the floor of the van.

"That all?" asks the man in the driver's seat, looking back.

"Yeah, go!" says Forty-one, sliding the door closed.

I don't know what's happening. Everything is a jumble.

Blinking, my eyes detect a hood over the governor's head. But as we drive through the streets, I know I have at least stopped George from shooting her. So what is this? Another plot?

A hood is quickly slipped down over my head.

"What's going on?" I call out and get a slap across my face.

"Don't worry," says a voice that sounds familiar. "None of them can track us, not this vehicle. Can't cut off the engine either." He laughs and I guess it's the driver who's speaking. "Not powered by electro-volt. It's pure dino fuel. Old-style engine. A classic. You ever ride in a van, Fritz?"

My ears perk up at my name. Who knows my real name?

"Doctor Richards...?" I dare question. No slap this time.

"Yes, Fritz." He chuckles like he's happy he's fooled me for these two years. "We all have our parts to play. This is mine. I hide in the spotlight, ready to act in the shadows."

"What? You're part of this...what *is this* exactly?"

"It's a plot, obviously."

"What plot? By who?"

"Us. It's all cliques within cliques, circles within cohorts, groups within offices, departments, agencies, whole government wings – all vying for power, waiting, scheming, then acting."

"Who are you?" demands the governor, muffled by her hood.

Nobody moves to slap her to be quiet.

"All plotting to save ourselves," my doctor goes on, "or, with some luck, rise above the others, all of the others, and take charge of the whole thing – be in charge and smash anyone trying to come after them – *us*, that is. It's the entire nature of human endeavor. It's that try, try, try again thing."

"What do you want with me?" cries the governor.

Crouching by the governor, Forty-one says: "Ma'am, we're taking you to what they call 'undisclosed location'. We don't mean you any harm. We intend to use your safety now and your safe return later to get our friends out of jail. Maybe some other concessions."

"Like not forcing 'extra' males into two harmful paths," I offer for the sake of discussion.

"That's another one," says O-Eight from the front.

Dr. Richards snorts at that, then the van makes a sharp turn, hits some bumps, and we race straight through a checkpoint. Sirens wail when we fail to stop. The van swings left and right, jostling us inside as it races through the streets.

The night is much more quiet and I know we have left the city. I feel trees rising around us as the road bends and turns, leading us into another world. Eventually we slow, rolling over gravel.

We stop, engine off. The van's side door slides open and we are dragged out, pushed inside some kind of building.

23

SIBLING RIVALRY

WHEN MY HOOD IS REMOVED, I look straight across and see the governor, still with hood over her head. She sits on the floor like me, legs extended toward me. She has lost a shoe. The other has lost its heel. Her hosiery is torn. The gray slacks she wears are also torn at the knees, probably from when she fell as they dragged her, or when she banged them against the door runner of the van. Through the rips I see blood. Her gray blazer has been pulled down from her shoulders to help hold her arms in place and like me her hands are tied behind her, forcing a couple buttons on her white blouse to pop. At that moment I feel pity for her. She is, after all, my big sister.

"What's that?" asks someone in a strangely gruff voice. I guess my thoughts spilled out as mumbled words. "Yeah, we're supposed to call her Big Sister. But that's a joke."

She actually is my big sister. But it doesn't matter to them.

"Now we wait," says another. Both men sit at a table to the side of where I am on the floor. He turns to us. "By now our demands have been delivered to your office. That's if he doesn't get distracted. Then it's a matter of time, how long depends on your staff, *Madame Governor*." He says her name in sarcastic tone, then laughs.

"Can you let her sit up more comfortably?" I ask.

"Why do you care?" It's O-Eight, getting up from the table and coming over. He squats before me, looking down at me.

"Common courtesy," I mutter.

"Was that common courtesy the way they treated you down at

the Department of Social Order? Was it?"

"But they let me go."

"Eventually." O-Eight snickers. "Why they letcha go? What deal you make with them, huh?"

"I didn't make any deal."

"No, but you got a special badge. What's that about, huh?"

"I guess...." I wonder why they leave me tied up, like I'm part of the governor's entourage. "Maybe they felt bad for how they treated me. That's what I was told."

"Or they wanted you to work for them," says the gruff voice. It could be Forty-one. "That it?"

"How else would he get out of that interrogation then get special status and a pension? They must be working together." I know that voice as Dr. Richards, counselor and weekend automobile hobbyist. "I knew there was something about you, Sixteen."

"Call me Frank," I say, irritated by him. "I didn't do anything."

"Now listen here, Sixteen or whatever your number is," O-Eight growls, "there's lot more than you and me that wanna put this bitch away. Lots of different reasons, most of all is we gotta get back our freedoms – the right to do what we wanna do no matter if ya think it's good or bad, or something in between. The point is it's what we choose to do, nobody else interfering. Got it? There ain't no 'greater good', only individual...uh...what's that word?"

"Agency," Dr. Richards answers.

"Agency," O-Eight confirms. "Do what ya want. And this bitch, she wants to put us all in her prison state."

"Please don't call her that," I say, trying to remain calm.

"Bitch? What's wrong with it? It's a word," O-Eight snarls. "Lets her know what I think of her."

"I don't think she deserves that name." I cough, clear my throat. "Could you let her sit up? Get comfortable, at least? She's not going anywhere, so she might as well be comfortable as we wait."

O-Eight stares at me from his squatting position, then stands.

"Yeah, I see which side you're on."

"Actually," I speak up, "I was only at the school to get my sons. I went in with a guy named George, don't know his number."

"That bastard!" snorts Forty-one. "Always getting in our way."

"He was planning to shoot the governor. Had a pistol." I see the governor stir at that information. "I tried to get the pistol away from him but I failed. Then he was going to shoot me, and chased me, but I joined the audience and he couldn't get me there. Then I got swept into that smaller room."

"Perhaps it would've been better that way," the governor speaks through her hood.

"Please take that off of her," I say. "We don't know where we are so what harm does it do to remove it?"

"If he had shot you," the governor finishes, ever defiant.

Exhaling loudly, I no longer care. She's the same as before. Plain hateful, and unwilling to acknowledge me, or her mother, her family heritage, her childhood experiences. Maybe she really isn't one of us.

"Forget it," I say. "I don't care. But I'm not working for her."

That impresses O-Eight. He goes over, jostles the governor, and jerks off the hood.

"Hmm," says O-Eight, "not much of a looker."

She blinks in the light, shakes her head to move hair from her face. Her eyes glare at me when she focuses.

"I knew it was you," she says. "Why else would you be there?"

"My sons attend that school," I respond, holding back my anger. "I was trying to get them out. They already have my younger son marked for that transformation project of yours. Neither he nor his parents want that. Not the military option, either. None of the options. We don't want any of that forced on us."

"See? Those are the freedoms we mean," says O-Eight.

The governor squirms, gets herself into a better position, sitting upright on the floor, her back against the wall.

"They will find us," she says firmly. "They will kill all of you."

Forty-one laughs. "They won't find us. We're in a goddamn state park, a place that's long been closed. Nobody comes here. Everybody says it's haunted."

"Oh," she says. "I know the place. It's where police killed those squatters who refused to give up the land. About a hundred of them – men, women, children. They made a big pyre to burn the bodies."

Dr. Richards gasps. "How awful."

"History," the governor says with a sigh.

"That was before I was born." I look up at the ceiling, count the rafters. "So what's this building?"

"Park office," says Dr. Richards. "Used to be."

"That's the history we need to forget," the governor says. "Needs to be forgotten. It continues bad feelings and keeps us from building our Ideal Society."

I see a figure moving just out of my view, then comes around to flop down on the floor beside the governor. It's Dr. Richards. He puts his arm around her shoulders like they are lovers.

"How's my gal doing?" he asks, pretending to kiss her cheek. He playfully pulls her against him using the arm wrapped around her shoulders. "Still having fun?" He regards me, gives a wink. "Older women, huh."

"Please don't hurt her," I say.

"Nobody's gonna hurt her. She needs to be in good shape to hand her back. When we get our demands met."

O-Eight is clear on the plan.

"How did you get involved with these two?" I ask Dr. Richards.

"It's simple. I decided what I wished would change in our cold, gray city. I could see the direction her policies were taking us." Then he turns serious. "I was already a counselor, Fritz. Got my diploma in Psychological Arts at City University. The policies put a damper on who I could treat, who I was allowed to help. It was much better – and more lucrative – to listen to graduates from rehabilitation, as boring as it may be – no offense intended."

"I told you the truth," I speak up.

"I'm sure you did. I marked your sessions as adequate. You got your food boxes, didn't you?"

"Yes, but—"

"Sometimes you have to go along to get along." He grins, an odd side of him I never would've suspected. "Know what I mean?"

"And these two?"

"I also treated them. They had a common complaint. I listened to them. It made sense. If we could make a difference, if we could affect change, if we could in one fell swoop set the world right again, would we? Could we? Should we? And how best to do it?"

"We should," says Forty-one, "and we did."

"You're all in this together," I grumble. "But you testified at my interrogation. Never would guess you work together against me."

"Not against you. Against *her*."

"Whatever your plan is, it will fail," says the governor. "Our fine officers are even now on your trail."

"How 'bout we kill you now?" O-Eight barks.

"Stop!" I shout. "Leave her alone. You're getting what you want."

"Why do you care?" asks O-Eight. "What's she to you?"

"She's my big sister."

O-Eight frowns. "That's just what she wants people to say: she's our Big Sister, gonna take care of us, protect us, like this bitch could ever do that."

"Not without keeping us all under her control," Forty-one adds.

"Control can be a beautiful thing," Dr. Richards says. "When you get it, you want to keep it. You want to get even more. It becomes an illness, you might say."

"And she's going to have the vice-president killed," I blurt out.

They stare at me. The governor closes her eyes.

"She's already sick with some new virus, they report," says Dr. Richards. "She's not supposed to make it."

"See? Then she'll be appointed as the new vice-president."

"So her and her husband will *rule* together: President and Vice President Wornall. It's perfect."

"Then President Wornall better watch out. Better pay attention to what she does," says Forty-one. "He could get sick, as well. If you know what I mean."

"Yes, it *is* perfect," the governor speaks up. "It is the best way to run this nation and make it prosperous once more. You cannot deny that. It will work. Trust me."

"Trust you?" Forty-one laughs.

"You can't be serious, Bobbie, can you?" I ask sincerely.

She regards me with disdain. In a different situation she might have me dismissed, have me removed from her presence. Have one of her guards slap me. Now she's forced to confront me.

"What's your part in this?" she asks calmly, eyes narrowing.

"I have no part in this. I went to the school to get my sons. I got swept up in this thing. They think I work with you, but I don't. Tell them. Please."

"He doesn't work for me or with me." She chuckles. "We have no connection whatsoever. My staff mistook him for someone else. We corrected the mistake and sent him on his way. On his way with some compensation. That's the end of it."

"It's not the end, Bobbie!" I have to take a breath, angry as I am. "I want my sons safe from your barbaric policies. Let them go free. Let us out of your cold, gray city, dammit!"

"Listen to these two," says Dr. Richards, almost glowing. "Here's your true history, everyone."

"There is no history between him and me," says the governor. "And why do you call me Bobbie. My name is Roberta. My surname is Chesterfield. My marriage name is Wornall."

I level my eyes at this woman. "You are Bobbie Chesterfield, as you say, but your mother is also my mother. She's Isla Baumann, a woman your father bought and abused. She gave birth to you and to your brother, Abe. That is the true history. Years later I was born to Isla."

She's used to laughing away accusations and tries it again, but I see something in her face that acknowledges the truth of what I say.

"Fritz, if that is your real name – Eleven-Sixteen, officially – you are way in left field, looking under the bleachers, missing the ball completely."

"So it is true," says Dr. Richard, smugly.

Her face hardens. "Do I need to deny you a third time for it to count?"

I grow bolder. "So who called for prosecuting me for that video I made of our mother telling her stories?"

The governor looks down, then meets my eyes. "I did."

"You did. Put that on the record."

Our captors are enjoying the family drama.

The governor squints. "As I have told you previously, we simply cannot have people believing that their governor is a child of poor Southern stock, born from a bought-and-paid whore, nor raised in a forest or sneaking into the north for a better life."

"I watched Abe's funeral on streaming." Something is boiling in me. "You looked so *unsad*, like you couldn't wait to get back to your wonderful office. What did you do?"

"Everyone knows it was an accident, him falling off the combine, getting cut up underneath it."

"Was he pushed?"

"It was an accident. His sons know the truth."

"They know how much better their lives became after he died."

"I made no deal with them." She glances about the room like she expects sympathy from our captors. "They are business men. They know how to run a business – or a city. They can help us achieve our Ideal Society and make it flourish, so I put them in charge."

"In charge of the food supply," Dr. Richards snaps.

"We need to rebuild," she presses, sounding desperate. "We have to make hard choices to get back on the right path. We have to make a society that will sustain us and protect us from any and all harm. Remember how the world collapsed for a few decades all because of peoples' fear of the unknown, and the wars?"

"But why the repression?" I ask. "Why the strictness? We need to get along with each other, right? Not pushed to divide ourselves into classes and groups and cohorts pitted against each other."

"Only an efficient, productive society can endure," she insists. "There is no going back. We cannot afford to go back to what was."

"We have to go back."

"To what? All of the horrors our parents and grandparents had to survive through?"

"That struggle made us a good family."

"There are better families, Fritz, ones we form from our common aims, our joint struggle. Those are the people we trust, not people we might happen to share some genetic traits with."

"Mother would've hated you."

"Perhaps. Yet my father would love what I've done."

O-Eight gives her leg a kick and she cringes at the strike. "Time to shut up. Before my head explodes."

"Please, Bobbie, just take back your new policy on extra males. That's all I ask. Then let us leave the city. Me and my family. I'll never return and your secrets will be safe."

"There are no secrets. I'm not your sister."

"You are my big sister," I declare. "I proved it before you tried to scrape the truth out of existence. Our mother said so."

"Here," says O-Eight, holding a pistol in his hand. "Maybe you wanna use this. Maybe you need this more than us. Don't matter if she lives or dies. We'll have our demands or not."

"I can't do that." Filled with rage, I struggle to hold back, afraid what I'll do. "She's my sister. I swear it. It's the truth."

"You swear it?" asks Dr. Richards, leaning forward.

"I do."

"Then say it."

"I love my big sister."

He motions for Forty-one to untie my hands. He does. I rub my wrists. *What now?*

"Look at him," O-Eight sneers. "He loves his big sister." The way he says it in a sing-songy voice doesn't amuse me. "Pitiful boy. What choice does he have now? The fool." He hands me the pistol. "Do it."

Are there any bullets in it? Is this only a test?

Holding the ancient weapon in my hand, I think of the stories I read of my grandfather shooting marauders in the forest camp, the same place where I was born. If I'd grown up there with the same dangers, I'd know how to shoot. I'd know how to protect my family. But it's just a hunk of metal now. I'm useless.

"You point it at her and pull the trigger," O-Eight instructs.

Forty-one stares at me, a grin playing on his face. "He won't."

"Yes," says O-Eight. "I think he will. He has to."

"No," I whimper. "I can't."

I stare at this woman, handsome in her maturity, broken yet still defiant. She gives me nothing, no reaction, the same stony face that glares down from the posters.

"You've been delusional since I first encountered your video," she says. "And now it's come to this. Why did you come to the school to hear my speech? Obviously you're obsessed with me."

"Not obsessed," I mumble.

Her mouth tightens, a thought coming into her head. "You, Fritz, are nothing but a weak little man." She glares at me. "We should've pushed you off that ledge on the mountain when you were a baby. Save us both a lot of trouble. I heard Allie suggesting it, going to say you fell, but Amy knew Isla would be distraught. Lucky you. I froze as they discussed it. I feared I might be next. Now look at us."

I take a long breath. "I remember that moment."

All the moments in the past, leading to this moment. I've made a lot of mistakes, I know. But how will I remember this moment when I reach the future? Will there be more? I dismiss awkward memories that flash through me, letting me slip down into a fox burrow.

I hear her voice soar through my head, an echo of past speeches, the crowd cheering, and I want it gone.

"You gonna shoot or what?" O-Eight grunts.

We all hear it at the same instant.

O-Eight scrambles up, looks around. Forty-one gets to his feet, takes a stance. Dr. Richards smiles with satisfaction, as though the moment he's been waiting for has arrived.

The governor regards me, concern on her face, worry in her eyes. Maybe a regret or two poking her mind.

The front window shatters as something is tossed inside—

Boom!

The concussion throws me down flat, knocks the others over. We can't hear anything. Uniformed officers burst through the door. A pair surround the governor, checking her. Others quickly take care of her captors with the directed energy weapons: a beam, a bit of smoke, an eruption of the body in pain and death.

One officer turns to me. "This one, too?"

I'm not sure who he's asking, either the rescue team's leader or the governor herself.

A shot crackles through the storm. I'm not sure I hear it clearly. Someone has fired and the bullet hits the governor. I see her wince, see the red spot emerge on her abdomen, staining her white blouse. Her tending officers pull her away.

She gazes back at me and, grimacing, says: "Him."

The pulse strikes me like a stone wrapped in fire. I freeze in that fire, feeling a blast furnace sear me from inside, my mind breaking apart, sloughing off memories.

"Free. My. Sons," is all I can get out through clenched teeth.

It must not have been on full power, because after a few seconds that feel like days, my body just falls limp and weak, immobile on the floor. Dead captors are being dragged out, bodies mangled by energy bursts. As Forty-one turned to confront officers, he caught the pulse under his arm and it went out his cheek, leaving his head a withered melon. I can't look at O-Eight's body, now in three pieces. Dr. Richards got it best: still intact, looking like an extreme sunburn as he hunches over the table.

And me? How do I look?

Two officers gather me. The governor has already been removed from the cabin.

"This one, too," says one officer to the other.

I can't shake the pistol loose from my finger that's caught in the trigger guard. I never meant to shoot. She's my sister. The noise startled me. I jerked, finger flexed. Pointed at her already. I never meant to shoot her.

But I can't make myself speak. I want to tell her, but she's gone. I have to tell someone, but my mouth won't work. My tongue has shriveled. My lungs can't get air.

In that instant I know exactly how it's going to be.

The pistol is wrenched from my hand as the room fills with light.

And out of that blinding glory comes a little boy, looking maybe four years old. He raises his hand in greeting. He seems to know me.

"Come on, Fritter," says the boy.

He takes my hand as I recognize him as me when I was little.

"Let's visit Mama. She's over there with Grandma Hannah and Grampa Sandy. And the others. They're waiting for us."

24

TUBA TUESDAY

Dear Faith,

I hope you are doing well. You may not know me, but I'm Frank's wife. You may know him as Fritz, his birth name. He mentioned you a few times because you wrote letters to him. I wanted to let you know just how much he appreciated you writing to him. He said it made him feel happy that someone in the family thought to share the details of their lives.

However, I must inform you that Fritz has died. I don't know all the details – only what's been reported on the streams. You may have heard the news. He got into some trouble, had to go to rehabilitation. But he finished it with no problems and got a new job. He seemed to be doing well.

Later there was an incident at the school our sons attended. The governor was speaking there and a group of criminals captured her. Frank got swept up with her. They believed he was part of her group but he was only there to support our sons. According to reports, he managed to protect our governor and help her get to safety when she was wounded. Fortunately she is fine now. She was rushed to a hospital and doctors were able to restore her with no disability.

Unfortunately, Fritz was killed in that struggle. The Governor has praised him for saving her. She also accepted his last request to let our sons leave the school. In fact, she held off her new policy, and after she recovered she rescinded that policy statement regarding the determination of extra males. Now inclusion in a similar program is completely voluntary, with certain incentives.

I'm speaking of Roberta Wornall, *née* Chesterfield, our governor, who is married to the president. I don't know how much news finds its way out to you there. I only mention it by way of telling you how Fritz died. I thought you would want to know because of how you two are related. She told news reporters he saved her but got shot in the crossfire during her rescue. It was enough that we could be awarded compensation for his death.

Anyway, not to burden you with a lot of old news, I wanted to let you know that we plan to head west to find a new home. I thought our first stop may be to visit you. No obligations, of course. Just a visit. We won't expect to live with you. We have compensation cards from Widow Services so we can stay in a hotel, if one is available in Skinner Canyon or the nearest town. If you could help us get settled, show us how to do things in that environment, we would be much obliged. We will bring you and yours some gifts.

When I say 'we' I refer to my two sons, Frank and James, and our daughter, Maggie. Frank was about to graduate from the school, but James was at risk of being forced into the Governor's new program against his will and our wishes. Thus it was good that Fritz acted to save him. Maggie is still in the primary school and she hopes to play the family tuba someday. Oh, don't worry. We are not bringing that thing with us.

I know the story behind that tuba. Perhaps you do, as well. Frank never stopped talking about his mother and her father playing it. The noise laws they have in the city won't allow us to play it in public or in housing units. They have put it in a museum for Musical Arts. I take Maggie there from time to time. It's open on Tuesdays, what they renamed 'Seconday'. We call it Tuba Tuesday. She gets a thrill seeing it and knowing that her father, and those before him, used to play it. They have a sample of its unique sound on a recording if you want to hear how it sounds. Maggie loves pushing the button over and over until a guard sends us on our way.

And the notebooks Fritz thought were so precious – I dare say, the cause of all his troubles – well, they have found a new home, too. They're in the History Archives, under glass in a display case. You can read some of them, the opened pages, if you can read the cursed style they're written in. Of course, they've mislabeled them, calling them fiction, but you and I know the truth. Not many would recognize what your parents and grandparents went through during the great pandemic and the decades of troubles that followed. It's good you could grow up together in the National Park and help each other.

Now we are lucky to have a modern city, says our governor; in fact, a modern state. And soon the nation, with her marriage to President Wornall. Now she is set to become the new Vice President, sworn in right after the funeral of Vice President McDaniel, poor lady. The way she suffered during her year-plus of infirmity makes my whole being shudder! And the plans they have declared for us here! Fritz opened my eyes.

I'm sure I've bored you long enough with this letter. I've cut my finger twice on this old paper. Please forgive the blood marks. But I understand you folks out west don't have streaming service or the electric communications we use here so this is the only way to get a message back and forth. I wish you a healthy and happy life there, and I know – I hope – our family will make better choices once we are in a new place.

I pray that all is well with you. We will see you soon. Arranging tickets today, in fact. It's a five-day journey even on the express but we can afford it – have to afford it. We must leave this city before everything gets worse. Thanks to Fritz, however, I can see how Big Sister's nefarious plans will proceed, and it won't be a good place to live in the future, I'm certain.

Anyway, Fritz sends his love as do I and the children.

Bless you, my dear sister-in-law!

Yours,
Sandra

+ + +

Hope you don't mind a writing machine!!!

Hey there Sandra!!!

I'm glad to make your aquaintance. Thanks for sending a letter. We ain't got many for a spell so I'm guesing something happened to him. So sad. I sure will cry for Fritz. He was always kind to me, even sent some credits while ago when we was in need. Sorry for you & the kids.

It's awright for y'all to settel out here but it's dry & hot so maybe y'all won't like it none. But it's quiet most times, on account of no-body wanna live here. You wouldn't know it was even part of the same nation, just like wild territory.

Yep, plenty of lawless folk here, making their own way. Raymond was like that. But you know by now he done got shot and died. He's buried out back here, the only place that take him. Folks still count me as his wife, tho we weren't never wedded official.

I make my days gardning then sell them vegtables in a market in town & we do awright. If you smart like Fritz said you can prolly teach kids. That'll be good here. We ain't got no teachers so kids are dum. & we don't want no dum kids here.

I'll be looking for you. Maybe this letter gets to you after you leave but anyways I tried. I'm sending you this here reply. I wish you a good trip. Can't wait to meet all y'all.

Bestest regards,

Cousin Faith

P.S. I really don't mind a tuba. We ain't got no music here but some banjos.

GENEALOGY

Grandma Hannah's Line:

Sandy Baumann = Hannah Whistler
                Isla
            Frank =   (& Sandy = Lorraine, Frank's wife's twin)
                Cherie   Polly
        Trey (drifter) =
                Iris
        Sven (drifter) =
                Jenny
    Ajamu (preacher) =
                Ellie
            Big Joe =
                Raymond
        Sandy (return) =
                Allie
    Fred (custodian) =
                (stillborn)

Isla's Line:

        LJ (Big Joe's son) = **Isla**
                Amy June
        Lionel Chesterfield =
                ⇨ **Bobbie** & Abe
            (brothel guest) =
                    (Lily, died in infancy)
                Ajamu =
                    (miscarriage)
    Frank (after she returns
            to national park) =
                    Fritz (Frank Jr.)
            Julio (marshes) =
            LJ (return) =

LJ's Line:

LJ = **Isla**
    Amy June
      = Lori*
    (Calvin - died from snakebite)
    Grace - nurse at military hospital
    Faith - goes with Raymond out west
    Hope - sleeps around

Raymond (brother to
    both Isla & LJ) = Lori*
        Eve

    *Lori was Big Joe's wife, widow after the wars.

Fritz's Line:

Frank = **Isla**
    Fritz (Frank Jr./Sixteen) = Sandra
        Frank III
        James
        Maggie

**Sally's Line:

Sally Wilson/Winston = Buck Sadler (Book 2: *The Way of the Son*)
    Sara
      = Rick (doctor from island)
    Alice = professor
        Eden (Thirteen) = Thirty-nine?
        = Gary

**Sally lived with Hannah's sister Kristin and sons George and
Clay, along with Rick, until Kristin's death. Winston was her
married name but she was separated from him.

ACKNOWLEDGMENTS

In writing a novel a lot of influences come together in seemingly random fashion to initiate the story idea and propel the writing forward.

The *Flu Season* trilogy began with a deliberate thought-experiment based on the film *A Boy and His Dog* (1975), a sardonic adventure set in an odd post-apocalyptic landscape, based on Harlan Ellison's short story. I gave my novel the working title of "A Boy and his Mom and her tuba". However, I couldn't work on it as the SARS-CoV-2 ("covid-19") pandemic worsened. Only when the crisis was coming to an end did I find a way in and started *The Book of Mom*.

I didn't focus on the initial days we all experienced, when everything was immediate and real, but further into the future, when the worst we experienced had gotten worse: say, six years into the future. Book 2 *The Way of the Son* continues the story and we pass through another year of the post-pandemic experience. Everything is irrevocably broken and the only way forward is to rebuild from scratch.

In Book 3 *Dawn of the Daughters*, the rebuilding begins but our family isn't aware of it for a while. When they enter the new society, they find it being rebuilt in horrible fashion. Book 4 *The Book of Dad* shows us the beginnings of a society heading toward something akin to Orwell's world in *1984*.

I always select music to help create an appropriate soundscape for my writing. The aural support unlocks my muse. I found the ideal soundtrack in the following music: Jeop Beving (entire album *Henosis*; "For Steven"); Peter Sandberg ("Butterfly"; "Remove the Complexities"; etc.), Juliano ("Fallen Sun"; "Eternity"; etc.), and Max Richter ("November"; "Mercy"; "Infra 5"; etc.).

Special thanks goes forever to those who worked the front lines during the pandemic, some of whom lost their own lives alongside their patients. Our gratitude is immeasurable.

ABOUT THE AUTHOR

Stephen Swartz is the author of seventeen novels, including this current volume, as well as short stories and poetry for anthologies and literary journals. He's also published scholarly articles and a Ph.D. dissertation on the role of identity in student composition pedagogy. He has taught English at several colleges and universities over a thirty-year career. While teaching English courses at Langston University in Oklahoma during the past decade, Swartz realized his ambition to publish a few previously written novels. Thanks to the notoriety of the Amazon Breakthrough Novel Award competition, the first of them, *After Ilium*, was published – followed quickly by *The Dream Land* and *A Beautiful Chill*. Other newly written novels came in yearly succession.

Prior to attending graduate school and earning an M.A. (English) and M.F.A. (Creative Writing), Swartz lived in Japan for five years where he taught English at the middle school and high school levels. His experiences there helped inspire him to write his novel *Aiko*. Swartz also taught summer courses at a university in Beijing, China in recent years. His wide travels and interest in cultures and languages has propelled his fiction into explorations of situations where the main character is often a stranger in a strange land and must find ways to adapt – much as he has done during a lifetime and career of various excursions.

He borrows from those experiences for the *Flu Season* trilogy and this sequel.

www.ingramcontent.com/pod-product-compliance
Lightning Source LLC
Chambersburg PA
CBHW070830250626
47159CB00003B/721